# GIGI TEMPLETON

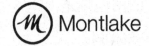

Published by Montlake, Seattle

www.apub.com

Amazon, the Amazon logo, and Montlake are trademarks of Amazon.com, Inc., or its affiliates.

ISBN-13: 9781662517907 (paperback)
ISBN-13: 9781662517891 (digital)

Cover design by Letitia Hasser
Cover photography by Wander Aguiar Photography
Cover image: © Pic Media Aus / Shutterstock

Printed in the United States of America

*This is a story about taking chances, and I applaud everyone who takes big or small steps forward to follow their hearts and achieve their dreams. It is also dedicated to my beloved rescue pup, Gracie Faith, who was my inspiration for Ollie. You brought us so much joy and were the best companion an author could ever have. I had fun writing this series with you. RIP, my friend.*

# Chapter One

"T-R-O-U-B-L-E." Chance Reed let out a low whistle. "All caps, bro. Stamped right across her forehead."

"No clue what you're talking about," Avery Reed commented as he flipped bavettes and hangers, separating out his rares, medium rares, mediums, and well-dones.

He scowled inwardly at the last classification.

*Way to mutilate a prime cut of beef.*

But this wasn't his rodeo. It belonged to his cousin Jack Reed. And Jack's cohost, Jillian Parks. YouTube sensations with a BBQ channel who were cooking up their specialties while entertaining a large crowd at the massive outdoor kitchen, in addition to their live stream audience.

Whereas Avery was filling in the gaps on the event lawn with a trio of wagon-wheel-style grills, arranged in a semicircle that allowed him to maneuver between the grates to stay on top of the colossal production.

"You never were any good at lyin'," Chance said. "You've been stealing glances at that blonde the entire time she's tried to make her way toward you, with a plate of Jillian's potatoes Romanoff that pairs well with . . . oh, yeah." He studied his palm, as if it held CliffsNotes to this impending drama. "Steak."

Avery smirked while he tended to his grills. "Got no time for a pretty thing like that. Can't you see we have meat to serve?"

"There's an innuendo in there somewhere," Chance said. Then laughed.

Avery snatched the metal tray from him and piled on the well-dones he'd put on before this new round of proportioned slabs.

His older brother continued. "She's a looker, for damn sure. And that outfit she's wearing. Lord have mercy. I tip my hat to her."

"What'd really help in this situation," Avery contended, "is if you'd get these steaks to the carving station to rest so they don't cross the line into no-man's-land. Ain't serving up jerky today."

"Someday, bro, you're gonna meet a woman who knocks you right out of your cowboy boots. Probably best that it's not this one. She's got 'city slicker' written all over her."

"No, she doesn't," he retorted.

Chance hooted. And said, "Gotcha! So you *have* been checkin' her out."

"Fucking help me move this beef, man. I don't have all day to wait around on you. Jack's gonna wind down this shindig in an hour, and I need to clear my grates. Go fetch me another couple of trays."

The inaugural Memorial Day Weekend BBQ Bash had been a huge hit. Today's soiree was centered on the true spirit of the holiday—to commemorate the fallen. Lots of people had spoken throughout the day about their lost loved ones, as well as recognizing heroes from around the Southwest. To counter the somber mood that brought on, various bands performed on a makeshift stage, and there was plenty of dancing on a laid-out parquet floor to celebrate what the nation had earned in return. Freedoms people still fought for.

Also to kick off the summer season.

An abundance of food had the paid guests wandering from station to station. The scents permeated the vast knoll fringed by oaks and flower beds. The animated conversations assured the Reed family that this had been a stellar idea of Jack's. Hundreds of people attended the long weekend of festivities, and the TRIPLE R—Reed River Ranch— would benefit from their patronage.

Not to mention, Jack and Jillian's online subscriber/viewer numbers would soar. Avery didn't know too much about that, but Jack's older sister, Wyatt—and her eleven-year-old son Alejandro, a social media whiz—had promised them impressive stats and higher monetization. *That* part he grasped. When it came to running a multigenerational ranch of this magnitude, improved finances were imperative. Every single season.

Chance returned with two more trays, and Avery filled them, saying, "I was a little worried we were going to run out, but we budgeted just right. I've got several more to fire up, then I'm done here."

"These'll be gone before they're even rested," Chance told him. "But by all counts, I believe everyone's had their fair share. Salads and sides are holding up as well, though Jack's likely low on brisket and chicken. And I suspect most of the kegs are dry."

"Not a surprise, especially with Jack having hired shuttle buses to get guests from town to the ranch and back."

"No drinkin' and drivin', so they can imbibe until their coupons are gone. Also makes for minimal traffic out here. No excessive vehicles to disrupt anything." As foreman of the ranch, Chance was the authority on environmental impacts to the "establishment." He added, "Our main road and the offshoots could accommodate the influx, but it'd make for a hell of a haul and open us up to potential injury lawsuits, walking on dirt and gravel—not exactly conducive for the ladies and their heels."

"True fact," Avery concurred.

"Including your new admirer. She keeps shooting inviting looks your way, but every guy she passes stops to chat her up. She might be hitched before she even reaches you."

Avery gave a half snort. "Again . . . I don't have time for—"

He groaned under his breath.

The blonde had broken free of her latest diversion and was on the move. Headed straight for Avery's grills.

"I'll leave y'all to it, then," Chance said with notable humor.

Avery resisted the urge to roll his eyes. Because she really was a stunner. Damn near making his heart stop.

It'd been a hell of a long time since he'd been enticed by a woman, when there was a constant stream of activity here at the ranch to occupy every waking hour. Feeding three chucks a day to a dozen or so cowboys and plenty other ranch hands from sunup to sundown—and restocking and prepping in between and afterward—consumed his energy. Also satisfied his culinary creativity. He never served the same meal twice in any given week. That held true for the desserts.

But the blonde was impossible to ignore. He couldn't even step away and let his assistant, Ritchie, answer any questions she might have.

Avery was riveted where he stood.

"So," she mused in a silky voice as she sidled up to the largest of the grills in the center of his workstation. "This entire place smells like a carnivore's heaven, and I'm thrilled I gave up being a pescatarian."

"We don't talk much religion around here, honey. Folks get to be what folks wanna be."

She smiled. Vibrantly.

Avery felt a physical jolt to the gut.

Shit. She was her own electrical storm with her pearly white teeth and the flare in her golden-amber eyes, with a hint of orange around the irises.

Tiger eyes, his mother would call them when feral cats wandered onto the ranch. Rare and captivating. The blonde's were multifaceted with incredible depth—so that Avery practically fell right into them.

Quick to catch on that he was only joking about not knowing the meaning of *pescatarian*, she said, "I do have an insatiable desire for seafood. Particularly a succulent Maine lobster. Or a perfectly prepared Chilean sea bass."

"I've got neither, unfortunately."

"As expected at a meat lover's food fest. Since arriving here, I've been craving a filet with hollandaise and some of that brisket in the smoker."

*Jesus, she has an appetite.*

He liked that. Though that wasn't all that appealed to him.

4

She was dressed to the nines on this sunny Monday afternoon. She wore a flimsy top with wispy shoulder straps and a drapey neckline that revealed the inner swells of her breasts. The material was a shimmery metallic black and silver, and the strands pulling from her sides to her back to hold it in place were also whisper thin.

The front V'd at her waist, showing off an inch or so of her tanned, toned stomach. Her full-length black skirt had a tight banding low on the hips and a slit up her left leg. Her leather ankle boots had pointy tips and crystal accents at the chunky heels—prudent because, while it was just a stroll along decorative pavers from the shuttle to the lawn, stilettos would stick into the soft earth like tent spikes.

As dangerous as navigating the roads, backing up Chance's statement.

And hell . . .

Now that Avery had gotten a good look at her . . . Chance might be right about her being city. Not his jam at all.

Though she spoke with a light accent.

Not that that proved anything.

The rest of her was a walking advertisement for all the frilly stuff some women were into, including Wyatt. Her influence on him when growing up on the ranch was probably why he cataloged the pertinent details. The sleek hair pulled up on the sides with sparkling clips, the remainder flowing like a satin curtain down her exposed back. The smoky effect around her eyes and the thick, velvety lashes. All of which ensnared him.

Then there were her words . . .

Avery shifted from one foot to the other as he felt an uncomfortable tightening in his groin.

"Insatiable desire," "succulent," and "craving" were terms that could be his undoing with a woman like her.

Especially when wicked ruminations were creeping around the fringes of sensible thoughts that were centered on cooking—not rumpling bedsheets.

"What do you recommend, cowboy?" she asked, batting those lashes. Keeping Avery fixated on her fiery eyes and her suggestive comments.

Red-hot lust was a branding iron he knew best to avoid. Avery was as committed to the success of this ranch as Jack—and everyone else— was. He had no intention of blowing his role by getting all wrapped up in long legs and rasping sighs. Or the most beautifully sculpted face he'd ever seen.

*TROUBLE* for sure.

However, he couldn't help but play along.

"You talking about what's on the menu?" he taunted, their gazes locked.

Her irises deepened in color. "You have to direct a girl to the appropriate selections when she's inundated by them."

"Mmm . . . ," he murmured. "You're no girl. Though I can certainly lead you down the right path."

He mentally harangued himself for not being as witty or as seductive as he suddenly wanted to be. But it'd been ages since he'd hit on a woman.

Thus, he stuck with what he *wasn't* rusty at.

"Let me introduce you to my award-winning smoked-paprika tomahawk." He gestured toward a two-inch-thick bone-in steak. "Or the hailed porterhouse—a strip and tenderloin cut, so you get the best of both worlds—with my top secret seasoning." He pointed that out too. "While I do advocate for a bacon-wrapped filet mignon or a rib eye smothered in cowboy butter with sautéed mushrooms and onions, I find I can elevate the flavor of the other two better. Both have excellent marbling, similar to the rib eye."

"My mouth is watering."

So was his. For a different reason.

"I'm torn," she said. And executed a playful pout.

Not a look that would lure him under normal circumstances. But she was damn pretty.

She told him, "I've never tried a tomahawk. Or a porterhouse—that reminds me of those restaurant commercials that declare if you can eat a seventy-two-ounce one, it's free." Now she cringed. "Seventy-two fuckin' ounces. Good Lord."

He chuckled. "Yeah, they make you eat all the fixin's too. Dinner roll, salad, appetizer, baked potato. Shoot . . . now I'm hungry."

"I can't believe you're not snacking while these are cooking up. The spicy, savory aroma is driving me wild."

"I suppose I'm more distracted by the visual stimulation."

Okay, that was moderately better on the flirtation scale. If the heat in her golden eyes was any indication.

She teased him a bit as she said, "There are plenty of women to choose from here." She paused, cleared her throat, and added, "I mean, if that's what you're into."

"If that's your roundabout way of asking whether I'm straight—and single—then I'm doing a piss-poor job at my attempt to woo you, as it were."

"'Woo' me. That's so sweet." Her laugh was soft and luxurious. His gut clenched, and his blood turned to magma.

Goddamn, he was losing his shit over her. Nothing *sweet* about that.

Also . . . he felt, deep in his bones, that she was someone he wanted to know better.

Somehow, he sensed her inner beauty might exceed the outer beauty.

Could be her unwavering gaze that inspired this notion. Could be her entrancing smile. Could be that she was still standing here with him, when there were men wound around the proverbial block to nab her attention. Many of whom appeared to be more high society than Avery Reed could ever aspire to be.

Sure, he had accolades and a champion pitmaster belt buckle he occasionally bragged on. But he was otherwise humble to the core.

That might have been a different story when he was on the BBQ circuit—and well beyond—had his dad's reckless antics not, inadvertently, brought Avery down a peg or two. Caleb Reed could be an ornery son of a bitch, more often than not. He wasn't a man to even try to reason with. His wife had learned that early on—and had left the ranch when Avery was seven and Chance was nine. In the ensuing years, Avery was convinced the phrase "dumpster fire" had been crafted specifically for Caleb Reed.

*Asshole.*

But that wasn't the topic on deck.

Beauty wanted a steak. And, again, a woman who didn't exist on bird seeds impressed the hell out of him.

He said, "I'll send you to the carving station for a filet that's medium rare and rested."

"Hmm . . ." She tapped a manicured finger against her glossy lips. "I've changed my mind. Lady's prerogative and all that." The slight curving at the corners of her mouth made her smile a coy one.

"Feel free to tell me what you're interested in, darlin'." That was casting a wide net.

She brightened. But evaded his underlying inference.

"You sold me on the others." She pointed to the first cut he'd shown her and said, "I'll have that one there. And . . ." Her finger drifted toward another juicy steak. "That one too."

"I don't serve 'em straight off the grill—"

"But those are the ones I want," she insisted in a sultry tone. Lifted her gaze. Fluttered her lashes again. And queried, "So that's what I should have, right?"

Avery's jaw clenched for a second, stifling another chuckle.

Then he replied, "If you say so—"

"Don't you dare let a 'ma'am' slip out," she lobbed back. "I don't want us gettin' off on the wrong foot, cowboy."

"It's never meant as ageism," he assured her. "Just a word of respect."

"Granted," she conceded with a nod. "But . . . don't call me 'ma'am.'"

He couldn't hold back a laugh this time. "Well, I wouldn't want those pointy boots of yours injuring my pride and joy, so I promise to refrain. Though it'd be helpful if I knew your name."

She studied him briefly. Then said, "You have no idea who I am."

His brow rose. "Should I?"

"Well," she continued in a more modest tone, "not necessarily. Other than you're a widely recognized pitmaster, and your cousin is an acclaimed grill master with his own YouTube channel. And I'm a BBQ cook-off host. Layla Jenson. A pleasure to meet you, Avery Reed."

Despite her warm intonation, his spirits took a dive south.

"Sooo, you're here for Jack. His celebrity star *is* skyrocketin'."

"*Not* here for Jack," she hastily said. "Or Jillian. Much as I adore them both on-screen. But they're not the format I'm promoting."

"Now I'm confused," Avery admitted.

"Plop those steaks I'm requesting onto my plate," she told him, "and between the time it takes for me to explain what I want from *you*, Avery, and the time it takes me to settle back into my chair at that table over there . . ." She glanced over her shoulder, then returned her gaze to him. "These'll be in excellent condition."

He was intrigued.

*Mesmerized* was more like it.

Not the least bit wise, but . . . it was what it was.

"I'll bite on this line," he said as everything within him pulled taut.

He couldn't possibly fathom this convo having anything to do with his BBQ status, since he really hadn't had one of late. He'd left the circuit eleven years ago. With his reputation intact, despite his dad's having been sullied.

Perhaps it was something else she had on her mind—though whether she actually was coming on to him remained to be seen.

From the quickened rise and fall of her chest, however, he found it hard to believe the scorching chemistry *wasn't* mutual.

And speaking of something on the cusp of getting hard . . .

But he kept himself in check. He wasn't some awestruck schoolkid.

Well, the *awestruck* part might be accurate.

He grabbed his tongs to do her bidding.

"We've been filming cook-offs on our YouTube channel, *Light Your Fire*, for the past few years," she said. "We're on season five and doing something a little more adventurous."

"So no backyard chili competitions?" he quipped. Searching for some levity and safe ground before he got trapped in her molten irises.

*Light your fire, indeed . . .*

"You are correct," she asserted. "No amateur hour here. While we have done a southwestern chili contest with all ingredients cooked over an open flame—with extraordinary regional variations—we only seek out seasoned BBQ buffs. Not at the celeb level, but ones who can bring their A game and can teach realistic recipes to aspiring, midlevel, and even more advanced 'cuers."

Avery loaded her plate.

She added, "So, yes, Jack and Jillian are notables and on our radar. But this current battle royale is for Best Bunkhouse Cook."

His head snapped up.

She grinned. "Ah. Got your attention there."

That earlier internal song and dance about him being humble flew right out the window.

Avery prided himself on his job on the ranch and valued his awards from the circuit. His dad might have wrecked both their careers in that world, but Avery had gotten out while the getting was good and had preserved his championship standing.

That sentiment was reinforced when Layla said, "Throughout the entire Texas cowboy community, your name repeatedly comes up as an exceptional bunkhouse cook, Avery. And you have huge love from fans in Kansas City and Memphis—from BBQ superstars, no less. That's astounding!"

Avery's hackles rose. Sure, the compliments were more than welcome. He just wondered how much research this woman had done on him.

As in, did it involve his dad? Had she dug into the "Caleb years" that still haunted Avery?

He gazed at her—with scrutiny—not wanting to believe her presence here today had anything to do with dredging up his past. Or turning it into some sort of commentary or, God forbid, a documentary.

True fact, there was enough drama for a lengthy shit show on Netflix.

And if Caleb ever returned to the TRIPLE R . . . Holy. Hell.

Avery couldn't go there in his mind. Bad blood was one thing. Nearly destroying a dynasty, a generational legacy . . . that was indefensible.

But . . . Layla Jenson seemed genuine. Pitching an authentic concept to him that she hadn't fully outlined—yet her enthusiasm for it was palpable.

So much so, Avery let his guard down enough to ask, "Exactly what are you proposing, darlin'?"

◆ ◆ ◆

She'd hooked him!

Layla bit back what could've been a very audible sigh of relief—or an explosive *squee*!

She was making a big play for a sixth season of the show she'd helped to create, and that meant the current season five had to kick ass.

Luckily, she'd been able to sign a half dozen bunkhouse chefs to this endeavor. But her executive producer wanted four more. And the only reason she hadn't reached out to Avery Reed immediately was because she knew he was a part of this Memorial Day weekend festival, and filming live segments would pull him from his duties. Or make him flat out say no.

Therefore, she'd had to bide her time. No easy feat. When Layla recognized a gold mine, she went after it with gusto.

She'd wished to merely swoop in and call *Action!* from the second this season's format had been hatched and green-lighted. But it hadn't taken long to discern that Avery Reed couldn't be included in the initial launch, with everything else he had going on. Even now, she understood she'd be putting some pressure on him to join the competition.

Yet so much of that pressure had already been mitigated, she reminded herself. She and the production team had laid sound groundwork that ensured Avery (and everyone else in his position of not being able to break away from ranch responsibilities) wouldn't be put out.

To that end, she told him, "We're working with the top ten names in bunkhouse barbecue. The greatest concern from a production standpoint is that we're mindful of these chefs' obligations. We're not interested in being disruptive."

"Yeah, but . . . cutting loose from feedin' the 'boys—"

"No need to cut loose," she interjected. "We come to you."

He put their discussion on pause with a finger, then accepted two trays from a man who was maybe an inch taller than Avery's six-foot-one stature (yes, she'd researched his stats) and possibly a couple years older than his thirty-one years.

Confirmed when Avery told her, "Meet Chance, my older brother. Foreman of the TRIPLE R."

She couldn't shake hands, hers were both full with the weight of her plate. And there were open flames between them. But she smiled and said, "Quite pleased to make your acquaintance, Chance."

"Likewise, Miss Layla."

He took her in from head to toe. As had every other man she'd encountered today.

Unlike her lukewarm reaction to them, this cowboy's gaze actually *could* trip a breaker within her, he was that devastatingly handsome. He carried on the obvious Reed family traits of thick dark hair and hypnotic blue eyes. And half-assed grins that were swoon-worthy.

But . . . alas . . .

Only Avery incited the distinct crackle through her veins.

*That* man was a thunderbolt of magnetism and vitality. He might not think he was sparking her interest outside her current vision quest, but there most certainly were sparks.

He possessed an evocative quality she couldn't quite define. Something elusive that made him stand out from the crowd. He exuded a masculine vibe, absolutely. Also a mysterious one, equivalent to a secret one knew existed but couldn't uncover. An outer shell that couldn't be breached.

Not yet anyway.

But with some effort, who knew what might be revealed . . . ?

That sent exhilaration down her spine.

The complication, however, was that Layla had her own secrets not to be uncovered. Her own outer shell not to be breached.

Making her hypocritical for wanting to delve deeper into him while being careful not to divulge too much about herself.

Her horrific past was meant to be dead and buried—never to be exhumed. She was a new person now. With a new name, a new persona, a new life, a new . . . *everything*.

Bottom line, she was here to engage with Avery for the sake of the show. For the sake of her career. That was where her sole focus ought to be. Not on how rugged and sexy the man was.

She had to concentrate on how he'd make a spectacular addition to a production she desperately hoped would have more seasons and gain a bigger audience. Not only because she needed this job; it also offered exposure and acknowledgment to a subset of cooks who represented a glorious culinary culture that made one's toes curl and their stomachs growl.

Okay, yes, she'd once been a BBQ connoisseur. As her daddy had been. But somewhere in her early twenties, Layla had lost her way. And, to be honest, she'd become a food snob. One who preferred fine dining in a ridiculously expensive restaurant versus a grassroots event such as this.

She'd returned to her own roots, though. And was happier for it.

After the brother carried away the steaks from Avery's station, she informed him, "We have some incredible traditional grill and smoke masters on the show, but none who match your expertise with the pit when serving a large group of people. Working with an earth oven and conquering that perfect temperature with the right coals and embers is an artform, Avery. As you know. And that, combined with your overall barbecuing skills, could win you this title."

"Honey, I do have plenty of 'em," he said. "Not really chasing after another."

"Just think about this," she implored. "We're filming this week in Cheyenne. But the crew's available next week. That gives you plenty of time to recover from this extravaganza."

"I don't need recovery time." He winked.

And that did crazy things to her body she couldn't begin to process. Even made her hands tremble as she held her heavy plate.

"I'll be up before the sun rises tomorrow to prep a feast fit for kings, after all these wranglers and ranch hands have done to make this bash a success. Helping to clean up and reset the scene every day, while ensuring the cows and horses are tended to." He gave a nod. "They've done this family a solid. As always. It's gratifying to me to reward them with chucks that aren't slapped-together by-products. We take care of our own on the TRIPLE R."

Emotion swelled within her, taking Layla by surprise. Her daddy would have said something akin to that, if only she were still in contact with him.

She swallowed down the lump in her throat but knew her eyes were a bit misty, due to Avery's conviction as much as the wayward ruminations on her daddy. Which she always kept tucked away. Her new persona came with the need to distance herself from him. He just wouldn't understand all that had happened to her—why she literally didn't look like the daughter he'd raised.

Pushing the painful notion away, she told Avery, "That's the spirit that will win this competition. Yes, the quality of food, the cooking techniques, and the unique recipes are the primary focus. But *why* you stretch the limits to deliver the best you can is the underlying heart and soul of this contest."

She tried to collect herself, but there was a burning sensation in her core that went hand in hand with all the research that had led her to seek out Avery Reed.

She emphasized, "I swear our team won't flip a well-oiled operation on its side, cowboy. Just . . . give it some thought."

His shrug was noncommittal.

She further reminded him, "I'll be over there with my assistant, Brodi. The redhead who always looks like she's vibratin' in her seat. She has a million to-dos running rampant through her whiz-bang brain. Plus, she's always starving—all those calories she expends vibratin'."

Layla laughed at how earnest those statements were. She also beamed on the inside because Brodi was a miracle worker with a heart of gold—and Layla's bestie.

She told Avery, "Think the tomahawk and the porterhouse are gonna rock both our worlds." She smiled again.

Then she carefully turned to go, given her load. Also before she gave a bit more away of herself than she'd intended. And ruined the steaks with her delay in delivering them.

Though it was difficult to drag her gaze from Avery.

His low snicker indicated he was well aware.

Damn. This wasn't going to be an easy mission.

Sure, she'd seen photos of him on the internet. And she'd thought he was hotter than hell. That, however, had not prepared her for the *reality* of the man. His strong build and commanding presence. Also his reserved—perhaps purposely controlled?—disposition mixed with natural charm and dry wit.

She'd expected a more overpowering personality, having watched clips of him on Jack's show and then from the recent street festival in the nearby town of Serrano, where he'd been grilling fajitas with another cousin, Luke.

In effect, what she'd anticipated was a cowboy Casanova.

But the Avery Reed she'd met today was more of a cool drink of sparkling water. Hitting all the right spots on a hot summer day. Leaving her tingly all over . . . yet not fully quenched.

Because she'd only had a sample of the man.

And she couldn't deny . . .

She was thirsty for more.

# Chapter Two

"Is he signin' up?" Brodi Brooks pounced the second Layla returned to the table they shared with eight other people. "I have the contracts on my phone, ready for printing. He can review them early this evening, and I'll scan them at the business center at the hotel in town, or if they have a scanner here, we can—"

"Slow down, my overzealous assistant." Though that was one of the things Layla loved about the five-foot-five dynamo.

"How slow can I go? I can't get y'all to agree to use electronic contracts and signatures, so I have to plan for all the extraneous variables. Printin' and scannin' . . ." She made a face. "Gah."

Layla laughed. "Lots of these cowboys and ranchers prefer to flip through papers, not screens on their computers."

"And yet Jack Reed has his own socials blowing up. Total techie."

"I think that's more his producer's and his nephew's doing. His sister's as well."

"Regardless, I—"

"Just be patient with the process. Avery requires a multipronged approach," Layla told her. "He's got his hands full with this event and other duties. I floated the concept and will let it sink in. Then I'll mention the other specifics at the right times."

"Aren't we supposed to strike when the iron's hot?"

"Not hot enough yet," Layla murmured. And sliced through the mammoth tomahawk steak, placing a hunk on Brodi's plate. She did the same with the porterhouse.

Toppings for the steaks were being passed around the table, but Layla was a purist and wanted to catalogue the flavor profiles Avery had captured.

Before she took a bite, she added, "I haven't hit him with the true zinger yet. I just need a little more time with the man."

Brodi leveled her with a look. "I'm confused as to whether you need time with the *man* or the *cook*."

"Ha, ha. Try the steaks."

"Oh, I intend to devour the steaks. Just wondering if that's your thought with *the man*."

Layla's stomach fluttered. When it really shouldn't. But, hell . . . there was just no getting around the fact that she was deeply attracted to Avery. Perhaps she had been from the get-go, in this season's developmental stage.

She'd been prepared, in theory, to encounter him.

Again, in reality . . . *good Lord.*

He was just so . . . *there.*

So wide. So muscular. Somewhat imposing. Taking up lots of space and all her air. In an arousing way.

Even with him wearing a leather apron as he tended to his steaks, Layla got the full visual of broad shoulders and defined pecs.

More than how his looks would boost the show's ratings, he'd had Layla at "no one treats a porterhouse with more TLC than me." The declaration he'd made on Jack's live stream months ago. That intimate statement and his accompanying smoldering gaze had lit a blaze within Layla—a fiery one she'd never experienced before.

Not exactly a sensible acknowledgment on her part. But an inescapable one.

Brodi broke into her thoughts, saying, "I can't tell if I want to climax over the scent coming off these steaks or gorge myself on what will surely be melt-on-my-tongue ecstasy when I taste them."

Layla nearly spewed the sip of cabernet sauvignon she'd just taken a sip of.

"What?" Brodi asked, undeterred.

"There *are* other people at this table," Layla reminded her.

"Who aren't paying a lick of attention to us anymore. Girl, they're all trying to clean their plates as fast as they can and go back for more until we're cut off from this chow-down orgy."

"Oh, my gawd." Layla did a brief face-plant into her palms. Then said, "I'll never be able to say for certain what I adore most about you. Your colorful and candid observations, your pertness, or your brilliance."

"Eeegads!" she quipped, though with a wince. "It's the 'brilliance' part that's killin' me, isn't it? Like, I'm just too much in my head, right? When I should've been making the rounds since we got here. Flirting and stuff. But eeeww . . ." She did her signature grimace emoji imitation. "IRL interactions . . . hashtag: ThankYouNoThankYou."

"You're doing fine," Layla assured her. "You said hello to the people in our immediate vicinity."

"Then promptly ignored them." Brodi sighed. "This is a meat market of dual varieties. I'm not up for a schmooze fest. I just wanna eat and figure out how this bunkhouse cook-off is going to pan out."

"Another key factor to add to my list of heartin' on you. However . . ." Layla sipped again, since it seemed to be a safe moment in which to do so. "While we're promoting the show, it is imperative we schmooze. Pretend we're actual social creatures."

"You're killin' my buzz."

Layla laughed. There was always something *killin'* Brodi Brooks— in a good way or a facetious one.

Layla said, "I endured forty-five minutes of trying to get to Avery. More significantly, trying to get him *alone*."

"I'd say you have a competition of your own going on, but he just waves the ladies away from his grills, sending them straight to the carving station. He's all tunnel vision, attuned to his times and temps.

Well. Until you came along. Bet he burnt a few steaks when he caught sight of you."

"Not even one, I guarantee it. He can do this in his sleep. Goddamn, he'd be so awesome on our show! We have to snag him."

"While scarfing down amazing eats," Brodi said in between bites. "Holy cow, I can't get enough of this cow!"

"Yeah, Avery Reed has genuine talent." Her gaze drifted to him. For about the millionth time today.

He finished his steaks and stripped off his apron. The tug of leather against his shirt released two snaps on his flap—opening the shirt to the middle of his expansive chest.

His bronze skin and chiseled muscles made her pulse pound. The way the short sleeves of his shirt hugged his biceps sent a tickle along her clit.

And the overall effect of him . . .

*Holy Christ.*

Layla wanted to shred the remainder of the material and put her hands all over him. Taste every inch of him. Take him deep in her mouth and—

*Whoa, wait—whhaaat?!*

*Layla, Layla, Layla!!!*

*Inappropriate thoughts about a potential contestant!*

She gaped.

"What just happened?" Brodi asked, covering her mouth because it was full.

Layla snapped her jaw shut and shook her head. "Nothing."

She considered there wasn't anything specific in her contract that said she *couldn't* canoodle. She had no sway with the judges.

Still, it was neither professional nor practical.

She reminded herself this was a corporate outing. Her executive producer had landed the two tickets for today's grand finale, and Layla and Brodi had made it here from their last filming location, in Santa Fe, to spend a couple of hours absorbing the ranch scenery and enjoying the feast before Jack concluded the party.

By the looks of things, it'd take a major announcement onstage to get these people moving toward the shuttles and off the property; there was way too much jubilation going on. Still food to ingest, still shuffles around the dance floor to take, still friends to make.

She'd thought this venture would be predominantly about barbecue. She'd been wrong—it was also a networking smorgasbord.

Although Layla typically kept to herself in private settings, making her and Brodi kindred spirits, she had a knack for marketing when surrounded by this many people—and that inherent trait had burst forth as soon as they'd arrived.

Brodi was more inclined to be the behind-the-scenes guru. And that was a nice complement to Layla's efforts to gain more recognition.

Problem being the latter was a catch-22 of its own making.

Layla was driven by her need to succeed. Conversely, she was still hindered by a past that had her constantly looking over her shoulder—and staying as far away as possible from her father and her other relatives and former friends to keep them out of harm's way. Which meant, at the end of the day, she and Brodi would go back to their hotel rooms and their somewhat solitary lives.

Brodi's by choice. Layla's by necessity.

Although she was thrilled to be among the land of the living again, she was still a woman who was waiting for the other shoe to drop. Knowing she'd done everything she could to escape a monstrous "situationship" and make it so that the man who'd brutally attacked her couldn't find her, identify her. Yet she still harbored doubts—and fears—that he would. He was that powerful, that persistent.

Not exactly the issue at hand, though.

Layla had more to discuss with Avery.

She polished off her meal as he wound his way through the crowd and the tables and disappeared inside the main house.

Brodi slipped away, only to return with refills on their wine. Bringing along individual crème brûlées.

"I can't fathom how I have room for this," she said, "but I do."

"Yeah, that looks divine," Layla concurred. The berries on top were the perfect supplement to the meat they'd consumed. "We had salads as starters, but those rich potatoes Romanoff and the Dutch oven rolls pretty much made me regret eating rabbit food when we could be sparing space for everything else."

Brodi grinned. "For what these tickets cost, I'm pretty sure our management team will be pleased we've stuffed ourselves to the gills."

"And now I'm thinking . . . ," Layla mused as Avery emerged from the covered patio, wearing a new shirt—this one pewter colored to match his jeans, hat, and snakeskin boots—and wove his way toward her, "that I could use a little cardio."

"Please tell me you're not just referring to dancing. Because that cowboy has been scopin' you like a prized steer and—" Brodi's brow furrowed. "Perhaps we're taking the culinary adages too far. Let me just say . . . you're for sure in Avery Reed's crosshairs."

Warmth flooded Layla's veins. "Lucky me."

She applied a new coat of vanilla-scented lip gloss.

Seconds later, Avery strode by her table, holding out his hand.

What did Layla do? She placed her palm in his and let him lead her to the dance floor. With neither of them saying a word.

She did glimpse back at Brodi, whose eyes were huge.

Avery pulled Layla close and murmured, "You do two-step, right?"

"You do apologize for being condescending, right?"

He chuckled. "Not my intent. I'm just not sure where you're comin' from. Not just geographically."

"I can two-step," she assured him. And let him hold her right hand at chest height as she flattened her left palm against his shoulder. He was the leader; she was the follower.

They fell into step with the others moving counterclockwise about the floor. He guided her when he wanted to turn her and steadily brought her back to him. They worked in sync with each other through eye contact, body movement, and some sort of cosmic connection.

Layla had learned this dance from her daddy when she was small enough to start out by standing on his boots. Then being in rhythm enough to go through the quick, quick, slow, slow motions on her own.

It'd been eons since she'd danced with anyone, yet with Avery . . . it all came back to her.

When the music changed to a slower ballad and he held her a bit more firmly, she broke the "dancer's space" to snuggle close to him.

She twined an arm around his neck and inhaled his crisp cologne that mingled with his male heat.

"You get all fancied up for me, cowboy?" she inquired.

"Well, if you'd wanted to nibble on me because I smelled like barbecue, I'm not sayin' I would have minded."

She laughed. "You've spruced yourself up with a refreshing fragrance, but I still get the hint of mesquite woodchips, so . . . I'll say you found the perfect balance."

"That you can tell the difference between my preferred smoky flavors—mesquite, oak wood, and hickory—is impressive. But I'm more pleased I didn't find you in the clutches of another man when I returned."

"I'll confess that marketing our channel is important, but Brodi and I are here primarily to convince *you* that our show is a worthy endeavor."

He groaned. "We're back to that."

"Let me just tell you that we've got the production process down to a science, so it doesn't interfere with your operation. We film segments over the course of five days: a specialty meal of your choosing to get us started, then a breakfast, a lunch, a dinner, and a dessert."

"Think I want to talk more about you nibblin' on me."

The mere thought sent liquid fire through her veins. How she stayed the course was beyond her.

Though Layla did hear the sultriness lacing her voice as she continued. "We have three BBQ professionals to judge every segment—each of those scores go into the individual contestants' lockboxes, not to be revealed until the finale. Even I don't see them."

"Very pins and needles like."

"Exactly. The suspense is an additional driving force to keep viewers tuning in," she said. "I'm the one who interacts with the cowboys you feed—and with you. All via testimonials and short interviews. But I have absolutely no say over the judging. I do not provide a score. I don't provide personal opinion of the food. I'm only the host."

He turned her again, pulled her to him. Sending a delicious shiver down her spine.

She said, "Here's the kicker, Avery." She stared into his gorgeous blue irises and told him, "The winner gets one hundred and fifty thousand dollars."

His brow quirked.

"Yeah. And the runner-up gets fifty grand."

His jaw worked.

"There's a total win here. I *feel* it," she asserted. "Again, I have no input and no stakes. I'm literally Switzerland. But I am instrumental in which contestants we select. And yet the truth is, I didn't have to advocate for you, Avery. All I did was mention your name—*everyone* voted yes. We just couldn't interrupt your current focus. Though . . . if next week you can allow us to—"

"Darlin' . . ." He let out a low grunt. Dipped her with a strong hold, then brought her upright and sealed her to him, leaving her breathless. "I don't just answer to myself. No one in this family does. Everything that goes on at the TRIPLE R is meant to keep us in the black. Year over year."

She went up on tiptoes and craned her neck, so her lips were but a wisp from his. "One hundred and fifty thousand dollars, Avery. Fifty K at the least. You gonna tell me that's not a substantial bounty for this ranch?"

He gritted his teeth. Guided her around the dance floor some more, keeping her in his tight embrace.

She added, "Maybe you once competed for the glory of it. Maybe you want a new glory. But the fact is . . . you have incredible potential to take the cake here, cowboy. And I swear to you, on my mama's own grave, God rest her soul, that we won't be a nuisance. You do you, let me interview you in snippets, and let the judges taste what you've cooked up. You'll go about your regular day, Avery. Just bring your best recipes and your expertise to the table. That's all."

It was like Christmas morning when you were eight and your dad promised you that if you did your chores and kept your mouth shut while he nursed his hangover, you could open your present.

With there being absolutely no guarantee there'd be a present.

Because your mom had long since left and your alcoholic father only knew it was Christmas because your ever-vigilant uncle had brought over a tree and your beloved aunt and tried-and-true (though mostly pesky) cousins had helped to decorate it.

Kind of an extreme comparison, but the key correlation here was that you were asked to deliver the goods with no more than unicorn dreams to back up your effort.

Not only that, Avery simply couldn't afford the distraction.

Conversely . . .

The dollar signs flashing in the back of his head were difficult to ignore.

As was Layla's soft smile. And her gently arched brow.

Not to mention her silky voice as she added, "I have experience in the champion BBQ world. Long ago, yes. And now more recently." Her eyes clouded for a moment, intriguing him. "Suffice it to say, *I'm* no amateur. But, again . . . I'm only the face of the competition. I don't contribute to the result. So you can be assured that what happens is solely up to the judges. Although . . ."

She executed a smooth turn and moved right back into his arms.

"As a cocreator, I have a vested interest in this entire production," she told him. "I want a real winner."

Avery wasn't certain what she knew about him, what she saw in him.

But he for sure felt a charge between them.

So he took the bait. "What else do you need today?"

"To see your cooking facility. I'll take some pics and add them to your dossier."

He frowned. "I have a dossier?"

This alarmed him.

But she was still breezy. Damn near feathery in his arms, without the hint of tension in her body. So he held fast to the idea that she hadn't dug *too* deep.

He didn't take her for the duplicitous type. Someone who might come off as being wholly on your side, reeling you in . . . only to blindside you. With a dossier on your epic failure of a father.

Jesus, he hated how harsh that was.

But both he and Chance had lived the reality. As had the rest of the family. So there was no untethering himself from it.

Layla said, "There's nothing invasive in your file, I promise. Just all your awards. Some articles that evaluated you against your younger cousin, Jack, noting you both use different techniques. Various displays of your rig and your grills, and how those changed over the years as you gained notoriety—and skill. How you inevitably turned to maximizing the pit."

"Trying to control something that's seriously not meant to be controlled." A component that had fascinated him from the moment he'd learned food could be smoked in a trench.

"Earth ovens take attention and dedication," she said. "And you've slayed the outcome."

"Hmm. Never heard it put it that way. Why don't you make the introductions with Brodi before I whisk you off to my lair."

Her amber eyes sparkled as she teased, "Thought we were checking out your operation, cowboy."

"It is my principal domain."

"Then let's have a look-see."

He gave her a final twirl before escorting her off the dance floor, holding her hand and keeping her close. Just in case some other gent got the misguided notion to step in.

He hadn't marked his territory since a high school crush, but he suspected he'd done it quite thoroughly now, after raiding Jack's closet and returning from the main house.

Avery lived down the hill, closer to the bunkhouse, where the ranch foreman prior to Chance had resided until he'd retired. Right around that time, Avery had taken over as head cook because his uncle had ordered Caleb—the previous chef—off the premises for good. Avery had been nineteen.

That was the year that their competitive BBQ team had imploded. As usual, thanks to his no-count dad.

Not anything he wanted to get into with Layla. Chance had remained in their family home, and Avery had moved into the foreman's house, which made sense because it was closest to his industrial kitchen, just a two-minute ride on his utility task vehicle from his driveway.

When they reached Layla's assistant at her table, the redhead was fervently typing on her phone and barely noticed them.

Layla cleared her throat. "Incomin'," she said.

Brodi's head snapped up. "I was just scrolling through posts about today's—and this entire weekend's—activities here at the TRIPLE R. Ginormous hoopla. This is a sensational event that has created a firestorm on socials. Unbelievable!"

"Which gives us a fantastic foundation for bringing Avery onto the show," Layla commented.

"I've neither confirmed nor denied my involvement," he reminded her. "Just giving you a tour, darlin'."

"And I just wanted the two of you to meet," Layla said. "Avery Reed, this is Brodi Brooks."

"It's a pleasure." Avery tipped his hat with his left hand, not willing to relinquish the right one still holding Layla's.

"Ditto." Brodi smiled up at him. And asked, "Sure y'all don't need those contracts now?"

"Not quite yet," Layla said with a pointed look.

Brodi heaved a sigh. "Fine. Just text me when you do, and I'll email them your way. I'm hittin' the first shuttle out of here." She raised a brow at Layla. "But you're not going with me . . . ?"

"Avery's going to let me see his official workspace. So I'll catch up with you at the hotel."

"I'll be luxuriating in a bubble bath, so don't come bargin' through the adjoining door. Knock first."

"It was only that one time in Boulder! And only because your music was so damn loud."

"No such thing when you've got Kane Brown, Kenny Chesney, and Morgan Wallen cued up."

"You were playing Taylor Swift," Layla countered.

"But I love her!" Brodi jumped from her seat, passed Layla's slim clutch to her, kissed her on the cheek, and then said, "Don't you ever go giving me fits about being a Swiftie. If she could grill up a sirloin to blow your mind, you'd be stalkin' *her*."

Layla shot a look at Avery. "I'm not stalking you." She groaned playfully. "That much."

He chuckled. "See how put out I am?"

"And here's my chance to employ the perfect exit strategy," Brodi said as she snatched her own bag and stuffed her phone inside. "You two enjoy your evening. I'm off to bliss out in my bear claw tub."

"We'll walk you to the shuttle," Avery told her. More of a protective command than a mere suggestion, not that he had any sort of concern about her safety. They had security crawling all over this place, and the crowd had been tame all weekend. Rowdy during the music they liked, of course. But not disorderly.

Still, regardless of Chance indicating earlier that the kegs were all but dry, Avery had no qualms shepherding both ladies.

They skirted the still-full tables and took the path that rounded the large main house.

Brodi said, "At first, I thought we'd arrived at a ski lodge, rather than a ranch."

Being in Hill Country, the terrain and the climate were a bit different than what most would expect. Not full-on Rocky Mountains imagery, though they had rolling hills and an occasional snowfall. Not all desert landscape or dusty plains with drilling rigs. But a lush mixture of trees and meadows. Creeks, ponds, lakes.

"Our outbuildings are more indicative of Texas architecture," Avery offered. "Most of the housing, though, features rock trimming from our river. Denotes part of our heritage of livin' off the land."

"So there's fish in that river?" Layla asked as she beamed up at him.

"Naturally, that's where your thoughts would go," he said in an amused tone. "We have largemouth and Guadalupe bass. Rainbow trout. Sunfish. It's not lobster, darlin', but I promise you it all cooks up right."

"With your seasonings, I'm sure."

"And they say the way to a *man's* heart is through his stomach," Avery jested.

"Nothing wrong with a woman who recognizes tasty cuisine when it's wafting under her nose."

"I do find that highly arousing."

She laughed. "So I'm turning you on because I'm a foodie."

"No, darlin', everything about you is turning me on."

"Oh, for the love of God!" This from Brodi—with a long-suffering sigh. "If you two don't get a room *soon*, the whole planet might spontaneously combust."

"Sooo melodramatic." Layla snickered. "We're just joking. No serious flirting going on yet." She batted her lashes at Avery. "Right, cowboy?"

His cock twitched, and he had to speak around the lust swelling in his throat. "Not yet."

Because he couldn't ratchet this flirtation up a notch the way he wanted to. Not when Brodi was present. Not when other partygoers were making their way toward the shuttles.

Avery wanted Layla alone—the very reason he'd consented to show her his setup, despite still having monumental reservations about agreeing to be a part of her competition.

That'd bring to light all that he preferred to keep in the dark.

Brodi stepped onto a full-size tour bus, and Avery directed Layla to the section of the circular drive where the family and staff vehicles had been rounded up. He greeted the two men from the private security company, and they pulled back the barricades to create a gap. Avery went to his truck, opened the passenger door for Layla, and then climbed behind the wheel. He dropped the visor, and his keys fell into his palm.

He had enough room to maneuver past the first shuttle that was filling up. Two others waited on the opposite side of the fountain that was in the center of the driveway.

As he and Layla headed down the hill with other trails winding toward the right-hand portion of the ranch, he asked, "Where you from, darlin'? I know it's not Serrano. I would have seen you in town. Can't miss that pretty face."

Out of the corner of his eye, he could see her staring at him. Like she was assessing how much personal information she should offer.

That spiked his curiosity.

Eventually, she said, "My unofficial bio reads a bit different than my public one."

"Swear I won't rat ya out." He tore his gaze from the windshield and winked at her.

Layla's dreamy sigh made his chest constrict.

No doubt, he was playing with fire. She was too beautiful by far, and the way she stared so intently at him, her tiger eyes shimmering, he was a moth drawn to the flame. One that could burn deep if he kept traveling this path with her.

She settled in her seat with the belt on and said, "Had a feeling I might end up being an open book with you."

"Why's that?"

"Because you look like a heartbreaker, but you don't act like one."

"So I really do suck at stakin' my claim."

"Oh, you did just fine when we were on the dance floor. Make no mistake, cowboy."

He glanced at her again. She smiled.

He'd say the tightness in his chest eased, but this was the sort of sexual tension that required a more specific release.

"And PS," she said, "I'm here with you, right? When I could be with Brodi on a bus. About to take my own bubble bath."

"You're here to see my kitchen," he reminded her.

"Is that what the kids are calling it these days?"

He chuckled.

"Yes, this is the prime opportunity to get a gander at your inner workings," she told him. "So I can report back to my crew. But stealing a few minutes alone with you is even more appealing."

Precisely what he'd been thinking earlier.

"So it's not just about the 'cuein'," he ventured.

"No, cowboy, it is not."

Well, then. That was setting the record straight.

He veered off, taking the smooth, dirt-packed lane to a conglomeration of buildings, pointing out which was which. "Stables and corrals. Barn for tack, supplies, hay, and whatnot. Silo for feed. Bunkhouse. Chuck hall, as I call it. Then farther down is my house."

"It's all so stunning," she said as she took in the scenery, with random thickets and wildflowers, miles of green pasture, the river running in the backdrop, along with the rising hills in the distance.

"We've got the acreage for a substantial operation and the right people tending to all the jobs needed to keep the moving parts moving."

He pulled up to a large red cedar log cabin with a hunter green metal roof and an elaborate deck.

"Don't move. Give me a sec." He shut off the engine and went around to collect her, helping her down to the graveled drive.

He cupped her elbow as they crossed the lush grass to the porch, with Adirondack chairs, sofas, and accent tables for comfortable conversations. Or reading a book, listening to podcasts, playing a guitar. The wranglers and the other ranch hands didn't have much downtime, but there was plenty of room to accommodate playing poker or tossing lawn darts. Whatever they chose in order to unwind and decompress after supper.

Layla told him, "Y'all make every space useful and inviting."

"I did mention the staff are deserving."

He pulled back the creaking screen door and plugged in the code to the entrance. Gestured for Layla to precede him.

"Oh, wow," she said on a rush of air. "This is huge."

The walls on either side of the door were lined with refrigerators and freezers, with shelving units at each end for ingredients, spices, backstock. The left portion was dedicated to stovetops and ovens. The right was for triple sanitary sinks, a commercial-grade dishwasher, and the two metal prep tables with casters that were folded vertically and pushed off to the side until needed. Beyond all this was a long butcher-block counter for serving, with a gap in the middle that Layla passed through to survey the dining room, though all the tables and chairs were collapsed and set against the wall.

As her gaze fell on them, Avery explained, "We're typically only in here during inclement weather. Clearing the space makes it easier to mop the floor throughout the day as we come and go."

"Yeah, this is all immaculate." She whipped out her phone and snapped pics.

Avery then unlocked the double doors leading out back and showed her the kitchen setup there, with mini fridges, a workstation with a dual sink and six burners, a grated cowboy grill, a flat one, and five other types of grills and smokers, plus meat lockers.

"And there's the pit," she mused with awe.

"Give me a Dutch oven, banana leaves, burlap, foil, anything I can wrap food in, and I'll deliver a winning meal."

She clapped her hands together, lighting up like a slot machine with all sevens.

Somehow, that tore at his heart.

Reminded him of all the potential he'd had to keep collecting titles.

How much he'd *wanted* to collect more titles.

Because in doing so, he was elevating his game and honing his skills for the greater good—the ranch.

"Once again," she said with emotion, "that's the spirit, Avery Reed! In addition to your big *Why*—going the extra mile to serve those who serve your family—this will have viewers rooting for you. And those endorsements count toward your overall ranking."

"If I agree to be a contestant."

"Why wouldn't you?" she challenged.

He groaned. "You do realize you're deflecting, right? Any reason why you have difficulty talking about yourself?"

He stared her down as she hedged.

His brow crooked.

She said, "I'm not exactly getting *your* life history."

"You did research me, correct?"

"I'll confess I got distracted by the photos." Her cheeks flushed. "And it had nothing to do with all the BBQ on display."

Avery's thoughts shifted to more lascivious ones. Like getting this woman naked and trailing his fingertips along all that honeyed skin he already knew felt like satin under his touch.

"To my credit," she said, getting on track again, "I did note all the accolades and the belt buckle. Kinda surprising you fell off the map when you were only nineteen. Though subsequent features all mentioned you'd taken on the role as executive chef here."

She peered up at him with the melty eyes that were going to be the death of him if he didn't at least get one kiss out of this excursion. He could resist plenty, just out of being finicky about where he placed his affections.

But not where Layla Jenson was concerned.

"So," she continued. "Case closed, I guess."

He hadn't forgotten the topic of conversation. *Him.*

Avery's teeth ground. Not only over the raw desire hitching up several notches but also because he debated how he wanted to address his own elephant in the room. She wasn't fully forthcoming with her "unofficial bio," so maybe she needed a little tit for tat. For him to prove he was worthy of hearing her story after he'd provided some of his.

Since it was barely five o'clock and the sun was still shining—and he could use something to cool him down, *not* due to the sun still shining—he put her on hold for a minute. He pulled two beers from a fridge and sat with her at a picnic table under a shady tree. He popped the tops off and handed one over.

"You want a glass, darlin'?"

"Hell, no." She snickered. "I can even do shooters, cowboy."

He chuckled, though it did nothing to alleviate the pressure he felt, pretty much from head to toe. More wickedly so in all the sensitive places in between.

They tapped rims, and he took a long drink.

Then he said, "I got the short end of the stick in some ways, when it came to bein' on the circuit. Had the talent but not a conducive team infrastructure. More accurate . . . not the team leader I required."

"Your dad was part of your crew. I didn't get the chance to look him up."

"I'm glad," he told her with instant relief—in that vein. "He's the bad seed. Destroyed everything we'd been striving to attain."

She sipped before saying, "I'm sorry for that."

"And I'd prefer it if you left him out of the equation. No point to rehashing his destructive ways. He obliterated our future on the circuit. And almost bankrupted this ranch. So when he was banished from this property by my uncle—Jack's dad—I took over his position as bunk-house cook. That's all I've been focused on for the past eleven years."

Which he loved.

But as he and Layla stared at each other across the table, her cook-off proposal hypothetically laid between them . . . Avery couldn't deny he did face temptation he might not be able to refuse. Not just her but also this unexpected opportunity.

Who wouldn't love the prospect of becoming a comeback kid?

Problem was all the dirty laundry would come back with him.

He sipped some more, mulling all this over.

She didn't give him the full-court press. She merely stated, "Chances are damn good you've improved upon your already stellar techniques."

"I like to think so. It's different when you're not working in an antagonistic environment. When you can experiment or perfect a trick of the trade without someone breathin' down your neck and constantly criticizing you."

"That's the beauty of our competition, Avery. You get to demonstrate all you're capable of in your own world, under your own conditions."

She left that sentiment to taunt him as well.

He drained his beer. So did she. He locked up the facility and got her into the truck again.

She gazed out the windshield, then the side window. "Sure is one hell of a setting."

"Not even as spectacular as when the sun's goin' down over the river."

She shot a look his way. "Is that an offer, cowboy?"

"Well, since you're here . . . you might as well see it."

"Sunset's not for a couple hours," she said with a hint of mischief in her eyes.

"I can give you a tour of my house. Make you dessert."

She laughed. "I had crème brûlée. And oh, my God, I can't justify eating for another week."

He wagged a finger in the air and chastised, "Don't go getting birdlike on me. A cowboy likes a woman who knows her way around home-cooked meals."

"To be honest, I split the steaks with Brodi."

"I assumed so. Still. Those cuts weren't for the faint of heart."

"No, they were not. And I feel better that we got some exercise on the dance floor."

There was a veiled insinuation about more of a workout to combat the calories, he was sure. But didn't want to be too presumptuous.

Then again . . .

He didn't have to be.

She leaned in close and whispered, "Perhaps we can work up a new appetite."

"Sunset it is," he murmured.

And started the truck.

# Chapter Three

His house was identical in architecture to the chuck hall.

"Y'all like your amenities," Layla commented as they rolled to a stop in front of Avery's porch, which was also well appointed.

"When you spend the majority of your time on a ranch, honey, it's nice to have creature comforts."

"I do not discount that." She unlatched her seat belt and was about to reach for the handle on the door.

"Whoa, whoa," he said. "No lady opens her own door around here if we can help it. No offense."

"None taken." She gave him an appreciative look. "Manners are never frowned upon in my book."

Yet she scowled. Before shaking her head.

"What was that about?" he asked.

"I sorta lost that perspective for a while."

He helped her out of the truck again. As they ascended the steps, he prompted, "How'd that happen?"

"You're getting good at roundabout questioning."

Avery shrugged. "Not so roundabout. And I'm willing to put effort into knowing you better. More importantly, the *unofficial bio*."

He disengaged the digital lock and ushered her inside. Security wasn't this tight around the ranch, not with the gate to the entrance being monitored with a camera and requiring a code. But Avery harbored qualms over his dad somehow getting onto the premises—and busting into his house or the chuck hall. That was how deep his worries over Caleb's return ran.

As he closed the door behind him, Layla said, "The 'hidden' details aren't something I share with people. Only Brodi and my executive producer. I need a level of discretion. Or disassociation from my past. A degree of trust. Or . . ." She blew out a breath. "I don't know. I just feel a basic instinct to safeguard myself."

His gut twisted. "From what?"

"Life," she retorted. Then glowered. "No. That's too victim-mentality for me."

She bounded down the step of the raised hardwood platform at the entrance and wandered about the spacious living room, the bar area with a pool table, and more sofa seating off to the side. Even took a peek at the kitchen with dining for six and additional seats at the island.

When she returned, Avery was still standing in the foyer, under a chandelier emitting an amber glow, like the pendant lights hanging throughout the exposed-rafter, split-level home. There were two antique-looking ceiling fans on pulley systems. Lots of medium-brown wood and brushed-aluminum accents.

"This is sensational," she said.

And not filled with unpleasant memories the way his childhood home was. How Chance lived under that roof of stifled and oppressed dreams, where too much male testosterone and violent tendencies had reigned supreme, was beyond him.

Although maybe being two years older than Avery, Chance had accumulated fonder recollections of their mom, and that was what made his existence in a previously volatile patriarchal establishment more tolerable. Bearable.

Cutting into his thoughts, Layla said, "I'm guessing there's an extraordinary view from the second floor."

"Of the river or . . . ?"

She laughed softly and gazed up at him with glowing eyes. "Your wooing's improving, cowboy."

"Let me lead the way." The stairs were off the gaming room.

The mezzanine opened to the living space below, then wound toward the back of the house with three bedrooms, including his master suite.

She maneuvered around him as he halted on the other side of the threshold.

"Wow," she muttered as her attention fell on the focal point of the floor-to-ceiling, wood-trimmed windows and doors that looked out on the balcony, fringed by trees, and the verdant pasture beyond, leading straight to the gentle rapids.

Avery flipped the switch for the rock-accented gas fireplace taking up a far corner where a sofa and two chairs were positioned.

Layla crossed to the doors and stepped outside, breathing in the fresh floral-scented air, from rosebushes below. Avery joined her at the railing.

"Definitely something to be said for rural living," she commented.

"It's peaceful, most of the time." He didn't bring up the shouting matches from his teenage years. "Can get a little loud when there's cattle to herd or the cowboys want to blow off steam, cranking the radio and throwing back beers and tequila. Though . . . that noise doesn't actually drift up to this room, so."

"Your own slice of paradise." She glanced at him and added, "Kinda big for just one person."

"I don't spend all that much time here. So I guess I don't notice if I'm ramblin' around in too much square footage."

"Regardless . . . it's beautiful, Avery. All of it."

"*You're* beautiful, honey." He gave a snort. Shook his head. "That's about the lamest thing I could say. You must hear it constantly."

"Not always," she murmured. And inched toward him. "And not from a man like you. Until now." She rolled her eyes. "That probably only makes sense to me."

His arm raised, and his fingertips almost grazed her cheek, but she ducked away. His arm dropped to his side.

She let out a quavering breath, gazed back at him, and said, "Sorry. Involuntary reaction."

His brow furrowed. He didn't press, though. Instead, he asked, "What's the view like where you live?"

"Persistent, you are." Her light tone returned. "And tactical. I live in San Antonio. So lots of plush greenery, like here."

"By way of . . . ?" His gaze didn't falter.

She groaned. "I'm the one who asks the questions, Avery. That's my job."

"I haven't given a yes or a no yet, so we're not really interacting in a professional capacity. Correct?"

"But I should be. I want you to say yes."

"Give me one good reason why."

"I gave you one hundred and fifty thousand reasons why." Her expression turned pointed.

He wasn't deterred. "There's no guarantee I'll slide into a money spot."

"Trust me, Avery," she said as she closed the scant gap between them and stared up at him. "I wouldn't be this invested if I didn't believe you have the winning combination."

He stared back, his jaw working.

She continued. "I advocate for every contestant. They wouldn't be on the roster if they didn't have what it takes to clinch this competition. It's just that . . . with you . . ."

She seemed to search for the right words. Looked damn convincing that this was highly important to her, critical even. Not just for her career.

"Layla—"

"Wait. Hear me out." She splayed a palm against his chest. "I have a sixth sense about these things. About what makes a champion. Yes, you've already proved your worth in that vein. But that was some time ago. Yet today at Jack's event . . . you fully reemerged. Sooo many people were gushing over you and your steaks. Recalling that friendly cook-off

40

you and Luke had with Jack and Jillian on Jack's channel. Discussing how you can come across as being devilish on-screen, but when there's no camera rolling . . . you're the real deal, Avery Reed."

Her eyes misted.

She whispered, "Damn it." And turned away.

"Now hold on a minute, darlin'." His fingers tenderly curled around one arm, and he brought her back to him. "What's honestly going on here?"

She gazed up at him again. And said, "You don't fade into the background, Avery. Nor do you purposely outshine anyone. You're comfortable in either role. This BBQ bash was Jack's signature event. You commanded your own grills without stealing his and Jillian's thunder. You were just you. And that impressed the hell out of everyone. Including me. *Especially* me."

"I do aim to please," he jested.

She gave him a pretty smile. "I'm not just talking about your cooking, cowboy. I'm talking about *you*. My female viewers will go crazy for you, Avery. That's a given. But all fans of barbecue will cheer you on. That's a promise I can make. They'll want their own pit in the backyard—and they'll have a reference as to how to properly build and use it. Because of you."

His gaze narrowed.

She nodded in silent confirmation of her statements, that he could make that big of an impact on an audience. Like Jack and Jillian were doing with their shows, her podcast and blog, and her cookbook that had basically become an overnight sensation once she'd teamed up with Jack.

Hell, Avery wouldn't mind publishing one either—or several. He'd certainly created enough recipes over two decades. But, really . . . it was the mechanics of what he did to ensure those recipes successfully came together that he wanted to impart.

And so, what . . . ?

He was considering doing this?

Avery reeled.

Layla further averred, "It matters to me how emotionally invested my viewers are, more so than just them being entertained or educated. I want them to really know who they're rooting for—and why. And with you . . ." She sighed. "I can just feel, deep in my soul, that you've got all the right stuff, cowboy."

He still had roadblocks to skirt, though.

"Layla, remember that I have a past that could interfere with your assumptions."

"A rap sheet?" she half joked, though with a raised brow.

He snickered. "No rap sheet."

"Well, then. Pasts can be overcome, Avery."

She said this with such conviction, he had to push back a little. "Can they?"

She gnawed her bottom lip. Then let out a puff of air. "I can attest from personal experience that one can check their baggage at the door if they so choose. With the caveat that sometimes it's easier to do that when they have a *trap*door."

"Now my mind is burnin' with curiosity."

"Precisely why I have two bios."

"Give me the actual one," he quietly insisted.

She didn't speak for a while. Avery didn't poke and prod, allowing her to gather her thoughts. For as much as she wanted to lead him to water and vice versa, it was a process for both of them.

"I grew up in a tiny town near the northwestern Texas–New Mexico border," she told him. "My mama had been a Sunday school teacher, and my daddy is a farmer. We have horses and chickens. Goats. Acres of corn and cotton. Nothing like this land, by any stretch. A very small setup."

"Nothing wrong with that."

"Nope," she concurred. "We only required a few day workers to help out. And me feeding everyone when I was old enough. Though that started when I was pretty young."

"Your mama . . . ?"

"She died while giving birth to me."

His gut clenched. "I'm sorry to hear that."

"My daddy didn't tell me until I was ten or so—only initially indicating it was right around the time I was born, and that it was natural causes that took her. He didn't want me to blame myself."

Avery sucked in a breath.

"He would've kept it from me my whole life, I'm sure. But bits and pieces came out here and there. Eventually, the puzzle was complete."

Avery contemplated this and carefully said, "I understand how painful that would be for you and for him. But . . . why would you need to conceal that from the general public? Your audience?"

"Oh, cowboy . . ." She rolled her eyes skyward. Then glanced back at him. "That's just the beginning."

"Gotcha." He still had sordid secrets of his own. Ones best left in a taped-up box and shoved under the bed. Better yet, dumped into a pit and burned.

Except that might taint the pit in the proverbial sense.

She said, "I have backstory that's no one's fault . . . everyone's fault . . . my own fault." She gave a shrug of one bare shoulder and contended, "But that's not why I'm here."

Avery's emotions warred with that revelation.

On the one hand, she was right. This was supposed to be about him joining her competition.

On the other hand . . . he wouldn't have invited her into his home—and he was sure she wouldn't have accepted that invitation—if they weren't moving beyond the pretext of her wanting him on her show.

He told her, "We're mixing a lot of peripherals here, trying to get to know each other. Think we'd both prefer to build Rome in a day, but . . . maybe what we really ought to do is spend some time living in the moment, with what's happening right here and now."

"A smart cowboy is a sexy cowboy." She gave him a simmering look. "I did mention to Brodi you're more the type to need layers."

"I like to iron out the wrinkles before puttin' on the shirt. That's not always possible."

"No, it's not. In most instances." Once more, she flattened a palm over his pecs and solemnly said, "In this particular instance . . . I can see us putting the cart before the horse."

"Aww." His head bent to hers, and he said in a low tone, "This is gonna be our thing, honey? Poor idioms?"

"Well, if we were kissing," she murmured as her lips lightly brushed his, "we wouldn't have to shame ourselves with them."

"You are sheer genius."

She laughed sweetly, her warm breath blowing over his cheek. "I just can't seem to help falling under your spell, cowboy."

"Didn't know I was casting one." He gave a sharp grunt. "Goddamn, there we go again."

"We should remedy this before it gets out of hand."

"Oh, I'd say plenty's about to get out of hand."

His lips tangled with hers. No tongue, just delicate, flirty kisses that had her fingers curling around the material at his chest as her other palm pressed to his obliques. She leaned into him, but he was mindful not to twine an arm around her and haul her up against him, the way he was dying to do.

Flames seemed to lick at his groin, sending a heat wave upward to his gut and blazing through his veins.

He cautiously gripped her hips, not exactly sure what had triggered her when he'd almost touched her face earlier. Not wanting to startle her or jerk her out of *this* moment.

And really, the slow burn was fine by him. It gave him time to taste her, to breathe her in, to listen to her soft moans.

Granted, the intimacy arcing between them made Avery ache for her in a way he couldn't ever recall feeling. So that the need to take this all a step further mounted within him.

His tongue glanced over hers, playfully.

She sighed again. And reciprocated.

It would have been all seventh grade–like, but then she repositioned her hands and freed a couple of the pearl snaps of his shirt. Well, Jack's shirt, but . . . that was of no consequence at present.

Her nails grazed the inner swells of his pecs, and that seared him to the core.

She whispered, "Way to launch a subtle attack."

"You were in on the strategy."

Her lips curved against his. "Mm, it's a very productive one."

She pulled apart the flap, right down to his belt buckle, where the shirt was tucked in.

"So much for the slow burn," he muttered.

"I couldn't stand the suspense a second longer."

Her gaze flitted to his exposed torso, taking him in with hungry eyes.

She released the material in her hands and twisted her arms around herself so she could unlatch the clasp in the middle of her back. Avery coiled his fingers in the minuscule straps at her shoulders and eased away the shimmery top, laying it out on the chair next to them, then returning his attention to her.

"Son of a gun." A carnal sound tore from his mouth as he absorbed the sight of her before she moved into his loose embrace.

Her breasts nestled below the ledge of his chest and the skin-on-skin contact set his pulse racing and had his adrenaline spiking.

She circled his neck with her arms. Whisked off his hat.

They both kept the kisses sultry and provocative. Not too heavy. More . . . teasing and taunting.

Avery had the inclination to move in for the kill. But this was a tricky endeavor, on many levels. And the last thing he wanted to do was spook her. Push too hard, too fast.

He wasn't prone to giving up the reins, but he sensed Layla needed an acclimation period. They hadn't gone from zero to sixty, no. Although they'd only just met—and not for *this* reason—he knew there was much more to learn about her. Much more she had to wade through too.

Admittedly, these were fleeting notions. What really occupied his brain was how she melded to him, how fragile and yet firm she felt in his embrace, how she couldn't seem to get enough of his mouth on hers and the feel of their bodies sliding against each other.

It was tormenting and titillating at the same time.

Eventually, he couldn't stop himself from walking her backward, into his suite. She tossed aside his hat, neither of them caring where it landed. He guided her toward the four-poster bed. Slid the zipper of her skirt along her hip and let the garment fall to the hardwood floor.

The erratic beats of his cock matched his heart rate.

He unfastened his belt buckle.

She knelt before him, popping the button on his jeans.

But Avery gently gripped her upper arms and said, "I don't want you on your knees, darlin'. I want you in my bed."

Layla's blistering gaze drifted up his body as though the vision of him excited her as much as his words did.

He brought her to her feet, lifted her slightly, and set her in the middle of his California king. He slipped off her boots and joined her, not quite settling between her legs, instead propping himself up on the mattress and gauging her response.

Clearly sensing his trepidation, she said, "I haven't been with anyone in a very long time, Avery. And I wouldn't be here with you this evening if I wasn't absolutely certain it was a good decision on my part."

"If that's your way of telling me you're selective, then I'm flattered."

"There's a bit more to it than that," she confessed. "But suffice it to say . . . I want you, cowboy."

"Music to my ears."

His head lowered to hers. This time, their kisses were deeper, longer, hotter.

Her fingers threaded his hair. He kept himself braced with one forearm alongside her as his other hand skimmed over her collarbone to her breast. He caressed the mound, swept his thumb over her pebbled nipple. And felt the shudder through her.

He didn't break the kiss. Didn't give her a reprieve from the massaging either. And that seemed to spur her on. Her tongue toyed with his, and her fingers around his biceps dipped into the flexed sinew, keeping him near to her. She writhed on the plush comforter. Arched her back, melding to him.

A foreign sensation tingled along his spine. An inky darkness edged the corners of his mind. He could lose himself in every little detail. How she clung to him, squirmed beneath him, matched his wicked tongue tangling.

His erection strained against his zipper. He should've at least let her free him, but no. He'd had the compelling need to take over.

And yet . . . that still wasn't happening.

He was no more in control of this encounter than she was.

He dragged his mouth from hers. Stared down at her parted lips and her sparkling eyes. Her blonde hair fanned out on a pillow.

Then his gaze roved her body, committing every inch of her to memory.

His gut clenched.

Goddamn, she was a sight to behold.

For endless moments he was mesmerized. Stuck in a vortex of lust, where all that registered were sensuous curves, long legs, and honeyed skin.

Sure, the lacy black thong was also ingrained in his brain. But the overall presentation was so stimulating, Avery couldn't catch his breath.

His fingers skated over her stomach, making her flesh quiver.

Her thighs pressed together, as though that simple gesture had ignited a firestorm within her.

He definitely felt it.

"Layla," he murmured, "you're the stuff fantasies are made of."

She stared at him. "What hooked me the most, at the party—even when you were just stealing glances my way—was how you looked at me like . . . like . . ."

"Like you're nothing I've ever seen before?"

"Yes," she said on a hiss of a breath. "Exactly."

"Darlin' . . ." His hand glided south, to her bent legs. He coaxed her knees apart. Trailed his fingertips along her inner thigh, gradually inching back toward her apex.

All the while, their gazes remained locked.

"I just can't think of a more stirring sight than you," he murmured.

"You have all the right words to go with that bedroom voice of yours."

"Just bein' honest."

"I admire that about you. I don't take you for a player."

He winced. "Wouldn't know where to start, truth be told. Got too much going on. No time or energy or desire for games and head trips."

Her gaze didn't waver as she quietly asked, "You wouldn't hurt a woman, would you, Avery Reed?"

"Someone broke your heart, darlin'?"

She gnawed her lip for a second or two.

Then she said, "He broke more than that, cowboy."

# Chapter Four

Layla wasn't quite sure why she was saying so much.

Then again . . .

Maybe she did know why.

Everything she'd said about Avery previously seemed to be true. She'd always been an excellent judge of character and had learned how to read people at an early age. Something that was inherent, but which had also been honed by her daddy's insights, mostly centered around the people who came and went from the farm. Typically strong, earnest workers. But there'd been some shady characters from time to time. Layla could recognize shifty eyes and smooth lines—even hitches of breath when a lie wasn't rolling off the tongue as easily as one thought it might.

There were other traits to look out for. Body language. Fidgeting. Trying too hard to sell a story.

She'd not had any of these things in mind when she'd fallen down a dangerous rabbit hole in New York. One she shouldn't have been teetering on the ledge of to begin with, but sometimes ambition could be a blinding temptation. And she'd been lured by it.

Eventually, she'd come to her senses and had heeded the perils. Had attempted to coax the party doing wrong to right their axis. That was when the trouble had started.

Avery said, "I have no cause to hurt anyone."

In her heart, she believed him. Deep in her soul, really.

She swept a lock of dark hair from his forehead and said, "I didn't need that affirmation from you. Not sure why I posed the question. Maybe just because . . . it's natural due diligence on my part."

"Don't go second-guessing anything about me, Layla. I am the epitome of 'what ya see is what ya get.'"

She smiled. "That's what I figured. I suppose I just needed to hear your answer."

His gorgeous blue eyes clouded. Squinted with scrutiny. "You're not afraid of me, are you?"

She searched her feelings for an absolute truth, so that she could put some closure on this conversation she didn't want to have. Her head rolled back and forth on the pillow as she said, "Not at all. I like you, Avery. I told you I thought you were the real deal. And I meant it."

"I just want you to be sure—"

"Kiss me, cowboy. And then decide whether you want to keep talking."

His cloudy irises cleared.

No. They flared with heat.

"I could do the kissin' thing all night," he admitted.

"Well, you are my ride back into town, so that makes me your captive audience of one."

"Sun hasn't even set yet. That gives me all the time in the world to win you over."

"Thought we established that you already have."

"Well, I like to be thorough."

As evidenced by the scorching lip-lock he delivered.

His tongue delved deep and with such finesse, she forgot all about their brief interruption. Sure, it was prudent for Layla to be cautious. One thousand percent. But reinventing herself had also reset herself. So that she wasn't swayed by "shiny objects" dangled before her like a carrot, and instead had returned to and remained grounded in the values her daddy had taught her.

And by the way Avery kissed her, she didn't have much difficulty leaving her broken *everything* behind her for the evening.

His hand was still between her legs, and it drifted over her thong. Lightly, so that she wondered if she'd imagined the faint touch, she was so desperate for it. But then he rubbed her through the lace, a soft caress that teased her.

She buried her fingers in his hair, and her spine bowed again, so her nipples brushed against his hot skin and hard muscles.

He swept aside the material, baring her, and massaged her dewy folds. A moan rose within her throat but had nowhere to go with his mouth sealed to hers.

He circled her clit, and that incited more sparks. Then he eased a finger inside her, stroking her until she was dripping wet, and he could work in a second finger.

Darkly erotic sensations swelled and threatened to burst wide open at any moment.

All it took was the strumming of his fingertips against that magical spot within her and suddenly—

All those sensations collided and erupted.

She broke their kiss and cried, "Oh, my God, Avery!"

Her pulse pounded, and her entire existence seemed to incinerate. Lightning quick.

He kissed her temple as tiny orbs flashed behind her lids. Somewhat akin to a cosmic explosion.

She let out what might have been a giggle.

"Didn't think that was anything to laugh about," he grumbled.

She glanced at him. "I saw stars, cowboy."

One corner of his mouth quirked. "Good news, then. That was my goal."

She pulled his head to hers and kissed him, languidly. Once more getting all wrapped up in how amazing it felt to share this intimacy with him.

He withdrew his fingers from her and palmed her breast, kneading with a hint of pressure.

Dragging his mouth from hers, he flitted his tongue over her nipple, then suckled.

A small whimper fell from her lips.

"That's more like it," he whispered.

Then he shifted and peeled off the scant bit of lace that was in his way. He stood and toed off his boots. Shucked his clothing.

*All* of his clothing.

Layla drew in a rasping breath. "Oh, my."

He snickered. "As good a view as the other scenery on this ranch?"

"Words fail me."

"Toying with me now, honey?"

His roguish grin made her stomach flip.

"No, I'm being serious."

He reached for the handle on the nightstand drawer, pulled out a box of condoms, and then glowered—at the box.

"I'm going from bad to worse," he lamented.

"How so?"

"I can't remember when I bought these, and the package isn't even open."

She pressed her lips together for a moment. Then tried to keep the humor from her voice as she asked, "Should we check the expiration date?"

"Indeed, we should." He shook his head. "This is embarrassin'." He inspected the box and then turned more optimistic. "Oh, well. We're in luck."

She laughed. "Now I'm the one who's flattered. I think."

"Nice to know I'm still in your good graces."

"And not merely one of a stable full of women waiting on their chance with you?"

"If there are even just a couple," he said as he yanked open an end and extracted a half strip, "I haven't noticed."

"As I said . . . there were plenty of eyes on you today."

"I was only interested in yours. Stunning as they are."

He tossed aside the outer package and opened one foil packet.

"Now would be the best time to back out, darlin'."

She crooked her index finger at him. Gave what she hoped was a come-hither look, and told him, "More of you is what *I'm* interested in."

"Can't argue with that." He sheathed himself and returned to the bed. He pulled her to him and added, "Seems I've won the lottery."

"Don't get me started again on what you could win, Avery Reed."

"We did agree to no more talking."

"Unless it's of the dirty variety."

"That I can happily manage."

An electric current thrummed through her veins. "I don't doubt it."

He settled on his back with her straddling him. His hands clasped her hips, and he held her steady as she splayed her palms over his abs. The man was a chiseled-to-perfection hunk of virility, and she took a few seconds to admire the visual, let it burn straight to her core.

Her heart rate quickened. She had the desire to leave feathery kisses over every inch of him. But the need to feel him inside her superseded everything else.

Her hand skated downward. She curled her fingers around his wide shaft and guided him just so, the head of his cock nudging her opening, then penetrating just enough to taunt her. And make her gasp.

His jaw worked. His chest heaved.

"Goddamn, you're tight," he murmured.

"And so wet for you."

He kept her in place for several suspended seconds, not allowing her to take more of him just yet. As though he was the one who required adjusting to the feel of her.

Raw intensity exuded from him and called to something primal within her, strengthening their connection. She hadn't been seduced this time. She'd set her sights on Avery Reed. No denying it.

She sank farther onto him, her inner muscles clenching and releasing, eliciting a carnal groan from him.

Her hips undulated, and he loosened his grip, moving with her.

Their gazes held, their breaths escalating in time with each other.

He was thick and throbbing within her, creating a scintillating hint of friction as he filled and stretched her.

"Jesus, Avery," she said on a sliver of air. "You feel incredible."

"I want you to feel *all* of me." His hands slipped to her ass, and he pressed her down onto him, as his pelvis lifted, so that she took him deeper.

She moaned. "Oh, God . . ."

Her skin tingled, and her breaths turned to mere wisps.

"That's it, darlin'. Ride me slow and easy."

She didn't have much choice, sensing anything else would have them both out of control in a heartbeat. Not to mention, their pace was sexy and seductive, drawing her into an unfamiliar world of dark pleasures. And she wanted to stay here a while.

Her hands slid over his pecs as she lowered herself to him, her nipples grazing his hot skin.

She gave him a flirty kiss, then said, "A girl could get used to this."

He chuckled, though it was strained. "I'd like to tell you we're gonna go on and on this first time, but you're testing my restraint and stamina."

"We just got started . . ."

"Yeah, but goddamn . . . you're squeezing my cock, and it's making me half out of my mind."

"That I can't control," she told him. "And you can take full credit."

"Like me deep in your pussy, do you?"

Her insides ignited.

She clenched a bit more fiercely and felt the tension that seized him.

"So much for slow and easy?" she quipped as she sat up again, bracing herself against his rib cage.

His palms glided up her sides, and he cupped her breasts, caressing with a scintillating amount of pressure. Enough to heighten her arousal, which already seemed to be off the charts with the sizzle arcing between them.

His hips bucked in a more assertive tempo that had feathery sighs falling from her lips. She matched his pace, but suddenly it just didn't seem to be enough.

"Avery . . ." Lust blazed through her.

He kissed her, and that only intensified her cravings, adding fuel to the fire.

"Like that," she whispered. "Oh, my God, just like that."

He pumped into her. Stroking that ultrasensitive spot, making her more and more crazed for him.

She was instantly addicted to the flash of heat and the vibrations that lit her nerve endings and pulled every fiber of her being taut. There was a breaking point coming. Absolutely. Just . . . not yet.

He kissed her once more. She repositioned her hands, clutching his shoulders at the rise of his traps, her fingers curving in as she pressed her upper body to his.

"I can't take much more of this," he ground out.

Suddenly, he sat up, one arm twining around her. He maneuvered onto his hip, and that gave him leverage to shift into a faster cadence that led straight to a crescendo for her.

Without any warning, those tenuous threads snapped, and she called his name.

"Oh, my God," she panted. "Oh, my fucking God."

Tremors rocked her.

Avery wasn't done.

He carefully flopped her onto the mattress and draped her thigh over the small of his back. He palmed a cheek again, angling her just so, and drove into her, with confident strokes.

She dug her nails into his side, while the other hand tangled in his hair.

"Yes . . . ," she murmured, opening further to him, drowning in the bliss. "Right there, Avery. *Right there.*"

All the sensations blossomed. She could barely catch her breath, and her hips gyrated in a demanding rhythm, having no idea where she came up with it, but Avery matched her.

The next fiery wave crested, and she shattered. "Oh, Jesus!"

"Yeah, that's it. Squeeze me tight, Layla."

She did, milking his cock.

"Keep doing that, darlin'," he said in a gruff tone. "Just keep doing that."

She couldn't stop if she tried. Something feral took over, and she wasn't inclined to curb it. She wanted more. So much more.

She continued to wriggle beneath him, clutching and then releasing him.

"Goddamn," he whispered as his body tensed, every muscle turning rigid. "Fuck . . ."

He pumped a bit harder.

Seconds later, his sturdy frame convulsed—as though she could have brought him to his knees, had he been standing.

"Holy Christ," he said on a near growl.

Then he surged inside her, his hips jerking, his cock still stroking.

Heat and exhilaration ribboned together, twining with his climax echoing within her. And then—

"Avery . . ." The only word she got out before another orgasm burned through her. "Oh, God, that is so . . . *hot.*"

Liquifying her until she was limp and boneless.

And deliriously happy.

"Greedy of you, baby," he teased. His face was buried in her hair, and his lips brushed the crook of her neck. "But I'm willin' to give you whatever you want."

She'd slayed this beast of a man. This magnetic force that possessed talent and charm . . . and a humble nature.

Oh, but good Lord, did he have plenty to be arrogant about!

He roused himself with a soft grunt and notable difficulty—enough to cause another laugh to escape her.

"Were you planning to take a nap, cowboy?" she asked.

"Well, I certainly wouldn't mind staying in this very position for the rest of the night."

Her heart melted.

He planted his hands on either side of her shoulders and hauled himself up, though he still lingered close.

Avery gazed down at her. "You just might be the holy grail, honey."

"Ha, ha." She swatted at him, liking this mischievous side of him as much as the broody one. "Not a chance."

"Says you." He shook his head, then seemed to force himself to withdraw from her and move away.

As though it was the last thing he wanted to do.

"I'm gonna take a shower," he told her.

"Okay if I join you?"

"Don't go expecting me to be a gentleman and keep my hands off you," he warned with a wicked glint in his eyes.

"I'd be disappointed if you kept your hands off me, cowboy."

He reached for one of hers and tugged, helping her from the tall bed. She snatched the strand of condoms from the nightstand and set them on a stool in his nicely appointed bathroom.

While he rid himself of the condom he was wearing and then turned on the water that fell from an overhead rain feature, she collected fresh towels and a washcloth from a slim cabinet with frosted glass doors. She removed the clips from her hair and entered the spacious corner shower. Two wire racks mounted one on top of the other held glass containers of shampoos, conditioners, and body washes, in various scents.

She turned a mockingly suspicious eye on him and asked, "Sure you're not married?"

He chuckled. "Aw, honey. When would I have the time to be?"

She couldn't argue with that logic. Knowing he must have a hectic schedule. She did as well. Even when she wasn't in a different city every week for filming, she was always on the go, scouting talent and searching for inspiration for her next season. Forever praying there would be a next season. This particular platform was an obsession of hers, due to its free-flowing format and the control she had over the subject matter.

Also, losing her job would mean having to find another one, which would mean trying to land an interview with an incomplete résumé. She'd only been Layla Jenson for five years. So, no prior work experience and no college or high school degree could be listed or verified. And she wasn't inclined to show anyone the document proving her legal name change from Tess Billings—or hand over her Social Security card.

With the online system this crew used, she entered her own information and got paid via electronic transfer. The fewer people who could connect dots, the better.

She'd been able to get her foot in the door with this project because she'd come across a YouTube docuseries by a fellow film student from NYU with a new home base here in Texas. Todd Holden had been a trusted friend of hers in college. Also, someone she'd helped out in a bind he'd not wanted anyone to know about, and Layla had kept his secret while they'd rectified the situation.

Though she wasn't anyone to lord something over another person, she knew he was grateful and would reciprocate if she reached out to him.

Now, she needed Todd and his people to continue with these episodes.

In a roundabout way, all of this made it imperative that Avery became a contestant. While also making it precarious that she was in this compromising position with him.

*Impossible not to be.*

Her gaze roved his body, and all the tingles returned. *Like that.*

Maybe they'd never dissipated.

Her insides lit up as he moved in close to kiss her.

A fleeting one because she pulled away—before they got carried away—saying, "I have to get this makeup off, or I'll turn into a melting clown face."

"Can't see the point of you needing it at all," he commented.

That was a prickly topic, so she skipped over it and said, "Give me a minute."

She selected a facial wash from a rack and squirted it onto her damp cloth. She gently scrubbed while Avery opted for a gel and soaped himself up.

"You really should let me do the honors," she said after rinsing off the silken foam and letting her hair run clean of product.

"I'm ready to lather *you* up." He filled his palm with the body wash that matched her choice of herbal scents and rubbed his hands together. "So, yeah . . . I'm not capable of *not* touching you."

"Am I complaining?"

She turned from him to wring out the cloth and hang it on a hook at the end of a rack. He stepped behind her and glided the luxurious suds over her hips and into the dip of her waist. His front grazed her back, and she wiggled against him.

"That'll lead to all sorts of chaos," he murmured.

"Hence me coming in here prepared."

"Speaking of things that are about to come . . ." His hands swept up to her breasts and kneaded them as he nipped at her neck.

That had her anticipation mounting, and she kept grinding against him.

"You get me all fired up," he whispered. As evidenced by the thickening of his cock.

Excitement skittered through her. Yet she wasn't ready to abandon the sliding of slippery skin on skin. His mouth wreaking havoc on the side of her throat. His fingers and thumbs pinching and rolling her nipples, beading them. Sending sparks to the heart of her.

She reached behind her to grip his hips as the water sluiced over them, clearing away the bubbles.

Eventually, she turned in his arms and said, "Now that you're sufficiently recovered . . ."

"Told you it wouldn't take long."

He shut off the valve and opened the doors, grabbing up the towels. He passed one to her that she wound around her body. He slung the other one low on his hips. Gave her the third one for her hair. She rubbed her crown and then the strands, which immediately began to curl as she patted her face dry.

When she glanced up at him, he seemed to be debating over the appropriate thing to say. Finally settling on, "You steal my breath, darlin'."

Her eyes misted. Her heart stammered.

He grinned. "Just so you know."

Layla couldn't speak for a moment or two.

First, she was astounded by how easily he complimented her, how sincerely. How it wasn't difficult at all for him to lay out his cards, not holding any aces up his sleeve. Not that he was wearing any. Point being . . . he was true to his word about not engaging in games.

Second . . .

Well, that was a more complicated component to dissect. Layla couldn't help but wonder whether Avery Reed would be so enthralled with her if she didn't look the way she did now.

Yes, she wanted to believe they'd still feel that kismet-type connection that had struck like lightning when they'd first met. Something she hoped ran more than skin deep, was more instinctive in nature.

What had her stumbling was that she didn't want Avery to make this attraction about physical appeal. At the same time . . . she did.

And that brought on the trouble of trying to maintain a balance between honest reflections versus hypocrisy. Wasn't she reacting to his overall appearance too?

Yes, she was.

Though she did remind herself that she was entrenched in something more significant—her primary focal point was on his skills and abilities, and his personal interactions. Mainly with her, sure. But she didn't dismiss how he'd put huge effort into helping to make Jack's bash a success. Or how he was concerned for Brodi's well-being and had escorted her to a bus. And, certainly, how he was ever vigilant with Layla in all capacities. He kept his eye on her. He kept her close. He touched her mindfully. Sensuously, yet with respect.

With passion too. That was not to be overlooked.

She didn't have a full summation of all she was trying to capture here. And perhaps she was premature in wanting to wrap these notions up in a tidy package.

The two of them weren't a match made in heaven, after all.

Not with their life trajectories shooting off in opposite directions.

So she tabled the entire jumbled discourse happening in her brain, rested a hand on the sexy cowboy's abs, gazed up at him, and said, "You look like a man who could use a bit more relief."

She spared a glance at the bulge the plush white material could not conceal.

He laughed, albeit strained. And told her, "You do tend to get me all twisted up, darlin'."

She whisked away his towel. "Let's see what I can do about that."

"Why don't we see what sort of gratification we can *both* get."

He nabbed the strip of condoms. Then gave her a scorching kiss.

His arms twined around her, and he lifted her, walking them toward the double vanity. He hoisted her higher and set her on the granite countertop. Pulled her towel away.

He kissed her ardently while she clutched his biceps. Got lost in his intensity.

Within seconds, he was pressing into her.

She gasped. Rocked back on her ass to tilt her pelvis. Raised her legs and anchored him to her with her feet at his tailbone. Her head fell on her shoulders, and he kissed her neck, his teeth gently scraping, his tongue soothing, his mouth suckling.

"You get me wet," she whispered. "So fast."

"Happy to oblige any cravings you have."

"You're doing fine with that. Trust me."

"Just so you know . . . Jesus . . ." His breaths turned razory. "I can hardly keep my shit together with you."

"Stamina's not the objective here," she told him. "Your recovery time is stellar. So . . . multiple orgasms on both sides are something to strive for."

"And I'm willing to deliver."

He slipped his forearms under the backside of her knees, spreading her legs wide. She braced herself with her palms against the vanity, keeping herself poised for more. Which he gave her. He pumped into her, making her pussy contract around his shaft.

"Take what you want from me," he murmured. "All of it."

Her lids drifted closed and she gave herself over to the feel of him pushing deep. The frenetic energy coursing between them. The insistent stroking that had them both racing toward an erratic, mind-blowing completion. Knowing they'd start up again soon thereafter.

The thought of an entire night with Avery Reed sent her soaring higher. Until the tether with reality broke free, and she caved to the fantasy they were weaving. And fell to pieces under his spell. Again.

He was right behind her.

The throbbing of his cock had her inching toward that finale he'd given her last time, where the sensations he prolonged mixed with the overall thought of him and rippled through her, eliciting yet another beautiful release.

"That's just the most amazing finish to a most amazing interlude," she murmured.

"'Interlude'?"

"Well, I'd call it a fuck, but . . ." Her brow rose.

He nodded. "But that's not what it was."

"Doesn't feel like it."

"Is that a problem for you?"

She reveled in the afterglow, not jarred by his question, just whisking her fingers through his damp hair and smiling at him.

Eventually, she told him, "We aren't on the same plane—I mean the spatial one. Though, also the literal one. I have a flight to Cheyenne tomorrow. I'll be there for a week. I have three to four more weeks on the road, depending on your decision, which I'm not influencing. I gave you the spiel. It ended there. Ball's in your court, Avery."

"That notwithstanding, you do make an excellent point about your itinerary. Mine's set in stone too."

They stared at each other.

He added, "I just need you to know that I don't think of you as simply a one-night—"

"No need to say it." She brushed her lips over his.

"It's not something I can easily define."

"Me either." She kissed him once more. Then asked, "Do we have to?"

He didn't seem to have an answer to that. Rather, he cleaned himself up, wrapped his towel around his hips, then scooped her into his arms and carried her to the bed.

He set her on the end and peeled back the comforter and sheets that she crawled under.

"What can I get you?" he asked. "Scotch? Bourbon? Water? Or—"

"Water would be great, thanks."

He crossed to the wet bar and retrieved an individual bottle from the mini fridge to pour into a cut-crystal tumbler. Then he reached for a decanter and splashed two fingers of amber liquid into his own glass. Presumably, the scotch.

She accepted her drink from him. He sipped his, set it on the nightstand, and slid in next to her. Coaxing her to him, so she snuggled against him, her head on his shoulder.

His fingers combed through her hair. He said, "I like the curls."

She was quiet for a moment. Then something—maybe the honesty growing between them—compelled her to delve into her past. "I started straightening them in college. Wanted to look more 'refined.'" She sighed. "It worked, to an extent. I even dropped the accent."

"Not sure I know what all that means."

"I wanted to be someone else, Avery. Not the demure farm girl. Not the quiet one who cooked and cleaned and blended into the woodwork, with no one taking notice of her."

"I can't fathom that."

"I didn't look like this back then."

They both fell silent.

Then he urged, "Tell me more."

"It's not a Cinderella story," she said. Though she reflected on that statement and amended it. "Sort of was for a brief time. And even recently," she conceded. "I got the YouTube channel in the wake of my personal disaster. I landed within a new sphere of influence—one that's infinitely more on the up-and-up."

"Sooo . . . what does all that entail?"

This wasn't a comfortable conversation to have. But she chose to throw him a bone. For numerous reasons. Including the fact that Avery was genuine. She wanted to be as well.

She told him, "I left the farm for NYU. I studied finance, with a minor in broadcasting."

An unlikely tandem curriculum. But she was fascinated by large fiscal transactions and wanted to interview visionaries with unique start-ups. She'd dreamed of being a corporate spokesperson or a TV personality on a program specializing in economics. Unfortunately, her knowledge and concise, astute delivery weren't enough to fulfill those aspirations. It wasn't mentioned in any job description, but "non-pretty people need not apply" was the order of the day if you were to be the "face" of an entity.

A double-edged sword. She hadn't had the right looks when she was Tess Billings and had a clean slate. Now she possessed the facial features producers wanted, but she couldn't pursue a bigger gig without answering a lot of questions and filling in blanks she didn't want to fill in.

As Tess, things had gotten all topsy-turvy when even media internships were out of her grasp. But then someone had rescued her—literally from the bowels. An up-and-coming real estate mogul named Christopher Courtland.

She told Avery, "While I was still in school, I took a part-time job in the research division of a real estate investment firm that was just getting established. I shared a desk with two other employees in a cramped room with six additional people and spent hours upon hours on the internet and the phone, trying to unearth golden nuggets for the powers that be to capitalize on. I had a knack for it. Received promotions and better pay. But I didn't make it out of that windowless office in the basement."

Not even for a receptionist position. She'd thrown her hat in the ring and was told that wasn't her forte, no matter how pleasant and hospitable she was. Once again, it was code for her not having the "right look."

"By the time I graduated college, I had a list a mile long of leads that had been turned into successful acquisitions. One day, I got a visitor in the small room. A new associate who was extremely aggressive. Young and hungry. He needed backers to build a conglomeration that would secure commercial properties for urban hubs—restaurants, nightclubs, entertainment centers, boutique shops, workshare spaces, et cetera. One-stop, integrated services in sophisticated environments to replace strip malls, spread-out marketplaces, and the like. Building vertically, not horizontally."

"A more concentrated 'downtown'?"

"Yes, on major corners, so that if your outdated strips or downtowns were failing, these modern siloed hubs would be your respite."

"What about living spaces?"

"Phase two was buying up surrounding properties to convert into luxury micro apartments and hotel rooms. The entire premise was focused on independent mini communities."

Avery continued to stroke her hair. "I guess that's not a bad idea."

"No. And yet . . . yes. It cuts you off from your larger neighborhood. It's almost like permanently cohabitating at an all-inclusive resort or on a cruise ship, where you stay within the confines of your plotted existence."

"Ah, gotcha." He paused. "But then again . . ."

"I know, Avery. You want to equate it to the TRIPLE R, where all your resources are accumulated, and this is where you gather for the better part of your day. And I don't discount that. I'm just saying that within major city limits, with a populace not all working toward a common goal as y'all do on the ranch, it's a bit more challenging to achieve."

"Granted. So what happened?"

This was the very moment her narrative turned dicey.

She said, "The ambitious associate needed someone on his side who could mine—and extract—information and data. Someone who knew the precise questions to ask, for sure. But that person also had to be able to talk with others so that they didn't come across as interviewing, or researching, or—"

"Spying?"

"I suppose that's an accurate enough term."

He harrumphed. "You were the spy."

Not even a query on his part.

She felt deadweight in her stomach as she confessed, "Without quite knowing it."

"How's that possible?" he carefully inquired, so as to not offend her, she assumed.

"Because I was too naive to realize I was being used in that capacity."

Avery shifted. She rolled onto her back, stretching her arm to deposit her empty glass on the nightstand next to her.

He stared down at her, "I can't imagine anyone pullin' the wool over your eyes, darlin'."

"But they did," she contended. "And, no, I'm not going to feign full innocence here. I accept culpability. It's just that . . . I didn't recognize from the onset what my actual role was."

His brow quirked. He needed more from her.

She said, "I was invited to a swank fundraiser. Met some wheelers and dealers. And just through my typical inquisitive fashion, I gleaned some beneficial information. I passed it on, thinking that if someone had imparted it to me—a virtual nobody—it couldn't be that proprietary. Perhaps that was why they didn't censor themselves with me. *Because* I was a virtual nobody. Who was I going to tell?"

She stared at Avery with a solemn expression.

And added, "I didn't know what this information might be used for. I shared it in casual conversation with the person who'd sent me to the party—not as a guest but as an infiltrator, I eventually figured out."

Avery lay back down. Brought her to him again.

The sun was starting to set, and Layla admired the view while they were both propped against a mound of pillows.

Not wanting to miss the subtle display of lavender, pink, and gold that gradually intensified, she waited for some time before she spoke again.

"Turns out," she said on a sigh, "the majority of intel I collected was pertinent. My reward was gowns, shoes, jewelry . . . for other galas." The *shiny objects* she'd been seduced by. "People paid more attention to me. I got caught up in being someone. *Finally* being someone."

"That's what you wanted the most?" Avery asked.

She gave a slight nod. "I would say 'at the time,' but I'm accepting of the spotlight at present, so I can't pretend I don't like some form of notoriety."

With the anonymity drastic reconstructive surgery afforded her, in a sense, she didn't have to worry too much about being recognized. Not by Christopher, who'd never looked that closely at her anyway. A man who'd not had any trouble taking out his rage on her when she'd tried to quit the game—and attempted to convince him to do the same.

The additional security of staying on the YouTube platform was that Christopher had never watched a video or channel in that format in his life that she was aware of. Sure, chances existed that he might troll social media to find her. But she convinced herself they were slim. Not impossible, but slim.

Avery said, "Nothing wrong with liking being in front of an audience. Jack supplements ranch finances with his channel."

"I do enjoy hosting a show. And it is my sole source of income."

"So now you're more in control of what your intents and purposes are?"

She grinned, though somewhat shakily. Considering she wasn't fully out of the woods. However . . . "That's a wise observation. And . . . yes. Other than I can't really blow this opportunity because—"

She stalled out, needing a moment to collect her thoughts. Reel herself in.

"I'm not gonna say more." She gave him an earnest look. "I offered my pitch to you. I let you know the stakes—not just what's involved with the competition but that I have to remember my role and not complicate it."

"Meanin' no fraternizing if I sign?"

"I have to keep this job, Avery. And again . . . we're not on the same page. I'm somewhere else tomorrow. And somewhere else a week later. Tonight, though . . . I'm right here."

"Enjoying the sunset."

"It is spectacular."

They gazed out the tall windows, watching the vivid colors painting the sky deepen as twilight encroached.

Avery said, "Just one more question."

By his grim tone, she suspected he wanted to know the conclusion to her previous situationship—what Christopher breaking more than her heart meant.

Her insides roiled. She said, "I don't want you to ask the question I think you want to ask. Best not to know the answer, Avery."

Her hand splayed over his abs.

She was tucked against him, their legs intertwined.

There was an uncertainty that lingered between them.

More than one.

But for now . . .

They were living in the moment.

# Chapter Five

Avery made love to her two more times before they drifted off to sleep.

He woke with her backside pressed to his front, his body and arms wound around her. Her hair smelled of the scent he never used—tea tree-lemon-sage. Apparently, his housekeeper provided it in the event he had company of the female persuasion. And he didn't deny it was an enticing combination coming off Layla's soft waves as they brushed his skin.

His internal clock had him rousing at half past four, and he didn't want to disturb Layla. He definitely didn't want to unravel from her. But he had work to do.

Yet, for the first time since he took over as bunkhouse cook, he wasn't in any hurry to slip from the bed and get on with his busy day.

Her curves melded to his hard muscles. Her breaths were deep and measured, an enticing rhythm. She was so alluring, he could lay here for several more hours, just absorbing the sensuality of her. The feel of her.

That wasn't a luxury he could partake in, though.

Avery believed Layla would comprehend that, having studied bunkhouse routines for her show.

He tried not to wake her, but that was impossible, given how tangled up they were. As he stirred, she did too. She glanced over her bare shoulder and said, "Sun's not up yet, cowboy."

"I start before sunup, honey. Gotta prep. Lots of mouths to feed, and I make everything from scratch."

"Of course you do," she said with admiration.

"You just go back to sleep. I'll bring you breakfast later."

"My flight's not till this evening." She yawned. "I have time to drive to San Antone with Brodi, pack, and then catch the plane."

"So get more z's, and I'll see you in a bit."

And yet he still didn't move. Something to consider. He wasn't in the position to be this wrapped up with a woman at the exact time he needed to get himself around and to the chuck hall.

Thus, he forced himself to swing into high gear. Kissed her temple and climbed out of bed. He dressed, refilled her water glass, then left.

He took his UTV from the house to his bunkhouse kitchen. He parked and passed through the screen door, inhaling the woodsy fragrance of oak woodchips and lit fires, those being the two cowboy campfires that warded off the early-morning chill and offered auxiliary grates for cooking.

He could see the entire outback seating straight through the primary kitchen. The setup was further illuminated by tall lamps and ground lighting, the latter so no one stepped on any snakes nesting in the grass.

His assistant, Ritchie, came in through the far doors and said, "I've got your chimney starters goin', sir."

"So I smell. Nice job, Ritchie." Avery eyed him and added, "Didn't think you'd be up so soon, after the weekend activities. I'm sure you're exhausted."

"Are you kidding?" he asked with unbridled enthusiasm. "I can't even believe how great that bash was. I had a blast!"

"You were spot on with your prep too," Avery assured him. "Jack's accountant will reconcile the party funds and then distribute bonus checks to the staff. Including you."

Ritchie shook his head. "I didn't do all that for extra money, sir. I did it because I love this ranch and all the people. And, damn!" His hazel eyes glimmered as he said, "I learned so much. We cook for a crowd here but *not a crowd like that!*"

"Hence the reason I told you to sleep in for an hour to recuperate."

"I could barely sleep even after breaking down all the grills and cleaning 'em last night. Cowboys did all the heavy lifting for us, getting everything returned to their proper places."

"We couldn't have pulled this off without all the help." And Ritchie hadn't been the only one to follow Jack, Avery, and Chance's direction to keep the event running smoothly from day to day.

Ritchie further contended, "I for sure couldn't let you down. Not this morning, when everyone's gonna be feeling the strain and be hungry as hell. I have the utility carts loaded with the dishes and rollups. And the coffee urn's a-brewin'."

Avery's gut twisted with pride—and gratitude. He respected the kid's work ethic. Though "kid" was borderline patronizing, and that wasn't Avery's nature.

Ritchie was twenty-three. He'd come to the ranch at nineteen—the same age as Avery had been when he'd taken over this position. In his four years with Avery, Ritchie had floundered and flourished. He'd been a homeless orphan when he'd wandered toward this stretch of Texas, outside Serrano, and one of the cowboys had given him a ride. Problem was, Ritchie hadn't had anywhere to go. So he'd ended up here. And had demonstrated mad skills that Avery appreciated.

He told Ritchie, "You grab those ramekins for me so I can parse out ingredients, and we'll get this show on the road."

"Yes, sir." Ritchie nearly bounced on springs as he moved behind Avery to collect what was needed. Only seconds later, he turned toward Avery, set a large bin on the metal prep table Avery had unfolded, and asked, "What is all this?"

Avery spared a glance his way. Grinned. Then he laid out his knives on the table.

"These have my name on them," Ritchie said, emotion tinging his voice.

"Yeah, I noticed that."

"These are aprons like yours. Grillin' gloves too."

71

"Yep."

Ritchie sifted through the bin. The two black leather aprons had "Ritchie 'Right Hand' Matthews" in red scripting centered at the top, with "TRIPLE R Chef" stamped below his name and moniker. The two brown ones had green lettering. The sets of gloves matched.

His gaze shifted to Avery.

"I never expected this," he said. More choked up now.

Avery nodded. "'Cuz you're modest, Ritchie. You keep your attitude in check and do what needs to be done."

"I learned that from you, sir."

"Makes me even prouder." Avery wouldn't lie . . . he felt the tug of emotion too. Seeing this young man grow from scrawny and unstable to sturdy and loyal—as hardworking as all the wranglers and ranch hands—filled Avery's heart.

Ritchie was too old for Avery to think of him as a son, and yet . . . he sort of did.

Ritchie pulled the items from the bin and spread them out. He gazed at them as though they were gold bars. And then pulled in a deep breath.

Avery said, "You earned those, Ritchie. Don't think twice about it. Just suit up and check on our woodchips while I get the food rollin'."

Ritchie did as instructed. Though his *thank you* lingered in his eyes.

Avery gave another nod—of acknowledgment.

"I just want you to know I'm not ever going to let you down, sir."

"I don't doubt it, Ritchie. And you can call me Avery or Pitty now." His own nickname.

"Yes, sir."

Avery held back a chuckle. "Get to it, all right?"

Ritchie yanked off his cloth apron that was stained and also frayed around the edges. He selected a black one because that was what Avery had on. He figured Ritchie might consider this a team uniform—and he wouldn't be off the mark.

Hell, they fell so easily into step with each other, Avery knew they'd have a good chance of coming into the money with Layla's cook-off. If he was allowed an assistant. Not that he couldn't rustle up a meal for the wranglers, the additional staff, and the three judges all on his own. It was just that Ritchie provided the additional hands one found beneficial for mass production.

*And so . . . what?*

Avery's head cocked to the side with his mental contemplation.

Was he leaning toward a potential win, a new title, cold, hard cash?

*Why wouldn't you?*

*Been there, done that in the reasoning department,* he reminded himself.

For as much as Layla dodged her past—to whatever extent that might be—Avery had the ability to lay low on the ranch to keep his at bay too.

But he had to wonder . . . was he now merely hiding out because it was convenient, and he was accustomed to his routine? Or did he fear that getting back on any kind of BBQ circuit would resurrect the troublemaker in his father?

Then again . . .

Was his dad even alive?

Sometimes people who faded into obscurity didn't have obits or notices to next of kin. It wasn't as though anyone at the TRIPLE R was Caleb Reed's *in case of emergency* number. When he'd damn near destroyed this place by draining the coffers and was stripped of his own titles following drunken tantrums that warranted assault charges, his brother Royce Reed—Jack's dad—had basically declared he was dead to the family anyway. Not easy words coming from a man who was so dedicated to providing for others that he'd worked himself into his own early grave in support of his legacy.

Evidently, some things couldn't be forgiven.

Purposely tearing down what others had put so much effort into building up and sustaining—when so many lives and futures were at stake . . . Being a selfish, greedy, horrendous SOB offered others some clarity when it came to cutting the umbilical cord.

How it'd all affected Avery was a barbed wire fence he still felt twisted up in. Because he'd been the one on the circuit with a madman, and he'd been well aware his dad was an alcoholic and a gambler. One with plenty of debts. Avery didn't know how they'd gotten paid because they were heftier than the team's winnings. Then his uncle Royce had pieced together the paper trail and realized his older brother was stealing from him. Syphoning money from the family, the entire ranch. Bleeding them dry.

Something Avery couldn't comprehend.

He curbed these thoughts for now and tempered the anger they incited. He had food to serve.

He grabbed a crate of eggs from one of the large refrigerators and cracked half of them into a bowl that he set under the standing mixer to whip up, then started another batch. He chopped ham and veggies for Denver omelets before slicing and dicing ingredients for his avocado and tomatillo salsa verde.

Ritchie busied himself cutting home fries to parboil and pan-fry. While they were in the roiling water, he made a big bowl of fresh fruit cocktail.

They met up at the grills outside, and Avery dumped the chimney starters into the long firebox to get his heat going. Ritchie supplied the cleaned grates for one half and the flat griddle for the other portion. Once the desired temperature was reached, Avery arranged his plump breakfast sausage with a hint of cayenne on the grates, along with asparagus wrapped in applewood bacon. He got the ham and veggies cooking up and then poured the egg mixture onto the smooth surface and spread it thin with his spatula.

Ritchie set up the buffet table with plates and the rolled-up napkins with flatware. Then completed the beverage station with mugs, glasses, and spoons, adding pitchers of milk, and cranberry and orange juices.

The aromatic scents enticed the cowboys, and they filed in, filling up their cups as Avery folded the oversize omelets, cut portions at an angle, and piled them on platters that Ritchie delivered to the buffet table. Avery transferred everything else to their respective platters and then retrieved southern biscuits from his trench, to be served with either his homemade gravy or his honey-and-cinnamon butter.

The conversations came to a standstill as the chow line formed and then everyone dug in.

"Go on and join 'em," Avery told Ritchie, who always waited until Avery indicated it was break time for them before they cleaned up.

Avery poured hot coffee and made a plate for himself, then sat with Chance at the round table off to the side that the two of them occupied. Unless Chance was eating at the main house, where he got the opportunity to have discussions with Jack and Mateo—Wyatt's husband and the ranch rep for auctions and other business—without them having to carve time out of their day for meetings.

Didn't take much brainpower to know why Chance was hunkering down with Avery this morning.

Sure enough, his brother jumped right in. "You left the party before it officially came to a close."

There was humor in his tone.

Avery glowered at him. "I did my duty and turned my station over to Ritchie. Don't hassle me, bro."

"No hassle. Just sayin'."

"No need to say anything. I got the job done."

"Thoroughly," Chance concurred. "Not an empty belly to be found on that lawn. Some were even asking for to-go containers."

He snorted. "For the price of those tickets, I'm not surprised. Then again . . ."

"Yeah . . ." Chance drew in a breath. "They gorged themselves. On top-grade meats, no less. Not to mention all the sides and desserts."

Avery ate some of his omelet, then washed it down with coffee.

He told Chance, "If the profit margin is favorable, I'd be good with doing this twice a year. Maybe quarterly."

"Don't know what sort of draw we'd get if it wasn't perceived as being 'exclusive.' However, if we made it a smaller scale so it wasn't so costly for us and the guests, that might be one more revenue stream for the ranch."

"Just that Jack doesn't like the disruption, right?"

As Chance sliced into his sausage, he said, "I can't argue with that. George and his landscaping crew have to revive the lawn from not only the foot traffic and the tables and chairs, the carving stations and pop-up tents, but also from the dance floor and the stage."

"That's a good point." He sipped some more, then ventured, "Could be Jack needs to evaluate what the impact is on the surroundings."

"Sure thing."

Avery groaned.

Chance glanced up from his plate. "What?"

"Something interesting has cropped up—and I'm not certain how it might bear upon the overall environment, but if all were to go well, it most definitely could pump up the operations' bottom line."

Chance's brow rose. "That's always important to Jack. Hell, to all of us. What's simmerin' in your head, little bro?"

"Not my idea, just so you know. It's Layla's."

Chance chuckled. "How intriguing. I wasn't going to mention that I saw you leave yesterday with her and her pretty little friend."

"The friend is Brodi. Spitfire. You'd like her."

"Oh, whoa." He lifted his hands in the air, in surrender. "Don't go getting me all knotted in your shoestrings."

"I wear boots, dumbass."

"And, clearly, you *did* get knocked right out of them by Miss Layla Jenson."

"Inescapable," he murmured. And polished off his omelet.

Meanwhile, Chance hooted and lightly slapped his thigh. "Didn't I predict that was gonna happen? Christ Almighty, I should hang a shingle and start charging for fortune tellin'."

"If you wouldn't mind getting over yourself, I could use some actual advice."

Chance settled down. Gave him a sincere look and asked, "What seems to be the problem? Because that was obvious mutual attraction between the two of you. From the get-go."

"Not claiming otherwise. But she didn't come here to kiss and cuddle with me. She came here to recruit me."

"I'll find out about the latter later—tell me more about the kissin' and cuddlin'." He wagged his brows.

If Avery hadn't already eaten his biscuit, he would've thrown it at Chance.

Then again . . . why waste a perfectly good biscuit?

He shook his head. And said, "On a need-to-know basis—meaning this goes no further—she's still in my bed."

Chance whistled under his breath. "Well, color me jealous."

"Times a lot, I promise you. She's . . ." He clamped down on his lip, not wanting to utter a word that wouldn't do her justice.

"It's like that, then?" Chance mused.

"Multiplied by infinity."

"I think that's redundant," Chance said. "I'll consult Jack on that."

"You'll do no such thing," Avery admonished. "He'd want to know why you want to know, and that would circle back to me. And Layla. Jesus. Why are we making this so complicated?"

"I'm only following the commentary, bro. You're the one chasin' your tail."

"That is a true statement."

Avery was the one instigating all this uncertainty. For good cause.

He said, "Look, I'll tell you straight out that she hosts a BBQ cook-off channel, and she wasn't at the event to enlist Jack. Her project's different."

"How so?"

"They're looking to crown a Best Bunkhouse Cook."

"Hot damn," Chance said, keeping his voice down when it seemed he wanted to shout from the rooftops. "That's yours to win, Avery."

"Comes with a hefty purse too. For first or second place."

"So you signed on the dotted line?"

He scowled. "Can't do that right off the bat. Again, gotta run the flag up the pole, starting with Jack. And ensuring your activities with the wranglers aren't interrupted. Layla swears they have the production crew honed to be unobtrusive. If so, then great. But there's a little more to it than that."

Chance's head tilted to the side. "Such as?"

"Dear ol' Dad."

"Ah. Him."

"Yeah, him."

Chance cleared his throat. Rested his elbows on the table, his chin on his clasped hands.

"So you see my dilemma," Avery said. "One of three, really."

"Maybe."

"How's that?" Avery challenged.

"Hear me out. First, we've seen neither hide nor hair of the man in over a decade. He's not welcome on the TRIPLE R. Brute force and embezzlement follow a person around like a ball and chain. And we've alerted our team to keep him off the grounds. Not to mention, the gate code has been changed countless times since Uncle Royce gave him the boot."

"And it's been quiet on that front, as you said. Just seems to me that if there's money to be had, he'll come sniffing around."

"That could very well be. Not just related to you. If he's learned of Jack's channel and this past weekend's BBQ bash, he could have dollar signs flashin' in his eyes over all that as well."

"And seeing me in a competition for upward of a hundred and fifty K would also draw him out."

"Wow." Chance whistled. "That's a nice chunk of change."

"Bringing me to issue number two." Avery pushed aside his plate and drained his coffee. He said, "If I win, there are some bare necessities I'd want. New hat and a couple pairs of jeans. Some cooking equipment that will enhance what Ritchie and I do. Not anything that Jack should have to spring for beyond my budget, more gourmet—per our choice. I don't want to tap the ranch funds for stuff Ritchie and I pipe dream about."

"That's commendable. And I see where this is going. You know Jack's not gonna accept money from you, Avery."

"If I just so happen to find myself in the position to offer it . . . what would you suggest?"

Chance wiped his mouth with a napkin and dropped it onto his plate. He pinned Avery with an earnest look and said, "We'd have to get Mateo involved. He's the top negotiator around this place. And he knows how to speak Jack's fiscal language. Also knows how to work around Jack when he's being stubborn."

"Like how he got Jack to accept a bull from Luke's poker earnings."

"Just like."

Avery mulled this over. Then he approached the end of the trifecta, saying, "Third quandary is that I might be more invested in Layla Jenson than just the possibility of making a fistful of cash."

Chance grinned. "That's a given. She had you at 'carnivore's heaven.'"

"Listening in, were ya?"

"I drop eaves when warranted."

"You're not as amusing as you think you are."

"I don't have any trouble makin' the ladies laugh. You, however . . . you're an odd duck for sure."

"Duck . . . oh, fuck!" He slapped his hands on the table.

"What the hell was that all about?"

"Turducken would be my specialty meal for the contest. I fucking can't go wrong with that. I make it for the 'boys on major holidays, and they scarf it down."

"Avery, they scarf down *everything* you make."

"Could just mean they're starving because you've got them out on the range all day."

Chance's guffaw garnered attention. But then the wranglers went back to eating.

He said, "See? Can't really be bothered by anything else when they're chowin' down—on *your* food."

"Okay, fine. But why am I an odd duck?"

"You get in front of a camera, and you're as big a ham as Jillian's puppy. In reality, though? You're nose to the grindstone. All work and no play. But boy howdy, did you take an instant shine to Layla. Bet you had a bitch of a time hauling yourself out of bed this morning."

Avery rubbed the hint of stubble he hadn't bothered to shave, since he'd be showering and cleaning up later, when he was done here and before he had to prep for lunch.

"She's not exactly the kind of woman you want to leave. And it's not just her looks, Chance. Like Jillian, something haunts her. Something bad happened to her. There's a tentativeness about her. About us. And with whatever it is she's running from, I can't unpack all the Dad drama *I'm* still outrunning. There's a deep-seated humiliation embedded in all that, and I can't eject it. Not when I feel he could show up here one day, out of the blue, and send us spiraling again."

Chance sat back. Drummed his fingers on the table as he said, "The scenes he caused on the circuit were never your doing, Avery. No one ever blamed you."

"How can you say that when the slightest thing set him off? If he was drunk off his ass—which was all the goddamn time—and even the tiniest of detail was overlooked, he'd go apeshit, being the loose cannon that he was. Tongs once fell from the table into the dirt, and instead of getting a fresh pair, he erupted. Toppled the table. Our entire competition's meats went flying. Not an isolated incident, by the way. We'd be done for the day. Hours and hours *and hours* of work—wiped out. Money lost, not made."

And God help them all when Jack was pulling ahead with the scoring. Caleb would rant and rave as though Satan had possessed him. He'd even accused Jack and Uncle Royce of cheating.

Absolute BS. They wouldn't. They didn't have to; they were that good. A source of contention on his dad's side that Avery had to ponder as well, given Jack's newfound celeb status.

Although . . .

"You and I don't share his temper," Avery continued. "If I entered Layla's contest and didn't win, I'd be bummed, sure. Because it'd mean something to me to stand out. Especially after all this time. Yet it wouldn't be the end of the world. I'd move on, do what I've been doing. But if Dad got word . . . if he somehow found out they were filming here on the ranch . . ."

His gut clenched.

It wouldn't just be mortifying if Caleb invaded the production, got in Avery's face in front of the cowboys, the judges, the audience . . .

It'd be horrific if he went on one of his bombasts in front of Layla.

Not only that . . .

"The man has violent tendencies," Avery stated. "I don't want him around our people. Plain and simple."

Again, especially Layla. Because Avery suspected she'd been involved in some sort of volatile altercation—or plural. He sensed she'd found a safety zone. He wouldn't wreck it. Not even for a hundred and fifty thousand dollars.

He'd finally reached his answer?

He groaned.

The options he weighed were not to be taken lightly. This was a hell of an opportunity to pass up just based on a what-if. This truly was a contained environment. Chance would see to it remaining that way during the filming.

And the ranch could use the additional funds.

Not to mention . . . Avery really was enticed by a new title.

But there was something about the woman that held him back.

That was why he needed to speak with Jack. Not for permission. Rather, for a different kind of advice.

The love of Jack's life, Jillian, had come here as a recluse, for reasons that were also violent. She'd thrived. So much so, she'd been able to return when there were *hundreds* of people crawling around this place—and even clamoring to get close to her.

She hadn't overcome her fear of crowds. She'd kept to her own safe space during the weekend events. Had stuck by Jack's side, but had still, in effect, been immersed in the activities. She and Jack were learning to work with her phobia.

Avery needed to find similar confidence in protecting Layla from his father, should he weasel his way back into their lives or onto the property. Jack would offer the proper tips. He always did.

So for now . . . the answer was to discuss this with his cousin.

He told Chance, "I want to do the cook-off. I want to win that money. I just need to make sure nothing goes awry."

Chance speared him with a knowing look. "I hear you loud and clear. Me and my crew have cattle to move and horses to tend to. But that security we hired for the party might be our best bet to man the gate."

"I don't want to add to the expenses, Chance. Just . . . let me get a handle on this with Jack. In the meantime, I've got a woman waiting for breakfast. I need to finish here and whip up something for her."

"The omelet with a Bloody Mary would be my suggestion."

"Perhaps this is the reason you're not married. Gotta go above and beyond." He shook his head, gathered his dishes, set them in one of the busser bins, and then shut down his operation.

# Chapter Six

"I smell something sinful," Layla said in a sleepy voice as her eyelids drifted open.

"Could be me, though I wouldn't say sinful. I need another shower."

She gazed at Avery standing at the foot of the bed, setting a tray on the bench that ran the width of it.

"I'm willing to let the breakfast go cold in order to join you." She flashed a flirty smile.

"I can wait. You might like this."

Regardless, he pulled the snaps on his shirt and tossed the material aside.

"I'm confused," she said. "Are we eating or getting all sudsy in the shower again?"

He chuckled. Grabbed the tray and rounded the bed to her side. She shifted to give him room. He set the tray between them.

"Oh, my." Layla gasped. "Eggs Benedict over croissants?"

"Freshly baked."

"And salmon instead of Canadian bacon."

"Bit of a twist."

"Plus, potatoes with asparagus spears, heirloom tomatoes, and bacon bits. A mimosa. Yogurt parfait. How you spoil me." She batted her lashes at him.

He grinned and said, "Figured you might be witherin' away up here."

"Just woke, so perfect timing. And a whiskey glass full of wildflowers. Aren't you just the sweetest?"

"You're my first overnight guest. Not sure I got it all right."

Her heart fluttered. "I'd say you nailed it, cowboy. Mind if I devour?"

"Not in the least."

She cut into the egg first, sampled it, and sighed. "Perfectly poached. And that hollandaise with dill. To die for."

"Complements the squeeze of lemon. As well as the salmon with chives."

"Jesus, Avery. You just . . . threw this all together, didn't you?"

"I've made it plenty of times, so it wasn't difficult."

"And yet it's five stars all the way." She set her fork aside. Sipped her mimosa. And added, "I think you're extraordinary."

"They're just eggs, Layla."

"Be cavalier if you want. I'm not only talking about your breakfast. I'm talking about you, in general. The yogurt parfait would have sufficed this morning. Or some avocado toast. Yet you can't help yourself. You have to satisfy palates."

"Isn't that what gourmet cooking is all about?"

"Sure, in some respects." She sipped once more, then countered with, "If you were to serve simple fried eggs and sausage patties to the wranglers before the sun rose, would they complain?"

"Well, at this juncture, they'd expect it to be on either a sesame seed bagel or a toasted English muffin, with some melted cheese and a side of grits."

"Damn, that sounds good. And I think I lost my point. Aside from you being thoughtful and inventive. Not offering status quo."

"If you're trying to persuade me—"

"Told you I wasn't doing that. This is just me appreciating your talent."

"Thank you for that."

She took a couple more bites, then realized there was only one fork.

"You're not sharing with me?"

"I already ate, darlin'. I'm going to take a shower, which is sort of counterintuitive given that I'm gonna make love to you one more time, then drive you into town so that Brodi doesn't think I've kidnapped you."

"The hardship," she said, knowing there was a flicker of excitement in her eyes. "Fabulous food and a hot cowboy getting naked with me on a stunning ranch. I'll for sure tell her not to file a missing person's report."

"Be that as it may . . . ," he said as he stretched toward her and kissed her. "You do have to be in Cheyenne tonight."

"Doing what I love best," she confessed.

He climbed off the bed and proceeded to divest himself of his clothing.

Layla was torn between the enticing view and the scintillating scents from the tray.

Only when Avery disappeared into his bathroom did she continue eating. While sighing and moaning—not just over the breakfast.

She finished her meal as he returned, still dripping wet, the beads rolling along his thick neck, then splashing onto his collarbone and trickling down his chest.

He moved the tray to the bench again. Folded back the covers and slipped in next to her.

"We might need some sort of patch or twelve-step program to curb this addiction," she said as he pulled her on top of him.

"Only if we're tryin' to break the habit, darlin'."

◆ ◆ ◆

His words stuck in her head.

While Avery drove her back to town, Layla squirmed in the passenger seat, not finding a comfortable position because her inner thighs burned like she'd just run a marathon and her pussy pulsated with all the memories of being filled.

Christ, she'd always joked about Brodi's hyperactivity, and yet Layla could barely sit still.

Avery shot a glance her way and asked, "Okay over there?"

She rolled her eyes. "I feel as though I've been tased—in a fantastic way by an electric cattle prod."

"Am I the cattle prod?"

She laughed. "Don't go getting cocky on me, cowboy."

"Swear I won't."

Layla tried to settle down.

But then Avery went and said, "I *am* the cattle prod, right?"

"You lit me on fire. Is that satisfactory?"

"Sounds appropriate."

He pulled in front of the boutique hotel she was staying at and came around to collect her.

She'd snatched up the shirt he'd been wearing when they'd danced, had tucked the ends under, and tied the tails at her waist. Her sparkly top was a bit much for this time of the morning. Plus, she didn't want to be arriving in a garment she'd left in the previous evening.

Not that wearing a cowboy's shirt provided a different connotation.

Fact was, she wore it because it smelled faintly of Avery.

She left him at the elevator. Inviting him up would only lead to more sexy times. And she had to get on the road. Also, he needed to head back to the ranch and prep for lunch.

She showered and changed into jeans and a loose tank. Put away his shirt in her bag.

She met Brodi in the small parking lot, ready for the ribbing she was about to get.

"Don't suppose you brought me a doggie bag," Brodi immediately chided.

"The hotel has a complimentary breakfast. Guessing you partook."

"I did. Surprising. That feast last night should've fueled me for a day or two, but then I started thinking about what we're going to experience in Cheyenne with all that bison, and I just couldn't stop myself from cowgirlin' up to the buffet."

"Yeah, I didn't exactly say no to Avery's offering this morning."

Brodi clapped her hands together. "That's a good one. Did he also cook for you?"

Layla blushed. A new affliction. She rose above it, though, and said, "That's what I was talking about."

"Sure, it was."

Layla slid behind the wheel of the rental car and strapped herself in.

"On a more serious note . . . ," Brodi began.

Layla cut her off with a finger and a quick glance her way. Then she started the engine.

"First, we're not cajoling Avery," she told her assistant. "Second, what happened between him and me, happened between him and me. I can't take it back. I wouldn't if I could. He's that incredible. But the perspective we need to maintain is that I did my job—and then I did him."

Brodi exploded with laughter.

Layla smiled. "Well, it was a mutual effort, but you get my drift."

"Bet it was damn hot."

"That it was. Although . . ." Layla pulled into the light traffic and approached the four-way stop. Waited her turn, then headed out of town. "It wasn't just steamy sex."

"Down and dirty?" Brodi asked with hope in her tone.

"Well . . . once or twice. Also slow and easy."

"Good Lord, girl! How many times did you two go at it?"

"I lost count, to be honest."

"I hate you." Brodi gazed out the side window. Heaved a breath. Then stared at Layla. "I love you. But I hate you."

"Please. That sex fest you had in Ruidoso last season makes us all squared up."

Brodi sighed. "Neither one of us has gotten laid much since the show launched. But an occasional cowboy ringin' your bell . . . that's just pure sunshine."

"It's more than sunshine," Layla admitted.

Brodi shifted in her seat so she could stare at Layla. "Is it, now?"

"Nothing to be done about it, though, so settle down."

She took the interstate toward San Antonio. Changed the topic of conversation to their next gig. Played music when that subject ran dry.

She dropped Brodi off at her apartment and then drove to her own. She unloaded her tote bag and assembled a larger suitcase for her coming week, including Avery's shirt again, despite his scent fading from the material. Didn't matter. It was symbolic having something of his mingled with her stuff.

After catching up on emails and socials, she departed and picked up Brodi. On the flight to Cheyenne, they discussed the next few legs of the competition, with or without Avery's participation.

They went their separate ways when they reached the hotel. Layla hung her clothes and took a bath.

She was just about to turn in when her phone jingled. She connected, recognizing the area code.

"Aren't you resourceful?"

Avery chuckled. "Brodi texted me your contact info, so I'd say she's the resourceful one. I never gave her my number."

"That little funny bunny," Layla said. "She's playing matchmaker. Though . . . I thought we were managing that all on our own."

"Are we?"

She heard what he *wasn't* saying. "I grasp that we're not quite gelling—at the same time that we're gelling. Isn't that weird?"

"Honey, just focus on what you need to accomplish this week."

"I always do."

"And let me whisper a few sweet nothin's to you."

"That would make my lonely evenings much better." She removed her robe and slid under the covers. "What would be perfect, however, is if you knew how to video call me."

"Oh, Jesus. That would require me to ask my nephew Ale, and that would lead to him wondering why I asked, and then he'll potentially inquire of his mother the need for me to suddenly know how to video call."

Layla grinned—though he couldn't see it. "You get all wrapped around the axle over every detail. I actually find that to be thrilling."

"Pleased I can—"

"But it'd be more thrilling if we had the visual when we're nowhere near each other."

"Then I'll figure it out."

"Maybe just ask Brodi. She'd happily set you up."

"That's one hell of an assistant," he said.

"And BFF. She knows all my secrets. Keeps them."

He was quiet for a moment. Then he murmured, "I want to know all your secrets."

"Thought you were going to lull me to sleep with seductive words."

"I can do that too."

Her heart constricted. He wasn't invasive in the least. Layla just had qualms about how much more she should reveal. No, she didn't expect Avery to sell her story on the street. He'd also keep it to himself, she was sure.

Discretion wasn't really the issue. Yes, it was important to her. Vital. But she didn't take him for the sort who'd betray her confidence.

What disturbed her was how he'd react to hearing what she'd gone through.

Even initially having explained to Todd, her college friend and now boss, why he didn't recognize her or know her new name had been traumatic—for him as much as for her. Then confessing it to Brodi because Layla and Todd accidentally used her identities interchangeably as they were both getting accustomed to her significant alteration. It'd confused the hell out of Brodi to not know if she was Layla Jenson or Tess Billings.

So for now, she told Avery, "Make up a dirty bedtime story for me, cowboy. And we'll deal with the rest later."

"Ask and ye shall receive." Granted, disappointment tinged his deep voice. But he played along. "Tell me what you're *not* wearin', darlin'."

Avoidance was a tricky beast. Avery had never realized how much so until he'd met Layla. Until they'd both woven a web that was sticky as all get-out because they wanted to know things about each other but were having a hell of a time relaying their own truths.

Avery had started this new journey by discussing his concerns with his brother. Now it was time to branch out to Jack.

On Wednesday morning, Avery fed the cowboys and then drove up to the main house with his own contributions to the family breakfast.

"Excellent timing," Wyatt said. They were all getting situated at the table when he strode into the large kitchen. "And darned if whatever you brought us doesn't smell as delicious as what Jack's cooked up. No offense, Jack."

Jack shot her a smirk. She laughed.

Avery set the platter with his beef-and-egg breakfast nachos on a trivet and removed the foil. His aunt Brett whisked the potholder rack out of the way so Avery could place his tray of iced strawberry parfait in the center of the table.

"One thing's for sure," said Jack's producer, Garrett Jameson, "we never lack for food around here."

"Gotta keep the tanks full," Chance commented. He'd texted Avery earlier, saying he was prepping assignments for his crew so they could hit the ground running after Avery and Ritchie served them; he'd therefore missed the meal Avery had cooked for the bunkhouse.

"You made these nachos just for me, right, Uncle Avery?" This from Hunter, who shared his mother's blond hair, fair skin, and energy level.

Though his twin brother, Alejandro—who bore the family resemblance of dark hair and blue eyes—was equally spirited.

"You have to share, dummy," Ale said.

"No name-callin'," Mateo, their father, chastised. "Neither one of you will get nachos."

"But I didn't do anything!" Hunt was quick to plead his case.

"I apologize," Ale begrudgingly told them all. "I knew he was jokin'. I was jokin' back."

"Be nicer about it," his mother said.

"Y'all get started before this goes cold," Brett instructed. "Well . . . 'cept for the dessert."

Avery took the chair opposite Jillian and grinned at her. "You're still here."

"Yeah, about that . . . ," she murmured with mischief in her tone.

"We've been keepin' a secret," Jack chimed in.

Wasn't that becoming the bane of Avery's existence?

Farther down the table, next to Garrett, Jillian's podcast producer, Mindy Vonn, turned giddy with a smile and a glint in her eyes—indicating she knew what this secret was.

Avery's gaze slid back to Jack, at the head of the table. His recently claimed position, though he'd overseen the ranch since his daddy had passed, when Jack was nineteen—apparently a coming-of-age *age* around here.

With one phone call from home, Jack had left college, the chance at pro football, land and livestock management economics, and Jillian Parks behind.

Ten years later, he and Jillian had unexpectedly reunited.

Jillian said, "Turns out, I've had a terrible time cultivating my new line of hybrid chili peppers for next year's hot sauces and spicy dry rubs. And I discovered it's because leaving this ranch was the worst thing I could have done for my creativity."

"Mm, we're sayin' it's the ranch that brought you back?" Jack's brow lifted. "Is that right, darlin'?"

A collective laugh rumbled through the kitchen.

"Yes, Jack. All the people."

"'All the people'?"

She leaned toward him and smiled charmingly. "You too."

He chuckled. "Thank you for that, darlin'. I was starting to fear I wasn't as special to you as I thought I was."

"Topping the charts, I promise."

"Y'all stop with the fluffy commentary," Avery said, "and tell us what's going on with you two."

"I'm sticking around a bit longer," Jillian informed everyone. "Only going back to Seattle to pack up, sell some stuff, and then . . . I'll be living here permanently. As Jack's wife."

"Oh, my God!" Wyatt cried.

And then literally cried. As did Brett. Mindy's eyes misted as well.

"Well, isn't that just the damnedest," Avery muttered. Though his aunt heard him and shook a finger at him for cursing.

"I'm not surprised," Garrett said. "The way you've been making audiences swoon and cheer you on. It was too real not to see this coming."

As hugs ensued, Jack replied, "*We* didn't exactly see it coming. Lots of obstacles in the way."

"All of which you hurdled." Avery gave his statement consideration. Talk about polar opposites who'd had zero common ground, other than peppers.

*And their growing devotion to each other.*

That was a sentiment he found intriguing. Jillian's path had altered as her recovery had changed her life and the way she'd dealt with her previous isolation.

Whereas Avery and Layla's issues were related to career ambitions. Putting a million miles between them, even when she was in San Antonio for a day or two out of the week. Avery couldn't drop everything to travel that distance. Couldn't ask her to do the same when she only had so much time for a turn and burn.

Getting more deeply involved with her would only prove to be disastrous. He knew it in his soul. Was convinced she did too.

And maybe that was why they weren't being so forthcoming with their darker thoughts.

The cook-off might be fated. But a romance? That seemed a bit of a stretch.

He let those notions percolate as Jack continued.

"We have other news," his cousin said.

Jillian was already radiant. Now she beamed.

"Keeping this only in the family, within these walls for the time being," Jack expounded. "But it seems our reckless abandonment has led to me knockin' up my bride-to-be."

Another volcanic response from everyone at the table had them on their feet, with tears flowing and more hugs ensuing. Avery joined in with the latter, very carefully squeezing Jillian and congratulating her.

Then he shook Jack's hand. "You know how to bring home the gold, cuz."

"To be fair, she came to me." He winked.

"Whatever. I'm happy for you."

"And I appreciate that."

"Shotgun weddin'!" Chance called out as he joined their semicircle.

"That's been a decade in the making?" Jack countered.

"Yes, but the end result did come about quickly," Avery reminded him.

"Sure as hell hope the kid looks like Miss Jillian," Chance said, "without a trace of your ugly mug, Jack."

Avery roared with amusement. "Dude, we all look alike!"

Chance gave this a moment's thought, then scowled. "So I just insulted myself."

"You never were the sharpest crayon in the box," Avery retorted.

"Hey, now . . . what did I just say to my sons?" Mateo asked as he stepped into the lighthearted fray. "Be better examples."

Avery knew they already were. With the exception of the occasional cussword slipping out.

As he glanced around, he couldn't help but note that this family was a tighter, more cohesive, and certainly a more tranquil unit when no one was creating drama and trauma. Putting their personal goals and desires above everyone else's.

That'd been his dad's problem all along.

And as much as Avery hated to admit this about his own father . . . they were all better off without him.

He knew Chance had a valid point that Caleb Reed returning to the TRIPLE R was a long shot—and it'd be made clear before he could pass through the gates that he wasn't welcome here.

So maybe doing the show didn't quite warrant his paranoia. Maybe it was just the fact that he and Layla existed on different ends of the spectrum that caused him to drag his feet.

That was a matter to resolve with her. For the moment, he returned to the table with everyone else and polished off the meal.

While his aunt, Wyatt, Jillian, and Mindy cleaned up—with help from Garrett and the twins—Chance went off to catch up with the cowboys and Mateo headed into town on business. Avery followed Jack into his office.

"You don't usually attend breakfast here at the house unless you have something to discuss," Jack said, diving right in.

"All's well at the bunkhouse," Avery assured him. "Chance would have alerted you otherwise. And Ritchie and I have everything under control with our cookouts."

"Yet you're takin' a chair in front of my desk." Jack eyed him with interest.

"Indeed, I am. Got something to mention. Make sure you're comfortable with it before I proceed."

"This wouldn't have anything to do with Layla Jenson, would it?"

Avery's head snapped back. "Chance told you?"

"Nope. I recognized her from *Light Your Fire*. You think I don't research BBQ channels so I'm not mimicking anybody?"

"Not a lot of ranches this size have the owner 'cuein', grillin', and smokin' on live streams."

"Actually, there is plenty of competition. Jillian and her hybrids and sauces add diversity, so that's helpful. But that's not what we're talking about, is it?"

Avery rested a booted ankle on the opposite thigh and clasped his hands at his prized belt buckle. "If you know who Layla Jenson is, and are familiar with her show, then you probably know this season's theme is for Best Bunkhouse Cook."

Jack grinned. "Had a feeling that was why she was here on Monday."

"According to her, there are ten contestants—me included if I agree."

"Why *wouldn't* you agree?" Jack asked.

"Situations."

"Hmm." He seemed to mull over Avery's curt response. Then he said, "From what I've seen, they use each cook's everyday facility as their set. Bring in their own production people. Layla hosts. Doesn't seem too drastic in terms of our operations. You go about your normal day, and the judges sample and rate the product you produce."

"Yes."

"Where's the complication? That's your domain, Avery. Between you and Chance figuring it all out, I don't see where my approval is needed. I'm giving it, but you don't have to seek it."

"I appreciate that, Jack. Just a little more to the story . . ."

"That being?"

"I don't want to bait my dad."

"Ah." Jack was quick to catch on. As Chance had been. Because it was an eyesore one couldn't look away from. He said, "I'm confident we can mitigate that risk. We have the resources to keep him off the property. Any other issue?"

"Aside from not wanting Layla Jenson to know anything about Caleb Reed?"

Jack sat back in his chair, nodded his head, and said, "It's best your dad's not a factor in our familial equation anymore. While my mom and I do find value with atoning and redeeming, there are some lines to be drawn in the sand. I don't think any of us would ever believe Caleb is a reformed sinner. It's a bad thing to say, I will admit that. We're supposed to accept those who choose to repent. But it's been eleven years. And I haven't received a penny toward the enormous chunk of change he stole that almost put us under. I haven't heard word one from him. No one has."

"I'm on board with the 'forgive and forget' mentality, Jack, when earned. But it's a fact that if someone is willing to provide reparation, they make an earnest move in that direction. As you said, it's been over a decade. So if he comes skulking around after I've joined the competition, that's an obvious motivation to heed."

"We can keep an eye on all of that," Jack assured him. "If you want to do the show, Avery, do the show."

"Thing about Layla . . . ," he said as he circled back. "She's got her own issues. I don't want mine adding to them."

"You think I have some insight?"

"Jillian didn't arrive here as a whole person, Jack. But she's sure morphing into one."

"That's not from my assistance alone, Avery. This entire family took her in," Jack said with conviction—and emotion. "That's what we do. She faced adversity and powered through. The more she saw we accepted that, the more she opened up to everyone."

"So you're telling me to be patient."

"I don't know the extent of your feelings, Avery, but—"

"They're pretty extreme."

Jack only gave a half smile this time. "That's a fine line to walk. You want to explore something further, but . . ."

"But my life is here on the ranch. Hers is everywhere else . . ."

Jack sighed. "I'd contend that geography could be addressed. Truth is, though, I never intended to leave this ranch either. Not even for Jillian. She knew that."

They stared at each other.

Jack continued. "It's a jagged pill to swallow, and it might even sound chauvinistic. That's not what it is at all. I have a legacy to protect and people to provide for."

"As do I."

"Well, ten years later with Jillian—"

"Ten years?" Avery shook his head as his gut clenched. "Layla will have been to dozens of ranches. Might have even gone global. There's no way in hell this woman is single ten years from now. I can't believe she's single today."

Jack's eyes narrowed. "What are you really getting at, Avery?"

He groaned. And confessed, "That I already know the ending to this story. Not how the competition will work out. But how me and Layla will. And . . . I don't know . . ." His eyes rolled upward. "I saw you after Jillian drove away. Seemingly for good." He released his hands at his waist. Sat forward. Pinned his cousin with an intent look. "Wasn't a comforting sight, Jack."

"And you'd prefer to nip whatever this is with Layla in the bud to save yourself."

"To save her too."

Jack took a few moments to digest this. His eyes darkened in color. His expression turned shrewd.

Avery grew wary. Jack was going to say something profound and implore Avery to consider every possibility. Avery wasn't quite sure he could navigate those waters.

He'd never met a woman who'd dug her nails into him so deep, so fast. The hold Layla had on him was palpable . . . and predictable. At least, the outcome was predictable.

Jack also sat forward and rested his forearms on his desk, tapping a couple of fingers against his brown leather blotter.

"The suspense is sucking the life out of me," Avery drawled.

Jack gave a wry laugh. "Yeah. That's the thing about scenarios such as this."

"How fucking common are they? I don't know squat about what I'm feeling, Jack, but if this is love at first sight . . . I'm screwed."

Jack slowly nodded his head. "On the surface, yes."

"To my core, Jack."

Jack's eyes widened.

Avery's gaze didn't falter. "I took one look at her, felt a jolt in my gut, swore off engaging with her in my head, and then proceeded to invite her *to my home*."

Now Jack grinned. "You realize that says it all? You've never had a woman at that house."

"I've never had a woman on this ranch, period. I don't bring my occasional flings here. These are—"

"Sacred grounds."

"In our sense of the word, yes."

Jack let out a sharp exhale. "People make long-distance relationships work all the time, Avery. Not a new concept."

"Yeah? Were you and Jillian planning to date long distance? How do you think that would've worked out for the two of you? *You* in particular, an all-or-nothing sort of man? Oh, wait. I just answered that question for you."

Jack glowered. "I never believed there'd be a simple solution, Avery. And, yes, I was miserable every day she was gone from this ranch, from my bed. But I have an obligation here, so *I* powered through."

Avery continued his stare down. Bit the bullet. And demanded, "Did you know she'd come back to you? Somewhere in your heart or soul, Jack. Did you *know*?"

# Chapter Seven

Layla was at her production team meeting at the hotel in Cheyenne, covering all the details for a few upcoming weeks' worth of episodes.

Todd said, "We have the photo layout of the kitchen—all an inside operation. Here's how we want to do the blocking." He laid out the pictorial spread. "Audio and lighting are configured. We just need to confirm it all works in reality. As usual."

That translated to staging at the actual site. They wrapped up the meeting and hit the road. While the crew did their orchestrating and testing, Layla chatted with contestant Willet Hayes.

"We have your menus, but I'll also ask you to describe your recipes and ingredients as you're bringing the food together," she explained. "You'll have forty-five minutes to serve your cowboys and the judges. The last fifteen minutes of the show will be devoted to comments by the judges. They'll rate your offerings and lock your scores in your individual vault. After we cut, I'll do more interviewing to get your comments and others' as well. Those are testimonials that will be included in edited snippets of the episodes, for promotional purposes, and to fill in any gaps when the recorded version is uploaded."

"Contract says I can start meat beforehand, if I'm smokin'."

"Yes," she said. "And you'll want to make as big a splash as possible with your debut course."

"Then I'm ready to go when y'all are."

"Fantastic. We'll finish up on our end and start in about a half hour."

Willet rubbed his hands together. "I'm shootin' for the stars here."

She smiled. "That's the perfect attitude."

She was about to continue, but Brodi appeared at her side and said, "You have a call you want to take."

"Oh-kay." She narrowed her eyes at Brodi's cryptic delivery. She always told Layla up front who was on the line. Layla turned back to Willet. "If you have any additional questions, direct them to Brodi. And good luck with the competition."

Layla took her phone from Brodi and stepped away.

"This is Layla," she said.

"This is Avery," he replied.

She laughed. "I'm surprised."

"No, you're not. You knew I'd say yes."

Excitement shimmied through her. "I knew you'd say yes."

"We can accommodate the filming next week."

She resisted the urge to break into a happy dance.

"I'll have Brodi get the legal docs to you, and then marketing will send some graphics your way to approve. Add a comment or two for us to personalize them. Take some selfies or have someone else photograph you so we have current pics. They don't have to be professional, or studio-type images. In fact, we prefer it if you're just you in your natural element. No Photoshopping or poses that aren't suitable for you."

"Easy enough."

"For you, certainly. You're incredibly photogenic, Avery." And she had to keep herself from fanning her face as heat burst on her cheeks.

She really wasn't thinking of her research; she was envisioning him yanking apart the snaps on his shirt and revealing his sculpted chest and ripped abs.

She bit back a sigh. Tried to compose herself. Difficult though that was with the sexy images flitting through her mind.

This didn't work in her favor, because next Wednesday she'd be up close and personal with him again. And having to pretend he didn't melt her into her cowgirl boots.

Forcing herself to focus on business, she told him, "Check out our past eps if you can find some time. Our live streams are meant to appease our audience, yes. But we also encourage contestants to view recorded versions in order to get a feel for the format. Our first few competitors for this particular season are veteran reality TV show participants who were willing to set the bar. This provides other challengers the chance to strategize."

"Gotcha."

"Listen, I have to go so that I can get my thoughts all organized around today's ep. Champion grill master smoking bison brisket."

"Bison. No shit? That's a clever undertaking. I'm sure he'll be attuned to developing the smoke ring."

"A certain aesthetic the judges will evaluate," she said.

"Doesn't add flavor or tenderness, though; that's key. What else does he have going on?"

"Scalloped corn, baked beans, and potatoes au gratin."

"Complementary sides, though a little bland. Regardless, I've got my work cut out for me. You get to yours, darlin'. I'll have Ale hook me up with his tablet so I can watch."

"I'm so glad you decided on this, Avery!"

He laughed. "Hard to pass up. And as an added bonus, I get you at the ranch for a few more days."

"Cherry on top of the sundae. I'm off."

She disconnected before she squealed with delight over this coup. Or moaned in ecstasy over thoughts of more time with the sexy cowboy.

"All's well?" Brodi asked as she swooped in to snatch Layla's cell from her and hold it while Layla hosted the show.

"You giving him my number before I did was crafty of you."

Brodi shrugged with nonchalance. "Just facilitatin' the process."

"Sure. I told you I was taking the competition aspect in strides. So what was it you were facilitatin', exactly?"

Brodi waved a dismissive hand in the air. "You know it doesn't hurt to have a fairy godmother. You could use one."

They stared at each other.

Brodi's brow crooked.

Layla snickered. "Jesus. I'd say you're too intrusive, but last night's pillow talk with the man was hot as hell. He has a to-die-for bedroom voice, and he doesn't shy away from the juicy language."

"Somehow, I sensed that about him." Brodi smiled. "And look at you, all glowing like you just spent a week at the spa."

"I'm only glowing because we have a phenomenal lineup for this cook-off. And now . . . we need to get to it."

Layla left Brodi and approached Todd. "We have our top ten. Moved Avery into the slot we wanted him in—next week. His pit work will be a great interruption from grills and traditional smokers, and he also has an exquisite setup. Marketing will go nuts over him. So will the viewers."

Todd eyed her curiously. "And you?"

"What about me?" She feigned ignorance.

"Oh, please," he scoffed. "I've known you forever. This is the first time I've seen you blush—over a phone call."

"To be fair," she said, "he does have a whiskey-burn intonation that curls toes."

"Uh-huh. Yours, presumably?"

She shrugged and asked, "Is that an issue?"

"You have no voting authority, and you don't interact with the judges beyond interviewing them during the samplings. They don't even stay at the same hotels we book for you and the crew. I don't expect you to be celibate, Layla. Especially not with that face."

"You do realize that, as a rule, I don't think about this face."

"You're not the one staring at it. I still do a double take from time to time."

"You got me there." She confessed, "I pass a reflective surface and startle myself. Lots of complications when you become someone else. Figuring out your new identity is one of them. Even five years later."

He twined his fingers with hers, bent his head, and whispered, "What that asshole did to you was insidious. That you survived is unfathomable. But the way you rose from the ashes, Tess . . . that's incomparable."

Her eyes glistened.

He added, "I'd win awards if I did a documentary on you. That's not how I roll, though. You want privacy when it comes to your background. I'm glad I can give it to you."

"Thank you. You've helped to save my life."

"You did that on your own, sweetheart."

"No. There was someone else who rescued me—my plastic surgeon." She swallowed a lump of emotion. "But I can't exist without having you on my side, letting me do what's most important to me, what I've always wanted but had door after door slammed in my . . . well." She sighed. "You know I wanted to be a broadcaster. You made that dream come true."

The ugly duckling syndrome was a painful one. The twist in her case had been excruciating.

But this time around, Layla had relied on her gut instincts. She hadn't ignored her good judgment. And continued to push forward because of it.

Todd told her, "I respect you. Don't think I'm gonna hold you back in any way. You keep evolving. It's a beautiful thing to witness."

He kissed her cheek. Just before a drop hit it.

Todd was quick to whisk the tear away.

She'd never imagined having faith in any man other than her daddy after she'd been so viciously attacked that she'd required extensive surgery to repair the damage. Yet some men came shining through.

"Thank you," she murmured.

"Get ready for the show." He grinned. "Layla."

"Right." She let out a long breath. "Layla." She inhaled more deeply. Nodded. Exhaled. And said, "I'm ready."

She checked her makeup as the crew moved into place. Dabbed on extra lip gloss. Ran a brush through her straight hair.

Maybe someday she'd have her own stylist on set. For now . . . she did her best. Thought of Avery joining the lineup. And smiled with excitement.

"That's the exuberance that brings in the crowd," Brodi said. "Let's rock this show!"

◆ ◆ ◆

"Yowza, that's an opponent to fear." Jillian grimaced.

Avery sat back in his chair in the living room of the main house and winced.

Ale had done him a solid by tuning him into *Light Your Fire* and mirroring it from his tablet to the large flat-screen mounted over one of the fireplaces. Showing Avery how to do it in the process.

Willet Hayes had slayed his bison.

Avery slid a glance toward Jack. Who shrugged. And said, "Impressive, absolutely. But turducken in a trench? Come on, Avery. A chicken wrapped in a duck wrapped in a turkey, stuffed with dressing, and smoked till the skin's golden brown and the meat falls off the bone with juices running? You've mastered that before, and you will again."

"My sides are gonna be crucial."

"Jillian's specialty," Chance said. "Consult her."

"I think he's too busy drooling over Layla," Jillian commented. "My goodness, Avery, she has enough charisma to choke a cow." Her eyes narrowed. She cringed. And added, "That was the weirdest thing to slip from my mouth. Where in the world did I hear that?"

Avery laughed, then told her, "Trust me, cowboy sayings creep up on you at the darnedest times. Not a one of 'em makes a lick of sense."

"I'll keep that in mind. In the meantime, starchy and light flavorings will pair well with your poultry," she assured him. "Add cranberries to your stuffing for an extra zap of flavor."

"Good call." Avery contemplated this for a moment, then made his selections. "Balsamic zoodle sauté with mushrooms, roasted sweet potato fingerlings, truffle parsnip puree, and maple-bacon brussels sprouts."

"That would go fantastically with riesling," Jillian said.

"Shoot." Wyatt sighed. "It's only the beginning of June. We won't get a meal like this till Thanksgiving."

Jack glared at her.

"Just sayin'," she retorted. "Name a time *ever* that you've made us turducken?"

Mateo gestured to both of them and said, "You two aren't helping me get my point across with the boys."

Both of his sons looked perplexed. *Innocent until proven guilty.*

Avery said, "They just tease, Mateo. You've got nothing to worry about with them. If only we could replicate them, none of us child-free peeps would be terrified about what to expect if we reproduced." He gave a low chortle.

No one joined in.

Avery's jaw clenched as he realized what he'd just said.

Jack told him, "Those sayings? Let 'em go. Because apples fell so fucking far from the tree with you and Chance, there's nothing to worry about."

"Jack," Wyatt admonished. Not about the sentiment, just about the swear word.

"I apologize for that," he said to Hunt and Ale. To Avery and Chance, he reiterated, "Nothing to worry about. Avery, you're just riled up because someone's shining a spotlight on you, and you're concerned it'll bring your dad back into the picture."

"Jack." This from Brett. She gasped. Then she slid her gaze toward Avery. Tears pooled in her eyes as she told him, "That's not for you to be upset over. He did what he did. It's not a reflection on you or Chance."

"I did say that," Chance offered. "But I think there's a deeper issue here. To be discussed elsewhere and not interfere with the boys' gaming time."

Avery nodded. "We're done with *Light Your Fire*. Ale, you and Hunt set yourselves up."

Wyatt and Brett collected the coffee tray and the dessert plates, and Avery gathered a few empty wineglasses, following them into the kitchen.

The first thing Brett said when the three of them were alone was, "If you're anxious about genetics, Avery, you can wipe that from your mind. Reeds aren't violent types."

"Caleb Reed is," he countered.

"That's a bit beyond my reasoning, I won't lie," his aunt said. "But as a whole . . . it's not hereditary. Not something you or Chance exhibit or should be concerned about."

"But could it show up in our kids?" he solemnly asked.

Brett stepped toward him and gently cupped his chin. "I've known you your entire life. The only thing I have to say about you shying away from having children is, don't do it out of fear of a self-perceived, inherited disposition."

"What about abandonment?" Wyatt quietly asked. "His mama did walk away in broad daylight, not ever looking back."

Avery felt the knife twist. Not that that was Wyatt's intent. She had a point to make as well, another query as to why neither Avery nor Chance were the least bit interested in wives and their own families.

Brett dropped her hand. Shook her head. More tears filled her eyes.

She told Avery, "Ruby didn't abandon you and your brother, per se. She left because she thought everything she did was the wrong thing and that she irritated your father with every breath she took. She hoped not being around would calm him down a bit. For yours and for Chance's sake."

"He was the exact same way on the circuit," Avery said. "Nothing calmed him down—not for long."

"She didn't know that," Brett informed him. "The trophies and the prize money appeased him, and that was all she really saw."

"They weren't easily won with him around."

"*That* she didn't see."

Avery's head dropped. He stared at the floor for a few moments. Tried to get his bearings.

Then he glanced up at his aunt and told her, "There is a very lovely lady who I think had her own volatile past. I won't subject her to mine."

He started to walk away.

"Avery, wait." It was Wyatt who called out to him, catching him in the hallway. She placed her hand on his arm and said, "As much as you want to shield someone from the world, you can't. Jack wasn't able to do it with Jillian all those years ago. He had to come back home after that first year at SPU. She moved on. Then she was trapped in a terrifying situation. Literally. Now they're—"

"You really can't compare us, Wyatt, much as I appreciate you trying to do so," he offered. "Jillian will find serenity and security on this ranch. Layla Jenson will not. Her life's meant to be elsewhere."

The more he said it, the more he'd get it through his thick skull.

Avery spent the next several days strategizing his menus for the show.

Early Monday evening, Layla video called him. Because he could do that now.

"Landed safely late last night," she said.

"Thanks for texting me and letting me know."

"Thanks for wanting to know."

They were both quiet for a few moments. Then she said, "Got my errands taken care of today, packed a new suitcase, and am headed toward the hotel in Serrano soon."

It was five o'clock, and Avery was folding foil packets for grilling—white fish and veggies in a sauce of garlic, lemon, butter, and red pepper flakes. He had his phone propped on the table, with some sort of pop-up kickstand thingy Ale had mounted to the casing. Quite helpful.

"Well, with that drive, you'll miss dinner here, darlin'. But I can always make you something special."

He mentally smacked his palm to his forehead as the words jumped from his tongue, without his brain having a say in the matter.

For fuck's sake, he'd resigned himself to this not being a viable, sustainable relationship. He'd stated the inevitable outcome when he'd been in Jack's office. His fate had been further sealed when Jack had admitted he hadn't believed Jillian would come back to him after she'd left the ranch.

That revelation had rocked Avery.

Deep down, he'd been convinced that Jack hadn't lost all faith when Jillian returned to Seattle. Then again, the sight of him for weeks after she'd left had proved he held no hope for a third chance at romance between them.

Admittedly, it'd been difficult for anyone else to reconcile in their minds that something wouldn't trigger another reunion for the star-crossed lovers. But it didn't happen.

And then it did.

And maybe that was the crux of Avery's problem. He wanted to think miracles occurred and stars aligned, not only for random, fleeting moments, but for the long haul. He'd not wanted to accept that Jack and Jillian were over, even though that was exactly the way that hand had been playing out at the time. Then lightning had struck and *bam!* They were together again. Getting married. Having a baby.

Avery couldn't be happier for them.

Unfortunately, it didn't rally any hope that kismet would favor him and Layla.

She could be here for a bit of time. But it'd only be temporary. She clearly had wanderlust running through her veins.

She seemed to be contemplating something similar, as she paused as well. Like . . . was this a wise thing for them to do?

But then she said, "I don't mean to be any trouble."

He almost snickered at that sentiment. She had been even before Chance had spelled it out.

"Honey, I'd be disappointed if you were in town and not wanting to see me."

*Way to shoot your own foot, Pitty.*

*What is wrong with you, man?*

Oh. Right. He was falling in love.

"I'll let Brodi check me in on my phone," Layla said, "and I'll see you in a few hours."

Perhaps the vid calling was a mistake because it obviously skewed his judgment whenever he saw those stunning tiger eyes.

Regardless of the repercussions swirling in his mind, he asked, "You know the way, or should I send someone for you?"

"I hit that long patch of road and then look for those TRIPLE R gates leading to your part of paradise."

He gave her the gate code. And added, "I'll leave the door unlocked. Come on in."

"See you soon, cowboy." She dropped off.

"Got yourself a hot date?" Chance asked with a grin.

"I just can't say no to one more night with that woman."

"Seems you'll likely get six of them while she's filming here."

"Could be. Though that'll only make her hopping on a plane on Sunday to wherever the hell she's going next all the more agonizing."

"You are turnin' into a glutton for punishment, bro. I'm a little worried."

"Be a lot worried," Avery told him. "I sense this will all blow up spectacularly in my face."

Chance's gaze narrowed. "You're willing to take that risk?"

"You heard me invite her to the ranch, didn't you? When I've contended all along it's a mistake."

"Well, who knows?" Chance clasped his shoulder. "Maybe it'll be your *best* mistake."

"Go take a shower. You smell like a stall that hasn't been mucked out. I've got work to do here."

"I'll be back for supper." Chance chuckled as he ambled off, no doubt comically mourning Avery's imminent romantic demise. Which he was bringing upon himself.

He completed the packets and got them on the grates while Ritchie set up the buffet table.

Following the fluid execution of the cowboys' meal—thank God one thing in his life was smooth sailing—Avery went to the house to clean himself up and change into a tank top with drawstring pants before he collected wildflowers, putting them in whiskey glasses scattered about the house.

Then he crafted appetizers and a meat and cheese board. He selected a cabernet franc he was fond of. Turned on the Bluetooth speakers and a country western playlist that Ale had downloaded for him. Lit wood fires in the two downstairs hearths for ambience.

Then he just sort of . . . waited it out.

Fighting a grin.

Knowing that all the tumult was warranted and yet . . . letting it fall by the wayside as he thought of Layla on her way to him.

# Chapter Eight

Layla was shocked she didn't collide with Avery's truck in the side drive.

Her gaze was on the house.

More specifically, the front porch.

She managed to pull alongside his vehicle without incident and shoved the shifter into Park. She shut off the engine but left the keys in the ignition, knowing no one was going to steal the rental the production company had provided her with because Layla didn't have her own car. Not much point when she was rarely ever home.

Avery came down the steps to open her door, and while the sight of him momentarily diverted her attention, it quickly returned to the deck. All lit up.

Not vibrantly, obnoxiously lit up.

Warmly, beautifully lit up.

She slipped from behind the wheel. He closed the door, rounded to the passenger side, and retrieved her "necessities" bag. Her suitcase for the week was in her trunk.

She stared at the scene before her, with nary a breath in her body.

Candles emitting a soft golden illumination and multicolored blooms alternated up each step, on both sides. Same for the top and bottom of the railings. He'd added twinkling lights to the base of the two planted trees on opposite ends and had draped lightweight blankets over the sofa and chairs that were laden with pillows. Soft music floated from the house.

All rendering Layla speechless.

He grinned and said, "A more proper way to introduce you to my home."

Layla's heart constricted like a big fist was squeezing it tight. Tears pricked the backs of her eyes. Emotion clogged her throat.

She opened her mouth to speak, but still . . . no words flowed.

"You do like candles, right?" Avery asked in a hesitant voice. "We had all these left over from the BBQ event. The glasses too. Wyatt— she's my cousin—suggested all this, but I arranged everything myself." His brow knitted. "Maybe I went overboard."

Layla tore her gaze from the subtle opulence and the entire entrancing setting.

"You just went around picking flowers for me?" she asked, stunned.

"Well, to be fair, we do have a lot of them."

Now her heart nearly splintered. "Avery." The only thing she could say before tears pooled in her eyes.

She pressed her hand to her trembling lips as her gaze slid to the most romantic display she'd ever laid eyes on.

Finding her voice, though it was frail, she said, "No one's ever done anything like this for me."

"I find that hard to believe, darlin'."

"Believe it, cowboy." She glanced up at him. "No one."

She noted his consternation and had to remedy it.

She brushed away a few drops, slipped her hand in his free one, and said, "It's lovely, Avery. Thank you."

"I just wanted you to know . . ." His voice trailed off. He gave a slight shake of his head. Let out a strangled sound—and tried again. "That I like you being here. And you can visit anytime."

She twined her arm around his, snuggling close. She inhaled his fresh masculine scent. Let more tears fall.

"I'm not sure this is good or bad," he confessed. "You crying . . . us getting more tangled up with each other . . ."

"I can drive back to Serrano," she offered. Though it was the last thing she wanted to do.

"What about all this food I made?" he teased.

She gazed up at him. "I'm sure the wranglers will find room in their bellies."

"Ain't that a fact."

They stared at each other. Until she thought all these feelings would choke her.

She said, "Let's just see how the evening goes. Yes?"

"I'll give you three guesses on how it's gonna go."

"But I only need the one." She craned her neck, gave him a soft kiss, then batted her damp lashes.

He grinned. "My thought too."

He guided her up to the seating area, depositing her tote at the screen door. Through it, she could see more golden accents. So he hadn't just concentrated on this one spot for them. That practically liquified her as she sank onto the sofa and he sat next to her, reaching for the bottle of wine and then pulling the cork. He poured them both a glass, and she positioned herself to face him so they could tap rims.

"You're ruining me for all other men, cowboy."

"That's sort of the point, honey."

"Consider me sufficiently wooed."

He chuckled. "I just didn't have a better term for it."

"It's elegant."

"Bringing all these tears to your eyes isn't."

He grabbed a napkin and dabbed at her cheeks. She didn't pull away.

Perhaps that was why he said, "Something happened to you, and I don't know what it is, Layla. But you aren't afraid of me."

"No," she said with absolute conviction.

"Even though this . . . thing . . . between us is unsolvable."

"I won't give up my career." She was adamant about this. "It's what I've wanted almost my whole life."

"I can't give up this ranch. It's who I am."

"I already know that, Avery. It's another reason I wanted you on the show. Your devotion is commendable." She smiled and added, "As amazing a coup as it would be if I could steal you from this place and take you on the road as my cohost . . . I have no delusions of being able to do that. No. Point-blank, I wouldn't even suggest it."

"Interesting how we've already arrived at this stage. And yet we're not relenting."

"Knowing we should?"

He sipped. Sighed. Then said, "I won't deny I ran through all the what-ifs, with the accompanying, 'Why would we torture ourselves?' Seems we're destined for misery."

Her stomach knotted. Because she couldn't reject his statements, contradict them.

"Well, I'm here now . . . ," she simply said.

He kissed her and murmured, "Doesn't that just make my night?"

He poured more wine and angled the tapas plate her way.

She told him, "Not to be more of a downer, but I have to start thinking of a concept for next season, now that we have this roster nailed. I need a proposal for our sponsors."

"Have you considered food trucks?" he asked. "There are some serious BBQ offerings to be had. Not just in the Southwest but all over the country."

He winced.

She caught it.

She chewed on a tomato-basil cracker with mozzarella and a drizzle of balsamic vinegar. "You're providing me with options that will take me to the West Coast? The East Coast?"

"Maybe Canada and Mexico."

She stared at him. "You really do understand what drives me, cowboy."

"Not saying it's easy to accept. But you have a great platform, and you love what you do. Why wouldn't I support that?"

She leaned in close and swept her lips over his. Stared into his eyes again. She whispered, "*You* might be the holy grail."

"It's not a far-fetched notion to say I'll always be here. Pretty much etched in stone, truth be told."

She considered this. "You're almost a three-hour drive from San Antonio."

"And I can't make a jaunt your way and be back here for breakfast with no sleep."

"That whole 'no sleep' thing *is* enticing." She kissed him again. And said, "Bottom line is . . . I wouldn't mind coming to you."

"You have the access code."

She knew it was judiciously given out.

Still . . .

"Monday nights in your bed is enough for you?" she asked.

"Nope. Not by a long shot."

Okay, that said *so* much.

"But I don't want to dissect that right now," he told her.

He put their wineglasses on the end table and pulled her into his lap. His fingers combed through her hair. She'd not straightened the long curls, since he'd said he liked them.

She kissed him. Faintly at first. Enjoying the heat oozing from his every pore. Thrilling over how he wound his arm around the small of her back, keeping her close.

Her fingers released the snaps of his shirt as their lips twisted and tasted.

This was definitely a glorious way to end her workweek, right before she started up again on Wednesday.

And knowing her next segment was here on the ranch, she could overlook the agony of only getting one night a week with this man. She didn't bother to wonder how long that might last. He could get tired of the lack of physical contact sooner rather than later. Not to mention the emotional disconnect.

She was in his arms now, and that mattered most for the time being.

Her nails grazed his abs, and the muscles flexed. He wriggled a bit, as though to get comfortable against a tightening crotch.

She whispered, "There's nothing like a cowboy getting all worked up. Not that I've had experience with one until now."

"You just keep doing what you're doing, darlin'."

"In that case . . ." She kissed him more passionately. He responded fervently.

And there they went again, getting lost in each other.

She shifted so that she could straddle him.

He eased her shrug over her shoulders, and the humid air drifted over her flesh. Her thin-strapped top rustled in the gentle breeze, caressing her skin as much as his fingers did as they glided down her arms. Making her shiver.

Their languid pace and the sultry atmosphere had her melting into him.

In between sensuous kisses, she murmured, "This beats the hell out of a lonely hotel room."

"Let's not talk about lonely, honey. We won't be doing ourselves any favors."

"Point taken."

"Just keep kissing me."

She did.

Song after song played in the background. Stars glittered in the sky. Crickets and frogs found their own perfect harmony. She glanced around from time to time, when she needed a breath, and marveled at the tranquil surroundings and the flickering of the faux candle flames.

His hands slipped under the chemise material partially covering her and found the clasp to her strapless bra. He unhooked it with a finger and thumb, then peeled it away, tossing it aside. He palmed her breasts and massaged with a tinge of insistency that conveyed his need for her, but also his contentment with maintaining their leisurely pace. Relaying how much he held himself in check, when she sensed he wanted more.

That sent a ripple of delight through her.

She suggested, "Why don't we take this party upstairs, cowboy?"

He didn't hesitate. Didn't say a word. Just stood in one stealthy movement as she wrapped her legs around his waist. Though she unraveled from him at the door so he could use a remote to turn off the candles and another for the tunes.

"We'll get the rest later," he said but snatched up her bag to bring it inside.

He closed the door behind them.

Layla observed the same assortment of candles and flowers leading up to the mezzanine. There were scattered petals along the corridor to Avery's suite.

She glanced over her shoulder. "You don't do anything halfway, do you, cowboy?"

"I'm sure I forgot something," he admitted. "This isn't my norm."

Yet he flipped on the gas fireplace, "lit" more candles, and tapped another playlist. Voilà . . . the romantic mood continued.

"My pulse is wicked fast," she told him as he pulled her into his arms again. "And there are some insane things happening between my legs."

"Which is where I want to be."

"Ah, we always find our way to the right juncture."

"That unto itself is a sexy connotation."

He wasted no time getting them naked. Jerked back the bedding. Pressed her down onto the mattress as she spread her legs for him.

Her hands skated up his biceps to his broad shoulders. She sighed serenely. "You have a strapping build, Avery Reed."

"Feel free to take full advantage of me, honey."

She nipped his lip. And said, "Can't help myself."

"Ditto." His gaze slid over her.

Then he inched down a bit, his lips skimming over her collarbone to the tops of her breasts. His tongue curled around one pebbled center, flitting provocatively. He moved lower, teasing her stomach with butterfly flicks.

Exhilaration rippled through her as his fingertips grazed her slick folds.

"Why does it feel like an eternity since you touched me?" she murmured.

"Because we should be doing this every night."

"There is that."

Irrational yet desirable.

She said, "At least we get these stolen moments."

"I have huge thoughts on how to maximize them."

"I was hoping . . ."

His tongue drew lazy circles around her navel. He bit lightly at the rim. She threaded her hands through his lush hair. Her lids drifted closed.

Layla's body begged for more, but she didn't urge him on. He'd reach his destination when he was good and ready. Sure enough, he maneuvered himself in the V her thighs created, and his warm breath blew over her exposed flesh, making it quiver.

He spread her folds with his thumbs and fluttered the tip of his tongue over her clit.

A whimper escaped her. She sucked in her cheeks, holding another one at bay.

But she had no control over the writhing of her body.

He teased the knot of nerves with more of the quick flickers. Toyed with her folds with long licks. Then traced her opening with his tongue. All so electrifying and decadent.

She gripped his biceps, holding him in place. He knew what she wanted—and she knew he was going to give it to her.

Two fingers penetrated her, and she couldn't stop the next rasping breath from filling the quiet room.

"Avery . . ."

"Baby, let me get you off. I want you crazed for me."

"*Sooo* close."

He put extra effort into his combination of fluttering and stroking. Pushing her higher.

Until she shattered.

Moments later, he was sheathed and inside her.

And that was only the beginning . . .

# Chapter Nine

Avery splashed bourbon into a glass while Layla gussied up in the bathroom.

She emerged wearing what Avery considered to be the most sinfully angelic outfit imaginable. She had on a lacy bra with low-cut cups that barely covered her pert nipples and a satin bow in the center of her plumped-up breasts. The skimpiest of lacy panties. A satin and lace robe, one side slipping off a shoulder.

The ensemble was all in cream, and it enhanced her honeyed skin and her soft blonde curls.

And made his blood boil.

Avery took a deep drink. Groaned. Then said, "I could pretend to be cool here. But . . . you'd see right through me. Damn . . . you make me hard in a heartbeat."

She cozied up to him on the sofa. Sipped from his tumbler. Then smiled beguilingly. "Precisely what a woman likes to hear."

He chuckled. And said, "You didn't have to 'slip into something comfortable' for me. Naked was just fine. Though . . . I do appreciate the lingerie."

"Picked it up earlier today."

"Just for me?"

"Just for you."

He battled contradictory thoughts, as was the constant case for him where she was concerned.

He'd barely dressed after making her come again, following going down on her. Easy to rid himself of his boxer briefs now.

The problem here was that Layla looked like a dream come true.

He told her, "I don't want you to take everything off—because it's hot as hell. But I *do* want you to take everything off—because you're making *me* hotter than hell."

"One of your superpowers, Avery Reed, is that you are earnest to the core."

"Got nothing to hide, darlin'." He cringed at his untruth. "Except a past I don't want coming back to haunt me. Or the competition."

She eyed him quizzically. "Is this why you've been uncertain to join? Everyone else we approached jumped right on board."

"I can understand that. It's not just about the money—though that's a substantial lure. But getting to demonstrate what we do on a daily basis, what we do best? That's the real appeal."

"Yet you were dodging it."

"Yeah." He took another drink. "I don't want my father seeing an episode and coming out of the woodwork."

"The Caleb Reed I didn't fully research. Because I was too smitten by his son."

"You got a thing for Chance, darlin'?"

She laughed.

It soothed his soul, reducing the typical disconcertion he felt when mentioning his dad.

"Quite the jokester you are." She kissed his cheek and added, "Granted, he shares similarities with you. But when it comes to me, Chance doesn't resonate the way you do."

"Glad to hear it."

She rested her head on his shoulder and told him, "Chemistry's a crapshoot, cowboy. You never know when it's going to zap you."

"Or fade into oblivion . . ."

She glanced up at him. "That's true. It can change over time."

That sentiment hung in the air, tainting the otherwise pleasant fragrance from the wildflowers.

Layla sighed. "Seems we keep returning to how we're not a match made in heaven."

"Yet we know precisely what to do in the moments we're together." He placed his empty glass on an end table and stood, offering her his hand.

He led her to the bed, grabbed a condom, divested himself of his briefs, and sat on the edge.

"Let's compromise." He coiled his fingers around the slim strands at her hips and dragged her panties downward, letting them fall to the rug. Leaving on the rest of her lingerie.

She straddled his lap, taking him in all at once, sending a shudder through him.

"Fuck, Layla . . ."

"Always ready for you, cowboy."

She rocked her hips as his hands clasped them, forcing her to start slow. She clutched his upper arms, and her head fell back.

Avery left feathery kisses along the tops of her breasts, her collarbone, her neck. He flicked her earlobe with his tongue, and she let out a small whimper. He nipped a bit lower, then suckled gently.

"You find all the sweet spots," she murmured.

"Like that, do you?"

"I like everything you do to me."

He loosened his hold on her, and she picked up the pace. Wound her arms around his neck. Kissed him.

Avery's hands slipped to her ass, massaging while she rode him. An inferno roared through his veins.

She was so damn tight, so slick. Opening further to him, taking him deep.

He kissed her bared shoulder. Her satin-and-lace robe cascaded down her back, between his legs, grazing his skin. It was delicate and sensuous, like the woman herself.

Her eyelids drifted open. She smiled invitingly, driving him wild.

"I know what you want," he whispered.

"Of course you do."

She untwined her arms. Reached behind her to flatten her palms on his thighs, near his knees. Arched her spine. Let all those lustrous curls tumble along the satiny material.

He increased the tempo, his hips bucking.

"Yes . . . like that . . ." Her breaths were wispy, her voice faint. "Just like that, Avery."

He shifted his hands, circling an arm around her to keep her pinioned to him and freeing up his other hand to wedge between them. He rubbed her clit, and that incited moans that made him nearly lose his mind.

Her pussy clenched and released, working him into a frenzy to match their cadence. His pulse hammered and adrenaline raged within him.

Her first climax almost sent him over that searing precipice as she cried his name and milked his cock.

Stamina was never going to be his friend with this woman.

He stood, and she was quick to anchor her legs around him. He turned them and laid her on the bed. He thrust into her with all the passion he felt for her, all the lust that blazed through him.

She moved with him, lifting her hips, grinding against him.

"Oh, God, Avery . . ." Her nails dipped into his biceps. As much as they could because all his muscles were rigid, rock hard. "Oh, God, yes . . ."

Her chest heaved, her nipples peeking out over the scalloped trim of the lacy cups. The graceful cords of her neck pulled taut. Her lips parted. Her eyes opened.

He focused his gaze on hers, captivated by the glow of orange around her amber-and-gold irises.

If ever there was a moment he'd freeze in time, this was it.

She was more than beautiful. Felt better than anything on this earth he could think of—and even anything celestial. She was perfect. And in this one instant, *they* were perfect.

But the pressure mounting within him, stretching much too thin, couldn't be controlled.

The reins snapped.

"Oh, goddamn, Layla!" His body jerked. His cock swelled and erupted, splintering all of him. "Oh, fuck . . ." His next breath stuck in his throat. Epic fireworks went off in his head.

And his heart? Well, that now belonged to Layla Jenson.

*For better or for worse.*

"I'm having trouble thinking of what to say." Layla was tucked against Avery and couldn't catch her breath, even though they'd showered and were nestled on the sofa again, him in a towel and her in her robe.

They gazed out at the starlit sky. Spanish guitar music played in the background and mingled with the crackling of the fire.

Her legs were curled up as they shared a scotch on the rocks. He said, "Likely because we're knee-deep in each other, and yet we've only scratched the surface."

"There's more to the situation with your dad."

He countered with, "There's more to your New York experience."

"Question is . . . will tackling these things change our existing paradigm?"

"That we're two ships passing in the night? No."

His fingers were tangled in her hair, and he lightly massaged her scalp, adding to all the tingles she couldn't escape when she was near him. When she heard his rich, intimate voice. When she thought of him.

He further said, "One complication is that I might say or do something that could cause you to break your commitment to neutrality with the show."

"Not with the way it's structured," she insisted.

"But you are a cocreator, right? I saw the credentials when we watched Willet Hayes's episodes. That provides you a degree of influence."

"I told you it doesn't. And this is too important to me to compromise the premise, to jeopardize trust. I *need* this job, Avery. I owe someone a huge debt."

*Oh, shit.*

Her lips pressed together.

Why was it that every time she was with this man, she divulged more and more? It just slipped out with no red light to stop her.

He set the glass on the coffee table and shifted so he could face her, propping himself up on an elbow.

"What's this?" he asked.

It took her a few moments to compose herself. Then she said, "Someone did me a favor, Avery. An extraordinary favor. A 'be careful what you wish for' favor. It came with a hefty bill. I pay what I can on it. The people I used to know don't hand out freebies—there are always strings attached."

It wasn't even some sort of twisted matrix. It was a simple equation.

Regardless, Avery looked perplexed.

Understandable. She was only offering pieces to the outer edge of the puzzle, not the guts of it.

She didn't say more. Just reached for the glass and sipped.

"I need cash too," he said in a quiet voice, taking her by surprise.

She studied him for a moment. She wanted to ask why, but he hadn't forced an admission from her. So.

She passed him the glass, which he drained. She refilled it from the decanter on the coffee table.

Silence ensued.

"Maybe scratching the surface is all we should do," she told him.

"Maybe. But . . . that doesn't feel right."

"Agreed."

He said, "If I win any money, I want to give it to Jack—to pay him back for the money my dad stole from his dad."

She couldn't help the jaw-drop. Tried to pick it up off the floor, but that was futile. For several suspended seconds at least.

He continued. "Even the grand prize won't cover what's owed. But it's a dent. That's what matters." He groaned. And said, "No, what matters is that Caleb Reed's sons do what they can for the ranch, every single day. We can't right the wrong, change the outcome. Can't even say we're sorry because no one wants to hear it from us. No one's placed blame at our feet. But we do feel the shame."

Layla's eyes watered. "Jesus, that's heavy."

"Something we've had to live with since we were kids. Something we can't rectify. We just prove as much as we can that *we* want to be a part of the Reed heritage, that *we* will do everything in our power to add to the profit margin, to strengthen the operations, to keep this ranch going. Not just for those of us today but for future generations. For Hunt and Ale. For Jack and Jillian's child. For all the grandchildren, and so on."

Tears rolled down her flushed cheeks. Avery collected the box of tissues on the end table, and she pulled out several sheets.

"Your story is so moving, Avery—"

"It's not a story, Layla. It's a reality. And I'm not sharing it on the show. Not looking for sympathy votes, darlin'. I want a fair shake. I'm the best at what I do, or I'm a runner-up, or I'm nothing."

"But the audience—"

"Will see me being passionate about cooking for the people I care about. They'll see me providing the highest-quality meal I can crank out without exceeding my annual budget. But beyond that . . . my other motivations are mine alone. I want the title, yes. The money, however . . . that's all for the ranch."

"To pay back someone else's debt."

"It is what it is, honey."

"Avery." She let out another long breath, hearing the pain behind it—for the weight on his shoulders. And because they had so much more in common than they could've imagined when they'd first met.

She tried to put this in perspective, yet that was difficult.

She said, "Your aspirations are commendable, cowboy. I've told you that before. You are so much more than a bunkhouse cook, an uncle, a nephew, a cousin. You have an award-winning soul, Avery Reed." Her eyes misted again. "And as bizarre as it sounds, I felt that in my own soul. From the start. I can't even say how . . . I mean, I don't know why I thought this about you. Except . . ."

Something dawned on her.

"What, Layla?"

"I've skirted—until recently—the lessons I'd learned from my father. He taught me how to see beyond facades, to question intentions if they didn't seem aboveboard. My first year or two at college, while I was trying to reinvent myself, I kept those principles in mind."

She frowned.

"Didn't help me to make friends," she said with remorse. "I didn't trust anybody because they were in New York."

Now she winced, thinking of how narrow-minded and contradictory that was—because *she* was in New York.

"But once I started at the firm," she continued, "I was starstruck by the way people dressed, the jewelry they wore, the restaurants and the theaters they talked about going to. All of which I saw and overheard whenever I was summoned upstairs to present my latest findings. The associates all seemed so glamorous. They had multimillion-dollar, even *billion-dollar*, commercial sales to discuss. And while I knew they were under tremendous pressure, and a lot of their deals were as fragile as a house of cards, there was a certain confidence—*arrogance*, I now recognize—that I found appealing. Because it was something I lacked."

"But you had your own strengths to be confident about," he pointed out.

"Yes. In finance and definitely with my research capabilities. I mean, I should have been content with knowing those were huge contributions. A lot of those deals came about because of me. And maybe . . ." Shame rippled through her at the deeper thought here. She averted her eyes.

"Layla." Avery hitched her chin with his index finger under it and brought her attention back to him.

She sighed. "I was envious, Avery. A little angry. And I caved to those emotions. I stopped microanalyzing everyone. Took an 'If you can't beat 'em, join 'em' stance that came about right around the time the hotshot came looking for me. So that I was ready, willing, and able to be plucked from obscurity. Regardless of the reason. I didn't care what it was."

An agonizing, though humbling, admission.

With a shake of her head, she added, "My daddy wouldn't approve of that. So I didn't tell him anything about the firm and my involvement with it."

"Meaning you were already pulling away from him when you got involved with the associate."

"I was," she further confessed. "I kept telling myself what he doesn't know won't hurt him. But I'm sure it did anyway."

Another tear crested the rim of her eye. Avery gently swiped at it.

She said, "He would have wanted me to chip away at anything that appeared false to get to the truth. And it would have saved me, in a lot of ways, had I followed that advice."

"Nothing false about me," Avery offered with a light kiss. "Think you've seen that for yourself."

"Yes, I have."

"Simply put," he said, "Chance and I don't want to recap what we lived through, what we were trapped in, what still chases us. At least . . . we don't want it all on public display."

"Serious question . . . ," she asked, as she was prone to do. "If you win, and you put this dent in your dad's debt, will that alleviate some of *your* shame?"

Avery's teeth gnashed.

She nodded. And further inquired, "Why is that? Why won't it appease you, to a degree?"

"To a degree, it will," he assured her. "Yet overall, as an all-encompassing remedy? Layla . . ." He swallowed hard. "Money won't erase what's burned into people's brains. The fighting, the yelling. The fact that my mama walked out on us . . ."

He groaned.

Her heart broke for him.

She was about to tell him not to say anything more, but maybe opening floodgates was therapeutic. Especially when they'd been closed for so long.

He said, "My aunt Brett insists Mom thought she was doing right by the family, leaving us. She thought my dad's behavior, his drinking and his gambling, were due to him being unhappy with her. But Chance and I . . . well . . ." He blew out a harsh breath. "We think she took the easy way out."

"How so?" Her voice was thin and quavering.

"If she wanted to do right by her sons, she would've taken us with her. Not left us with a demon."

Layla melted into him, one arm coiling around his, the other wrapping around his midsection. Her face was in the crook of his neck as she said, "Now I get it, Avery. I know why it's hard for you to go through with this show. Your dad could turn it—*you*—upside down and inside out."

"His expertise."

She drew in a shaky breath. They had different circumstances, yes. But they both had unstable pasts and liabilities and complications with straightening their arrows.

"Avery," she said, "you're in an advantageous position, even if it seems risky. You have the talent to be in the money with the show. Also, we're shooting here, requiring an access code to get on the property. This is an ideal scenario for security and keeping out those not wanted. Correct?"

"The reasons I said yes."

"So focus on that."

"As long as your production company doesn't go for the dramatic jugular."

A valid concern.

She lifted her head and kissed his cheek.

"You have my absolute promise," she vowed. "I wouldn't want anyone airing my dirty laundry, Avery. And my executive producer protects me in that vein. We'll protect you too."

"Honey, if Caleb's still alive or out of prison, I'd be surprised. I can't even say whether he possesses the mental capacity to be as wily as he always was. But I will warn you that he proved to be a crafty snake in the grass when Chance and I knew him. He'll charm you to the core while robbin' you blind. And if you cross him in any way—real or perceived—he'll rain down hellfire on you."

Her heart wrenched.

"Fuck." He grunted. "That's why I don't want him associated with anything or *anyone* in my life. So now I'm back to thinking—"

"Don't you dare cancel on this, Avery." She stared intently at him. "Don't let your past memories hinder your present opportunities."

His gaze narrowed.

She said, "I'm not pressing on my behalf or that of the show's. The crew and the other contestants can pivot on a dime. They and the participants are ready to film. It's a fluid schedule. This has nothing to do with the show or me. You have to feel comfortable with your decision, naturally. But don't let a possibility that might not even be a factor ruin this for you."

His head fell back against the top of the sofa. His eyes squeezed shut.

Layla's fingertips trailed along his temple and down to his jaw, which was clenched. She rolled his head toward hers. Kissed him.

She said, "I very much comprehend where you're coming from, cowboy. More than you know. One thing I can guarantee is that my executive producer is on the up-and-up—I learned to trust Todd when he slipped up in college and then begged for my help because he wanted to fix his mistake. And then he was *my* salvation when I didn't know how to begin my new life. He supports mitigating risks. *Trust us.* Please."

Avery's lids opened, and he gazed at her for a few breathless moments.

"I've never left my front door open for a woman, Layla. I've never given one the gate code. I've never asked Wyatt how to impress one."

"I hear you, cowboy. I do." She kissed him once more. "Let's get through this week. Together."

He got to his feet. Scooped her into his arms and carried her to his bed.

Giving her his answer.

Layla had no need for her robe when she was under the covers with Avery. She wanted his skin against hers.

They continued to kiss. Then he had her on her back, settling between her legs.

And they started all over again.

"You got some hickeys on your neck there, little bro," Chance said, gesturing to Avery's neck.

"You should see her." Avery winked. Though Layla probably had makeup to cover the love bites he'd left on her.

Chance grinned. "I noticed when I was comin' up from the stables that you had an overnight guest."

"Who kept me up most of the night." He fought a yawn. "Not that I'm complaining."

"And I doubt it took much effort on her part."

"I will say, I had difficulty letting *her* sleep."

Chance bit into his stuffed breakfast burrito. Then snickered.

He didn't even have to say anything for Avery to know the direction his thoughts ran.

"She's worth my needing toothpicks to keep my eyes open," Avery said. "If I only get a snooze here and there for the next several days, I won't regret it."

"Yeah, except that you're supposed to be demonstrating your superior pit skills this week. So . . . don't slack off for the sake of a pretty face."

"Christ, Chance, she's so much more than that."

He chuckled. "You're easy to bait when it comes to Layla. Dude, you think I don't get she's *all that* for you?"

"Not practical," he mumbled.

"As if you get to choose."

Avery dipped his burrito in the pool of green pepper and poblano hot sauce on his plate and munched, so he didn't have to draw out this conversation.

The sun was on the rise, splashing vermillion, gold, and orange across the sky as the moon faded. A gentle breeze blew through the trees, though they all knew it'd be a hot and humid summer day.

Chance finished up and said, "We'll see you at noon."

"Vegetable beef stew with biscuits and Jillian's broccoli slaw in a light dressing."

"She's getting you to add healthy sides."

"Doesn't hurt. These cowboys stay with us over the years. Gotta keep 'em in good shape."

"They'll be roping most of the day. Excellent exercise. Adios, bro."

He departed, and Avery tidied up with Ritchie, who wrapped up the remaining chores as Avery made a breakfast plate for Layla, covered it with foil, and took the UTV to the house.

She was already showered and dressed.

"That's not exactly how I anticipated finding you, honey."

"Just trying to maximize our time together, cowboy."

"I had thoughts about what we'd do after you ate. Didn't involve clothes."

With a laugh, she told him, "We can work that in. I just thought that maybe you could give me a tour of portions of the ranch that I haven't seen. So much acreage to cover."

"I have the UTV outside."

She crooked a brow at him.

Thus, he prompted, "You ride horses, darlin'?"

"You do apologize for being condescending, right?" she said, repeating the question from when he'd asked if she knew how to two-step.

He smirked. "Let's saddle up, then."

Her gaze fell to the tray in his hands.

"After you have breakfast," he amended.

"Praise the Lord. Because the last time I had Belgian waffles topped with berries, powdered sugar, and maple syrup, with chocolate sauce on the side, and crispy fried chicken is like . . . never."

"Mexican chocolate, even better. And that jalapeño honey mixed into the coating on the chicken adds the spice to complement the sweet."

"As an FYI, I'm a sucker for hot-and-sweet Italian sausage simmered with peppers and onions."

"Duly noted. On a roll, coin-sliced and served on their own, or mixed with farfalle pasta?"

"Mm, farfalle . . . hadn't even considered that option."

"I'll work on a recipe for you."

"While I hope that my cameramen can keep me in their frames this week."

"Not much to worry about there, darlin'." His gaze slid over her. "You look just fine."

He delivered the tray to the coffee table. There was still a low blaze in the hearth. She settled in with her plate and sipped her cranberry juice.

Afterward, they went down to the stables, and Avery introduced her to a few of Jack's trained horses that weren't yet in the cowboys' rotation and needed a workout. She selected a coppery sorrel with a golden mane. Chose her saddle and added her tack.

She guided the horse into the open pasture, following Avery. They mounted and walked for a while as Layla and her horse, Sadie, became familiar and comfortable with each other.

They trotted toward a grove of trees, then broke into a canter until they reached the river. They carefully crossed the shallowest part and continued up a gently sloping hill. At the top, Layla rounded the horse and stared out at the endless pastures, the buildings, the cows being wrangled.

Her eyes glistened.

"I just can't imagine putting all of this at risk," she said.

She blinked away a couple of tears.

"Sorry." She let out a sharp breath. "I shouldn't have brought that up."

Avery clicked his tongue and guided his horse. They sidled up to her and Sadie. "You don't have to pretend I didn't tell you all that I did, Layla. And you're right. There's no justification."

"It's just so stunning," she said on a broken breath.

"So you can see why Chance and I would do whatever necessary to help the family retain this legacy."

"For sure. I grasped that even before I got this spectacular view. But this is a vantage point that really hits home."

"Yes, it does."

They shared a knowing look that was also full of uncertainty.

Layla could almost hear him asking, *Why wouldn't you want all of this too?*

Those weren't words he vocalized. Yet she felt them in her soul. And he wasn't off the mark.

Particularly when it came to sharing all of this with him.

*With him.*

But that wasn't what her endeavor was about. She had to remind herself of that.

Her life wasn't on one ranch. It was on other ranches, in other locations. On airplanes, in hotels, et cetera. Wherever the wind blew, she tumbled along with it. Wherever Todd approved her next venture, she was there.

Still. For these special moments, she could admire what was spread before her and could accept that Avery found so much wonderment in this place that he was willing to make a sacrifice and go for it with the competition. That "sacrifice" being a bit of pride because he didn't know if his dad would invade his life, the show's socials, any other avenue that would tweak Avery's nerves.

She told him, "You have a valiant cause, cowboy. Stay the course."

His gaze swept over the land below them. He nodded. And said, "It's worth rolling the dice, darlin', if I can hand something to Jack."

"I get it. Now . . . let's cross that stream again, and I'll race you back to the stables."

His smile was electrifying. "You never fail to amaze, darlin'."

They made their way down the knoll, eased over the smooth river rocks, and broke into a vigorous gallop.

Avery took the lead. Then dropped slightly behind. Then surged at the end, just barely beating her.

She laughed like she hadn't laughed in years.

He helped her from the saddle, and two stable hands took over to cool out the horses. Avery kissed Layla for endless minutes.

Only when his internal clock apparently kicked in did he pull away. And tell her, "I've gotta get food prepped, honey."

"Can I help?"

He gave her a quizzical look. "You do that?"

"I served the day workers at the farm, remember?"

"Yeah, I remember."

"Been a long while since I've cooked. I pop frozen dinners in the microwave when at home or order room service when on the road."

He winced.

"But I haven't forgotten how to do this, cowboy."

"Layla." His expression softened. "Honey. If you want to ride horses and cook and make love here on the ranch . . . you'll get no protest from me. It's everything else that's working against us."

"I know." She didn't have to say more. Just followed him to his UTV and then freshened up at the house in quick order so they could get back to the chuck hall.

# Chapter Ten

"These stockpots are fantastic," Layla said as she put four of them on the outdoor burners while Avery grilled sirloin and Ritchie chopped vegetables.

She added beef broth and seasonings, bringing the liquid to a boil. They assembled the stew and let it bubble.

Avery added a three-berry cobbler to the earth oven.

"I'm not privy to noncompetitive meal prep," Layla told him. "I'm only seeing what happens when the cameras are on. So this is a different angle for me. I want to document this, but that wouldn't be fair. I don't have this kind of footage with the other contestants."

"So maybe just enjoy our behind-the-scenes moments." He winked.

She fanned her face. "I was only going to post ones that were PG-rated."

He chuckled. "Those are few and far between."

"And I'm good with that."

The stew simmered until the meat was tender and the flavors blended.

They served the wranglers and ranch hands. Then Avery and Layla sat with Chance.

Avery's older brother asked, "You joining us for supper at the main house tonight, Miss Layla?"

Avery would have kicked his brother's shin under the table. But he was curious as to Layla's response.

She said, "That hasn't been mentioned to me yet. And I should probably go back to Serrano. Though . . . if there's an official invite issued, I'm happy to accept."

"I did tell you the door's open," Avery reminded her.

"To your house," she pointed out.

"All one and the same, honey," he told her.

He noticed a tremor running through her hand, and she set aside her spoon. She shot a look at him. "Didn't we ascertain we might be on the verge of a slippery slope?"

"Yep. Question still stands," he said.

"I did like how we just worked together. Is there a specialty you take to the table at the main house?"

"Usually a dessert."

"Great idea." She glanced around, zeroed in on his garden, and said, "Lemon and blueberry empanadas with a drizzle? Carrot cake cupcakes?"

"This woman totally gets us," Chance said as he piled his silverware on his empty plate. "We eat later in the evening. After the wranglers are fed."

"Jack cooks at the house?" she asked.

"That's his territory," Avery told her. "Jillian's, too, now that she's moving in. They're getting hitched and having a baby."

"Oh, fuck!" Layla exclaimed. Then clamped a hand over her mouth. Briefly. She said, "Pardon my French."

Avery and Chance exchanged a look. That was Avery's phrase.

Someone needed to take away his shovel. "Knee-deep" with Layla was turning into a shallow grave for him.

She continued. "I knew there was more between those two than cohosting his BBQ channel. You can't manufacture chemistry like that. It's damn sexy. They hooked me from that call-in Jillian made." She gave the gentle giggle that always made Avery's stomach pull tight. "I will confess to replaying the section that featured you, Avery. Very witty. With that perfect balance of charm that provided another sizzling component."

"That's my cue to exit stage left," Chance joked as Avery and Layla stared at each other.

Avery barely heard him.

He told Layla, "You should've just called me that very day."

"Didn't have your number."

He chuckled. "Like Brodi couldn't get it for you."

"Point taken." She shrugged. "But I had to do some research first. I prefer to know who I'm approaching with my competitions. Though, yes . . . I should have just called you. That very day."

"You're here now. That's what counts."

Her smile was the sweet one that built upon the smoldering sensations she evoked. Making him think he could drown in lust and be a better man for it.

Though there was a different L-word tickling the back of his brain.

He wasn't the type to subscribe to instant infatuation or anything beyond that. Falling in love was supposed to take time. You were supposed to *know* who you were falling for.

Granted, every bit of herself that Layla revealed drew him in. Beyond that, her actions spoke volumes. Not only in how she interacted with him but with others. And how they responded to her. She didn't hide her passions or cower from getting involved in fragile matters of the heart.

Solidifying for him that love at first sight actually *did* exist?

Still a touchy subject. However, the cons didn't outweigh the pros. Not yet anyway.

As the cowboys cleared out, Avery, his assistant, and his . . . *what?* . . . girlfriend (?) handled the chores.

Then they started prep for the next meal. Steak tacos with Mexican-style pickled red onions and cilantro, hangers, chili-cumin roasted corn, and southwestern potatoes.

While the cowboys ate, he and Layla ducked out to go to the house and clean up. Well, to do more than that.

Later, they took the desserts up to the main house.

Avery felt a bit awkward introducing Layla around, knowing his entire family saw right through him—she wasn't just the host of the show he was starring in this week. Reeds were great at ribbing each other, but they took it easy on Avery. Probably because this was the first time he'd brought a woman to supper.

Much to his relief, there was plenty to talk about as food was passed around the table that didn't center on him and Layla, though casual questions were dropped . . . just so that the others could learn more about her. She didn't deflect. Not only, he suspected, because they were noninvasive queries but also because she wanted to be forthcoming.

When the desserts were served, he said, "Layla's ideas."

"And Avery's recipes," she added.

"You've never made either of these for us before tonight," his aunt chided him. All sly-like.

"She's just making good use of my garden," Avery explained. His gaze shifted to Jillian. "Along those lines, how are you planning to move your operation on-site?"

"I was offered use of the guesthouse as a commercial slash certified kitchen," she told everyone. "With the bedrooms being available for my podcasting and storing my supplies."

Avery slid a glance toward Jack. "You think of everything."

"It was my mom's idea," Jack said. "Makes perfect sense. Jillian's operation is expanding by leaps and bounds. She'll also continue to cohost with me."

"And I'll help her tend to her crops," Aunt Brett chimed in. "We have plenty of land surrounding the guesthouse that George will get ready for her to cultivate her chili peppers."

"Guess you could say this *family* thinks of everything," Jillian declared.

"I've already discerned that," Layla replied.

"We're also building storage for Mom's pottery, to sell online and at her craft fairs," Jack said.

"And," Jillian added, "we're using the kitchen and storage in the guesthouse for Jack's new business venture as well."

Avery eyed him with interest. "And that is . . . ?"

"Barbecue sauces and syrups," his cousin announced.

"Oh, snap!" This from Chance. "I've only been sayin' this for over a decade."

"Do not grief on me," Jack said. "I didn't quite realize I could add another revenue stream without it draining my brain and energy. But Jillian has optimized her production process, and Mom and I are on board."

Some of the weight that had resided in Avery's chest for most of his life lessened. "That's incredible, Jack. All of you."

The potential for additional capital was a huge advantage. The more padding of the coffers, the less Jack had to stress.

Something very serious to consider. Avery recognized that Jack's dad had been mired in financial deficits and faced the ever-changing environment that affected livestock owners. There was always something to throw a wrench into the works. And when his own brother became that wrench . . . things had declined.

Avery knew it hadn't been simply about the fiscal constraints that had been created. He understood that his uncle Royce had been betrayed. By Avery and Chance's father. And all Uncle Royce had done, in turn, was figure out how to make ends meet, how to maintain an empire, how to keep an eye on his nephews and ensure they knew they were a part of this family, regardless of their dad spitting on this very soil.

This inspired Avery to tell them all, "I'm moving forward with *Light Your Fire*. It makes sense. I have the skills. And . . ." His gaze flitted to Jack. "If I come into the money, it's yours."

Okay, yeah, he was supposed to consult Mateo on how to weave those funds into the ranch's books before he blurted anything out.

But Avery had to take a stand.

The entire room fell silent.

Jack glared at him. With too much emotion in his eyes for it to not spear Avery to the core.

"That's a no-go."

"It's a for-sure-go." Avery held his gaze. "I intend to win. And that's cash for the ranch."

Avery shoved back his chair. He offered his hand to Layla, who joined him.

He said, "Y'all enjoy the desserts. And know I'm committed to this."

He led her out.

◆  ◆  ◆

Layla fought the tears. They wouldn't do her or Avery any good. They wouldn't do the situation any good. That was for Avery to iron out with Jack.

The complexity she grappled with was that Avery had a sound ground on which to stand: doing whatever he could for his family.

She admired that.

They undressed without disturbing the tranquility. They slipped between the sheets. She nuzzled against him.

Quiet moments consumed them.

Eventually, she said, "Y'all have an integrity that's heartwarming."

"It can also aggravate us."

"Not so. There's an underlying desire to be all that you can be. Everyone is invested in that, Avery. Straight down to your nephews, who also contribute. And your auxiliary people, like Garrett and Mindy. Cowboys and ranch hands."

"Our universe encourages personal growth and group cohesiveness—all at the same time."

"Agreed." She added, "I respect that everyone can pursue their own interests. Develop them and turn them into monetized vehicles."

"We'll see about that."

She grasped his point. "You and Jack will have difficulty reconciling a cash award, if you win one."

"I'll deal with that when I win."

She kissed him. And murmured against his lips, "That's the preferred sentiment here. *When*, not *if*."

"I have sufficient motive to come through on the high side."

"Yes, you do."

His fingers grazed her upper arm. "Tell me more about your swing and miss, darlin'."

"Not sure what you're talking about, cowboy."

"You know."

The air turned stagnant.

She had to provide details as well.

Hers got grim here.

She sighed. Then said, "I followed a path I shouldn't have. Got too caught up in who I could potentially become after spending so much time as a wallflower."

She was ill at ease now. But didn't shrink away from the topic at hand.

She told him, "I had the perfect entrance into New York society. For a short span of time, I reaped rewards. Felt like royalty. Understanding I wasn't, but still . . . I was immersed in glitz and glamour. All I had to do was pull a few teeth."

"Till someone was on to you?"

"Yep."

She propped herself on an elbow and stared down at him. "I delivered misinformation. Could have been given to me on purpose. Or maybe I just misunderstood. I'd had a couple martinis during those particular conversations. Doesn't matter. The outcome was so horrendous,

I begged him to give up the game. To find venture capitalists who were on the up-and-up. To not get roped into shadier dealings."

She plopped onto the mattress and stared up at the ceiling, anger and anxiety roiling through her.

Avery asked, "What happened next?"

"He didn't like my earnest approach." She grimaced. "He didn't like anything I said after that, including that we should find a different project that didn't require so much espionage. Because that was what it'd become. Corporate espionage."

"But *you* weren't raiding bank accounts, right?"

"Oh, God, no." She sat up again and gazed at him. "I'm not even sure I can call myself the equivalent of the getaway driver. I was a communication vehicle, sure. But again . . . if you're willing to impart proprietary information during a cocktail party, it's bad on you for wanting to hang the messenger."

"And yet you still feel guilty."

He said this in a tender tone. So that she wilted against him.

"Yes, I do." Didn't take a rocket scientist to form the correlation between them. "I grasp our tie-in, Avery. Your dad set the winning stage while also building the gallows for you."

"I could've gone so much further with the competitions."

"And to be honest, he could have—*should have*—reveled in your rising status."

"But then he'd flip a switch and cause a problem. One after the other."

She cringed. "You wanted him to be honorable."

"And he didn't give a shit about that."

Avery let out a harsh breath. Glowered a bit.

Then he said, "You were a pawn too. And ended up owing a stash."

Her insides twisted. "Some mixed implications here, cowboy. I was lured, yes. Then I saw the light and tried to redeem myself. In the end . . . I did ask for the one thing I desired the most. And I'm happy to pay for it."

"Meanin'?"

"Meaning, I made a huge mistake playing spy, just to gain a sense of self-worth. I intended to return to my virtues. Recommended he do the same. After that . . . all hell broke loose. On my face."

Avery bolted upright. And demanded, "*What?*"

Layla tasted the ferric tinge of blood—and terror—she couldn't escape. But she didn't hold back this time. She told him, "He hit me alongside my temple with a bottle of brandy, so please don't ever offer me that."

A bad joke.

She continued. "I blacked out for seconds, minutes. I don't know how long. When I came to, he wound my hair around his fist, hauled me up, practically dragged me into the kitchen, and slammed my face into the stainless-steel door of the refrigerator."

"You are fuckin' kiddin' me!" Avery was on his feet in a second.

She drew in a deep breath. Gazed steadily at him. And said, "Over and over."

Avery paced with so much pent-up agitation it made her stomach roil—so that she might've thrown up. That was also due to having just revealed her darkest secret.

His hands balled into fists at his sides.

She told him, "It was five years ago, so you have to let the rage go. Nothing to be done about it."

He whirled around. They stared at each other. The air crackled with more emotions and tension than she could dissect. All piercing and painful.

"Is this asshole in prison?"

She shook her head. "I never pressed charges. He knew people. People who tended to me in a private hospital that he paid off so that the police wouldn't be involved. A man who came in and whispered that he'd kill me if I uttered a word—not that I could speak. The best I could manage was to scribble out my desire for a cosmetic surgeon who *I* would pay for. I only had one request of him."

"Which was?"

*"Make me pretty."*

Tears pooled in her eyes.

Avery returned to the bed, perched on the edge. Not too close.

He tried to make sense of all of this, she could tell. Though it really wasn't complicated. Her train had jumped the tracks, she'd gotten back on the *right* rails, and had disappeared when she was well enough to leave the hospital.

She'd drained her savings account for the initial down payment on her surgery. Rerouted investments so she could rebuild her life elsewhere. Assumed Christopher had likely told HR that she wouldn't return to work for whatever excuse he made up. She changed her name, left everything behind her, and came to Texas.

"My first thought was to go to the farm. But I couldn't figure out how to explain this new person to my father. Nor did I want to put him in any danger. If he went off half-cocked. Or if someone followed me there. I laid low for a couple of years. Then got up the nerve to approach a friend from college who owed me a favor. Todd liked my pitch for a traveling cook-off show. I was trained in broadcasting, so it was a natural fit. And the audience seems to like my appearance. So. I sort of got everything I wanted, Avery. In the long run. Bear that in mind."

"Except there's still this monster out there who—"

"I don't think about the monster. Not as a rule." She hedged a moment. Then admitted, "I do still feel the need to look over my shoulder. That's why I haven't seen my daddy yet. But I've done a thorough job of burying Tess Billings. Even the payments I make to the surgeon are via electronic transfer. He's one of the very few who can identify me, so maybe I'm effectively paying him hush money. Though he's earned every penny. I'm not upsetting that applecart, ever."

Avery raked a hand through his hair. Let out a gnarled sound. Stood and paced some more.

"Don't go chasing your tail on this one, cowboy. Can't change my past. I can only move forward."

He gave her a staunch look. "But you still can't go home, Layla."

Her heart constricted. "That is a fact. For now anyway. Maybe someday I'll convince myself I'm a distant memory and no one's searching for me to make sure I never report what happened."

"You should report it," he averred in a quiet tone.

"Nope. He'll lawyer up with a legion I can't compete against." She spread her arms and added, "I'm happy with my life, Avery. The production crew is my family. There's a deeper sense of camaraderie with Todd and Brodi, of course. Those two know my story. And I trust them to keep it. Todd also knows I need a job that doesn't require a résumé or a background check. He can't support the show if it fails, though, so we do what we can to grow our numbers and increase monetization."

She strove for a bit of levity to lighten the somber mood, saying, "Having you on-screen will do wonders in that department."

His jaw clenched. There was a smirk trapped in there somewhere, but he was too amped up to let it out. She recognized the signs, was attuned to his characteristics. Also, she'd gone through this with Todd, who'd wanted to get on a plane and smash Christopher Courtland's face, so he suffered the way Layla had. It'd taken endless convincing that she would be fine without his retaliation to calm him down a bit.

Brodi had been furious as well, but she'd mostly just cried.

Now here was this strapping cowboy who likely would gain satisfaction from pummeling anyone who assaulted her. And he had a ranch full of other cowboys who would back him up, she had no doubt.

Causing her to say, "This stays between us, Avery. No one in your family needs to know."

They continued to stare at each other.

His irises were too dark and his jaw was too set for her to not accept this whole scenario as a personal affront to him. That he wanted to do something to rectify it, to make up for what she'd endured. And to take out his own fury on the one who'd hurt her.

And by God, the experience had been excruciating. She knew she was lucky to be alive. Surprised, really. It was a miracle what sort of shattering the body could withstand.

The same held true for the spirit.

She told Avery, "I believe in my heart that what goes around comes around. That karma can bite bad people in the butt. I'm praying his takes him down in one fell swoop."

It was a vicious thing to say, yet she didn't even wince. Didn't feel an ounce of guilt over saying it out loud.

Avery nodded. Because he got it.

"Chance and I once whispered in the shadows about how easy it'd be to loosen the latigo on our dad's saddle in hopes he'd take a fall during a dead gallop. Seemed fair, considering we had to lie to Uncle Royce once or twice a month if we had visible bruises and say we were bucked. Or that we were just roughhousin' between ourselves."

"Good Lord." She stared at him, her stomach churning again.

"We could never bring ourselves to do it. Of course not. We were just angry young boys wanting to end the bullying. But also protecting our father from jail time for abuse. It was a bit of a conundrum."

"A horrific one."

"You and I have violent pasts. Chance too. I'm guessing my mama as well, and that was why she left, before it escalated. If so, she saved herself, and I have to let go of the animosity I feel because she didn't take us with her. I wouldn't be shocked if Uncle Royce went several rounds with my dad when they were growing up. Caleb Reed didn't just wake up one morning fightin' mad. He's been that way since I've had a memory."

A menacing shiver cascaded down her spine.

"You definitely don't want him coming back," she said.

"No, I do not. No one does."

"Which makes it incredibly ironic that you're doing this show—which *could* bring him back—in hopes of paying off some of his debt."

"Aren't we a twisted pair, you and I?"

"I cannot deny that. And yet . . ." She crawled toward his side of the bed, untied the sash of her robe, and let the material slip from her shoulders. "There is something to be said for sexual therapy."

He guided her down onto the mattress. "It's more than sexual, don't you think?"

She couldn't deny the emotional bond they'd created on many levels. But she only touched on the immediate component, not wanting—at present—to delve into their deeper feelings for each other, knowing they were almost impossible to reconcile.

She murmured, "We're both tormented. But willing to see beyond that."

"Make no mistake, honey, I could spit nails right now."

She swept her fingers through his hair. "I grasp that concept."

"Sinkin' into you is the ultimate distraction."

"Then condom up and take me for a ride, cowboy."

# Chapter Eleven

Having reconnected physically with Layla helped to relieve some of his tension, yet Avery was still wound up over everything she'd told him. And the fact that he'd been damn close to the mark of her having a dangerous past.

The trampling that Jillian had suffered at a concert, forever changing her life, was a tragedy. Also an accident.

What had happened to Layla . . . that was a direct attack. The type of battery he couldn't comprehend, even having lived with a man who had a short fuse and a mean spirit. Who couldn't see past his alcohol-induced haze to recognize the damage he inflicted.

As kids, Avery and Chance had hidden this side of their father from their cousins as best as they could. Even their aunt and uncle, as much as possible. But the adults had their suspicions. Aunt Brett invited them to spend the night at the main house as often as she could, without infuriating Caleb by making him think she was trying to take his kids away. Uncle Royce stepped in a lot as well. Caleb would settle down, and life would go on. Until something else got his goat.

Family was family. You couldn't pick and choose.

But you could reach a boiling point and tell them to get the hell out. And stay out.

Avery prayed the exile stuck.

He got the cowboys their morning chuck, and then started in on the turduckens he'd smoke in his pit for the first round of judging.

Layla had had breakfast with him and Chance, and she was now observing Avery deboning the chicken and duck. Ritchie prepped the stuffing, since the cooks were allowed an assistant if they had one, given the size of the staff they fed.

Layla couldn't participate in any way other than ask questions. She set up her tripod in front of their workstations and attached her phone for video to document the process, but also, Avery deduced, to prove she wasn't involved.

Avery already had his primary and secondary pits heating up.

He said, "I'll smoke these at around two hundred and fifty degrees. Should take about five hours. Right around the time your crew and the judges come in, Layla."

"Making this a one-shot deal," she pointed out.

"Yep. I either nail the temp and timin' . . . or I blow it." Because there was no digging up the ovens and checking the contents. He wouldn't disturb his embers or risk losing any heat by opening lids. He'd also have to prepare another turducken and sides during the segment, to demonstrate, live, how it was done. He'd then pull the finished product from this batch in his pits. So it truly was his only chance to get it right.

He'd claim the tension through his muscles was due to the pressure of wanting this to go perfectly, to win the competition. Unfortunately, he was still worked up over all Layla had been through. And talking about his dad, his childhood.

The plus side was that she lit up when the cameras rolled, and every time she smiled, it thrilled him, warmed his heart. So that he could breathe and concentrate.

Well, the concentrating part wasn't quite so smooth sailing because he was a bit too transfixed on her. Though he was at a crucial step with the poultry during the live stream, so he forced himself to focus on the deboning process again, explaining in detail to the audience his best practices because it could be a tricky endeavor. Next, he discussed the stuffing mixture and added the cranberries Jillian suggested.

He'd need to roast the sweet potato fingerlings in the trench, and that was another piece of timing to configure with the overall temperatures, not wanting to burn the veggies in the firebox.

He checked his earth ovens, running a bare hand over them to discern the correct level of heat, then shoveling lava rocks mixed with applewood chips over the lids. The combination of scents above and below the ground permeated the outdoor kitchen.

The wranglers filed in and chatted enthusiastically with Layla about the turducken, having eaten it before from Avery's pit.

He demonstrated the balsamic zoodle sauté with mushrooms and pine nuts, the truffle parsnip puree, and the maple-bacon brussels sprouts.

Layla joined him, saying, "I can see why the wranglers love holidays at the TRIPLE R."

"They don't get the full day off, so we try to make the meals special."

"Seems like you do that every day, Avery."

"It is my goal, dar—Layla," he corrected himself. Could he go five days of shooting without calling her *honey* or *darlin'* on-screen?

Jack and Jillian—and her rescued Maltese, Ollie—were in the background, and they both stifled laughs. Though Jack nodded, as though he was well aware the struggle was real.

Layla said, "Aside from your seasonings, what is the one key ingredient you use with the poultry?"

"Duck fat," he told her. "Not only with the poultry but with the fingerlin's too. You can sauté mushrooms in it, and I also brushed some on the brussels sprouts. It's as healthy as olive oil or chicken broth."

She looked stunned. "I had no idea. I mean, it sounds rather . . ."

"Artery hardening?"

She nodded. "Exactly."

"It has a bad rap. But I swear it yields a velvety texture that'll curl your toes, darlin'."

*Fuck.*

Whatever.

She didn't seem to mind his slipup.

To her audience, she asked, "Who needs a fan?" She returned a dreamy gaze to him. "How'd you come across this gem, cowboy?"

He chuckled at her own term of endearment. Their cover was likely blown. Since she wasn't worried over it, he didn't stress either.

He told her, "Another one of my favorite meals to cook is duck confit—I use some of the fat it simmers in to toss with peeled and quartered potatoes. Stick 'em in the air fryer, and they crisp up fantastically on the outside but have a light and fluffy inside. You can dip them in anything you prefer—ketchup, mayo, spicy jalapeño fry sauce. Or eat as is, salted. Promise you, you'll never boil potatoes again."

"Sounds downright delectable. But . . . an air fryer? This coming from a pitmaster?"

"As you can see, my pits are full. I can dig another one, sure. Or simply plug in my baskets and have sides in almost half the normal time. Hell, I've even made salmon in them."

She gasped in mock horror.

The crew erupted.

"Does that disqualify me?" he teased. Knowing it wouldn't. He was doing true barbecuing today.

Confirming this, she said, "You're fine, Avery. I'm just taken aback. An air fryer is so . . . modern."

"And convenient. 'Specially when you have hungry cowboys who are on a tight schedule. Though it's really a backup amenity. Particularly when it's rainin' hard with thunder and lightning, and we have to be inside. We have generators in the event our main power source goes out, so that we don't lose cooking capabilities."

"Ah. Gotcha. That's a valid point. And impressive to have contingency plans."

"If I served peanut butter and jelly sandwiches, darlin', I'd fear a revolt."

Her smile was the vibrant one that further loosened the rope holding his soul hostage over all they'd shared last night.

"From what I've gathered, your bunkhouse staff is far from mutiny. They're advocating for a Michelin star."

With another chuckle, he said, "Not in my purview, but I'll take the compliment. Now if you'll excuse me for a minute, darlin' . . ."

With a camera following him, he left the grills to pull his poultry and fingerlings from beneath the dirt they were packed in. He and Ritchie placed the Dutch ovens on a metal table lined with foil and dusted off the remnants of earth and ashes.

Avery's heart thumped faster as they got closer and closer to the big reveal. Ritchie added the potatoes to the other side dishes on the buffet table.

Layla was next to Avery again, asking, "Can you tell us about the rocks used within your pits? They're not the signature TRIPLE R river rocks."

"No, I have drier stones to line them. The river rocks provide a smooth surface, but because they come from a waterway, they contain pockets of liquid that will boil and have the potential to be more explosive during the cooking process. We want to generate steam in certain instances but not incite a geyser."

She blushed. Turned from the camera.

His low laugh filled the void.

He also gave her a small reprieve from what was *apparently* an inside joke for them as he continued his commentary. "Understanding the materials you're working with and maximizing them is crucial. If I want to wrap meat in banana leaves or seafood in burlap, I have to take into consideration how they'll absorb moisture and smoke."

Composing herself, Layla said, "And what if you create too much moisture?"

She started to lose it again. As did Jack and Jillian.

Avery wanted to rise above. But there were myriad snappy, sexy comebacks playing on his tongue.

Thank God Ritchie unwittingly came to the rescue and said, "We're all good on our temps, Pitty." He set aside the meat thermometer. "And we're ready to slice."

The moment of truth was upon them.

Avery had to shove flirty banter to the back of his brain. This was critical. He couldn't afford to fuck it up. In fact, he sent up a humble word to the heavens that he wouldn't and then removed the first turducken from its oven.

The triple bird had the perfect golden, crispy skin and was trussed up tight. Avery snipped the heavy twine with shears. He cut down the spatchcocked center of the turducken with a large chef's knife and separated the halves, showcasing the tender, juicy meat and the layers of stuffing in between, steam rising off the entire display. Right in front of the cameras.

Ritchie held his exuberance in check as the production crew and Layla surveyed the outcome from all angles. Then he portioned the poultry while Avery carved into the others they'd retrieved from the pits.

They made up individual plates for the three judges and set out the rest for the buffet.

Layla joined The Three at their table and asked questions regarding the food as Avery sat with them and absorbed the responses. All positive. Verbal high marks for color, taste (including whether they tasted the smoke/fire), texture and tenderness, creativity, and presentation. As well as for the degree of difficulty. They commended him for using trenches.

As the judges tallied their scores and dropped sealed envelopes through the slit of a locked box, Layla interviewed the cowboys again. The shooting wrapped up, and the crew broke down their equipment and headed out with Todd and Brodi.

Jack and Jillian swooped in as the judges departed.

All as impartial as Layla had indicated.

Jack said, "Aside from makin' eyes at the pretty host, you did a damn good job."

"I beg to differ," Jillian commented. "He made *exceptional* eyes at the pretty host." She smiled up at Avery.

"Great, I'm the most obvious sucker on the planet."

"Two-way street," Jillian told him. "She was plenty doe-eyed herself."

"It's a wonder I could remember my recipes." He chortled, self-deprecatingly, yet with admiration for the woman who preoccupied his thoughts more than she should.

"I get the feelin' you scored big time," Jack said. "And explaining more about the firebox and the pits as you progress will garner more viewer love."

"That's right, Uncle Jack!" This from an excited Alejandro as he jumped out of the passenger seat of the UTV Chance had just pulled up to the outskirts of the chuck hall. Ale waved his mini tablet in the air and said, "Viewers are allowed to post their own polls and comments. And the show's accounts are blowin' up with shout-outs to Uncle Avery!"

Layla wandered over, and Ale thrust his tablet toward her.

"Look at this, Miss Layla! Your other contestants don't have this big of a reaction on the first day of filming!"

"Nor have those contestants likely secured a gold medal straight out of the chute." She glanced at Avery and said, "*Wow* times a lot."

He grinned.

She returned her attention to Ale, who was making his own eyes at her, of the googly variety.

Avery's nephew said, in the most professional tone an eleven-year-old could muster, "You have talent, Miss Layla. The audience likes my uncle, but I think the key to growin' your subscribers is . . . more of you."

"Whoa, kid!" Jack interjected.

Ale shot him a perplexed look.

Jillian said to her fiancé, "He didn't mean it the way you're taking it." She laughed. Then added, "He has a point . . . though not totally.

Of course the male demographic is going to want to see more of Layla. But I also believe that Avery's techniques are vital to focus on. Not to mention . . . he's easy on the eyes."

Jack scowled. "Maybe we ought to leave that all alone. We've got too many people eyeballin' each other."

She fluttered her lashes and said, "I only have eyes for you."

"Jesus, people," Avery scoffed.

"Uncle Avery!" Ale glanced up at him with reprimand in his gaze. "We're gonna have to start a swear jar."

"I didn't swear," he contended.

"It's on the list," Ale countered.

"Fine. I'll bring you s'mores tonight with sea salt and caramel. Your favorite."

"That's bribery," Ale replied.

Avery stared him down.

"I didn't hear a word," the nephew conceded. "I'll post what I have on our socials. Gotta go."

Chance said, "I'm playin' chauffeur while his mom and dad are having lunch in town with Luke, at his cantina. Aunt Brett is teaching her pottery classes, and Hunt wanted her to help him make something for Father's Day."

"Where'd Riley disappear to?" Avery asked. She was Jack's youngest sister and Luke's twin. She'd come out for Jack's BBQ bash and only seemed to be here and there afterward. Not that that was unusual for Riley Reed. She didn't know how to stay put.

Jack said, "She's working with Whit Tatum on more songs she's written."

Layla whistled under her breath. "If we could incorporate all these talents into the show . . . but, no . . ." She shook her head. "I haven't offered that op to anyone else." She paced for a few moments. Then drew up short. "Not that they've had anything on this level to offer. Homegrown chilies, specialty dry rubs and sauces, pottery, music?" She paced again.

Avery's gaze bounced between Jack and Jillian. Avery shrugged.

"You keep thinkin' on it," Chance told her. "If we can find an additional edge, let's do it. Now I have to get the kid up to the house to fix my laptop. Screen's gone all kinds of wonky on me."

"You changed the wrong settings," Ale said with comical exasperation.

"Well, I don't know which ones I accidentally changed, so you're gonna have to change 'em back. Earn your keep around here, boy."

"See y'all. Miss Layla." Ale tipped his hat to her.

A ripple of laughter through the group followed him and his uncle out. Though Layla's hand over her heart indicated it melted.

"Y'all are too much," she mused.

"I just think we have really good taste," Avery stated.

"Agreed," said Jack. Then he took Jillian's hand and added, "We've got to scoot too. Ollie has a vet appointment."

"Everything okay?" Avery asked.

Layla gazed at him like his empathy for the dog liquified her further.

"Just a checkup and heartworm meds," Jillian stated. "Kind of you to ask, though." She gave him a kiss on the cheek. Then turned to Layla. "The two of you sparkle. Thanks for letting us be on set."

"You're welcome to be here for the rest of the segments."

"With the exception of tomorrow, since we're in town for Jack's local TV hour, count us in," Jillian said.

After they left, Layla went back to grinding over how to add more of the grassroots razzle-dazzle to the upcoming shows. "It just seems like an epic failure on our part if we don't highlight what really goes on at this ranch."

"But you're in the middle of a live season . . ." Avery gave her a pointed look.

"That's correct." She tapped a fingertip against her lip. Then said, "And the other contestants mostly have food as their sole competitive component. One of them had a ropin' event in the background. Another had a hatchet-throwing tournament. That was ten minutes of sheer terror. Other than that, no one got too creative. It's not frowned upon. I mean, you have forty-five minutes to show off before the judges get their fifteen minutes of fame."

She wandered about some more.

Avery said, "Maybe you're too much of a visionary, darlin'."

She turned and faced him. "Telling me to stay the course, cowboy?"

He crooked a brow.

With a sweet smile, she walked into his arms. Kissed him. And said, "That's good advice."

She and Ritchie helped to clean up and prep for the evening chuck—kick-ass chili (no beans or tomatoes, this was Texas!), jalapeño-cheddar corn bread, and a butter lettuce salad with a creamy cilantro-lime-buttermilk dressing.

Later, they took the s'mores, chocolate lava cake, and the pull-apart cinnamon strudel knots to the main house.

The atmosphere was lively. No consternation, no confrontations.

Avery didn't believe for a second that Jack was going to roll over and accept funds from him. But they didn't argue about it tonight.

They followed up the meal with Ale's Reels from Jack's latest *Rub It In* shows that he cast onto the big screen in the living room. He'd also compiled highlights of Avery and Layla on *Light Your Fire*, rallying Jack and Jillian's fans to this new cause.

"These trailers are wonderful," Layla told Ale.

He beamed. "I can do more if you want, Miss Layla."

"You have free rein to post whatever you want on Jack's socials. Mention the competition in Jillian's podcast and newsletter," Layla said.

"All that's fine. If you can generate buzz, that'll give Avery a boon when it comes to viewer likes. For the show's socials, we have to stick with what our marketing team posts, to keep it all aboveboard. I can't get too carried away with one contestant. I have to be objective with everyone."

"I'm not sure what all that means."

Avery gently clasped his shoulder and told him, "Miss Layla has to abide by what all the other competitors are capable of doing. Not go beyond just because we can."

Ale's face contorted. "That doesn't seem fair at all. If someone's built a bigger, better mousetrap, why would they have to play on the same level of those who have a crappier mousetrap?"

Everyone fell silent.

It was a good question.

It was a complex question.

Avery asked, "What do you know about mousetraps, boy?"

"It's an online game I play."

"Okay . . ." He gave this thought and then said, "You can't reach a higher score without improvin' your product."

"I'd just be stuck at the beginning. Over and over."

Avery's gaze slipped to Layla.

"Again . . . is it cheating if we have more to offer?" he asked.

Her head tilted to the side. She studied him for a moment. Then she told him, "I know what you're both saying. And you're right in that bringing more to the table is an advantage. It's just that in this particular competition, the most important element is the food. As we ascertained earlier. And we don't want to take anything away from that factor while hyping a different one."

"Yeah, but . . ." Ale's brows scrunched.

Layla ventured, "You're talking about how the other contestants have been using gas, charcoal, and porcelain grills. Traditional smokers. Not a pit."

"Uncle Avery's upping the game. And *that's* acceptable." Ale stared at both of them with a whole lot of "duh" in his expression.

Avery's adoration swelled. But he tried to keep his—and his nephew's—feet on the ground. He replied, "The entire series centers on BBQ, Ale. How it's rendered isn't the criteria. How it's prepared, how it comes out, how it tastes . . . those aspects are the most critical."

"Well said," Layla remarked. "But how it's rendered *does* add a style component to the competition and is a consideration for the judges' scoring. What I'm unsure of is adding extraneous stuff."

Avery told Ale, "*Extraneous* stuff would be us throwing a shindig like your uncle Jack's party. That's not what this show is about. It's one meal at a time to be judged."

"I understand," Ale said. Though that was debatable. Regardless, he took the high road. "I'll just put together my vids, and we'll keep them on Uncle Jack's accounts."

"That's sensible," Layla told him. "And helpful."

Avery gathered her close and said, "Let's get a move on."

They bid everyone good night, and Avery took them back to his house.

While he turned on the fireplace, candles, and music, she changed in the bathroom.

When she strolled toward the bed he was sprawled in, he knew he was going to fall to pieces within minutes.

She wore a lacy pale-pink nightie that clung to every inch of her and had a scandalously short hem. The thin straps on her shoulders looked flimsy enough to disintegrate under a slight snap from him.

Her G-string was visible behind the lacy material.

He bit his lip. Eased his gaze from her golden curls to her shell-colored toenails before drifting back up.

"Holy hotness," he murmured. "If you were to wear only this all day long, I'm damn sure I'd never give a fig about feedin' wranglers or makin' desserts for the family or breathin'—ever again."

"Isn't that just the most beautiful thing you could say?" Her eyes glistened.

He told her, "I can't imagine a more stirring vision, honey." He clasped her hip and pulled her to him.

She settled right on top of him.

Exactly where he wanted her.

He flipped the covers over them, then ran his hands along her sides and down to her ass, which her nightie barely covered.

She left airy kisses on his chest. Flitted her tongue over his nipple, flirting with him. Making him even harder.

"Know what I like best about getting naked with you, cowboy?"

"Technically, darlin', you're not naked yet."

Her soft laugh ribboned through him. Tugging at his emotions as much as her slight writhing against him taunted his libido.

She said, "We create our own private space. A sexy cocoon. And when we allow it, nothing else exists."

"So my previous comment stands. You, me, and your lingerie . . . one happy little family."

She craned her neck to sweep her lips over his. "Thought the lingerie had been deemed useless."

"Not sayin' you're going to be wearing it for long. But I won't be the least bit upset if you tell me you bought this in every color available."

"That's how most women shop."

He groaned. "So I have more micro cardiac arrests to suffer through."

"Are you really suffering?" she teased.

"Well, the thong's still on, honey. So yes, I am."

"Then we should remedy that. ASAP."

# Chapter Twelve

Layla was up with Avery before the reasonable crack of dawn. They were filming his breakfast segment, and that meant she had to get herself around and head to the chuck hall with him, rather than luxuriate in his bed until he brought her a tray.

She wasn't disappointed, though. She was excited to interact with him throughout the process. The ingredients for his breakfast bake would be spicy, meaty, and cheesy, with golden hash browns and eggs sunny-side up included.

"I got my chimney starter going already, so the coals are hot," Avery explained when they were live. "For the first part of our cowboy casserole, we'll cook up some bacon strips in the Dutch ovens, just to get 'em heated. Then we'll remove the strips but leave the grease."

Ritchie had the cast-iron ovens set over the open flames of the grill Avery was using as his primer, for the benefit of the camera angles, and to accommodate Layla in the frame.

"I'm going to mix my cubed beef with garlic, cumin, ancho-chili powder, smoked Himalayan salt, and peppercorns," Avery said as he dumped each ingredient parsed out into a large bowl, drizzled olive oil, and used his gloved hands to combine it all.

He created his layers across each oven, with the beef on the bottom to brown first.

Then he said, "Hatch chilies are next so they'll sweat into the meat. You can go as fiery as you like, using whatever pepper you prefer. If y'all didn't know, our soon-to-be newest member of the family, Miss Jillian Parks, is the owner of Hotter Than Haba, and creates her own line of hybrid peppers, sauces, and rubs. The ancho-chili I'm using is her concoction."

Layla held a gasp in check. Shot a look toward Todd, who gave her a nod of approval.

The cowboy had smoothly slipped in something she truly wanted to highlight. Clever of him.

She didn't press her luck by asking more about Jillian's products. The name-dropping should suffice.

Avery continued.

"When you're working with chilies, leave the seeds in to intensify the flavor, but be careful when you do. Some pups like to stay on the porch rather than run with the big dogs." He winked.

*Oh, Jesus.*

The female viewers—even some of the males—had to be going nuts over how attractive he was. How casual. Earthy.

"I'm covering all this with the applewood bacon. The additional grease produced will seep to the lower levels, providing extra flavor. The potatoes go on top." He shredded them, and then in a cheesecloth, he squeezed out the moisture before arranging the thick slivers over the bacon. "Try to get as much water out of your hash browns as possible so they'll crisp up, not go soggy on ya."

Layla was loving all the "pro tips." A few of her contestants were so focused on assembly, they forgot to provide helpful details such as this. And, unfortunately, when she prompted them, she tended to throw them off their game, so she'd learned to refrain from coaching in that vein.

"I cover all this with cracked eggs and more seasonings," Avery announced. "S&P plus anything else that comes to mind. I'm choosing Mexican adobo to build upon the overall flavor profile."

"This aroma will be off the charts," she commented, her stomach flipping at that notion.

"Wait'll I add the cheese." He gave her a scorching look as he said, "Gonna get it all nice and gooey."

Sparks ignited between her legs.

She had to turn from the cameras as she felt the flush burst on her cheeks.

She asked Ritchie, "How long have you been with the TRIPLE R?" to distract herself—and because Avery had given him due credit, and she wanted to as well.

"Four years now, Miss Layla. Couldn't've ended up with a better outfit. Sheer luck of the draw on my part, but they all took me in like I was some long-lost brother. Gave me a bed in the bunkhouse straightaway. And that beats livin' on the streets."

Emotion flickered in his eyes. Layla prayed the cameramen captured it.

Now feeling a bit misty eyed herself, she said, "I see why they nicknamed you 'Right Hand.' My guess is you don't let anything fall through the cracks."

"Oh, you can be sure I sometimes do," he replied with a modest laugh. "But that's what's great about havin' a mentor like Pitty. Seems to have three-sixty vision. Never misses a beat, even when I do."

Ritchie's admiration shone through. He had immense respect for Avery—the entire operation and the people running it.

"I don't suppose you want to help me now?" Avery teased him. "If you're done flirting with the pretty host."

Ritchie chuckled again. "Sorry, sir. I sort of couldn't help myself."

"Can't say as though I blame you. But we've got a lot of work to do if you and I are going to win this competition."

Ritchie lit up even brighter. "Yes, sir!"

Layla's heart nearly exploded.

There was no denying it was the "we" and the "you and I" that charged Ritchie. The man he revered was calling him a team member—a significant one. A partner, even.

164

So noteworthy, Ritchie had to take a few seconds to compose himself. That only served to bring fat tears to Layla's eyes.

Okay, yeah, this family was totally upping the stakes. There'd not been this flood of feelings when she'd interviewed other contenders. They'd been so singularly driven, they hadn't engaged in this way. Or, again, hadn't had the big *Why* Avery did. Even Ritchie was a part of that concept.

Avery had several ovens to make, and as he completed one, Ritchie put the lid on and took it to the pit.

When he was done, Avery joined Ritchie, and he scooped coals from his firebox onto the lids of the ovens that were nestled over the rocks, covering them with glowing embers.

"The critical hit-or-miss here," Avery explained to the audience, "is that I don't want to overcook my eggs or my steak. Nor do I want to undercook my potatoes. So I have to surround the ovens but be mindful of what temperature I have from beneath and above."

He collected more firewood to keep the flames burning to produce additional embers.

He returned to his prep station, washed up, and assembled the apple crisps for the secondary pit, sprinkling his brown sugar–cinnamon concoction, combined with nutmeg, lemon, oats, and flour, over the fruit Ritchie had sliced. He dusted each filled oven with cayenne pepper and vanilla bean powder.

Layla's brow raised. "Always have to add an extra kick, eh, cowboy?"

He gave the low, intimate chuckle that made her breath catch.

"You know I like to add some spiciness to the sweetness," he drawled.

"Indeed, you do." The words tumbled from her mouth, unbidden. Followed by an audible sigh.

*Oh, dear Lord, Layla!*

She was all but wilting at his feet.

She cleared her throat and hastily said, "We have this recipe on our website. However, something tells me you cook to taste. Not to specific measurements."

"You're on to me, darlin'." He grinned. "I've been making this recipe for over a decade. I just know how to bring it all together. Tasting and adjusting is definitely imperative."

His gaze lingered on her, his brow twitching, discreetly. Her inner muscles contracted. She ducked her head once again, knowing she'd only give herself away if she looked at the camera.

She merely said, "Same with all your other recipes." *For their sexy times.*

He chuckled again. Knowing how he affected her.

Layla forced herself to remain in "host" mode. She returned her attention to the audience and said, "Lesson here is that you want to experiment until you find your perfect flavorings."

"That is one of the joys of cooking," he chimed in.

"I do like that part, yes. But eating is more my jam."

"And I appreciate your appetite, honey."

"Just have to work in some exercise to keep us on our toes," she replied.

They stared at each other.

Layla's brain blipped out.

Avery's teeth sank into his bottom lip. Briefly.

More microbursts ensued, deep in Layla's core.

On the other side of the counter, Todd's head cocked.

Brodi gaped, her eyes wide.

And the wranglers all gazed at them with blatant curiosity.

Layla shifted into Drive. She said, "Y'all, let's be serious for a moment. The average Joe needs to incorporate stretching and cardio into their daily routine. These cowboys are on the range all day, burning calories, so when they come to the table, they require sustenance. And not just from steaks. Isn't that right, Avery?"

"Darlin', I'm all for pork, poultry, and fish," he said, helping to bring the conversation around to something less provocative. "Just wait until I smoke a pig in my pit this week. Ain't never tasted anything so juicy and succulent. Well . . . once I have." He outright wagged a brow this time.

*So much for being discreet!*

It was borderline cruel to be so bound to her lust. All she wanted was to rid him of his apron, rip open the snaps on his shirt, and crawl all over him.

*Layla!*

*Are you just wallowing in the gutter of down and dirty thoughts??*

*Why, yes. Yes, I am.*

And it was impossible to stymie the trill along her spine and the pulsating in her pussy.

*So inconvenient.*

She held a long-suffering sigh in check.

Now she knew how Jack and Jillian must've felt when they'd so obviously been trying to hide their steamy attraction to each other while audiences were homing in on it with such ease.

Layla had already seen similar comments on the *Light Your Fire* socials. Part of her job was to engage with the viewers when they posted. She was accustomed to the broad strokes—answering questions about a particular recipe or a preferred spice that someone used. Queries about the BBQ circuit/world. Different techniques. And the occasional "Tell us more about Contestant X, Y, or Z."

For the latter, she provided official information, not specific commentary beyond her on-screen interaction with them. Especially when it came to female contestants. Layla didn't want to compromise them in any way, personally or professionally.

Nor did she want to encourage any sort of stalker mentality. That was the highest of priorities on her list.

Thus far, no incidents of the kind had plagued any of her cook-offs.

Save for this one instance of her lusting after the hunky cowboy here and not being able to control her reactions to him.

Telling her today's comments were going to be tough to tackle.

She collected herself for about the hundredth time and looked at the camera. "Now that I've given my PSA on being mindful of healthy choices, I'm going to reiterate that Avery's breakfast bake is served with an arugula salad."

He snickered. "And apple crisp, darlin'."

She shot him a sardonic look. "Way to sell me out, cowboy."

His sapphire eyes shimmered as he said, "As you alluded, these 'boys have a long, hard day ahead of them."

"And they're looking to eat. Do you start with the salad?"

"Just have to add the parmesan and almonds," he told her. "You should get some nuts in your diet every day."

Had anyone else said that, she wouldn't have flinched. But one corner of Avery's mouth quirked.

Her thighs went up in flames.

*Again . . . Not! Helping!*

Everything this man uttered held sexual connotations for her.

When she knew they either shouldn't or didn't!

Yet in her brain . . . they did!

*Oh, my God. I will die on the vine here, I'm so hot for this man.*

"Shouldn't you be checking on your casserole right about now?" she prompted. To take the pressure off her.

"I've got a few more minutes."

"How do you know that?"

"I just do."

"Can you be more specific?" she asked, latching on to the attention-diverting olive branch he'd offered. Sort of.

"Thing about the pit, darlin', is that you have to learn cooking conditions. Practice with temperatures and how you best achieve and maintain them. Increase or reduce as necessary. You have to subject yourself to trial and error. Till you've developed a sixth sense for how long certain things take to bake, smoke, simmer, what have you."

He was so smooth. *So Matthew McConaughey explaining what sort of boating person you might be in *Failure to Launch.*

All laid back, but with expertise driving his monologue.

Layla's questions withered as fast as she did.

Suddenly, he exclaimed, "Ah!" Clapped his hands together, and said, "We're ready."

*Thank God!*

Layla needed a reprieve from all the zings.

Avery and Ritchie retrieved the cast irons with wire handles and performed the obligatory dusting off with hand brooms. The judges were the first to be served again. While Ritchie tended to the buffet table for the cowboys, Layla got initial reactions from them, then joined The Three—and Avery.

"What I like most about this," Judge #1 said, "is that the bake is hearty and yet not so dense that it's chewy."

"And the moisture is just right," added Judge #2, "so that there's no sogginess."

"The eggs," Judge #3 commented with a sigh, "are sublime." She added, "Crispy edges and whites, and a center that oozes golden glory." She enjoyed another forkful from her plate. "And the spices are just right."

"These Scoville heat units are perfect for this early in the morning," Judge #1 added.

And so on . . .

Layla tamped down a triumphant smile on Avery's behalf.

*You are Switzerland.*

*You are neutral.*

The judges had questions of their own on technique, and Avery breezed right through them.

As was the custom, everyone dispersed. Even the wranglers cleared out after eating.

Layla sidled up to Avery as he was placing the judges' plates and flatware into a busser bin.

"I narrowly made it through that episode," she said. "Thing about you, cowboy, is that you possess self-awareness that's alluring. You know who you are. You know what you're doing. That's a wild combo that can tear through an audience like a raging inferno."

She showed him her phone.

"Look at these likes, loves, and flames—totally skyrocketing."

"Meaning Ale is currently going batshit crazy?"

"Do *not* say that in front of your family. That's a twenty-dollar term for the swear jar."

With a laugh, he said, "Honey, you've already learned how I keep that swear jar from becoming a reality."

"So you're saving that leftover apple crisp for Ale."

"To share with Hunt."

"What a good uncle you are." She kissed him. Then murmured against his lips, "What's my reward for assisting with the cleanup?"

"Do you fish, darlin'?"

"What?"

Maybe her brain was a bit scrambled from his nearness because she didn't catch on at first.

Then she did.

She perked up. "We're huntin' and gatherin' for lunch?"

"Plenty of fish in the river. And I've got some plants growing in a special spot for gooseberry-custard pie and black currant cake."

She closed her eyes for a moment.

He asked, "What are you doing?"

"Just calculating how many calories we'll have to work off."

"I do like how you think."

He kissed her. Not the least bit chastely. She was certain Ritchie was blushing from head to toe.

She pulled away and said, "We'd better get down to the river, or we won't have time to scale and fillet the fish. What are we making?"

"Depends on what we reel in. My hope is that we'll do southern-fried largemouth bass tenders and smoked lemon-pepper trout. I'll throw on some steaks to fill in any gaps. Add roasted potato wedges with a chipotle-ranch dip."

"I ate some of your breakfast—stellar, by the way. But I'm hungry again." She sighed. "Epicurean delight to the max."

"If there's anything in particular you want, just let me know."

"Oh, you know, cowboy," she said with a suggestive smile. "You know."

He led her toward the stables, and they saddled up again. He directed them through a different pasture, away from the cattle and the cowboys.

They rode down into a grassy valley where the river widened and was gentler. There was an outdoor setup of picnic tables, Adirondack chairs, a huge deck with a ramada top, and more tables underneath.

They secured the horses, and then Avery retrieved fishing poles and gear from a storage bin.

Layla said, "Good of you not to ask me if I can hook my own night crawlers. We're well aware how that conversation will end."

"With me eating crow."

He set the tackle box on a table and opened it.

"Moot, though," he continued. "We've got artificial bait. Spinners, cranks, jigs. Plastic worms. Take your pick."

Her gaze slid over the vast selection. She pointed to one quadrant of the trays and said, "I like the colorful ones."

"Then colorful ones you shall have."

She rigged her own line, and Avery whistled under his breath. Flashed her an *I'm impressed* look and then outfitted himself.

"You fly-fish as well?" he asked.

"Even tie my own flies."

"Figures."

They headed to the end of the pier and cast off in different directions, Layla somehow sensing this was going to be their own competition, especially given they had individual coolers.

She snagged a bass and glanced over her shoulder as Avery was pulling up a sunfish on his line.

"Awww, isn't she purdy?" Layla joked.

He smirked. "Have to start somewhere, honey."

"How's this for a start?" She showed hers that she'd scooped into her net.

Now he scowled. "I will never hear the end of this."

"And not just from me."

"Keep at it, darlin'."

They spent over an hour collecting fish. A nice bounty, if Layla did say so herself.

Not playing the sore loser, Avery said, "Let's get back and gut these."

She gave a slight pout. "But I wanted to skinny-dip."

"Then you'd better get out of those clothes. We have about a half hour."

She shucked her navy ankle boots, jeans, and a loose navy tee with a purposely faded circle in the middle and "BBQ Girl" stamped within, at an angle. Her bra and panties hit the dock while Avery stared at her.

Excitement shimmied through her.

She said, "Come on, now, cowboy. We've only got so much time."

She spun around and dove into the warm water.

As she surfaced, pushed her hair from her face, and wiped away drops from her eyes, Avery dove in.

She circled her arms around his neck and her legs around his waist.

"This is so refreshing," she told him. "This Texas sun can be unrelenting, despite it only being early summer."

"That's why we've got all these shady trees. Even around the chuck hall. Plus, portable AC units and fans that we can use outside to cool the air."

"I do admire how you extend the luxuries to your crew. We filmed at a smaller operation in Louisiana that was complete bare bones, and the wranglers were sweltering in the heat and humidity. Tasty alligator, though—blackened and with a Cajun hot sauce. The bobcat was interesting. Just needed more flavor; the meat was a bit bland. Not that I made mention of this. I sample but don't comment when it comes to the quality and taste of the food." It was sort of drilled into her to reiterate this. Mostly because she was pressing her breasts against well-defined pecs, and that held the potential to skew her objectivity.

Avery gazed at her for several seconds that seemed to hold them suspended in time.

Then he grinned. And said, "That you're willing to sample alligator and bobcat is one of the sexiest things about you, Layla Jenson. Not *the* sexiest thing. Your lingerie definitely gets my adrenaline pumping."

"And you have a whole pig and white-tailed deer on the menu this week. Talk about turn-ons."

"Not all people will agree."

"I don't get too wrapped up in 'the hunt.' But I can see where that can be offensive to others."

"True. Though that's hypocritical of me because we sell off our cattle to produce beef that ends up on people's plates. So."

"And hides that end up on sofas and jackets."

He nodded. "It's a sociological conundrum. My personal perspective is to each their own. I don't oppose vegan material rather than leather. I also happen to like plant-based food—just not as my primary meat source. And I do eat fish."

"Speaking of . . ."

"Yeah, we've got work to do."

She shifted around to his back, hung on, and let him swim them toward the dock. She took the ladder up to the landing, and he followed.

"Guess I should've grabbed some towels from the bin," he said.

"Give us a couple of minutes to disassemble our rods, and this hot breeze will have dried us."

"You do realize that a couple of minutes of us naked will just lead to me taking you right here on a picnic table?"

She instantly gave up on her rod. "Do we even need the picnic table?"

◆ ◆ ◆

Later that evening, Layla joined Todd and Brodi for dinner at the hotel in Serrano. A definitive Western establishment with heads mounted on the walls and peppers lining the menu.

"You're going to want champagne with your dish, sweetheart," Todd said. "In fact, I'm buying, and it'll be of the expensive variety."

She folded her menu and gazed at him. "I know our viewer and subscriber numbers are soaring. Did we hit some sort of milestone today?"

"Those numbers are exceptional, Layla. I'm almost thinking that Avery Reed can single-handedly give us the audience base and the additional sponsorships to warrant a sixth season."

She pressed her hand to her mouth.

Damn it, she'd *known* Avery was a gold mine!

"But that's not what we're celebrating," Todd said.

Her hand fell away. "What's the occasion, then?"

He waited until they'd all ordered from the server who'd appeared—and indeed, Todd did select a private reserve bottle of bubbly.

Layla's gaze narrowed on him. "You don't spring for premium alcohol all that often. You win the lottery, and this is your way of telling us?"

"No, Layla." His tone was level, though it had the potential to lean toward exuberant.

"You're freakin' me out, Todd," she said.

"Me too," Brodi added. "You look borderline . . . *happy*?"

"You gals are giving me a rotten reputation."

Layla laughed. "We're just accustomed to your even keel."

"Yeah, well. This is something significant to commemorate."

"And it is . . . ?" Layla prompted.

He held them in further suspense as the server returned, popped the cork, and let Todd sample. Following his nod of approval, the server poured flutes. Then she put the bottle in a chiller.

Once she left, Todd raised his glass and said, "This is to Layla's freedom."

Layla was confused.

Yet they all clinked rims and sipped.

Her breath hitched as Todd grinned, then took a longer drink.

She did as well.

"Y'all are killin' me here," Brodi moaned.

"Okay, enough with me drawing this out," Todd told them. "You clearly haven't seen or read financial news of late, Layla."

"What would be the point?" she asked in a dry tone. "That part of my life is over and done. And we all know I can't try for a national or international commentator position. So."

"Well, *I* keep an eye on financial journals." He placed his cell on the table between them.

She felt an odd stab in her chest.

A tremor ran down her arm, so that she set aside her glass.

She stared at Todd.

"What do you know?"

He inhaled deeply.

On the exhale, he said, "Christopher Courtland is dead."

# Chapter Thirteen

Layla's eyes bulged. Her heart nearly stopped.

Brodi let out a strangled squawk.

Todd rushed on. "Seems his first urban complex opened in Pittsburgh to great acclaim and with a huge penthouse party. He over-imbibed with a prescription cocktail and vodka. His housekeeper found him early this morning. Drowned in his own hot tub. Might have gone into cardiac arrest first. That'll be determined by the autopsy, and all confirmed from a toxicology report."

"The hell you say . . . ," Brodi murmured. "OMG."

Layla stared at Todd, myriad emotions slamming into her.

Some so joyous, she nearly bounded from her seat to scream *Hallelujah!* from the top of her lungs.

Some so bleak, she could have filled a bucketful of tears.

She had no idea which way the scales would tip, so she merely sat stock still. Tried to breathe. Tried to process.

Todd told her, "This means he's never coming after you, Layla. Never, ever. Or your father. He's gone, Layla. Down for the count."

Her brain tripped. Her jaw dropped.

She pulled in staccato breaths.

Todd's hand covered hers on the table. Gave a gentle squeeze.

Brodi was weeping, repeating, "It's over, Layla. It's over."

It just wasn't a notion she could reconcile in her mind.

"Take a look at my phone if you need to see for yourself," Todd told her. "I have the breaking news pulled up on my screen."

"It's just . . . so impossible to believe . . . to . . . to . . ."

She didn't have the words.

Tears pricked her eyes. She tried to blink them away, not wanting to make a scene.

She reached for her flute and sipped. And sipped.

Didn't quell the ringing in her ears or slow the hammering of her pulse.

"This is just . . . too much . . ." Her voice quavered. Drops seeped out of the corners of her eyes.

"I know." Todd's hand squeezed a little tighter. Reassuringly. "But you *can* believe this, Layla. It's fact."

"Oh, my God," she whispered.

For five years she'd been living in fear, even when rationality told her Christopher wouldn't discover her new identity. Somehow, she'd just felt that he would. That the henchman he'd sent to her hospital room that one time would keep tabs on her. And ensure she never told her story.

But . . . that was all over now. As Brodi still chanted between sobs.

Her ugly duckling/Cinderella trope was fully coming to fruition.

More than that . . .

"I can call my daddy," she said on a sliver of air.

Todd nodded. "You worried that connecting with him would bring Courtland or his people to his doorstep. You don't have to fear that anymore."

"Beyond that," she said, "I couldn't call him when I was laid up. I could barely speak. When I finally got my voice back, I could have reached out to him, yes. It'd just been so long . . . I didn't know what to say. How to say it. How to say . . . anything."

There was no way she'd tell her daddy what had happened to her.

The convenient out had been that communications with her father had dwindled when she'd started at the firm. And had halted altogether when she'd gotten involved with Christopher. Therefore, it was a likely scenario that her daddy had accepted that she'd pivoted to a different "crowd" and didn't have time for him.

Whether that was a true assumption on his part or not, she didn't know. Whether he'd put any effort into trying to locate her when she'd gone full-on radio silent, she also didn't know.

What was more prudent on her end was what she shared with Todd and Brodi.

"I could have called, certainly. Yes, my voice was different in New York—no accent and more formal. But I let that go. Reverted to what I was accustomed to when growing up. He would have recognized *this* voice."

Christopher would not. He'd never heard her slight southern drawl.

"I was just too paranoid," she confessed. "I also couldn't see him because there was no simple explanation to give about how drastically my appearance has been altered. I'm literally unrecognizable. Jesus, Todd, it took a litany of 'remember whens?' from NYU in order for you to accept that I'm Tess Billings. You had such a hard time seeing through to that."

"Definitely a jolt to the system."

"I could have gotten my daddy there too," she also admitted. "But not without telling him so much that would break his heart. All the things he'd want to know about my time in New York, which would wreck him." More tears fell. She dabbed at them with her linen napkin. "I just couldn't do it."

"That's a legitimate point for the past," Todd told her. "Because you also wanted to protect him from Courtland. But now . . ." He gave her a solemn look and asked, "Don't you see the bigger picture here?"

She stared at him.

He said, "You get your entire former existence back. I mean . . . aside from the facial differences. But Layla, you can have all your Tess Billings credentials back. Your high school diploma, your college degree, your work experience. And you can add *Light Your Fire* to your résumé, citing Layla Jenson as your stage name. You can return to financing. You can pursue your dream of being a broadcaster. You're no longer confined."

"And I do have the benefits of the facial differences," she added.

Through her shock, she heard the doors swinging open for her.

This was not something she'd thought of the past several years because it was too far-fetched.

To let down her guard . . . that was inconceivable. But now?

She didn't have to look over her shoulder. She didn't have to fear for her life—or for her father's.

"Wow." The extent of her verbal response.

On the inside, though . . . ?

Everything went haywire.

All the cracks and crevices within her were about to break wide open.

It couldn't happen here.

"I have to go to my room." She shoved back her chair just as the full tremors rocked her, so that she almost fell to her knees.

"Layla—"

Todd reached for her. But she made an immediate beeline toward the exit that led to the elevator.

"Layla!" Brodi called after her.

She barreled toward her escape. Jabbed her finger into the button numerous times as though that would bring the elevator to her faster.

Bile burned up her esophagus, and she pushed it down, though more teardrops fell. She swiped at her cheeks.

Brodi slipped through the closing doors in the nick of time.

She didn't hug Layla, evidently sensing they'd both crumble to the floor.

But she held her hand.

They stepped out on their level, and Brodi got them into the room. Released Layla's hand and let her dash into the bathroom. She collapsed before the toilet and heaved. Repeatedly.

Brodi was behind her, holding her hair. Mumbling, "It's all okay now, Layla. That asshole got what he had coming to him. Arrogant fuckin' prick. Those drugs were probably fueling him this entire time. And to mix them with booze? He must've thought he was invincible."

That was perfectly accurate.

That was how he'd been able to attack her.

With no conscious, no soul.

And no worry over repercussions.

Not from a *nobody*.

Not from anyone or anything.

But that negative karma had finally caught up to him.

As Layla sat back on her heels, she heard Brodi at the sink. She returned with a damp washcloth that Layla pressed to her mouth.

Brodi sat on the tile with her, stroking Layla's arm. More tears crested Layla's eyes.

"This is the best day ever," Brodi said. "You just have to take the time to release all the emotions. Everything that's been bottled up inside you for so long."

Layla nodded.

"Then really consider what this means. Todd's right. You're free of that wretched human being. You can move forward without all the doubts and the terror of whether he's lurking in the shadows."

Layla pulled away the small towel. Tried to get a full breath. Still impossible.

In a choppy voice, she said, "I need to absorb all this—it's not resonating."

"Right. Of course. Just keep in mind, Layla. You get to change your narrative."

"That's huge," she said.

"For sure."

Layla gave this some thought, but it was too fresh of a revelation to sort it out.

She told her bestie, "Go back downstairs. Enjoy dinner and champagne. Celebrate with Todd. Celebrate for me."

Brodi's eyes misted once more. She got to her feet and grabbed the box of tissues, handing it first to Layla, who snatched a few sheets. Brodi then blotted her own eyes before helping Layla to stand.

She went straight to the vanity and dug out her toothbrush and paste from the bag she'd brought with her from Avery's house, knowing she'd be sleeping here tonight. Todd had wanted to get together for a production meeting with her and Brodi. But "breaking news" had prevailed.

Brodi propped her hip against the counter. Sniffled. And said, "I don't really want to leave you."

"I'm grateful for that. But I could use some alone time."

Brodi nodded. "I understand." Still, she looked reluctant to leave.

Layla splashed cold water on her face and patted her skin dry. Then she hugged Brodi. For a lengthy spell. Choking them both up more.

But when she loosened the embrace and held Brodi's shoulders, staring into her eyes, she felt sturdier.

"Tell Todd I'll be fine. *Know* that I'll be fine, Brodi. There's serious emotional upheaval to work through, but you're right. This is the best day ever." She managed a weak smile.

Brodi breathed a sigh of relief. "You'll bounce back. No need to hurry it; just digest it all. Breathe." She groaned. "Easier said than done, I grasp that. Just . . . take care of you."

"I always do."

"You've had way too much shit to deal with, Layla."

"But that's all over," she said.

"Right. I'm going to touch up my makeup and join Todd." She gave a decisive nod. Though it took her a few seconds to proceed.

"I'm okay," Layla quietly averred. "Go."

She did.

Layla remained in the bathroom, gazing into the mirror.

Her mind was a jumbled mess. Dozens of thoughts converged, and she couldn't sift through them to home in on the salient points.

Thus, she gave up and went into the main room, bringing her cell with her, which Brodi had taken from her cross-body purse in order to unlock Layla's door.

She slipped off her ankle boots and her clothes, putting on a pair of peach-colored satiny short-shorts with a matching camisole. She climbed under the covers, resting against the mound of pillows.

She wanted to cry some more.

She wanted to laugh.

But both would border on hysteria, she suspected. And that might not be containable.

Her stomach churned with uncertainty and excitement.

There were such contradictory feelings swirling like a cyclone within her that she didn't know where to start in shredding them apart and piecing them back together.

As she contemplated this, her phone rang with the tone she'd designated for Avery.

A part of her thrilled over him calling. The other part wasn't sure she'd have the right thing to say if she answered.

But of course she had to answer.

Unfortunately, he'd mastered video calls, and that had become his preferred way to contact her when they weren't together.

Her phone was alongside her outer thigh, so he couldn't see her face—specifically, her puffy and bloodshot eyes, and her red nose. She didn't lift it. Just tapped the Connect button.

"Did Brodi tell you to call?" she asked, her voice raspy so that she winced. She wouldn't be covering up her emotional state.

"No, I was just hating that you're there and I'm here. But now I'm wondering what's going on."

She hiccuped. Wiped away another tear.

"Layla?" His curiosity was laced with concern.

"Don't stress over me, cowboy," she softly said. "I'm a bit of a hot mess right now. But in the end, I'll see the silver lining."

"I can hear something edgy in your voice, but I can't see your face, darlin'. Why's that?"

She got up the nerve to raise the phone.

"Aw, Jesus. What the *hell*, Layla?" he all but roared.

"It's not bad," she quickly said. "It's actually good, Avery. It's just . . ."

Goddamn the flood of tears that threatened her eyes again.

"That's not a happy cry, honey. I've seen enough of Riley's ugly ones over losing an animal on the ranch—that's what this is."

He shot to his feet and grabbed his keys.

"Avery, you don't have to come here! You have a pig to smoke for tomorrow's segment!"

"I have it ready for stuffing and trussing for my rotisserie, and I'll get it on the spit by three a.m. I have plenty of time."

"Avery—" Her voice splintered.

"Darlin', you look like you need me."

*Oh, dear Lord.*

The drops continued to tumble along her cheeks.

"I do, Avery. I really do."

Avery didn't have these kinds of complications in his life for a reason.

The cook-off notwithstanding, he had more on his plate than just barbecuing. There was inventorying to do, budgeting, cooking/baking/ serving supplies to inspect for chips or fractures or other defects—and he replaced them as needed. Not to mention ensuring cords of various hardwoods and piles of charcoal and lava rocks were ordered and delivered on time.

The spices had to be replenished as much as the meats and produce did. And with that came the need to plot out weekly menus.

Also, Avery and Ritchie were the cleanup crew.

All of this culminated in a tidy package demanding his tunnel vision.

Now he had the competition to think about.

And Layla.

For all his responsibilities, he couldn't let whatever was happening between the two of them capsize his ship.

And yet . . .

He told her, "You hang tight, honey. I'm on my way."

He was out the door in a flash, driving his truck into town.

Brodi was just coming out of the hotel restaurant with Todd as Avery strode in.

She said, "You are too amazing, Avery Reed." She gave him the room number, though Layla already had.

Avery's gaze slid to Todd, who assured him, "It's not bad news. Don't look so grim. She's sliding into an adjustment period."

"I have no idea what you're talking about."

Brodi gripped his forearm. "Just listen to her. This is a twist no one saw coming." She kind of hopped about, doing that vibrating thing of hers.

Trying to clarify the situation, Todd explained, "Layla's whole life just changed. Again." He extended his hand to Avery. "Thanks for caring enough about her to be here."

They shook. Then Todd dragged Brodi away.

Avery took the elevator. He stalked down the hallway to Layla's room and rapped on the door. Feeling a crushing weight on his chest, which she obviously saw on his face and in his eyes when she flung the door open.

"No, no, no," she instantly insisted. "Don't wig, Avery." She threw her arms around him. "It's not tragic—not for me anyway. It's everything I wished for and nothing I can make sense of at the moment."

"You're going to have to be more specific, darlin'."

"I know. It's just . . ." Her voice trailed off. She sobbed against his neck.

He held her tight. Led her to the armchair and eased into it, her in his lap.

"Let me try to tell you . . . ," she said.

"Take your time."

This seemed to bring her around. She stared at him.

"Oh, fuck. You really shouldn't be here." She shook her head. "I'm so sorry, Avery. You don't need to be caught up in my drama. You have so much more to be thinking about than me."

"Considering I'm caught up in *you*, honey . . ." He grinned. "I'm caught up in *everything* about you."

She kissed him.

Out of the blue and with so much passion, it took him by surprise.

He had no clue what was causing her trouble. And yet . . . her searing lip-lock indicated she wasn't grieving. Something else was the issue.

He ignored for the moment that whatever that *something else* was had her looking like she'd cried a river. He didn't believe for a second that it had anything to do with her dad. She would have told him straightaway. And again . . . she wasn't mourning.

Currently, he shut his mind off to all the queries plaguing his brain.

And kissed her back.

She worked the buttons on his shirt, making him regret he didn't have the snaps that took her no time flat to release.

His hand slid under the thin material of her top, and he palmed her breast, kneading gently. His thumb swept over her puckered nipple, and her body jolted.

He could take this slow with her, but he wanted her naked, immediately. If not sooner.

He unraveled from her so he could lift her into his arms and carry her to the bed, the covers already turned down. He whisked off her nightclothes, though not without admiring her in them for a few seconds.

Then he peeled his attire off and joined her—not before grabbing the condom in his wallet, a habit he now had in the event they ended up somewhere other than his bedroom. Like the dock.

He brushed her long bangs from her temple and stared into her red-veined eyes, which coiled his gut, until she smiled sweetly.

"I'll be okay," she promised. "Just in need of your company tonight."

That was a knife to his heart.

If she'd been in Cheyenne or wherever she was headed next week and the week after that, he couldn't get to her this fast. If at all . . .

Deserting the ranch wasn't an option. Even with Ritchie's help. That was too much for his assistant to take on by himself, serving all those cowboys three times a day. Jack and Chance would pitch in, of course. But they had their own obligations. As did the others.

Avery knew where his place was. A key issue unto itself.

Though he closed down his brain once more because he was here for Layla. Briefly, yet if it kept the smile on her pretty face, that was worthwhile.

He kissed her teasingly and whispered, "I'll just pretend you were missing me."

"That's not a stretch, cowboy."

Her nails grazed his arm up to his shoulder, then his neck. Threading his hair.

She took a deep breath and murmured, "Finally." Like she hadn't been able to get a full one in.

This torqued his insides further.

But her lips skimmed over his, and she said, "Just knowing you were on your way calmed me. And, yes, I realize that only convolutes our situation."

"Seems unavoidable."

"I'm sorry for that."

"I am too," he said.

"Yet here we are."

"Beats the hell out of being alone in my bed."

She sighed. "I'm not sure I could have made it through the evening without wearing a hole in the carpet from pacing. I felt too anxious. Too wired. Too pulled in a thousand directions."

"And now?"

Her eyes glistened.

Her entire demeanor softened, as did her sensuous curves beneath him.

"Now I can breathe, cowboy. Now I can let my past tortured thoughts disintegrate. Let the newly undefinable ones simmer until I'm in a better frame of mind to wade through them."

"I'll admit I don't understand all of this."

"I don't expect you to understand, Avery. Just . . . be with me tonight."

"That I can do, honey."

His mouth captured hers. He kissed her long and deep. Continued kissing her, until their chests rose and fell in time with each other, and she draped a leg over his hips as he sank into her heat and moisture. Until they were moving together in a sexy rhythm. Until all the sensations coalesced and erupted.

Until they found bliss that alleviated some of the tension, the strain, the uncertainty.

*This* he could comprehend. And accept.

Avery hated leaving her. It was becoming a hugely conflicting emotion for him, but it was also something inescapable.

He kissed her bare shoulder and whispered in her ear, "Get more sleep. I'll see you for the lunch competition."

He slipped from the bed and got dressed.

Before he reached the door, she sat up, pressing the sheet to her chest. "Thank you for getting me through the night, cowboy."

"It's still the middle of the night, darlin'. Close your eyes."

"I apologize for you losing some sleep."

He chuckled. "Don't even bother with that. Havin' you in my arms just charges me more for this competition." He winked. Touched the brim of his hat. And made his exit before he caved to another round with her.

He drove back to the TRIPLE R, showered, then joined Ritchie at the chuck hall. His assistant had donned a brown leather apron, so Avery followed suit—not missing how that made Ritchie's chest swell with pride.

Avery felt serious tugs on his heartstrings, for numerous reasons.

He appreciated how devoted Ritchie was.

He reveled in how enticing Layla was, how easily she gave herself over to him, not shying away from the excitement and the emotion that consumed them both.

He also cherished the offering he found on his cowboy buffet table while Ritchie was starting the fires in the trenches that would burn for hours before they put the pig in the pit.

The box had Avery's name on it, and inside he found a new collection of his aunt Brett's serving dishes with a colorful, decorative, southwestern-themed glazed shell.

There was a note.

He swallowed down a lump before he even read it.

*Dear Avery,*
*I made these special for you and the wranglers. Never wonder if your contribution isn't as valuable as anyone else's. No one ever worries over whether our cowboys are treated to the best meals. In fact, a day doesn't go by when we don't hear compliments from them about how the chucks get better and better. You do this for them—and for us. Every day. And we are blessed to have you.*
*Love, Aunt Brett*

He turned away for a moment.
*Well, fuck.*

He drew in some breaths. Squared his shoulders. Tried to tamp down the burning sensation in his lungs.

No, it wasn't the first time his aunt—or anyone else—had commended his efforts. And, yes, she had good timing with the contest, and using this as a means to express that paying his dad's debt wasn't warranted, even if she didn't actually write those words. He felt them in his bones.

She wasn't trying to remind him of his *Why* either.

She was just giving him a gift. As she did on occasion with her pots for flowers that spruced up the chuck hall. With her mortars and pestles for mixing spices, and the mortar-styled ramekins with matching mini ladles for serving. He was slowly building an assortment of ornate accessories, and he couldn't deny that adding these platters would make his buffet table shine. Not just for the show but long after. A tribute to him. To Ritchie. To the cowboys.

He cleared his throat, turned back to his assistant, and said, "Why don't you get these cleaned up, and I'll tend to the fires."

Ritchie peeked inside the box. "These are great!"

"Following that prep, I need you to set out all our burlaps. We'll have to soak them for tomorrow's venison roasts. Along with our woodchips." The dampness would be paramount for keeping the lean meat from drying out or becoming too tough.

"I'm on it." Ritchie carefully hefted the box of platters and took them into the hall.

Avery added thickly splintered applewood to his pits, needing them to get good and hot before he started his pig. He'd be cooking the mammoth animal over an open flame for several hours, and he wanted a nice sear right off the bat. The fat would trickle down as the pig slowly rotated, flavoring and tenderizing the meat.

In addition to all of this, Avery and Ritchie had to get breakfast going.

They had plenty of time, so Avery said, "Let's start a campfire hash with eggs and campfire bread with berries in the secondary pit. I'll do pancakes with sausage and bacon on the griddle and grill."

They had all the lighting they needed outside, despite it still being dark.

The morning progressed as usual, with the exception of Avery checking on his skewered pork at the right intervals.

He sent Ritchie for a nap before they got lunch around, for the cameras. When Ritchie returned and tied on a new apron, Avery made a quick trip to his house to shower and change.

Everything was moving along fine when the production crew showed up.

And Layla strolled in.

*Goddamn.* He rolled his eyes and grinned.

She was a vision in a white eyelet dress that had short sleeves and a flared hem. Her brown leather belt and matching cowgirl boots complemented the outfit. For the first time since they'd started filming, she'd left her hair in the loose curls he liked, her bangs flipped over to one side, falling against her temple in a sexy way.

She'd clearly dealt with her weepy eyes because they were glowing vibrantly.

Her glossy lips were damned tempting.

In fact, it took all the willpower he possessed not to swoop in and haul her up against him. Kiss her senseless.

But The Three joined the group. And Avery and Ritchie had a pig to "assemble" as their demonstration and they also had to pull the cooked one from the fire they'd been monitoring all morning.

Yet . . .

Layla in her flirty dress, with her fluttering lashes . . .

Christ. He still didn't know exactly what had gone down last night to prompt the waterworks. But there was a lighter air to her today. She was a fresh breeze through the outdoor facility, all soft and shimmery. And that got his heart pumping and his testosterone spiking.

He took command of his commentary, though it ebbed and flowed with her interviewing. He showed off his sweet potato casserole with marshmallows, candied walnut spring salad with thinly sliced apples, pineapple bread, and traditional pig pickin' cake.

His overall presentation was precisely what he was shooting for, with the right char to the pork and a tender inside. The side dishes had an extra wow factor displayed on his aunt's platters.

Layla admired the buffet table and said, "You're bordering on a restaurant instead of a chuck hall here, Avery."

"Oh, darlin', it's always going to be a chuck hall. Just doesn't have to be a generic one. And my aunt Brett likes to punch things up a notch. She gives pottery classes in Serrano and has an online store."

He didn't think he was pushing boundaries by sharing this. Neither Layla nor Todd seemed inclined to think differently.

So he moved on.

"*Family* includes everyone on the ranch," he told the audience. "We all rely on one another. We all help one another. We're all focused on the greater good. And we all reward each other, in whatever capacity we can."

Layla sighed as she stared up at him. Not finding words, apparently.

He chuckled and said, "Now I have to get this food in front of the judges."

"The . . . ? Oh, right!" She snapped out of her daze. "Absolutely right, cowboy!"

She shifted out of the way.

Not that he minded her nearly melting into him.

But he did want to complete today's challenge.

After that was done and everyone went their separate ways, he drove her up to the main house, where Jack and Jillian were filming their show at the outdoor kitchen adjacent to the patio.

When that segment wrapped, Hunt and Aunt Brett cleaned the stations. Ale played with Jillian's dog in the lush lawn. Garrett and Mindy disassembled their production equipment and discussed marketing opportunities.

Jack joined Avery on the patio to sip beers.

Layla slid into a barstool at the long counter.

Avery still didn't know what last night was all about. But perhaps she needed to discuss it with Jillian first?

# Chapter Fourteen

"You two make one hell of a team," Layla said as she accepted bottled water from Jillian.

"Same can be said for you and Avery."

She spared a glance over her shoulder and grinned at the hunky cowboy. He winked. She sighed contentedly and returned her gaze to Jillian.

"He's got *Light Your Fire* down in more ways than one," Jillian said with a teasing laugh.

"I can't and won't deny that." Layla was quiet for a moment, wondering how much she could divulge.

But according to Avery, this woman had had her fair share of trauma to deal with. And also came from a vastly different lifestyle than Jack's.

So Layla took a chance and said, "I see the appeal of this ranch. Without doubt. I also understand the hold it has on everyone." She quickly added, "Not in a bad way. But in a familial way. It's a lifetime commitment for most."

"Including a couple of Reeds who aren't here full time. Riley arrived before the bash and stepped right into helping out. Luke contributes monetarily . . . regardless of Jack grumbling about it."

"But . . . no sign of a white flag from Caleb Reed?"

"Not that I'm aware of," Jillian commented.

"Seems so—"

"Wrong?"

"Yeah."

"Depends on your perspective, I guess," Jillian said. "Jack feels this place is better off never hearing from or seeing his uncle again. Though, he is still waiting for him to repent."

"I suppose Avery is too." She gave this thought. "Thing about that is, you can hold out hope where there is none and be even more devastated in the long run."

"Meaning?"

"I was in a situation where I wanted someone to recognize his faults and atone," Layla told her. "While also fearing he never would. Avery walks a similar tightrope with his dad."

"Yes, he does. But . . . tell me more about you."

Layla shrugged. "I still have to suss it all out. I haven't even shared the latest with Avery. However . . ." She let the thoughts roll more freely through her brain. Then she said, "I had this terrifying experience that left me in the hospital. A ruthless attack. And I had to become someone else in order to 'disappear.' But now . . . the assailant is dead. And that changes everything."

"Oh, my." Jillian seemed to absorb this, then said, "I'm not sure what you know about me. But I ended up in the hospital, too, following a trampling incident at a concert. People stepped all over me. I lost a fiancé, who couldn't deal with the tragedy, and also an unborn baby. My friends and my shelter—my possessions. I almost lost my life."

A visible shudder ran through her.

Layla reached for her hand on the counter, understanding her pain, and gave it a brief squeeze as a sign of empathy. As Todd had done for her.

Jillian continued. "I gave up all hope in humanity and hid away for a while. Bought a small house in a quiet neighborhood and closed the door on everything and everyone."

"I did that, too, for a couple of years."

"Because you thought someone would come after you?"

"Or go after my daddy," Layla confessed. "I couldn't put him in jeopardy."

"Now this person is gone. And you're unshackled from your past," Jillian said with relief in her tone.

This knotted Layla's stomach. "Not exactly."

Jillian's brow crooked with curiosity.

"Certainly, it's liberating," Layla told her. "It's just that . . . for the last five years, I've lived with a different name, a different face. With a blank page for a past. I was Tess Billings for over two decades, and yet I feel as though I've been Layla Jenson even longer. In spite of how odd it still is to catch a glimpse of myself."

This was one of the more grueling parts.

"I had major reconstructive surgery. And when the bandages were unraveled and I stared into a mirror for the first time, I nearly passed out. A total *Man in the Iron Mask* moment when that mask was removed. I was shocked."

"I can't even imagine . . ."

"It was quite bizarre. But I was also blessed because it gave me a second chance," Layla said. "I wanted to look different, for vanity reasons. Well, professional ones too. More importantly, I *needed* to look different, for my own safety. And I did." She gave a small shrug. "I *do*. Changed my hair color and my makeup once I'd left the hospital, which was sometime down the road. The few staff members dedicated to my case moved me from room to room and even faked discharge papers so that anyone asking about me wouldn't know I was still there."

Jillian's brows knitted.

Layla explained, "The lie that was initially told was that I was in a car accident. The nurses knew better. And protected me."

"That's all very terrifying."

"No more so than being trampled," she countered.

"No one was seeking me out to do further harm, Layla. I was left all alone."

"True. And now that there's no longer a threat to me and my family. . . I'm looking at the potential to achieve all the dreams I once had for myself. I'm just not sure how to proceed. I like what I'm doing today. But I still have bigger aspirations. And am thus having an identity crisis. At the age of thirty."

"I can relate in a way," Jillian said. "I was told not to expect children. So I erased all thoughts of becoming a wife and a mother. For years. And now? Turns out I'm pregnant."

"Huge congrats there." Layla smiled.

"I could not be happier." She drew in a deep breath. Let it out slowly. And added, "This entire ranch adventure has been therapeutic for me. A reclusive insomniac who can now sleep through the night and get on a plane to join Jack in front of a live audience of over two hundred. I knew I had to step outside my box, and this was the perfect place to do it."

"I can certainly recognize that."

"I'm still wary of the crowds," Jillian acknowledged. "Yet with Jack by my side and all the Reeds supporting me . . . I've been able to stretch much further than I'd ever anticipated these past six years."

"That's really saying something for someone who gave up on humanity."

"Indeed. Also, it turns out . . . I *need* people. I enjoy the interactions. Being with Jack makes it much more comfortable."

Layla sipped her water. And said, "I believe in that."

"You know . . . ," Jillian hesitantly told her, "you could spend some time here. After the season's over. What better place to evaluate your next steps?"

They stared at each other.

Layla grasped her meaning. Jillian thought she could find catharsis on the TRIPLE R the same way she had. With a sexy cowboy.

And that thought wasn't so easily discarded.

Except . . .

"I don't think trying to ascertain whether I'm Tess or Layla while getting more deeply involved with Avery is wise. I learned some painful lessons as Tess that I don't want to repeat as Layla."

She spared another glance over her shoulder. Avery caught it and squinted his eyes, as though pondering her conversation with Jillian.

She tore her gaze from him and said, "It's weird to see life in a whole new light."

"For sure. But letting people help you through it isn't a sign of weakness, Layla. That's my lesson learned."

Layla nodded. "I hear you, Jillian. I truly do."

They tapped the rims of their waters.

At that point, the men joined them. Jack rounded the island to stand next to Jillian while Avery slid into a barstool next to Layla.

"Y'all were talkin' about us, right?" Jack asked in an affable tone.

Layla smiled. "In a roundabout way."

"Well, that's something," Avery said with a casual grin.

"I'm thinking that taking our minds off BBQ and competitions and all of our personal challenges might be in order," Jillian offered.

"In that case . . ." Jack brightened. Like the world needed that. The man was his own glow stick, radiating amusement and virility. "What do you ladies say to an evening out? We can have a late supper at Luke's. Invite Wyatt and Mateo. Chance. Garrett and Mindy—I'm sensing there's something going on there."

Jillian snickered. "Saw that coming a mile away, cowboy. Nice of you to catch up."

His smirk was a playful one. Then he added, "Mom won't mind watchin' the two hooligans."

"As if Hunt and Ale could ever qualify as that," Avery said in a droll tone.

"My dog might, eventually," Jillian joked. "He's becoming more and more of a circus act with this big audience on the ranch."

"Those boys love it when he hams it up," Jack told her. "They want to build a Westminster-style obstacle course for him on the event lawn."

"Oh, geez . . . Ollie'll love that," Jillian said.

"Indeed. Now back to the idea on deck—we'd all like a night out, right?" Jack asked as he clapped his hands together.

"I just need to feed the cowboys," Avery stated.

Layla was on board. "I wouldn't mind a traveling family dinner. Todd and Brodi can meet us there."

"And I'll call Riley," Jack said. "Tell her to bring her appetite for Luke's fajitas and her guitar."

"Little dancing never hurts," Avery mused.

"Sounds like we have a plan," Layla concluded. "I'm happy to help you with the chuck, cowboy. As long as I don't step on Ritchie's toes."

"Just be sure to wipe away the spittle from the corners of his mouth from time to time," Avery jested. "He tends to drool when you're near."

She leaned in. Kissed him. And whispered, "You don't?"

Jack hooted. "She got ya there." He whisked Jillian off. The kids followed, along with the dog.

Layla slipped from her seat and inched closer to Avery, winding her arms around his neck as she stepped into the V his parted legs created.

She kissed him deeply, loving that he responded fiercely, pulling her tight into his embrace. Tangling his tongue with hers. Hitching their breaths.

As she'd mentioned previously, in moments like these, time ceased to exist. So, too, did the push-and-pull conflicts. Which were amplified by Layla's newfound emancipation.

She could go wherever she wanted, whenever she wanted.

Be whoever she wanted to be.

Though at present . . . being the object of the hotter-than-hell cowboy's desire was all that mattered to her.

*At present.*

◆　◆　◆

Sharing bathroom space with Avery wasn't necessary, due to him having additional ones.

But Layla liked it.

Only downside was that they constantly got sidetracked.

Showering together was its own time zapper as they got handsy with each other. Then there were all the frozen moments that came from stolen glances, which led to naughty thoughts of staying naked and going at it again. And again.

But then Chance was barreling through the front door and hollering up at them to get a move on.

Layla simpered. "He just has no idea how distracting you are."

"Ditto for you, darlin'."

She sped up her primping while Avery dressed.

Meeting in the bedroom, they simultaneously sniggered at each other.

"Just doesn't seem to be a point to going out when you look like that, honey. And there's that big ol' bed over there."

She wore a spaghetti-strapped, fit and flare LBD with turquoise suede ankle boots that had fringes and some bling.

"Don't go thinking I'm not on the same wavelength, cowboy. You're something to look at when you're straining all your muscles over a fire or liftin' a sixty-pound pig. But you also clean up nice."

His outfit complemented hers. He was dressed all in black.

He plopped his hat on his head and held his hand out to her.

"Best we get a move on," he said. "Or Chance'll walk in on us in our birthday suits."

"That door does have a lock, right?"

He chuckled. "We're committed. Let's go."

She nodded. "I'm actually looking forward to this."

"Me too."

They took the stairs and met Chance in the living room.

He whistled and said, "My, my, Miss Layla. You just get prettier and prettier."

She kissed him on the cheek. "Such the flirt."

"Yeah, so stop that," Avery mock glowered. "I'm focused on one competition only. Lemme land the girl without me having to arm wrestle you for her."

"The victory is yours," Chance retorted with his hands in the air, in surrender.

Layla's hand fluttered over her heart. "Brothers fighting over me. Isn't that just the sweetest?"

"It'd be the one time I didn't let him win at something, darlin'."

Chance laughed. "*Let* me win? Are you feelin' all right, little bro?"

Avery grunted. "We'd better pick up Wyatt and Mateo now. She's probably tapping her toe, wondering where the hell we are."

"As if!" Chance guffawed. "I'll have to cajole them downstairs as well. Two of 'em can't keep their paws off each other when they're in the same room."

"Jack will have done the heavy lifting for you. He has to be chompin' at the bit to get Jillian into a social environment."

"Not like she doesn't have bodyguards," Chance said. "If she's feeling the slightest bit uneasy, she can just glance around the table to one of us—and know we won't let anyone get close if she doesn't want them to."

"Luke'll put us all in a corner," Avery commented. "Out of the way of the crowd. He knows not to push her boundaries."

Layla stared at Avery. Then Chance. Then Avery.

She felt the sting at the back of her eyes.

"Jillian's not even a Reed yet, not officially," she said in a quiet voice. "And you guys are already fixated on how to ensure she's not overwhelmed or anxious about being surrounded by people."

"Her phobia can't be discounted," Chance pointed out.

"More than that," Avery added, "anyone in our group who's uncomfortable for whatever reason deserves our support."

"Wow." She blinked away tears, though there were trickles at the outer corners of her eyes. And her nose twitched. "Don't y'all take the cake?"

"Please don't mention cake." Chance grimaced. "I'm starvin'."

"Let's head out." Avery herded them toward the door. "Jack and Jillian will take Garrett and Mindy into town."

Layla texted Brodi to alert her they were on their way.

The trip to Serrano wasn't a hop, skip, and a jump away but just the right length for Layla to ask Chance about his take on the show and find out more about the ranch routine from his perspective.

He was in charge of the wranglers, the stable hands, and the occasional day workers. He also coordinated all the movements of the cattle from pasture to pasture. The branding, the breeding, the vaccinating, the loading of sold cows, and the unloading of steers and heifers bought at auction.

"How do you keep your eyes open?" she asked. "That's exhausting."

"No more so than what everyone else does," Chance told her in a humble tone—not one she was used to from this Reed. "Mateo's gone from sunup to sundown, sometimes for days, attending auctions, Bureau of Land Management meetings, statewide ranching town halls, other TRIPLE R business."

Avery told her, "And Wyatt's got her hands full with a part-time job, coaching Hunt's soccer team, shuttling everyone around, managing Jack's analytics and marketing, and keeping things organized on the ranch."

"It's a fascinating paradigm," Layla said. One she didn't delve any deeper into at the moment because they arrived in town. Avery parked and then came around to collect her as Mateo assisted his wife out of the extra cab.

They entered the festive cantina, Luke immediately swooping in to introduce himself to Layla.

"Lord have mercy," he drawled, "I don't know why all you lovelies are bypassin' my joint and heading straight out to the ranch." He lifted the back of her hand to his lips. Kissed it faintly.

"Try not to swoon, honey," Avery joked without humor. "He's our smoothest operator."

And bearing the Reed men's devastatingly handsome looks. His hair was a tad lighter than Avery's, and his eyes were sky blue. The resemblance was uncanny, though there were absolute distinctions.

Luke Reed had "playboy" written all over him.

This notion was backed up as he shifted his gaze to Brodi, who'd just joined them, with Todd in tow.

"Thanks for the invite," she told Layla. Then glanced at Luke and said, "Whoa! Get out!"

He grinned. Quite devilishly. "Luke Reed, at your service, darlin'."

"Holy Christ," Brodi murmured. "What's up with these genetics?"

"Right?" Layla teased.

"Hey, what am I? Chopped liver?" This from Todd.

"You have a certain aesthetic with your sandy-brown hair and all-American looks," Brodi informed him in a feisty tone. "But you're my boss. I can't get gooey over you." Her gaze returned to Luke. "You, however . . ."

"Hey, what happened to hating on schmoozing?" Layla ribbed her.

"Well, he wasn't at the BBQ bash, so I didn't get the chance to decide if I wanted to schmooze on him."

Luke's laughter filled the bustling entryway. "I like her. I do." He offered his arm to Brodi and escorted her—and the rest of them—to the long table he'd had set in a far corner, as Avery had predicted. One that also faced the dance floor. "Y'all settle in now, and I'll have waiters take your drink orders. Already have the kitchen staff working on a spread for ya."

He winked—at Brodi, or in general, Layla couldn't discern.

But next to her, Brodi whispered, "I'm gonna need to change my thong."

"Oh, my God!" Layla exclaimed, drawing all the attention her way as everyone situated themselves.

"You can't tell me *you're* not all worked up," Brodi said.

Layla blushed. "I'm just excited about the fajitas."

Avery made a face.

"Not that your food doesn't thrill me as well," she told him. "It's just that I saw that segment of you and Luke grilling up fajitas at the street festival, remember? And I've been dyin' to try them ever since."

His brow skewed in a peculiar way, as though he wasn't sure he believed her.

She giggled. "I'm not hot for your cousin," she murmured in his ear. "Brodi, though . . . well, she just might be."

She left that comment as is.

The servers delivered beers, margs, and tequila. Water for Jillian, per her request.

They all toasted with their drinks, and then Luke and his staff laid out sizzling fajitas, tamales, and enchiladas—with chips, salsa, and guacamole.

The lights dimmed, and the neons came on.

Everyone at the table dug into the spicy food.

They were only halfway through the meal when Riley Reed blew in like the Tasmanian Devil.

There was absolutely no missing her.

She strutted in wearing a curve-hugging black mini in a tank style, with black-and-silver snakeskin thigh-high boots, carrying a guitar case in her hand. The locals went crazy for her. Like she was their biggest celebrity—even more so than Jack.

She high-fived and hugged people as she headed for the family table.

Layla shared a look with Jillian, who said, "She's her own magnetic force."

"Yes, she is," Avery agreed before he hopped to his feet to pull out the chair on the other side of him. Riley hugged her way around the table first. When she reached him, he said, "I want you to meet someone."

"Ah, Layla Jenson." They shook. Quite vigorously, on Riley's part.

Layla asked, "You're watching the cook-off?"

"Heck, yeah, I am!" she declared. "I would've stopped by the ranch, but I was having a breakthrough with Whit. Y'all," she enthusiastically announced, "he performed in front of *five* live people!" She flashed all fingers on her free hand.

"As opposed to five *dead* people?" Chance jested.

She shot him a sassy look.

To Layla, she said, "Whit suffers from stage fright. Records all of his performances. But last night, he allowed some folks into his back-yard where he's built his own stage. Boy howdy, was he sweatin' bullets. Pulled it off, though. Like a firecracker!" Her deep-blue eyes sparkled. "I'll have him entertaining an audience of twelve by the end of next week, mark my words! Before we know it, he'll be in Nashville with me, singing my songs."

Avery took her case from her, and she plopped into her seat.

"Is there a crush happenin' here?" Chance asked her.

"Could be." Riley's expression turned sly.

She was a stunning redhead who emitted the same energy as Brodi, so Layla knew they would hit it off.

Various conversations ensued, with more laughter erupting than was polite for a public establishment, and yet no one outside their group seemed to mind. Likely expected it from a family with charisma to spare. Also, Layla suspected the Reeds didn't get out that much as a collective unit, given all they had going on at the ranch, and individually.

When Riley'd had her fill of Luke's food, she shoved back her chair, grabbed her guitar case, and went to the opposite corner of the vast restaurant, where two men were setting up a drum kit and amps. The bass player tuned his guitar as Riley tested the sound system.

She told the crowd, "Y'all know my two best cohorts from high school, twins Ken and Len."

A round of applause followed.

"That commonality bonded us at first," she said with mischief in her tone. "Then we stumbled upon loud instruments in the music room while all the other kids were on the playground at recess—and were inseparable thereafter."

"Didn't y'all get busted for that?" asked an audience member with a deep, authoritative voice.

Riley searched the cantina for the culprit who'd made the query. She smiled. As vibrantly as all the other Reeds.

"Well, Principal Meyers, you weren't exactly Johnny-on-the-spot the first few weeks we were, uh, *practicin'*." She cringed. "But you did eventually sniff us out."

"I was just giving y'all the chance to get better," he retorted. And made a scary face.

Everyone laughed.

Including Riley.

"Considering music was part of the academic curriculum," she told her captive audience, "Principal Meyers did allow us to continue our experiment. Here's how we fared."

She struck the first chords, and the band launched into an upbeat tune that got people on their feet and filling the dance floor.

Avery had Layla in his arms before she could even catch her breath.

He pulled her in tight, given the limited space.

She didn't mind.

"I can't get over how dynamic your family is," she told him.

"We have our moments."

"Times a lot." She snuggled closer so she could speak softer. "Guessing I'm breaking plenty of women's hearts tonight."

"Again . . . I haven't noticed."

She stared up at him. "Maybe tilt your hat back a little, cowboy. So you can see properly."

"I'm gazing down on all I wanna see, honey."

She nearly missed a step as warmth oozed down her spine. But he had a firm grip on her. "Less flirtatious appeal would keep me upright."

"But do I really want you upright?" He flashed a grin. "I mean, all the time?" He shook his head. "No, I do not."

"Your attempt to seduce me is unwarranted," she assured him. "I'm going home with you, cowboy."

"Doesn't that make my night?" He kissed her.

She teased him a bit, saying, "Only because that's where my car is."

"Ha, ha."

He gave her a spin, and she cozied up to him again.

"This actually isn't a slow song," she mused.

"Do we care?" he countered.

She nipped his lower lip. And said, "No, we do not."

They kept to their private spot on the dance floor as Riley and her boys morphed from one tune to the next.

Until Avery let out a low groan and told Layla, "You rubbing against me like this is inciting all kinds of wicked thoughts."

"And you only have so much time before you're back to cooking for the cowboys."

"Not to mention, I bet Mateo's itching to get Wyatt home."

Layla nodded. "Points well taken."

Chance was ready to knock off, too, given he had an equally early morning on the horizon.

They waved to Riley, said their goodbyes to everyone else, and departed.

As Layla fell into bed with Avery, she said, "I have to be back in town tomorrow for the production meeting with Todd that never actually happened."

His brow raised, reminding her that she'd yet to enlighten him about what'd had her in tears.

"I'm too tired to talk about it," she admitted. "And the only reason I'd keep you up this late is if you wanted to make love to me."

"You know I do."

She smiled. "Then have at it, cowboy."

# Chapter Fifteen

Layla drove into town in the morning, at a respectable hour.

She met up with Todd and Brodi for brunch at the hotel.

"Is your virtue still intact where the sexy cousin who owns the cantina is concerned?" Layla asked her best friend.

Todd gagged on his sip of cappuccino.

Brodi gave an exasperated look. And said, "If you think I grew social butterfly wings overnight, think again. Girl, that good-lookin' cowboy gave me one songful worth of twirls around the dance floor after you vacated, and I was nothing more than putty in his hands." Her *eh* emoji face took over. "What am *I* to do with that?"

"Meaning you ditched him the first chance you got," Layla commented.

"Left Todd at the table and took the rental car back here."

"Yeah, thanks for that," Todd lamented. "Jack had to drop me off."

"Thought you were smitten by Riley Reed," Brodi replied in between bites of her bagel, smothered with strawberry cream cheese. "Didn't want to rush you off or anything."

Now Layla nearly spit out her latte. She covered her mouth for a second, composed herself, and demanded, "What's this?"

"Mm-hmm," Brodi confirmed. "That woman had him all twisted in knots."

"Gimme a break!" he proclaimed. Displaying much more emotion than normal. "She's jailbait for God's sake!"

"She's twenty-five!" Layla and Brodi said in unison.

"Six years younger than me. So . . . totally off limits," he averred. And sipped. Then added, "What on earth would I do with a tornado in a trailer park anyway?" He pointed a finger at Brodi and said, "I can barely control *you*."

"Some women aren't meant to be controlled," she lobbed back.

"Some women shouldn't be so exuberant that they make men crazed in the head," he countered.

Layla finally enjoyed more of her latte. Then ventured, "Is there something happening here that I should know about?" She flitted a finger between her executive producer and her assistant.

"He's. My. Boss. Said it once. Said it twice. Will keep on sayin' it." Brodi was done with her bagel and set her napkin next to her plate. She pushed back her chair. "I have emails to answer, and you two have shit to talk about." She stood, grabbed her purse, and marched off.

Layla's gaze drifted to Todd.

He draped an arm over the top of his chair. Waved a dismissive hand. And said, "I might have a thing for redheads."

"*That* one in particular?" Layla prodded.

"She gets under my skin. All her thoughts and ideas—and the way she's a workaholic, like me. Brodi's mind never shuts down. I dig that."

"She's also very pretty."

"Very."

"Hmm."

"Yeah. Hmm."

"Okay, then," Layla said. "Perhaps we ought to have that production meeting now."

"You still wanna get your travel on?"

"You know I do. We've got Tulsa, Whitefish, and that ranch outside of St. Louis on our agenda."

"We've got more than that going on." He reached into the stylish brown leather backpack he'd slung over one side of his wooden armchair and extracted a file folder that he dropped onto the table between them. He flipped open the cover and said, "Brodi compiled all the latest analytics on the show—your dark horse is racing toward the finish line like nothing we've seen before."

She sifted through the top sheets, marveling at the numbers she reviewed.

"There's more, Layla. Keep digging. We've got sponsors coming out of our collective ass. They want ad time galore. And if you delve deeper, you'll get to the companies that are seeking you out to endorse their products. Totally running the gamut. Clothes, boots, and hats. Cookware and all things barbecue—like grilling utensils, charcoal, and hell . . . even grills." He gave a half snort.

She set aside the pages and speared him with a look. "These sponsorships give us our sixth season."

"Seventh, eighth, ninth . . . whatever you want, Layla." His gaze didn't waver. "And those endorsement deals? They'll pay the remainder of your debt and set you up for life."

They continued to stare at each other.

Layla's mind whirled.

Todd nodded. "You loved those BBQ competitions your daddy would take you to when you were growing up. You talked about them in college because you and I were both from Texas."

"We were fish out of water at NYU."

"Yeah. And while you were trying to emerge as someone other than who you were, deep in your heart, you were always a country girl."

"I always was," she confessed. "I just thought all those glittery gowns and galas would make me someone more important, relevant."

She toyed with the corner of her napkin, hating how she'd lost her way. And yet . . .

"I didn't like being *just* the farmer's daughter, Todd. I had more interests than being on a tractor or stuck in a stuffy little kitchen. And yet . . ." She shook her head. "I loved cooking. I still do. I'd forgotten that along the way. Maybe because I felt stifled there. Or maybe because . . . that was my mama's kitchen before me."

A tear fell to her plate.

Todd said, "Sometimes we're desperate to break free of a box we think we're put in."

Her head snapped up. "Exactly. From the moment you told me Christopher had OD'd . . . I've felt like one of those windup toys with the clown on springs."

He grinned. "A jack-in-the-box."

"You crank it just enough and see a whole new world." She sat straighter in her chair. "Including the endorsements. I said no from the beginning, to minimize where my face is seen. Not anticipating anyone would recognize me, of course not. But there was still that niggling fear that kept me on a smaller platform. No offense."

"None taken. We had to build an audience—and you've seen our recent numbers. We're not small anymore, sweetheart."

"No, we are not."

Todd added, "We haven't even touched on the job ops Brodi's put in a separate digital file for you. But I had her print them all out. Just so you can get the full view of your career landscape."

"I told you the offers had no bearing because I couldn't provide details they'd want in the interviewing process."

"Now you can."

"Damn. Now I can."

"Make no mistake, Layla. I'm not abandoning you. I have other projects to work on, yes. But I'm always available to be your consultant."

She eyed him curiously. "What are you saying, Todd?"

"That you don't need me as your executive producer." He collected all the sheets into a tidy stack and returned them to their folder. Pushed it her way. "You can manage on your own, with your crew. And Brodi. All of your themes have been sensational—and successful. And with more sponsors in your back pocket . . ." He grinned. "I can't help but drop the reins and let you run wild."

Her eyes squeezed shut for a moment.

Then they stared at each other again. She blinked. He lifted a brow.

"You're . . . what?" she queried. "Giving me the show?"

"Well, you did conceptualize it. Are a cocreator. The host." He shrugged. "For all intents and purposes, other than you don't direct the cameramen or engage with the judges, you are in charge of this production."

"Yes, but I need a buffer between me and The Three—and someone whose expertise is managing the cameramen and the subsequent editing."

"Come on, Layla," he said. "You've got that all under control. If you want to continue with this premise and this platform . . . then continue. I'll back you. As will all these sponsors. I mean . . . really study the list!" He gave a wide-eyed expression and laughed. Then more seriously contended, "Or branch out. World's your oyster at this point."

Words she'd dreamed of hearing . . . but never had. Until now.

"That's what's so surreal," she murmured. "That's why the toy popping out of the box resonates with me. I've been trapped for so long. But now . . . I'm breathing the fresh air."

"Well deserved, my friend. Well deserved."

They finished their brunch quietly, each contemplating all the variables left on the table.

Then Layla said, "This was an enlightening get-together. I'm going to hit the ladies' before I head back to the ranch."

"Don't overlook all the possibilities. You can do as you please, Layla. You earned the right."

She gathered her tote, stuffing the folder inside. She left a kiss on his cheek and said, "I love you to pieces. You can't even begin to imagine."

"I understand I'm irresistible."

She laughed. "Yeah. That." She shook her head and added, "Don't let me hold you back. In any way."

"You haven't, and you won't."

"I appreciate all you've done for me, Todd. I just don't know where to go from here. Other than . . ." She gestured toward the hallway. "The restroom."

"Go."

She wove her way through the small conglomeration of tables toward the facilities. After freshening up, she exited into the alcove and took a moment to call Brodi on the housephone, just to ensure she was okay.

"Don't know why that man gets me all riled up," Brodi huffed. "Todd's got less charm and zest than that Luke Reed—or even Chance Reed. And yet I would've been fine in his dancin' arms all night long."

"You were the one to shun him," Layla reminded her.

"I like my job. I want to keep it!"

"Don't go thinking you can't have your cake and eat it too."

"'Scuse me?"

Layla sighed. "I'm not committing to anything. But Todd might move on from our production. Then . . . you're open to . . . whatever."

"OMG! Am I about to lose my job without even having *slept* with the boss?!"

"Not." Layla scoffed. "Wherever I pivot . . . you're welcome to go with me." She more specifically stated, "I *want* you to go with me."

Silence filled the line.

Layla didn't press for a response.

Emotion tinged Brodi's voice as she said, "I want to go where you go. We're a team, aren't we?"

"A damn good one." The pause between them was as poignant as when Avery and Ritchie shared a moment that said so much. That they were partners.

"Happy to hear that." Brodi sniffled. "See you tonight at the TRIPLE R."

"Try not to get Todd all in a dither on the ride out. I don't want y'all crashing."

"Not like I'm gonna give him a hummer on the drive, girl. Well . . . I can't guarantee that."

"Oh, my God. TMI while he's still *my* boss."

"I'm out. You do you—and Avery."

"Ha, ha. Though . . . that's a given."

"Just don't forget the little people on your rise to the top."

Layla swallowed a sudden hard lump. "I'm not on a rise. I have a cook-off to finish. And never, ever in the history of *ever* would I forget about you. A *non*-little person, by the way."

"How you flatter me. See you later."

"Love to you."

"Same."

Layla hung up.

She took a few deep breaths. Tried to silo all her thoughts so she could concentrate on the immediate picture, not the bigger one ready to swell in her head.

But her ruminations were disrupted.

"Tess Billings. Right?"

She jumped at the unfamiliar voice behind her. And the name he'd used.

"You are not a woman who's easy to get alone."

*Oh. Holy. Hell.*

The first terrifying thing to run through her brain was that the henchman had caught up to her.

A chill chased along her spine.

In a shaky voice, she said, "You must not have heard the news. Christopher Courtland is dead. No need to come looking for me anymore."

"I have zero association with Christopher Courtland." The accent was a southern drawl.

This perplexed her.

Layla whirled around to find a tall, muscular man in boots, faded jeans, Western shirt, and a hat standing not more than a couple of feet away from her.

"I've been lookin' forward to meeting you," he said.

She stared into blue eyes that ran in one family. Along with the height and the broad shoulders. The dark hair.

"Caleb Reed," she said on a quavering breath.

"In the flesh."

She wasn't sure who was more dangerous. Him or the henchman.

"What do you want, Mr. Reed?"

"Oh, no call for the 'mister,' Miss Billings. Neither my brother, nor our father, subscribed to that. Caleb's fine."

"Whatever you prefer. And it's not Miss Billings. It's Miss Jenson."

"I'm a little confused about the details."

Her blood ran cold. "You listened in on my conversation the other night? Here at the restaurant?"

"I do apologize for that." He removed his hat and placed it over his heart. All sincere-like. "I was hoping for a moment to speak with you. But then everything got a bit tense at your table."

"Yes, because someone died. So what can I do for you?" she asked as her trembling fingers reached for her cell phone in her bag.

"No need to call 911. Or anyone else." He raised his hands. Still holding the hat. "I only want one thing from you."

*What could that possibly be?*

And exactly how worried should she be that he wanted her alone? Panic skittered through her.

What Avery had told her about this man having a short fuse was still ripe in her mind. Along with Avery's angst—and his pain.

She took a step backward, only to bump up against the ledge of the shelf the housephone sat on.

His body was between her and the nearest exit. She was backed into a corner.

Her heart rate accelerated. Her breath got stuck in her throat for several seconds.

She'd been wary of being in this situation for the past five years. She just hadn't expected it to be her cowboy crush's father who was bearing down on her.

"Why are you here?" she demanded in as stable a voice as she could manage.

"It's a very simple request," he assured her.

Yet if he were telling the truth, she wouldn't feel the tremors shooting down her legs.

"What is it?" she asked.

"For Avery to win this cook-off."

Layla gaped. The panic increased.

"I have no say over that," she asserted. "I designed the competition to remove myself from any sort of persuasion or influence. I—"

"I want my boy to win." He took a step toward her; she had nowhere to go. "He deserves to win. Ain't got no one better on your roster who can do what Avery does. And the entire ranch setup . . . that can't be beat either."

"That all depends on how the judges feel. How the viewers weigh in," she told him as her stomach roiled. And in her peripheral vision, she wondered if she could skirt him and outrun him to the side door.

*Yeah. Right.*

"I don't think you're hearing me, Miss Jenson," he said in a strained tone. "I want Avery to win. You make sure that he does."

He gave her a pointed look. Then he moved away, toward that exit she'd been eyeing.

Something snapped within her.

Likely due to that newfound freedom of hers.

She wouldn't keep cowering. Not anymore.

"Hey," she called out—brazenly, though her insides seized up.

He halted. Spun back to face her.

Layla forced herself not to shrink away. She even hitched her chin. "Are you threatening me?"

He plopped his hat on his head. And said, "You ought to go see your daddy. You never know how long he might have, Tess."

He turned from her. And strode out the door.

# Chapter Sixteen

*Oh, my God.*

*Oh, my God.*

*Oh. My. Fucking. God.*

Layla was frozen where she stood. Certain all the color had drained from her face.

She was shocked she still had a pulse. Shocked she was still standing, what with her knees knocking together.

*What the everlasting hell?*

She stared after Caleb Reed, wanting to retreat, to get far away from here, in the event he came back.

And yet she couldn't trust her shaky legs to carry her so much as an inch.

The man had not seriously just told her to ensure Avery won the competition.

*Yes, he had.*

Being horrified and confounded at the same time was an odd mix.

It kept her immobilized until two women appeared in the hallway, heading to the restroom.

Layla forced herself into action, taking the exit Caleb Reed had. He was long gone, as was the vehicle he'd come in, evidenced by the lack of activity in the parking lot.

Though she maintained a weather eye as she unlocked the door to her rental, slid a gaze to the back seat—just to be sure no one was hiding out there—and then slipped behind the wheel.

She took the long stretch to the ranch, checking her rearview mirror for anyone tailing her.

There was a truck behind her, so she flipped on her opposite signal before the entrance to the TRIPLE R and pulled over across the way, letting the vehicle pass.

Her hands trembled as they gripped the wheel.

She waited for a spell, just to confirm the driver didn't execute a U-ey and backtrack.

All clear, she turned onto the dirt road and plugged in the access code. The huge arms of the wrought-iron gate opened toward her. She crept through them, stopped, and allowed them to close with no one following her in.

Her stomach was still twisted; her nerves still tweaked. She had no idea how to tell Avery about what had just occurred. Hell, she hadn't even told him yet about Christopher's untimely demise—and what it meant to her today. And in the grand scheme of things.

Now she had to explain about his dad—and let him stew over what this might mean for him.

For her as well?

She continued to sit in the middle of the ranch's main road, mulling this over.

She rehashed in her mind the entire conversation with Caleb. Considered his tone, which didn't seem to be quite as menacing now as it'd been at the hotel. She tried to configure his physical placement too. Sure, he'd been too close for comfort. But he hadn't crowded her.

And when he'd covered his heart with his hat . . . she'd felt genuine emotion on his part.

*I want my boy to win . . . Ain't got no one better on your roster who can do what Avery does. And the entire ranch setup . . . that can't be beat either.*

The man had said those words with conviction—not with an underlying sense of greed that he'd gain something from Avery being named Best Bunkhouse Cook but from the belief his son was good enough to clinch the competition.

He'd also touched on that extra component Layla wanted to home in on when it came to the encompassing TRIPLE R and the family dynamic.

Her heartbeat slowed. The tremors through her body diminished.

But she was still tangled in uncertainty.

Catching sight of Chance with his crew and the herd, she took an offshoot and traveled to the ridge just above them. She got out of the car and walked through the ankle-high grass and the wildflowers to the split-rail fencing.

Chance saw her and called out to his lead, she presumed, "Keep checkin' the tags on those cows. I'll be back." He galloped toward her, eased out of his saddle, and tied his horse. He tipped his hat. "To what do I owe the honor, Miss Layla? Finally come to your senses and realize I'm the prized stud on this ranch?"

She laughed, and it loosened some of the tension within her.

"I do appreciate your humor, Chance."

He gave a playful frown. "Aww . . . just can't win you over, can I?"

"You know where my affection lies."

"And yet . . . here you are." He eyed her with intrigue.

"Yes, well. I could use some advice. Related to your brother."

"Now, sweetheart, don't go dragging me between the two of you. If you've got something to say to Avery, you just speak your mind to him."

She blew out a breath. "It's not of the romantic variety, Chance. It's about your father."

His head whipped back. "Didn't see that one coming."

"If you'd stop flirting with me—"

"It's harmless. For the most part." He winked. Then asked in a more severe tone, "What does Caleb Reed have to do with . . . anything involving you?"

"He's been stalking me."

"Are you fuckin' shitting me?!" he erupted, hands flying in the air. So that he startled the horse. "Goddamn it," he groaned. He soothed his steed and then returned his attention to Layla. "How did you find out?"

"He cornered me at the hotel."

Though . . . that wasn't necessarily true, as she'd just mentally recapped. She was the one to back herself against the phone stall.

The rage visibly tore through Chance, try as he might to control it.

Through clenched teeth, he said, "If you're going to ask me not to mention this to Avery, you already know I'll say no to you, Layla. This is *not* something I'll keep from my brother. Or from Jack. From anyone on this ranch. Your safety is now on the line."

"Yes," she repeated. Then shook her head. "Maybe."

His gaze narrowed.

She was about to expound on all she'd dissected minutes ago, but the sudden thundering of hooves had her sparing a glance over her shoulder and up the ridge where Avery came barreling toward them on his horse.

"Fuck," she murmured. Gazing back at Chance on the other side of the fence, she said, "Here comes the cavalry. He'll want to know what we're talking about, and neither one of us can lie to him."

"You came to me because you what to hear how to manage this piece of garbage without bringing Avery into the equation—distracting him from the cook-off."

"You're smarter than you let on, cowboy."

He smirked.

Avery slowed his pace as he reached them. Then he flung his leg over the saddle and hopped to the ground. He tied the reins to the top railing and gave both Layla and Chance an inquisitive look.

"Something I should know about here?" he asked in a gruff voice.

"Oh, for Chrissake," Chance huffed. "I couldn't steal her away, even if I put my best effort into it."

Layla closed the space between her and Avery, kissed his clenched jaw, and whispered, "You're well aware of this."

He harrumphed.

She laughed softly.

"No sense in getting turned inside out over us," Chance told him. "You've got real fish to fry."

Avery's eyes rolled upward. Then landed on Chance. "Yeah, but no. Ain't got fish on the menu today."

Chance seemed to do a quick rewind and then nodded. "Right. Can't use a figurative term with the word 'real.'"

"He gets brighter every day," Avery quipped. "Honey, give him another forty years, and he'll be as ripe and wise as a turnip that's still on the truck."

She stifled another laugh. "Be that as it may, now that I've had a convo with him, I'm thinking I might be mistaking your dad's intentions."

"My *what* now?" Avery turned rigid—*like that.*

"Sweetheart," Chance said to her, "you should let me teach you the subtle art of easing people into uncomfortable situations."

She shot him a frustrated look. "I had to give this due thought first, Chance. Not be strictly reactive. Then I discussed it with you. As I did—saying it all out loud—I started to form a different opinion of this scenario."

Her gaze shifted to Avery. She explained the entire scene at the hotel, while he paced and hissed with fury. Ripped off his gloves and shoved them in his back pocket.

Then he gently clasped her shoulders.

"Did he hurt you?" he quietly demanded, with enough worry and aggravation to bring a tear to her eye.

"No, Avery, he didn't. He didn't touch me. Just told me he wants me to make sure you win," she stated. "And now that I have some distance from the incident, I have this sense that he wasn't implying what I thought he was."

"How so?" Avery asked.

She sighed. Shook her head to clear it. Then told both him and Chance, "I assumed he was threatening me, pressuring me into a scam. So that I'd cheat on your behalf, Avery."

"But you can't do that. You *wouldn't* do that," Avery averred.

"Correct on both counts, cowboy. And he wasn't outright encouraging me in that direction."

She gave this even more thought, reaching deep into her soul for this one.

"He was telling me to make sure that I *did* do what I could to help you. Keep you focused. Bring in whatever elements that are acceptable. He just wants you to be recognized for your talents, Avery." A hint of empathy and emotion seeped through her veins. She added, "He told me to go see my own daddy. That you never know how much time you have left with someone. That wasn't a threat either. That was a life reminder. And perhaps . . . there's something in his life that's got him feeling it's too short for bad blood."

"That is *all* on him!" Chance roared.

"I don't disagree," she said. "It's just—"

"Layla." Chance gave her a stern look. "You are sweet as a peach, darlin'. I adore the hell out of you for that. And I know you want some roses and sunshine to chase away the dark cloud that is Caleb Reed. But please don't buy into his manipulation."

"Remember what I said, honey," Avery commented. "He'll turn on you on a dime. Be a silver-tongued devil one second and a rattlesnake with a venomous bite the next."

She nodded. "I heed these warnings. But my gut is now telling me something different, Avery. He only seemed ominous at first because I've lived on the edge for five years, waiting for someone to steal behind me and take me by surprise. He did just that. Only . . . not to harm me. Hell, he had the opportunity to whisk me out the side door. No one would have stopped him or even seen him—there was no one else there."

This infuriated Avery further, making him jerk his hat off and rake a hand through his hair. His jaw worked. His shoulders squared.

She rested a hand on his upper arm and said, "I do have lessons from when I was younger, and my daddy helped me to see people—either for being genuine or for being grifters. I understand your father has always been the latter. But in hindsight, I grasp there was a solemnness to his actions and words today. He wants you to win, plain and simple."

"So he can swoop in and con Avery out of the cash—*that's* plain and simple!" Chance bellowed. "He'll extort you, little bro. Claim he'll go public with Layla and her show not being on the up-and-up. Putting her career and her reputation—Todd's and the crew's too—in jeopardy. So that you'll cave and give him what he wants. *Money.*" He pinned Avery with a firm look. "It's always about the money. Every single time. And you know this."

Layla's breath caught in her throat over his vehemence.

"Or he'll come up with some cock-and-bull story about needing help with a made-up medical condition," Chance continued. "That could be what his 'life's too short' premise is all about."

"That's a fair point," Layla concurred, finding her voice.

Chance glanced down at her and said, "I know you have a big heart, and you hold Avery's—and this ranch's—best interests in that heart. But I know my dad. And he's no saint, Layla. If your initial instinct was that it was a threat, go with it." His gaze landed on Avery again. "And we protect her."

"Never said I wouldn't."

Chance strode to his horse, unhitched him, hoisted himself into the saddle, and galloped off.

Layla was back to being sick to her stomach.

She stared at Avery.

He swept his fingers along her temple. Kissed her, and whispered, "Never think twice about having returned to your values. You want to see the good in people. But like you said, you've got instincts, and you've been trained well. Don't let my family drama mislead you, honey. This isn't just a misunderstanding that ended in implosion. All facts are grounded in reality and are indisputable. He sold us out before. He'll do it again."

He pressed his lips to her forehead.

"Avery—"

"Honey, I have this next competition to prepare for. You can go up to the main house, or you can join me at the bunkhouse to get Ritchie rollin'. Hell, you can just take a long bath in my house. Whatever you want. Just do me a favor and stay on the ranch. You shouldn't be out and about if my dad's in town."

"I'll join you," she said. "My take on this scenario compared to yours and Chance's doesn't mean I'll do anything risky."

"I'm holding you to that, darlin'. As will the family. They'll be by your side. And hoping you let them look after you."

"I don't want to be any trouble."

He kissed her tenderly and whispered, "Too late, honey. And we're all good with that."

She stared into his eyes. They were glowing with warmth and depth. Also . . . concern.

"I promise I'll behave," she said. "I'll go to the chuck hall with you."

"Go on up to your car, then."

He gave her a pat on the butt to lighten the mood.

"That borders on patronizing, cowboy."

He winked. "Not when I'm just lovin' on you, honey."

He returned to his saddle and loped off.

Layla watched him go. Feeling heart palpitations at the sight of him on his horse as they headed toward the bunkhouse.

It took her some time to get herself together. Then she climbed the ridge and got into her car. She dropped the vehicle, her suitcase, and her tote off before walking to the chuck hall.

The strain between her and Avery lingered. Ratcheting up her anxiety over the issue with Caleb.

But they got through lunch and cleanup. Then Avery and Ritchie worked on the venison for supper.

The smoke was so delicious as it hovered in the air, Layla hung around the fringes just inhaling the aroma.

The judges came in, and she remained far from them. Her concentration was on asking Avery and Ritchie the right questions, while also staying out of their way as they dealt with windy conditions when a stiff breeze rustled the leaves on the trees and swept through the outdoor facility. They had to maintain their pit temps.

While being served, The Three noted the right bark and tenderness, meaning Avery got all the textures perfect. His sides were winners too.

Judge #1 said, "What's also commendable is your overall presentation. You have wonderful facilities here, with all the bells and whistles."

"There are some things we'd like to add to improve efficiencies and up our skill set," Avery admitted.

"As it currently stands," Judge #2 offered, "y'all have created a welcoming environment and one that shows a high regard for your staff."

"We couldn't ranch without 'em, sir."

Judge #3 told him, "I was particularly pleased with your buffet table settings. Those beautiful platters made the venison more elegant, and the entire aesthetic was eye-catching. Also respectful of your cowboys and ranch hands."

"My aunt's been modest about the value of her pottery, but I have to agree that it livens up the meals."

"This has been a great series here at the TRIPLE R." Layla stepped in as The Three prepared to depart. "We have one final segment to go with bunkhouse cook Avery Reed and 'Right Hand' Ritchie. We'll see y'all tomorrow for tempting treats straight out of the Dutch ovens. Go on now—light your own fire." She gave her signature pearly smile.

One of the cameramen let them know when they were clear and the outro credits were rolling.

Layla had such a good feeling about Avery's segments, the smile didn't fade. Not even with thoughts of his dad hanging in the balance.

She sidled up to him and said, "Make *me* a promise, cowboy."

"Anything, honey."

"When you win, do or buy something nice for yourself. Not just what will benefit the chuck hall, but *you*."

"Layla, whatever benefits the chuck hall, benefits me. All of us."

She couldn't argue with that logic.

So she didn't.

◆  ◆  ◆

Jack and Jillian—who were in attendance again—congratulated Avery, with Jack saying, "Willet Hayes has nothing on you, cuz. Even with bison on the menu."

"I'm not going to let my guard down," Avery commented. "His food sounded to be spot on."

"But his presentation was nothing like yours," Jillian pointed out. "Nor were his sides as ambitious as yours—I can say that about the other contestants as well. And the judges know this is actual standard fare for you to serve. You couldn't have just pulled out those ovens on your first rodeo, with everything at the right cooking times, without having done this over and over. I think that's a key factor."

"Definitely not my first rodeo." He chuckled at her terminology.

"I'll make a cowgirl out of this woman yet," Jack teased.

"Well, I was only a transplant in Seattle," she reminded him. "I came from the Southwest."

"And I appreciate you supporting us," Avery commented. Then he clapped his hands together and said, "Now, Ritchie and I have some cleaning to do."

"That's our cue to exit," Jack replied.

"Figures," Avery mocked him.

Jack laughed. Then told Layla, "We put your groceries in the fridge. Y'all have a good night." He winked conspiratorially.

When the place was cleared out, Avery asked, "What was that all about?"

"I'm making you supper tonight. You finish up here—then come see me at the house." She kissed him in her flirty way. Then whirled around and flounced off, swaying her hips and putting ideas in his head that went well beyond eating. Hell, he could forgo any meal when she was around.

But he still had work to do.

"Let's get to it, Ritchie."

◆ ◆ ◆

An hour later, Avery came through his front door, hung his hat on the rack in the foyer, took the step down into the living room, and crossed to the kitchen, propping his shoulder against the wide opening. He admired the view of Layla at the L-shaped kitchen island, her back to him. She wore one of those body-clinging lacy nighties and a G-string. In lavender.

Something about the soft colors she selected and the way they complemented her blonde curls and her honeyed skin, and all her luscious curves, had his heart constricting as much as it made his cock twitch.

*Down, boy.*

She was in the throes of a fragrant creation that also had his stomach clenching.

His own cooking didn't stimulate his appetite too much because he was always focused on the prep and the outcome. The latter of which he did take pleasure in, of course. It was just that he had laser focus when it came to his job.

Well . . . except when Layla was present.

It took all the willpower he possessed to keep his eye on the ball when she was standing next to him, interviewing him, her alluring scent wafting under his nose to compete with BBQ, her lashes batting in an inviting way. Her smile sweet and sexy at the same time.

And while his mind was on "sweet," his senses became more attuned to what she was whipping up, with Garth playing in the background.

Which had him chuckling because he didn't think wild horses could drag his attention away from the visual before him. Though, technically, his gaze remained. On her ass.

She glanced over her shoulder, her brow hitching.

He said, "There's nothing patronizing about me enjoying what you have to offer." He pulled in a long breath. Let it out at a slow, measured pace. "Damn, darlin'. You get the juices flowing."

She turned to face him. She hadn't even bothered with an apron.

A low groan tore from his lips. His gaze roamed her body, landing on her nipples, puckered against the dainty material, and her chest rising and falling—pretty much in time with his.

"Now you're just torturing me," he murmured.

He ripped apart his flap and tossed his shirt aside. "You don't mind that I'm a little sweaty, do you?"

"Oh, God, no," she said on a sigh.

"And I'm not interrupting what you're cooking?" he asked as he unfastened his belt buckle while strolling toward her.

"Hot-and-sweet Italian sausages are simmering in the slow cooker, after I grilled them and got nice marks and the right coloring."

"I was going to make that for you."

"But you've had your hands full."

"They're about to be fuller," he whispered as he palmed her breasts. His thumbs skimmed over the beaded centers, and he felt the shiver run through her.

Her nails dipped into his biceps. "You have just the right touch, cowboy."

"You inspire me."

She bit his lip. "Feel free to ravage me."

"That is always on my mind."

His mouth crashed over hers. He kissed her deeply, tasting chardonnay and the hint of the basil and oregano she was using with the sausage.

One hand remained on her breast, massaging, while his other arm wound around the small of her back.

She melded to him, and that spurred him on.

His finger and thumb rolled her nipple, then pinched lightly. Jolting her.

She moaned into his mouth. Rubbed herself against him.

His cock pulsated in wicked beats.

There was no way they were making it to his bedroom.

He lifted Layla into his arms, and her legs twined his waist. He carried her to the end of the table, kicking away a chair with his foot. He set her on the sturdy wooden top, pushed her hem up, and whisked off her panties.

While she popped the button on his jeans and slid the zipper down its track, he nabbed the condom from his wallet.

"Oh, with the foresight," she mused with a twinkle in her eyes.

"Think we've established I have difficulty keeping my hands off you."

"I do find that to be incredibly appealing."

"Mm, don't get me started on what's appealing."

She kissed him with the delicateness that made him crazy. That had him warring between wanting to drown in her soft, feathery kisses all night or bury himself in her heat and moisture.

Either would be fine with him. She was so damn tempting, he just let the moments sweep them away.

Eventually, she murmured against his lips, "I chose the slow-cooker method in case you were feeling frisky. No need for me to tend to this part of the cooking process."

He let out a low laugh. "I'm more than frisky, darlin'. I'm burning up."

"We should get you out of your clothes."

"We should get you out of *yours*." And with that, he divested her of the nightie.

Then he shoved down his jeans and boxer briefs.

She wagged a brow at how ready he was for her and said, "I'm just as primed."

"Good to know. Can't wait another second." He sheathed himself.

"Nothing more exciting than that, cowboy."

He eased into her, and she flattened her feet to the table, her toes curling around the ledge for support.

His arm encircled her lower back again, and she gripped his biceps. Her pelvis tilted, raising her a tad off the table and angling her hips so that he could start a slow, smooth rhythm, sliding along her tight, wet canal. Inching deeper and deeper into her.

"Like that," she murmured. "Take your time."

"Got no choice," he confessed. "Baby, you squeezing and teasing me will send me over the edge in no time flat."

"I love that."

He pumped into her. Knew when he hit that magical spot because she clutched him fiercely with her inner walls and moved with him. Her head fell back. His teeth scraped over her neck, his tongue soothing. Then he suckled, and she moaned.

His cock thickened.

He stroked quicker, with more force.

"Yes," she mumbled. "Oh, God, yes."

He slipped his hands under her and cupped her ass cheeks. Drove into her.

Her arms wound around his neck, holding him close.

"Take us there," she whispered in his ear.

He thrust and gyrated with a natural finesse that she sparked, and then felt her body tense. She contracted around him. He grunted.

A second later, she cried, "Avery!" and fell apart.

He was right behind her, everything within him exploding.

More than just physically.

It took him a minute or so to get his bearings as he stared at her. She smiled, her tiger eyes glowing.

"Jesus," he said. "What you do to me . . ."

"It's mutual," she told him in a languid voice. "So don't wonder whether I have designs on someone else, cowboy. We aren't ideal or fated, and yet . . . I'm only interested in you."

A complex statement. One he felt straight to his soul but couldn't rectify.

He gazed at her for a while longer, cataloging everything about her sultry expression and the honesty in her shimmering irises.

Then he gave her a tender kiss.

And said, "I love you, Layla Jenson."

Her heart swelled. Her eyes misted.

"Again," she murmured, "mutual."

Her palm pressed to the side of his face, her thumb sweeping along his cheek.

"I know that won't keep you here forever," he said.

"In a perfect world, we'd be perfect together."

"Making me hate the imperfect world."

Her lips brushed his. Against them, she whispered, "Nothing we can do about that, cowboy. We're living with our personal circumstances. Some good, some tumultuous."

"Yeah, about that . . ." He let out a sharp breath, withdrew from her, and tidied himself up. Only put his boxer briefs on, though. For which she was grateful. He slid her G-string up her legs. Handed over her nightie. And said, "I still don't know what went down the other night."

"Let me get the peppers and sausage. I'm trying them with the farfalle you suggested."

She got to her feet and went to the granite counter to fill the bowls she'd already set out.

Meanwhile, Avery refilled her wineglass and poured chardonnay into the one she had for him. He set the table with place mats, linen napkins, and silverware at the opposite end of where their quickie had taken place.

"Sit," Layla instructed. "Let me serve you."

She brought him a dish, cranked shredded parmesan on the top, smiled provocatively, and then went back for hers.

"This broth has the right seasoning," he commented. "And those sausage coins are juicy looking."

"Taste the peppers and onions," she said as she joined him.

He did. Nodded. And told her, "You like them one or two degrees just after the limp snap."

"So they're not crispy. Nor mushy or slimy." She cringed. "Can't stand it when they cross that fine line and lose so much of their flavor."

He eyed her closely and asked, "You ever consider doing your own cooking show?"

"Please. Smoke a turducken? I wouldn't know where to begin."

"That's modest but untrue. You presented all the right questions while I was preparing mine."

"Okay, so I read recipes," she said. "I also learn from the contestants every season. Plus, I have my own concoctions from years past, on the farm. However . . . I really like the hosting part. Kindly remember I was once a wallflower."

"That's still not something I can wrap my mind around," he admitted. "But I do hear what you're saying. And that's why *Light Your Fire* suits you."

"In some ways, yes." She didn't say more, just sampled the meal and allowed Avery to do the same.

When he slid a sly gaze her way, she laughed.

"Sun-dried tomatoes and spinach," he said. "Excellent additions. And you think you couldn't have your own show."

He let that comment linger as he dove in.

Every now and then, he mentioned something a little different that she'd done with the flavor profile.

When he'd polished off his first helping, he told her, "That you didn't toss all of this in with the pasta that's still on the stove tells me you're going to hook me up with the key ingredients on a roll."

"You like it toasted?"

"Honey, I think I've made it evident that I enjoy everything you have to offer."

"So diplomatic." She kissed him, then left the table to assemble a second dish for him.

Which he devoured as she ate her pasta.

Afterward, they stored the leftovers, started the dishwasher, and retired to the living room.

Avery built a fire while she clicked through streaming movies on the TV and decided on one.

She brought him a bowl of rainbow sherbet and a glass of wine—both for them to share. She curled up in his lap with a lightweight throw over her legs and served him a few bites.

He snickered and said, "You're not even paying attention to the movie."

"Purposely dove into one I've already seen. So I can concentrate on you."

Her lips drifted over his jaw and down his throat. He had an arm around her while holding the bowl in his other hand. She held the spoon. And, on occasion, remembered to feed him. Then she'd reach for the chardonnay on the sofa table behind them, and they'd sip.

At one point, he hit the mute button and got serious.

"Tell me about the other night, in your hotel room."

Layla hadn't been avoiding this discussion. Just seemed that other things had cropped up and pushed it to the back burner. A night out at Luke's cantina. Avery's dad arriving in town. The competition.

And her still having to decipher all the implications brought on by Christopher's shocking overdose.

But Avery should know what she was dealing with and all the complex variables.

So she bucked up.

"Big doings in New York, cowboy."

His muscles tensed.

She was quick to say, "Don't get riled. There's a happy ending to that particular story."

His gaze narrowed.

"The guy . . . my ex," she started, then drew in a breath. "He's dead."

Repeating that continuously made it more real in her mind.

So she added, "Very dead. Like . . . dead-dead."

Yesterday, she'd even found the wherewithal to check out the news links Todd had sent her as a personal affirmation.

Avery stared at her. "How?"

"Became a victim of his own success, I guess. Overly celebrated with booze and pills. Didn't wake up from his victory lap."

"Holy shit."

"Yep. It's super bizarre. But not uncommon, especially in high-stakes sales. There were plenty of associates fueled by coke or other substances. So. He's one more person who probably should have spent some time in rehab."

"And yet . . . the fact that he didn't—"

"Is to my benefit," she said.

She approached the most difficult part of this conversation.

She told Avery, "I feel unchained from that part of my life, mostly. Still have one shackle to release, but I'm working on that."

"The surgeon you owe?"

"I bear no ill will toward him, Avery. He did his job, and I'm paying him for it. There's nothing shady there."

He was quiet for a moment. Then he asked, "If I were to win the grand prize . . . would that money cover the rest of your debt?"

Tears instantly sprang to her eyes. Her heart wrenched over his generosity. Over his concern for her.

"Quite heroic of you, cowboy," she whispered against his lips.

"I'll find another way to pay Jack," he said. "And he'll understand. Hell, he doesn't want me to pay him at all. But I feel the need."

"Avery . . ." She gave him a faint kiss and told him, "You're just too much. Wherever you and Jack land is between you two. As for me . . . I have a payment plan with the surgeon. He gets that I can't reel in cash like fish."

Avery scoffed, with a strained intonation, at her analogy.

She added, "He was a Good Samaritan. Just not a pro bono one. And again. I got what I requested."

Avery grimaced.

"Don't stress on this, cowboy. I've been doing fine. And I have some golden nuggets in a file that might pay off the remainder."

"Oh?"

"Yeah." She blew out a breath. "Seems that not being terrified of someone hunting me down to make sure I never tell my story has generated a lot of opportunity for me."

He whisked away a few drops that had trickled down her cheek.

"So no need for the tears," he quietly said.

"Those are for you being so sensitive and caring," she told him. "Nothing quite like a hunky cowboy with a heart of gold."

He chuckled. "You bring out my good side."

"Don't sell yourself short, Avery. I didn't inspire you wanting to cover your daddy's debt. That was in your brain long before I came along."

"So about these new opportunities . . . ," he prompted.

"Those. Well." She accepted his need for a subject change. "I can stick with the show after this season, and it'll be all mine. Or I can do something totally different. Hell, I can aim for a prime-time slot on a different platform. Sky's the limit now. Which is weird." She shook her head. "Because I always wanted it to be, and it never was. Till now. I'm not quite sure what to do with all that."

233

"Sounds a bit overwhelming," he concurred.

"And exhilarating. However, for now," she said, anchoring herself in the moment, "I have to keep my feet on the ground, not have my head in the clouds. I have a season to wrap. Maybe that's the other component of what your dad was saying—because he overheard my conversation with Todd and Brodi and got the gist of it all."

Avery groaned, presumably over the mention of his father.

"I'm just making the point that I can't lose sight of what I'm doing right now," Layla said. "We still have your last meal to film, and it's our final chance to make you shine. Which reminds me—you need to call Riley. I'm thinking that having her on set will be a fabulous enhancement. She's entertaining and easy on the eyes. And perhaps a little snippet of Jack and Jillian, with Ollie playing court jester, would liven the dessert segment. Also, including Hunt and Ale in the frames adds to an entire family rallying around the cowboys after supper." She nipped his lower lip, flirtatiously. "Then there's you. Plus, Ritchie. Swear that boy has his own legion of fans forming."

"Ritchie?"

"Believe it."

He seemed to mull this over. "I sorta can. Something about that kid—*man*—draws you in."

"Part of that is his respect and admiration for you," she said. "Other part is that he's honest and cute."

"'Cute'?"

She winced. "Geez, don't tell him I said that. Not cute, like a baby chick. Though . . . kind of. Shit, I'm taking this from bad to worse."

Avery gave her a commiserating look. Stroked her hair. And said, "Honey, we are all over the board tonight. I wouldn't mind carrying you upstairs to bed, and we'll wade through the rest of this in the morning."

"I do like how you think, cowboy."

They left the bowl and the glass and settled in his bed.

They still didn't have any answers or resolutions.

But for now . . . they did have each other.

# Chapter Seventeen

Layla was up early—relatively speaking, given Avery was already at the chuck hall—and showered, changed into a satin nightie in buttery yellow, and spread out her laptop and papers on the bed. She clicked through the snippets her marketing team had sent her from Avery's segments, in addition to trailers that had been created for all the competitors thus far, so that she could do a recap.

She approved Reels and memes that were positive reflections on all the chefs' efforts. Also some bloopers, even ones from Avery, because everyone had a snafu here and there, and that was something that humanized them during this challenge.

Not to mention, there were outtakes of Layla flubbing her lines during the live streams.

That was another great aspect of this platform. They captured everything on-screen, in real time, but they also produced an edited version that was more condensed. People who weren't able to invest in the full hour due to having a short attention span, not being available during the live stream, or not having enough time in their busy day could get the highlights in a pithy video.

However, Brodi's data reported they were doing a fine job of converting those recorded viewers into subscribers.

Todd was spot on with the ability to continue the series.

Then again—

"That's another sexy visual that makes me wonder how I leave this bed in the morning." Avery interrupted her thoughts.

She smiled at his deep, intimate voice, caressing her like a warm Texas breeze.

She sighed—with ample lust tinging her breath—and glanced over her shoulder as she lay on her belly, taking him in.

He said, "You sprawled over my duvet is hot as hell, honey."

"Come join me," she said as she sat up. "I've got news for you, cowboy."

"That you're equally fired up for me?" he asked as he perched himself on the edge of the mattress, so as to not disturb her layout.

She moved in close. Kissed him. And said, "You have more huge love—from the viewers. Also from various companies that want you to endorse their products but don't have contact information for you, other than through the show. In other words, me."

"Not sure what you're getting at, darlin'."

"Avery . . ." She snatched a stack of a half dozen sheets and held up the papers. "They're offering you money to promote their products on social media—be a BBQ influencer. A couple are interested in you being their sole spokesperson. And this is just the beginning . . ."

He dragged a hand down his face. As though trying to hide his grin.

"Like Jack?" he inquired.

"Yes, like Jack. He's got plenty of interest in sponsorships and endorsements. Jillian as well. But I'm talking about *you*, Avery."

He shook his head. "That's nice and all, but I don't have time to film commercials or pose for social media posts, Layla. I can't afford that distraction, even after the bunkhouse cook competition ends."

"Agreed. But similar to our current production, cowboy, they're willing to come to you. This ranch is too beautiful not to capitalize on as a backdrop, and your chuck hall is part of that aesthetic."

He stood and paced.

She said, "I didn't even have to vet these, Avery. They're household names. Brands you recognize—and use. With one stellar addition."

He halted. Turned to face her. "What's that?"

"The global top seller of cast-iron and enamel Dutch ovens." She whipped out a sheet and thrust it toward him. "Look at *that* name. Look at the number behind that dollar sign. It's a bona fide offer. My legal consultant verified it."

"You're kiddin' me," he murmured.

"Nope."

"I've wanted a couple of these ovens for Ritchie and me. Can't buy them with my budget, though. Considered purchasing them if I win, but—"

"Avery, they will *give* them to you," she asserted.

While he contemplated this, she grabbed her phone, rolled onto her back, crooked one knee, and rested her ankle against it.

She scrolled through comments that mentioned him, telling him what they said.

Mostly, she was searching for the few corporate accounts that had been more direct, stating they wanted him to represent their products.

But then she happened upon a new post.

"Holy shit." Her leg dropped. She sat up once more, her loose curls falling all around her. She hooked a forearm under the mass at her nape and draped it over one shoulder.

"What's the problem?" he asked, a look of alarm on his face.

Layla gaped. Blinked. Tried to latch onto a clear thought. Then she simply blurted, "Your dad left a comment on the *LYF* socials!"

She handed Avery her cell, pointing to the post.

He read, "'Excellent job, son. Best of luck to you. I'm proud of you.'"

Avery tossed the phone onto the bed.

Backed away.

"What the fuck is he doing?" he growled in a low voice.

Layla retrieved the phone. "He has a profile. He has a Facebook page."

She clicked on his pic. And what she saw blew her away.

"Oh, wow . . ." She could barely breathe. Didn't say more for the moment.

"Is it his mug shot? Home address listed as some prison where he's sentenced to life for being a mean son of a bitch?"

"Not quite."

The profile picture was of Caleb Reed with an attractive brunette and a young boy. A lit Christmas tree filled the background. The banner photo was of Avery's dad on a horse with the kid in the saddle, a small ranch behind them.

She opened his About Info and said, "He's married, Avery."

"Didn't know he was ever divorced."

"Apparently so. Her name is Grace. He has a stepson named Michael. They have a small ranch in Grant."

"That's a county over."

"And . . ." She stalled out for a moment.

"And what?" he asked with a tinge of *I don't give a rip but still want to know* in his tone.

She glanced at him and said, "Your daddy's a recovering addict. Been sober for four years now. Calls himself a 'ne'er-do-well given a second chance by Grace.'"

She passed him the phone again. And he actually took it.

Though he scowled and returned it to her a nanosecond later. "Means nothing to me, darlin'."

But she knew that wasn't true.

In a soft voice, she said, "Can't sit well with you that he has a new family. And it's okay to express that, Avery. To feel it."

His gaze locked with hers. "Honey, I'm not sure what I'm feeling."

She nodded. "I understand, Avery. Believe me, I do." Emotion swelled in her throat. "I couldn't grasp at first how reveling in someone's death was spiritually or universally acceptable. To be honest, I kind of feel as though *I'm* the monster." She glanced away for a second or two. "Maybe that's why it's taken me so long to tell you the man who abused me is dead. I wanted him to be. And now he is."

"Layla . . ." He joined her on the bed again, crinkling some papers, but who cared? "Darlin', from the moment I saw you on the event lawn, I wanted to know you better. I sensed your inner beauty would rival the outer—maybe exceed it. I was not wrong."

Her eyes misted.

"What that man did to you is *not* your fault." He stared intently at her and added, "You made mention that first day we met that the blame was on others—*and* on you. I don't believe the latter. You changed your trajectory. And paid dearly for it."

She nodded.

"You're still paying," he said with agitation. "But . . . point being . . . *you're* no monster. You're a victim of circumstance, who's risen above. So *reveling* in the demise of someone who could have killed you—*nearly did*—is not a character flaw. You have a conscience that tells you it is. But for the record, I can state that being free of an evil soul is something worth celebrating."

His lips brushed hers.

He swiped away one more tear.

Then he told her, "I'm going to shower now. You wrap all this up, so I don't further destroy your work when I make love to you."

He removed his shirt and boots. Yet he bypassed the bathroom and stepped out onto the balcony, through the doors she'd left open to let in the fresh air.

Layla watched him, giving him a few minutes to collect his thoughts and reconcile his emotions. Also because hers had clogged her brain and throat.

He gripped the railing, his head dropping between those impossibly broad shoulders of his.

She slipped from the bed and went to him, trailing her fingertips lightly up his spine, then threading them in his thick hair.

She said, "You don't have to wish your dad well in his new life, Avery. Doesn't make you a bad person, either, for being angry or hurt that he didn't take the initiative to improve himself when he was here at the ranch but is doing it for someone else. Whatever atonement he's working on, that's for him to achieve and for you to choose whether you accept it or not. And if you don't . . . that's not a poor reflection on you, cowboy."

"Easy to dole that out but not as easy to acknowledge it on your end." He glanced at her. "Am I right?"

She sighed. "You got me on that one. But I am embracing my liberation. You just have to decide if your dad being out there in everyday society with a different wife and child is worth investigating to see if he really has changed . . . or just let it go. Sweep him and his comment under the rug."

He nodded. Straightened. And gazed down at her. "I don't think I can bring myself to believe this change. There's always a catch with him. I don't even want to know what it is this time. I've got money to win so that I can assuage some of my guilt over having a thieving father. That's my focus."

He turned and stalked off.

Then did an about-face and returned to her.

"Aside from loving on you." He placed a tender kiss on her forehead, then sauntered off to the en suite to shower.

Layla stared after him, her heart wrenching.

She'd gone through therapy to help her get to a healthier mental state while in the hospital.

Avery and Chance had not. Other than with their family.

Though from what she'd gleaned thus far, they hadn't been wholly forthcoming about what had gone down in that house—or for Avery, what had happened time and again on the BBQ circuit.

Counseling wasn't something she felt comfortable suggesting. Not while raw intensity and uncertainty radiated from him over this convoluted twist. He needed a spell to think it all through.

Problem was, she'd only be adding to his misery tomorrow when she left him.

But that was twenty-four hours away.

In the meantime, she dried the rest of her tears and packed up her work.

She'd texted him earlier that she'd made herself oatmeal, so no need for him to bring her breakfast. She wanted to spend their last two mornings under the covers for whatever stretch of time they could steal.

In that vein, she was quick to rid herself of her nightie and slip between the rumpled sheets, him joining her not long thereafter.

They didn't bother with words. Just shared all they were feeling through gentle touches and a slow lovemaking that left her breathless and sated.

◆ ◆ ◆

The dessert competition was as invigorating for Avery as all the other meal prep was.

He had his ovens buried and now walked Layla, the judges, and the audience through his demo of the slightly spicy blueberry empanadas Layla had wanted a while back, his triple-berry cobbler, a moist red velvet cake, and his showstopper: a calzone filled with a chocolate and raspberry-chipotle filling, accented with chocolate chips and white chocolate shavings.

A lot to manage all at once, certainly.

But he had the recipes and the cooking down pat.

While he gave the live prep talk, Riley was in the background, in the camera's frame, strumming on her guitar and humming softly, so as to not distract the audience but to enrich the ambience. The campfires were lit and crackling, as were the fireboxes. A fine layer of smoke ribboned through the grass. Cowboys and ranch hands finished their supper off to the side of the outdoor kitchen. Ale and Hunt bounced a tennis ball for the dog, who paused dramatically, as though on cue, to roll onto his back or pose like a meerkat to incite belly rubs.

Ritchie set out the southwestern-style platters on the buffet table.

The rest of the family filed in, unobtrusively, taking the Adirondack chairs and the sofa that had been moved onto the back patio.

Having Jack and Jillian on the outskirts could do nothing but bolster Avery's favorability, he was sure.

While he could do without another post from his dad, he did appreciate that his cousin's fans were supporting him.

Layla was her usual enticing self, asking pertinent questions and drawing out his pro tips as she maneuvered with him like an intuitive shadow while he assembled remakes of what was currently baking in his pits.

The aromas mingled with the steaks he'd served to the staff.

When they reached a lull during the cooking segment, Layla went into full-on hosting mode, introducing the family members who were interacting with the cowboys. Then she directed attention to Riley, who'd brought Whit with her.

Riley stopped her humming and said, "We've got a snappy tune for y'all that is perfect for Jack teaching Jillian how to two-step."

"I'm sorry, *what?*" Jillian croaked out.

"I noticed you weren't on the dance floor at Luke's." Riley jutted her chin toward her twin, who was in attendance as well. "So that means Jack's givin' a live lesson."

Jack swooped in to twine an arm around Jillian, pulling her close to him. He said, "Darlin', cowboys like a woman in their arms."

"Ain't that the truth," Luke chimed in—and gave a sexy grin to the audience.

Jack told Jillian, "First, let's learn the carriage." He placed their hands in the correct position. "Now, Jilly, I'm going to walk you backward in two steps that are quick, then two steps that are slow." He demonstrated. Then said, "We'll move in a counterclockwise direction around Riley and Whit."

"Jack, it's hard to concentrate on the rhythm when you've got that sparkle in your eyes," Jillian told him.

He chuckled.

Layla pressed her lips together as though in awe of a swoon-worthy moment.

Avery would have given up the entire competition to get her wrapped around him. But he had to be cognizant of her career, too, not openly slant a bias his way where she was concerned.

Wyatt and Mateo joined in. As did Garrett and Mindy. Todd and Brodi. Then Luke, alternating with the boys to show them proper technique, letting them be the lead, to get used to it.

Avery gave his aunt a twirl or two before Chance took over so Avery could check his ovens.

Layla and one of the cowboys struck up an accord, and it turned into a lively hoedown.

When the desserts were ready, Ritchie retrieved the Dutch ovens, and Avery revealed their contents.

*Oohs* and *aahs* came from The Three.

The first one said, "I would have been so disappointed if you hadn't baked a cobbler in that pit."

Avery nodded. "Almost sacrilege not to."

"Agreed."

The second judge told him, "I've never had dessert empanadas, and now I'm wondering why. They're sensational."

"Thank you. I had a little inspiration there." He curbed himself from stealing a glance at Layla.

The third judge was silent for a while. Savoring the calzone.

Eventually, she said, "I simply can't think of a better combination. I was wary of the chipotle in such a delicate dessert, but it's fabulous. The raspberry with both the dark and the white chocolate complement each other. This is a dish that should be on a restaurant menu. All of the dishes you've served, actually. And the presentation is astounding."

"Thank you very much for that," he said.

"It's clear you know how to set a scene, Avery," Layla said.

The judges finished their samples and cleared out, along with the production crew.

Ritchie had a pep to his step as he started to clean up. Whit looked equally charged as he repeated over and over, "I think I'm cured."

Riley loaded up her guitar while wearing a cat-that-ate-the-canary expression.

The cowboys demolished the desserts.

Jillian said, "I get the allure of the 'turn' in the two-step. I mean, it's a twirl for me. And I just . . . like the twirling part." She was a bit giddy.

Jack gave her another spin, despite there being no music. "Darlin', I'll turn you to your heart's content."

"Somewhere else," Avery told them with humor in his voice. "I have to get this place reset for tomorrow morning."

Everyone pitched in.

Before he knew it, Avery and Layla were at his house, both aware of the short amount of time they had together. They didn't mention it.

Layla said, "We have last night's leftovers that I can heat up for you, since you couldn't eat with the staff because you were creating your ovens."

He drew her in nice and tight and said, "You must be starving too."

"I could eat." She smiled saucily.

"Me not feeding you is an oversight on my part that must be rectified ASAP."

"I'll survive."

"So you want something else to whet your appetite."

"Nothing quite like sexy kisses from a sexy cowboy."

His mouth sealed to hers. They were barely inside the house, still standing on the raised foyer platform.

When they came up for air, he mused, "Do I take her to the kitchen or straight to the bedroom?"

"Always start in the bedroom," she seductively said. "She prefers that."

He chuckled. "Whatever makes you happy, honey."

"Are you indicating food should come first?"

"Not when you're in my arms, darlin'." And with that, he scooped her up and carried her to his suite, then got them undressed.

The long and leisurely route held merit. He took his time exploring her body, curling his tongue around her beaded nipples, flitting it over her quivering belly. Nipping at her inner thigh. Tasting the cream oozing from her pussy.

That was where he settled in, continuing the languid pace as he sampled her. While she writhed beneath him. Moaned in her sultry way. Lifted her hips just so, pressing herself against his mouth. Silently demanding more.

He was willing to give it.

Two fingers penetrated her tight depths, and she gasped.

He stroked slowly as his tongue fluttered over her clit.

"Avery," she said on a wisp of a breath. "Oh, God . . ."

He suckled her clit, eliciting more moans.

He gradually picked up the pace until his fingers were pumping inside her as his tongue glided over her slick folds, then homed in on that pearl of nerves again. Teasing her, pleasing her. Causing her nails to dip into his muscles as she gripped his biceps.

"That's so good," she murmured. "So amazingly good."

Her body tensed, and her breaths turned shallow.

He suckled her clit once more, and she cried his name as she came.

Seconds later, he was sinking into her, losing himself in her. Absorbing the vibrations through her body from her first release. Giving her another one before he succumbed to the heat and the mounting pressure. Then offering the softer bonus climax that seemed to make her even more delirious.

He grinned, his lips curving against her neck.

She sighed, sounding blissful and content.

Neither dared to say a word, to not shatter the moment.

Really, there was nothing left to be said.

They'd known their fate all along.

Neither of them could nor would change it.

They'd had their "for better," no matter how fleeting.

Now they'd suffer their "for worse."

# Chapter Eighteen

*Leaving shouldn't be this hard.*

Layla packed her suitcase in the morning, having already showered. Avery was still feeding the cowboys but returned quicker than normal.

"Want me to make you breakfast before you go?"

"Thanks, but I'll grab something on the road," she told him. "Todd and Brodi left town about an hour ago so she can make her mani/pedi appointment in San Antonio. Then we've got some reviewing to do for the upcoming week, and I have errands to run. Clothes to wash. Repacking to do. Flight to Tulsa is an early one tomorrow."

"Making thoughts of our Monday nights together dissipate."

"Most times we don't fly out until later," she told him—though she heard his point loud and clear. "Brodi found a screaming deal to Tulsa that bumps us up to first class, and she never passes on that."

He nodded. "I understand."

They stood a distance from each other, the silence stretching between them.

Chitchatting wasn't going to get them through this moment. Nor was pretending that a part-time romance would work. She was already botching it by leaving today.

Not Brodi's fault at all. She didn't know what Layla and Avery had talked about. They hadn't really committed to whether one night a week would suffice anyway—had let the suggestion simmer. Probably because they'd known, even back then, this was an impossible venture.

She zipped her suitcase, and he grabbed the handle while she collected her tote.

"I'll walk you out," he said.

They left his room, in no hurry. In fact, their pace was so slow, she could practically hear their feet dragging along the hallway.

Layla took that time to think about where they stood. But facts were facts. She had three weeks to film the remainder of the season and then had the finale to shoot. Plus, she had Brodi delving into themes to consider for season six, if they chose to continue with this show, and that meant a lot of scouting would be on the agenda. Regardless of what she opted to do next, Layla would have travel on her schedule. No skirting it.

Avery escorted her to her rental. Put her suitcase in the trunk and then opened the door for her, taking her tote, then rounding the front of the car and placing it on the floorboard of the passenger side.

He returned to her, still standing there, racking her brain for something to say that wouldn't send either one of them spiraling.

It was too late for that, really. Her stomach twisted, and her eyes misted as she gazed up at him.

He swept his thumb over her cheek. "Don't go cryin' on me, darlin'. You'll break my heart."

*Not* the thing to say to a woman who was falling apart.

"This just doesn't seem right," she whispered.

"Doesn't *seem* right . . . or doesn't *feel* right?" he quietly challenged.

She nodded. He'd know what term was most accurate.

Admitting it out loud wouldn't help their plight, keep them from a further tailspin.

His teeth ground. His eyes darkened.

She told him, "We can't draw this out, cowboy. We're only torturing ourselves."

"No lie." He groaned. "Be sure to text me that you arrived home. And landed in Tulsa." He kissed her forehead. Kissed her lips. And murmured, "Safe travels to you, darlin'."

More tears crested the rims of her eyes.

This long goodbye was one of the hardest things she'd done since becoming Layla Jenson. It was downright excruciating.

"Honey," he said, as he tried to keep up with the streams along her cheeks. "Don't go leaving me in a worry." He hitched her chin with his crooked finger. "You have to drive."

She sniffled. Tried to blink away the last few drops. Was unsuccessful because they still fell.

He pulled her to him, and she cried on his broad shoulder.

For sure, her emotions had not been this tumultuous, this tormenting, over the past few years. Not until she'd met the hunky bunkhouse cook, his cowboys, his partner, his family. And had heard his story. All of it. The good, the bad, and the ugly.

And knew he was still drowning in the latter two, related to his dad. An old wound freshly opened.

It felt cruel and selfish for her to "move along" while he was just now confronting the resurrection of his father—because of her show.

She'd been instrumental in bringing Caleb Reed back into Avery's life.

And she was just going to walk away from that emotional upheaval?

It wasn't what she wanted to do.

But it was what she *had* to do.

She pulled away, brushed her hands over her damp face, and said, "If I don't go now, I won't go ever."

"So stay."

Their eyes locked.

For several suspended, unwavering seconds.

Her heart nearly stopped.

But then he heaved a breath and said, "Go. Layla. Go."

She nodded. Yet couldn't quite move.

He kissed her one last time—so exquisitely painful.

Then he directed her into the seat. Helped with her belt and even turned the key in the ignition.

Layla drew in a long stream of air. Reached for a tissue in her tote and dabbed around her eyes. Blew her nose.

She settled back and said, "Don't worry about me, Avery. I'll be fine."

She gave him a shaky smile. He gave a weak grin in return. Then closed the door.

Layla backed out of the drive and took the road toward the main gate, her gaze flitting to the cowboy in her rearview mirror.

Until he was out of sight.

"Well, that fucking sucks." Avery plopped into a chair in front of Jack's desk. Whisked off his hat and added, "You were miserable to the core when Jillian left this ranch, and I knew it. I saw it. And then I willingly—*willingly*—invited that same misery into *my* life."

Jack dragged a hand down his face, rested his elbow on his blotter, and scratched his chin.

Didn't say anything, though. As if he was well aware of how this conversation would proceed. One-sided, on Avery's part.

And he was right.

Avery lamented, "Can't compare the remainder of the situation to yours, Jack. Jillian went home to her peppers, but realized she could grow them here. Layla's got the world sprawled beneath her feet now that she's free from her past. And thirty-five thousand feet above the ground is where she prefers to be. A jet taking her to every destination she can think of for her show. And a few I recommended, goddamn it." He scowled.

"There is that proverb about lovin' something and settin' it free." This came from Chance as he entered the office and plopped onto the sofa facing the fireplace.

Avery's head dropped back on his shoulders, his eyes squeezed shut, and he let out a low grunt.

"The point is that it comes back to you," Chance contended.

Avery opened his eyes, rolled his head, and speared Chance with a sardonic look. "If it's yours to begin with."

"Well, there is that." Chance grimaced.

"You left the door open—literally . . . right?" Jack asked, drawing Avery's attention.

He sat forward and propped his forearms on his thighs, clasping his hands between his parted legs. "She also has the gate code," he said. "When we change it, I'll let her know."

"Maybe give her a little time," Jack suggested.

"To do what?" Avery asked. "Get back into her traveling groove and realize she doesn't have time to pop by the ranch because, oh, yeah . . . it's not just poppin' by. It's a three-hour drive from San Antonio."

"Bit of a haul when you've just flown back from somewhere and have to fly out the next day," Chance concurred in an empathetic tone.

Avery nearly reached for a fountain pen on the desk to stick it in his temple.

Instead . . . he said, with as much reason as he could muster, "I don't begrudge the woman having a career. In fact, I encourage it. I applaud it. She's had some tough shakes, and yet she perseveres. I admire and respect that. No matter how it affects me."

"That's commendable," Chance offered.

"There's more." Avery jerked his chair around to face his brother. "More than just the dad sighting at Layla's hotel, he's also posted on her socials."

"I haven't been checking them," Chance admitted. "Not really my jam."

"Nor mine. But he left a comment—for me. And he has a whole profile thingy that claims he's a reformed alcoholic and has a new family."

Chance's gaze narrowed. "Say again?"

"A wife and a stepson. Small boy. Maybe seven or eight."

"Jesus Christ," Jack murmured.

Chance stood. And paced. Aggravated, for sure. The contained fury rolled off him in waves, though he didn't erupt.

Avery could tell his brother was trying his best to think this through. As Avery had done . . . until he'd deemed it futile.

What the fuck did it matter if Caleb Reed was alive, remarried, living a county over, and apparently happy as a goddamn clam for his good fortune?

Chance whirled around and said, "I can't say as though I believe this."

"Yeah, I know the feeling," Avery told him. "Seems sketchy."

He glanced back at Jack, who was on his phone, scrolling rapidly. Then tapping. Then squinting.

"What's that all about?" Avery asked.

"Well, it appears to all be fact, except . . ." His gaze lifted to meet Avery's. "I don't buy it either. I mean . . ." He let out a sharp, humorless laugh. "What the hell, right? He's just goin' about his business like he never devastated anyone, never put this ranch in jeopardy?"

"That's my thinking exactly," Avery averred. "Which worries the crap out of me."

"Makes two of us," Jack agreed.

"Three," Chance chimed in. "I don't feel the least bit comfortable about this. Especially given the timing. Spidey senses are tellin' me this is a part of his ruse. And it could hit us hard if we're not careful."

Layla drove through Serrano to that four-way stop.

To her right was the road that would take her out of town and to the interstate. Get her back to San Antonio.

To the left . . .

She stared at the sign as the other cars took their turns.

To the left was the next county over.

Where Grant was located.

More specifically . . . where Caleb Reed's supposed ranch was located.

*Supposed.*

What a funny word. Subjective, hypothetical. Sarcastic, even, due to it denoting a lack of merit toward something that could be an honest reality.

Because Layla still felt tremendous guilt over having inadvertently brought Caleb back into Avery's life—Chance's and the family's as well—and her curiosity was burning a hole through her brain, she flipped on her left signal.

She used her speakerphone to call Brodi, asking, "Can you give me some directions to the Caleb Reed ranch in Grant?"

"Um, 'scuse the fuck out of me?" Brodi retorted. "Not!"

"Jesus." Layla hissed out a breath. "I just want to see for myself—"

"Then I'm turning this car around and meeting you there," Todd cut in.

"Why am I on your speakerphone, Brodi?" Layla demanded. "And for God's sake, Todd, you're over an hour ahead of me."

"So pull off to the side and wait for me to come back," he insisted.

"Or just let Brodi give me some guidance. These roads aren't really roads around here. They're farm-to-market routes, and I'm guessing I need actual GPS coordinates, not street signs."

"So," Brodi said in her best Meryl Streep voice, "you head down to the Robertsons' farm and—"

"Brodi. This isn't *The Bridges of Madison County.* And that's not even the correct line. It was the Petersons'."

"Whatevs." She sighed with exasperation. "Not helpin' ya out. Come to San Antone. *Now.*"

"What she said," Todd iterated.

"I'm already headed toward Grant, so either help me or don't. And do you even know the difference between a farm and a ranch?"

"I'm from Dallas, if you'll recall," Brodi said. "City girl."

"So let's be country girls for a moment."

"I swear to God," Brodi ground out. "You're out of danger, and now you're putting yourself back into it?"

"Maybe not," Layla said. "Just tell me where I'm going. Please."

If ever there was a true pregnant pause . . . this was it.

"Oh, for the love of—" Layla started to say.

"Okay, okay." Brodi huffed. "Two secs."

Layla just continued driving along. What else was she to do? There were no indications of where the hell she was headed. Just huge acreage with a farmhouse after huge acreage with a farmhouse. Then some ranches with horses and cows. Then more farms and general homesteads.

Brodi came back on the line. "When you see a community recreational area with picnic tables, ramadas, and lawns for soccer or whatever, drive past that and turn right."

Layla did as instructed, looking for a stoplight but not finding one. So she took the first street she could veer off on.

"And now?" she asked.

"Just keep driving. There's a barn you'll come across before the house. Take the dirt road there."

"Every road is a dirt road," she informed Brodi.

"If you pass the rooster signage, as it looks like from the landscape view, you've gone too far."

Layla was starting to think she'd gone too far when she'd bypassed the route to San Antonio.

But a gnawing deep inside her told her to stay on this particular course.

And when she saw the appropriate signage with hens gathered around a strutting rooster, she knew she couldn't turn back.

"I'm here. Give me forty-five minutes to call you back."

"Oh, girl, you're killin' me! Forty-five minutes??"

"I think everything will be fine," Layla asserted. "Just let me investigate."

"With your cell camera on."

"Promise."

Layla exited the car just as a woman came from the screened-in porch to greet her.

But Caleb emerged from the barn and called out, "Go on inside the house, Grace."

Layla instantly recalled Caleb's profile: "Ne'er-do-well given a second chance by Grace."

That said so much.

Grace smiled at Layla, nodded to Caleb, and did as he requested.

Caleb approached Layla and said, "Don't hold her guilty by association, Miss Jenson. That's a fine woman who doesn't need to be judged."

Layla stuffed her phone in her back pocket and held up her hands. "Wasn't judging her. And I do respect that you protect her."

"I could've done better in the past. I didn't. She has nothing to do with who I was before. My atonement is my own."

Layla let those words permeate her psyche.

Her personal ruminations had much to do with not being a hypocrite. Not looking down on others when she'd shamed herself.

Also . . . she placed value in penance.

That was one reason she was here.

The other was . . .

"Nice setup you have," she commented in as casual a voice as she could, given there was still tension arcing between them.

"Got a chicken coop that generates eggs we trade for produce around the county. My wife has goats and makes products from their milk—soaps, lotions, what have you. Sells them at craft fairs. We have pigs up for auction, and some heifers. And I have three pits that I work for various catering events. Weddings, anniversaries, birthdays, and the like. We turn a decent profit."

"So this is real."

"Is that why you came here? To see if I'm now on the up-and-up?"

Her eyes connected with his. "Is that a surprise?"

He chuckled, low and deep. "I guess not. Why don't you come in and have some iced tea?"

She tore her gaze from his, and it swept the ranch. Though she remained a bit hesitant, she nodded and said, "That'd be lovely."

She followed him into the house, to a modest-size living room. There were multicolored foam golf balls scattered on the carpeted floor, along with cutout numbers and equation symbols.

Grace brought her son over, who had light hair and freckles.

Caleb said to him, "Michael, this is Miss Jenson. She's a guest of ours."

"How do you do?" the boy asked with a crooked smile.

She shook his proffered hand as she said, "Quite nicely, thank you. And you?"

"Very well, thank you very much."

"Oh my, with the manners." Layla pressed her palm to her heart.

He shoved his hands into his front pockets, now beaming.

Layla glanced at Grace, who also extended her hand.

"It's a pleasure to meet you," Grace said.

"And you," Layla replied.

Grace stared down at Michael, telling him, "Put all your learning tools away, and you can watch cartoons."

"Yes!" he blurted. Then got to work.

Grace explained, "He's homeschooled, and I find that using the golf balls adds a visual and physical component to studying math and holds his attention. He's also an early riser, so if he can get through half his curriculum before lunch, he gets to watch TV during his 'recess.'"

"Interesting how he lollygags through the second half so that he's not in a rush to do his evenin' chores." Caleb grinned. "But ends up feeding the goats and the chickens anyway."

The free-flowing exchange with heartwarming levity confused Layla.

Seemingly catching on, Caleb suggested, "Why don't we sit?"

She followed him to the round table situated in the middle of the small kitchen that was brightened by sunflowers in ceramic vases and light-wood tones. It couldn't have been much bigger than her daddy's kitchen, and yet it didn't have that pressed-in feeling. She wondered why that was . . . whether the "stifled" sensations truly were linked to her mother's lingering spirit—and Layla wallowing in the remorse that she'd been the cause of her death.

Caleb pulled out a chair for her. He then washed his hands and retrieved two glasses from a cupboard as Grace got the pitcher of tea from the fridge.

Caleb poured while his wife collected two plates and forks.

"I have lemon bars fresh out of the oven," she said.

"And they smell wonderful," Layla commented, still perplexed by this whole scene.

Grace served dessert, telling Layla, "You're even prettier in person. How is that possible?"

Layla fought the twinge over the compliment. It was well received, yet her life was a dichotomy.

"I hadn't realized y'all were watching the show, until recently," she said as a buffer.

"I still have ties in the BBQ world," Caleb informed her. "That's how I heard of Jack's YouTube channel. Then Avery's name started cropping up, and I wanted to see how he was faring."

She nodded. "I got a little puzzled over what you thought I could do for him."

"You did it last night."

Grace bowed out of the conversation, saying, "I'll leave you two to it."

"Thank you for your hospitality," Layla told her.

"Anytime." She kissed Caleb's cheek, then returned to the living room with her son.

Caleb continued. "I don't think Avery would have included all those key components that are central to the ranch if he hadn't been encouraged."

"That wasn't just me," she stated, thinking back on Ale quizzing them all about the bigger, better mousetrap.

"Avery is damn good at what he does," his father said. "He just sometimes forgets that he has more to offer, only thinking competitions are about the meat. There's so much more that brings together a complete package."

"I saw him building upon that during the week. He just needed to count on his family to give him a little extra oomph," Layla said.

"And I figured you'd give an additional nudge in the right direction."

"Everyone's free to do as they please during their airtime," she reminded him. "But this was definitely a case of 'If you have it, flaunt it.' They did it to the perfect degree. Nothing overboard, not too fancy. Just a casual evening at the TRIPLE R."

"I'm glad it panned out."

She picked at the powdered sugar topping on the shortbread crust with her fork, giving herself a few seconds to word her next question properly. "Even though it happened at the ranch?"

He nodded. "That's his home. His sanctuary. The place where he belongs."

"Not everyone embraces that concept—at least not right at this moment. Riley likes living in Nashville, and Luke's in town with his cantina. And then—"

"There's me."

He sipped his tea. Set aside the glass. And said, "First, if you're wonderin' if I've traumatized my new family in any way, I assure you I pulled myself together before Grace and I got married. And she and her son have done nothing but strengthen my belief in redemption. She knows my past. She didn't absolve me of my sins. She accepts my faults but holds me to a higher standard. She'd never let me fall back on my bad habits and old ways. She wouldn't leave me . . . she'd kick my ass out."

"I like her," Layla said, her gaze level with his.

He nodded. "This is her family's home." He winced, then added, "Not that there's anything left of the family. They passed in a wildfire that spread through the plains during a camping trip. She was widowed. Michael no longer had a father. And somehow . . . I don't know,

Miss Jenson." He combed a hand through his hair. "I was making my rounds with the cowboy outfits in the county when the fire broke out, and some of us saved a few people. That's how I met her and her son. And we just . . . bonded. The three of us. Out of the blue. Can't even explain it."

Layla's throat tightened. She couldn't speak for a spell.

She and Avery had experienced something similar, the moment they'd met.

The connection had been visceral. She'd felt it in her soul.

But it wasn't a "meant to be" scenario.

However, it seemed that for Caleb, Grace, and Michael . . . it was.

She cut into her lemon bar. It tasted even better than it smelled. She took a long drink of tea and then told Caleb, "I guess for you, all's well that ends well."

"Oh, no. Not at all." He let out a breath. "That's never how I feel. Yes, I pray to the Lord every night that this isn't a dream I'm going to wake up from. And I do everything in my power to prove I'm now worthy of this life—that I'm worthy of Grace and Michael. This ranch. What we're creating together. But that doesn't make me a good man, Miss Jenson. It doesn't exonerate me."

"What's so different this time around for you?" she asked.

"Every single thing. This ranch feels like home. The TRIPLE R? It was just a pit of despair for me. My mama died of cancer not long after my brother Royce was born. About five years. So I did what I could to help out with taking care of him. But there was something that had shifted in my dad after her death. Royce became this crown prince, like he was the only gift our mom had left him. The favoritism wore thin with me. And I started to resent not only my brother but my family. And the ranch."

"Is that why Royce took over operations when your father passed?"

"His reign was decided well before that." Caleb ate a bite, sat back, then said, "And that bothered the hell out of me because I was the one working the pastures and the stables from sunup to sundown when

I wasn't in school and only taking that span of time as a break when I had classes to get to. Meanwhile, Royce was sitting in Dad's office, watching him reconcile the books and learning about ranchin' from A to Z from an intellectual, not a practical application, standpoint. He never mucked out stalls, is what I'm sayin'.'"

Layla could see where this was headed.

Caleb told her, "The animosity festered like an infected wound. And I was the pus."

He let out an agonized laugh.

Then he said, "Shoot, I shouldn't have made that analogy while you're eating."

She put the forkful in her mouth, chewed, and said, "Not much stands in the way of me and food."

He grinned, apparently liking that she'd lightened the dark mood.

"I'm guessing that's one of the many things Avery admires about you."

"He has talent, without doubt."

"Absolutely, he does. And it's unfortunate I hindered him rather than helped him."

"Why is that?" she pressed, feeling the secrets start to flow. "Why were you antagonistic with him?"

"Because he was too good. Making him one more person I was jealous of. Hell . . ." He took a long drink, then said, "I was jealous of Chance too. My own sons. Avery had mad BBQ skills from the start, and Chance had a way with the cattle and the cowboys that made him a natural leader. He was born to be the foreman of that ranch. And I knew it was only a matter of time before Avery usurped me as the bunkhouse chef. I just never felt like I had a place there. And it pissed me off."

"Did you ever discuss this with your brother?"

"Royce didn't have time for my pettiness. Rightfully so. He had his hands full from a young age. So I crawled into a bottle and let the booze soothe me at times, though mostly it just led to me making bad choices. Hitting rock bottom and then realizing I still had levels I could fall. The gamblin' gave me a high when I'd win. But losin' cost me more than I could cover. So I got clever and started diverting funds from my annual bunkhouse budget. Found other ways to funnel money my way. Hoping I could score a hefty sum on the ponies or at a poker table to pay it all back before Royce noticed it was gone."

"But you couldn't."

"No, I could not." He rubbed the stubble on his jaw. Finished his dessert and drained his iced tea.

Then he stood and crossed to the far counter, where there was an antique breadbox and three matching canisters in a pale-green shade.

Panic skittered through Layla, thinking maybe he was reaching for a weapon. She shoved back her chair and got to her feet—it was habitual.

Caleb's head whipped in her direction. He held up a hand. "Please, just wait. Nothing to fear here, I promise. I just want you to know . . ."

He groaned.

Then he removed the lid on the tallest canister and extracted four white envelopes and a thicker folio.

He said, "Part of my recovery is working a program that focuses on making amends to people I've wronged. Some of those amends aren't so difficult. Others are. Please sit. Let me explain."

He returned to the table. She slipped back into her chair. Now more curious than wary.

He spread out the envelopes, with names scrawled across the front.

One for Jack.

One for Brett.

One for Chance.

One for Avery.

Layla's breaths were shallow as she said, "I don't understand." Though she kind of did.

"Direct amends for your trespasses ought to be done in person," he said. "That's humiliating and humbling. Painful as all get-out, so that you don't have a scrap of pride left. But you can muscle your way through them in hopes of getting closer to forgiveness—and rebuilding your pride, your dignity."

He sighed. Ground his teeth.

Then he told Layla, "With some of the people you owe amends to, however . . ." He shook his head. "There might not be verbal words to express your regret. Your sorrow. So you write them down. And you pray that the person reading them can not only 'hear' your remorse but also feel it."

"Did you write one for Royce?"

"Yes, I did. I keep it in my nightstand drawer."

Emotion pricked the back of her eyes.

He wasn't done. He pulled the thicker folio from his back pocket and unraveled the twine around the fastening. Peeled back the flap and dropped the packet onto the table.

Bills of various denominations spilled out of it.

Layla gasped.

He said, "It's nowhere near what I stole. But I've been saving for years. I wanted to have more to offer Jack—and the ranch—before I handed it over. Now seems to be a good time, though. With the caveat that I'll keep paying on my debt."

"Oh, geez." Layla stood again. And paced.

A lump lodged in her throat, and she wasn't sure she'd be able to speak around it.

Caleb said, "I have the nigglin' suspicion that what drove Avery to join your cook-off was the prize money. And if he wins any, he's going to give it to Jack. Am I right?"

She nodded.

"And that's his way of showing everyone that he and Chance aren't like me—they're better."

Another nod.

He said, "Somebody raised him right. It sure as hell wasn't me."

"Oh, God." She couldn't contain the sudden waterworks.

Caleb was quick to grab paper napkins from the holder and hand them to her.

"I only ask one thing of you, Miss Jenson. Layla. To please take these envelopes to the ranch. I'm not welcome there, and again . . . I can't verbally express what needs to be said. It's cowardly. But it's the best I can do."

"I'm so sorry." She shook her head this time. "I can't." Through her tears and her still-constricting throat, she told him, "I'm not going back to the TRIPLE R. I have a flight to catch. I have a job to do. I'm just . . . I can't."

She sobbed into the napkins.

Why the hell had she come here?

Why had she put herself in the position of getting more emotionally invested in Avery? In the Reeds? In the entire ranch?

What on God's green earth had she been thinking?

Caleb said in a consoling voice, "No need to fret, darlin'. I'll give all this to Luke."

"That's a good idea," she said around a sniffle.

"Now, now." He gently patted her arm. "Don't let all this drama ruin your mascara. It's one more thing Avery won't forgive me for."

She lifted her head, blinked with damp lashes, and said, "You're right again. He's not going to forgive you for anything, Caleb. He's cut to the quick. I don't have to reiterate why. Just know . . . he's not wired to let things go. He might acknowledge your amends and your contribution toward your redemption. But in his heart . . . you're not his daddy."

More tears fell.

Caleb collected additional napkins. And quietly said, "I know that, Layla. But I kind of needed to hear it."

She stared up at him. Saw the mist covering his eyes. The agony rimming his deep-blue irises.

He wasn't giving a cock-and-bull story as Chance had surmised he would.

This was all genuine. She felt it in her soul.

Making it even more complicated that she'd initiated this entire conversation. Asked all those questions.

He wasn't an interview subject. He was Avery's father—despite what she'd just claimed. And she'd drawn out his darkest secrets.

Only to do . . . what with them? Stash them away, keep them to herself?

She had no idea.

She had no clue what was written in those letters. She didn't know if Avery would read his. Or if everyone else would hold in silence the information *they'd* gleaned, out of respect for Avery not wanting to be informed.

And that brought on another quandary.

How would Avery feel if he learned she'd visited Caleb and his new family?

She swiped at the rest of her tears, blew her nose, and dumped the wad of napkins into the trash bin.

"I have to go," she said. "But I do appreciate you being forthright—and forthcoming. You don't know me. You don't owe me a thing. Yet it still had to have been difficult to share your story with me."

"Every retelling is a stab to the heart, I won't lie. But I did this to myself, Layla. It's all on me."

She shook his hand.

He said, "I'll walk you to your car."

Grace met them at the door.

"Thank you again for welcoming me in," Layla told her.

"I don't expect we'll see you again," Grace said. "I'm sorry for that. But if you do find yourself out this way, know we'd be happy if you stopped by."

"You're very kind."

Layla stepped out onto the porch and unlocked the door to her rental with the remote. She told Caleb, "I'll be fine from here. You take care of *this* family."

"Count on it."

She slipped behind the wheel. They waved to her as she drove off.

As though they were relatives.

She stymied a new flow of tears. This wasn't her drama to get caught up in. What Caleb did or didn't do with those letters and the cash was none of her business. It was all up to him.

Embracing that theory helped her to reach a better frame of mind as she assured Todd and Brodi she was safe and made the long trek home.

She dealt with all her errands and took an OTC sleeping pill so she'd get a good night's rest. Was up and about early and picked up Brodi to drive to the airport. They discussed the week ahead while they were on the plane, and Layla also batted around ideas for endorsements, narrowing down a few she felt were the most sensible.

And prosperous.

There was that to consider.

Todd met up with them later in Tulsa, inviting them to the downstairs restaurant that was more of a nightclub, with dim lighting and dancing.

They had a high-top table in the corner to observe the activity as they sipped cocktails. Brodi's stool was a bit close to Todd's, Layla noted. And hid her smile.

Sure, she was envious they were able to explore their attraction to each other, while being on the road together. She did, however, fear both her friends getting involved and then . . . getting derailed by career choices.

Brodi had said she wanted to go where Layla went.

And Todd had indicated he was moving on from the production at the end of the season.

But again, it wasn't her place to intervene.

Or was it?

Should she warn Brodi of the impending heartbreak that comes with falling for someone who is on the opposite end of your spectrum?

Or should she just mind her own business and figure out what the hell *her* next steps were?

*No-brainer there.*

Neither Brodi nor Todd were the "fools rush in" type.

So she polished off her amaretto on the rocks and said, "I'm out." She grabbed her purse and added, "I'm letting you pay, chief. While you're still the chief."

He chuckled.

"Y'all don't do anything I wouldn't," she quipped.

"That leaves the door swingin' wide open," Brodi joked in return.

"Indeed, it does." Layla blew them a kiss, then headed to her room.

The best thing she could do right now was focus on the next several weeks.

And that's what she set her mind to.

# Chapter Nineteen

Avery was at the family breakfast table at the end of the week, thinking he'd done a damn fine job these past few days of not looking like a forlorn sad sack.

Yet Aunt Brett dropping a kiss on the top of his head as she set the skillet potatoes on a trivet and then Wyatt ruffling his hair before adding the stacked French toast with berries to the table had him scowling.

Jack delivered huevos rancheros, and Chance brought over the sausage and bacon platter, each of them giving him an empathetic look that made him groan.

"Y'all can knock it off about now," he said. "I had a life before Layla Jenson. I'll have a life after Layla Jenson."

"Yes, but why is it *over*?" Wyatt asked. "The romance. Not your life. Just to be clear."

He clicked his tongue. And said, "Duly noted."

More of the family came in.

*So the gang's all here to witness my misery.*

He slid a glance toward Jack. Who said, "I don't know what to tell you, cuz. Wish I did, but I can't predict this outcome."

"Outcome's already been decided," Avery deduced. "So let's talk about anything other than Layla. Or me."

"That's going to prove difficult," Luke said as he came through the wide opening to the large kitchen. He handed out white envelopes to

Avery, Chance, Jack, and Brett. Then pulled up a chair and fixed himself a plate.

Avery waved his envelope in the air and asked, "What's this?"

"No idea what's contained within," Luke told him. "I'm only the messenger." He didn't quite settle in, saying, "Oh, and there's also this." He whipped out a folio from his back pocket and placed it on the table next to Jack. "Compliments of Uncle Caleb."

"What the fuck?" Jack said under his breath.

His low tone didn't matter.

"Jack Royce Reed," his mother warned.

"I know, I know. But . . ." His gaze shifted from her to Luke. "What the heck is going on?"

Luke shrugged. "He came by my restaurant yesterday. Swore he wanted no trouble. Said something about making amends, but he knows he's not permitted on the ranch. So he asked me to pass these along. I stole a peek at the fat one, Jack. There's cash in there."

A collective gasp from the adults filled the otherwise quiet room.

While Ale and Hunt munched on French toast, several looks were exchanged.

Avery was the first to speak.

"I'm glad he's finally taking responsibility for his actions," he said, "but I don't want to know squat about what he's up to, what his plans are, or what he has to say." He stood, went to the island, and depressed the lever for the trash and recycle bins, tossing in his sealed envelope. "Makes no difference to me." He turned back to his family and said, "Y'all have a nice breakfast."

He stalked out.

◆ ◆ ◆

Three weeks without Layla in his bed was twenty-one days too long.

Avery had plenty to do. Without doubt.

267

But there were mornings and fleeting moments throughout the day and then the nights when he just couldn't stop thinking of her body pressed to his. Her beautiful face, her glowing eyes, her sweet smile. And her voice. He could almost hear her whispering in his ear when he was prepping a meal or taking a shower. When he was drifting off to sleep, with her on his mind.

They'd bypassed the Mondays they might have been able to get together at the ranch without even saying a word about it. The evenings had just slipped by. And neither did more than text here and there.

It seemed like wasted opportunities, yes. And yet . . . it'd become self-preservation. For both of them, he was sure.

Avery had stopped digging his hole.

Unfortunately, there was still the finale to get through, where the winners would be announced.

Brodi sent a detailed email of what he should expect, by way of a cameraman and technician showing up to include him in the live conference feed that would feature all the contestants.

The production was set up in the outside portion of the chuck hall, with the entire family gathered, plus the wranglers and the ranch hands. And Whit Tatum.

Avery paced anxiously along the back patio. He wore the outfit he'd borrowed from Jack the day he'd met Layla, hoping it was some sort of good luck charm. He had, after all, scored with her that evening (ha, ha). He prayed he did the same with the judges and audience, in a different capacity.

Jack propped his shoulder against one of the thick cedar columns and said, "You can't change the outcome by wearin' a hole in those floorboards."

"I'm well aware." Didn't stop Avery from pacing some more.

"Do you even care that much about the money?" Chance asked. "Or is it more about the girl?"

Avery's head snapped up. He gave a nod of acknowledgment for the weighty question. And said, "If I don't win, I'll do endorsements if

I can, to pay Jack. But there's no signing on the dotted line to get the girl back."

He and his brother stared at each other.

Then Avery's gaze flashed to Jack. Whose brow rose.

Avery felt its meaning straight to his core.

He let out a half snort.

"Don't get me going in that direction," Avery said. "She's not a ranch dweller, Jack. She's got wanderlust in her veins." He'd felt that way about her from the beginning. And it was something he wouldn't try to alter.

"Well, this live stream's about to start," Jack reminded him. "So you'd best get your game face on. Win or lose, you put on one hell of a show, Avery Reed. You should be damn proud of yourself. *We're* all proud of you."

That was crucial to Avery. And everyone knew it.

He took a moment to absorb the love and affection. And accept the surge of dignity that came with having done his absolute best with this show, with honorable intentions.

Then the tech removed the cover from the big-screen TV that was mounted on a rolling stand, and he connected to *Light Your Fire*, which hadn't yet launched. Though the logo and Layla's vibrant smile were front and center.

Avery pulled in a long breath. Let it out on a rush of air. Forced his bunched muscles to loosen.

It wasn't that he was so tense over whether he'd be in the top two.

He was nervous about seeing Layla. Downright nervous.

Mostly, he knew it'd be harder than hell to act casual when his pulse was racing and his adrenaline was surging. When his heart was pounding, his gut clenching.

Christ, he almost wrung his hands in anticipation.

He wasn't left in suspense, though.

Suddenly, there she was, welcoming the audience, excitedly talking about this finale, and then saying, "We have some epic clips from each contestant, and I have follow-on questions they'll be answering live, one-on-one with me. But first, let me remind y'all of who these fierce competitors are, each of them having a shot at fifty or *one hundred and fifty* thousand dollars—and the title of Best Bunkhouse Cook!"

Square images of the ten contestants appeared on-screen, three on either side of Layla lower in the frame, and four running across the bottom. She started in sequential order of their boxes, corresponding with the week in which they'd competed.

"We have Cramer Dillon up first," she said, "from the outskirts of Odessa, Texas. Y'all will remember Cramer's old-fashioned bunkhouse kitchen, with callbacks to some of the great German and Chinese bunkhouse cooks from the late 1800s."

The facility was small and tidy, just right for a wrangler outfit of six to eight, with a mix of antique and modern enhancements that made it efficient, yet authentic looking.

Layla posed her questions, and Cramer answered, his box expanding to share the screen with Layla only.

She continued through the contestants, displaying their setup and recapping humorous anecdotes from her time with them. Making her even more likable, more relatable.

When she got to Avery and all his family gathered around at the chuck hall, the cowboys and ranch hands in the background, she said, "Entering the TRIPLE R is like coming home."

The instant tinge of emotion to her silky voice almost choked Avery up.

He didn't need to glance around to know that was the effect she had on the women assembled.

"It's serene, it's majestic, it's overwhelming." She gave a soft laugh, apparently to chase away the hint of melancholy. "The green pastures stretch for miles and miles. The shady trees and bluebonnets are plentiful. Add to that a large herd of cattle and stables full of horses—not to mention all the homes and outbuildings—and you have a breathtaking generational ranch that is also home to champion pitmaster Avery Reed."

Scenes of the ranch morphed into Avery sharing the screen with Layla.

"How are you, Avery?" she asked. With a shimmer in her tiger eyes.

"Doing just fine, darlin'." He resisted saying, *Better, now that I'm seeing your beautiful face.*

But he was damn sure his own eyes gave him away.

Indeed, she smiled delicately and said to the audience, "I knew Avery was a contender when I researched him for the show. Certainly, he has the skill set. But when I met him in person, at the Memorial Day Weekend BBQ Bash that his cousin Jack Reed and Jack's cohost, Jillian Parks, orchestrated, I had the opportunity to view Avery's indoor/outdoor bunkhouse kitchen facilities. And learn specifically why he'd be fantastic for this cook-off."

Avery grinned, knowing where she was going with this.

Layla continued. "I heard the conviction in his voice when he indicated he'd be up bright and early the morning after the three-day event to feed the wranglers and the ranch hands 'a feast fit for kings.' Not missing a beat, not taking any downtime for himself. And that's because he feels the staff on the TRIPLE R are deserving of his best, *every day*. Because they give theirs. *Every day*."

The shimmer turned into glistening.

Off to the side, Wyatt sniffled.

Layla said, "And he not only backed up that commitment, but he also brought a level of difficulty and intrigue to the competition with his pits and his recipes. In addition, he's surrounded by a cohesive, caring—and talented—family, and has a competent assistant in Ritchie."

"Thank you for acknowledging him, darlin'," Avery said, "because he's earned it."

He shook Ritchie's hand. The guy swelled with pride.

Avery chuckled. "Don't go getting too cocky on me now," he teased. "I still need you here, not thinking you should be working at some fancy steak house in Dallas."

"Not even on my mind, sir," Ritchie asserted. "Got no cause to leave the ranch. I'm just a few solid tosses away from cornhole champion in our ongoing tournament." He winked.

Those "on set" erupted with laughter. Because there was no such thing happening.

Layla fanned her face. "Watch out, Reed men. Ritchie just might outshine y'all in the charisma department."

He beamed. "Why, thank you, Miss Layla."

"Okay, again. Maybe don't flirt with the host so much," Avery chided.

With a solemn look, Ritchie told him, "Wouldn't know how or where to begin, Pitty. The most flirtin' I do is with the hens when I need 'em to lay more eggs for breakfast."

This kept the family and staff in stitches.

Layla attempted to stifle a giggle but was unsuccessful.

Avery nodded and said, "Well, I suppose that's all the time I'm going to get. Right, Layla?"

"We are on a schedule," she concurred. "So y'all hang tight till we get to the scoring."

She moved on to the last three contestants.

While their camera was off, Ritchie said, "Sorry I ate up your time, sir."

"Ritchie, the scores are already tallied, and the winner already determined. This segment has no bearing whatsoever, other than for entertainment value. And you provided it. My hat is off to you."

That seemed to send Ritchie straight into the stratosphere as he bobbed his head like he was the damn rooster.

Avery had to walk away so he didn't burst. Not only with laughter but also with pride.

Though when Layla introduced the next portion of the show, he moved back into place, where the cameraman had done his blocking to ensure Avery was aligned with his angles.

"So now we're down to the moment of truth," Layla said with a more serious visage and tone. Except . . . "Well, actually there are two moments of truth." She rolled her eyes in a comical fashion. "My faux pas."

Todd appeared in the frame and set a vault on the table alongside Layla. He worked the combination, opened the door.

"We could have used some suspenseful music there," she said. "Couldn't spring for a soundtrack, Todd?"

He smirked. Then stepped out of the frame.

"Inside are the individual lockboxes for our fabulous cooks," she explained. "We have the combined scores for each of the meals that were evaluated. Five in total. Then there's the final score, which comes from the viewer analytics to determine which cook 'stole the show.'"

Wyatt quietly clapped her hands together, as though she was convinced this honor was going to Avery.

And if it did . . .

"The audience likability score is weighted and will be added to each contestant's overall standing," Layla expounded. "So . . . shall we get down to business?"

Avery was on pins and needles. He assumed his competition was too.

Layla started at the beginning once more, sharing the meal scores with Cramer, declaring for that particular round, "Out of a possible seventy-five stars, you've been awarded seventy-two! Excellent job!"

The others didn't fare quite so well, until she reached Willet Hayes, who received seventy-four.

Avery winced, on the inside.

Seventy-four was a high bar. With only one point away from perfection, Willet was going to be tough to beat.

Layla said as much, looking a little concerned, though trying to hide it. Luckily, she had this hosting gig down pat and kept her perky disposition.

"Now, Avery," she said after retrieving his scores from his lockbox. "You brought some alternate elements to your segments. A shift from grills to the pit. Plus, the pizzazz of the TRIPLE R, and your family.

Also, only you and one other bunkhouse cook serves this large of a group, Willet Hayes. While your technique—meaning your trenches—does count toward your scores for mastering your recipes, the size of the staff you feed does not."

He nodded. "Doesn't matter if it's an outfit of two or twenty, Layla. The quality has to be high and consistent."

"Very good answer, cowboy. Now . . . let's get to it."

He suppressed a groan.

Because, yeah, that's exactly what he'd like. Only not in the context presented.

She was all soft and sensuous in a pretty baby blue lacy dress with bell sleeves and a flared hem. She had on light-brown boots with blue accents. Her loose curls were draped over one shoulder. Her eyes were smoky, and her lips were rose gold, with a shimmer to the gloss.

Every inch of him ached for her.

But that was neither here nor there.

He tried to stay focused on the results she was about to reveal.

She reminded him, "The judges rate each meal from one to five. For a possible fifteen stars per meal. For your turducken, Avery . . ." She opened a small, sealed envelope and extracted three note cards to show the audience. She smiled. "You received a perfect fifteen."

So why didn't his chest loosen?

Yes, he knew why. *Her*. So . . . moot.

She moved on. "For your campfire breakfast, Avery . . ." She repeated the process with a different envelope. "You received fifteen stars."

Wyatt gasped. God love her for being so invested, but she was putting him more on edge.

Layla continued. "For your pig in a pit . . . a score of fifteen."

He could barely breathe. Telling him this contest meant more to him than he'd let on.

"Your venison, which the judges felt had the absolute correct amount of juices and smoke, has nabbed you another fifteen."

*Fuck, fuck, and fuck, yes!*

He had a chance here. Granted, there were three others who didn't have their scores yet.

But he did have a chance!

At this moment, winning was about more than giving Jack some restitution. It was about proving he'd always had the expertise and the talent to take titles. But something—*someone*—had held him back.

No more.

He was breaking through all that.

And if he won, it'd be his victory. Not anyone else's.

Though . . . he spared a glance at Ritchie, grinned, and amended that thought.

It'd be *their* victory. And he couldn't ask for a better assistant. Couldn't be happier that he'd mentored Ritchie in a way that he should have been mentored by his dad.

That was water under the bridge now.

Avery actually felt freed from that shackle, knowing money was flowing to Jack from Caleb, even if it took him till his dying days to pay his debt. Even if he never did fully pay the debt. It filled a slim crevice in Avery's conscience. And that was something.

"So," Layla said, "your last score for this round, Avery, comes from your desserts. And let me just tell you, heaven's missing a baker. The scents alone were divine."

He chuckled. "Honey, you might want to work on your pickup lines."

Her smile was the vibrant one that always stole his breath.

Hell, every smile of hers stole his breath.

She told him, "I'm shocked I didn't gain ten pounds just eyeballing those Dutch ovens when you removed the lids."

"Wouldn't bother me in the least, darlin'." He winked.

Her breath seemed to catch. And it had nothing to do with them potentially outing themselves. That was probably already a given, from the second the cameras were on them on day one.

"For your last offering, Avery Reed . . ." Her voice quavered—just a hint, so that he might have been the only one to notice, he was that attuned to her. "You have yet another perfect score of fifteen." She displayed the cards.

Applause from his favorite peanut gallery ensued.

Yet he heard Layla say, "Congratulations. That puts you in the lead."

*For now.*

He would have breathed a sigh of relief, but she still held him captive.

"With seventy-five stars, Avery, you are currently the chef to beat."

The cameraman cut him off so Layla could give the next contestant his scores.

Avery's family gathered around him. The cowboys and staff shook his hand, not only in a celebratory way but in gratitude for what he offered them, when he could just be throwing hamburgers and hot dogs on the grills to fill their bellies.

At the end of the first round, they were all back on-screen, live.

Layla made the grand announcement: "Our winner of the techni-cal, quality, and presentation portion of this competition is . . . Avery Reed!"

He and Ritchie shook once more.

Layla said, "Now for the curveball." She made a sketchy face and added, "The scores given by the viewers and subscribers can turn this competition on its ear. Although no more than twenty-five points will be awarded overall from the audience, they will affect each cook's cur-rent standing. What I say about that is, in addition to bringing your best recipes and practices to the table, at the heart of what you do as a bunkhouse cook has to be a genuine love and respect for the people you're cooking for. That's what drives you to get up before the crack of dawn and work until the sun goes down. What makes you determined to find the superior meats and produce that fit your budget—and get creative when you're running low on pennies."

Avery felt that to his core.

*All of it.*

"Also," Layla continued, "when you infuse personality into what you do, that's a bonding with those around you that makes you a superstar. Let's find ours, shall we?"

In his peripheral vision, he expected to see Wyatt biting her nails. But she and Jillian were huddled together, hands clasped, with confident expressions on their faces.

That made him feel good.

Jack gave a thumbs-up.

Aunt Brett blew him a kiss.

Mateo gave a fist pump.

Garrett had a solid nod.

Riley and Luke gave a shared *You got this* look.

The twin boys and the dog . . . well, hell's bells, they were riveted.

*Humph.*

He grinned.

Perhaps he didn't need the title after all.

The support of this ranch was what mattered the most.

And he knew Layla was rooting for him too.

So.

He was ready when she went back through the lockboxes, containing their final envelope. Though she changed the order of contestants as she read the results, making it random to ratchet up the intensity, the excitement.

*Clever girl.*

Some scores increased substantially. Some barely moved the needle.

When it came down to Willet and Avery, he further admired her strategy.

*Dramatic effect to the extreme.*

She said, "Willet Hayes, you have an audience rating of . . . twenty-five!"

*Oh. Fucking. Shit.*

Avery felt a jerking low in his gut. This was no longer about a needle. It could come down to the thread.

"In the event of a tie, I've created this twist," Layla said. "The two cooks will decide whether to do a head-to-head cook-off of the judges' choosing for all the glory . . . or split the first- and second-place prize money between them—and share the title."

"I'm not sharin'," Avery said.

"Neither am I," Willet agreed with a grin.

This had become an all-or-nothing moment.

Though . . . that wasn't totally true.

Avery's audience score could place him below Willet . . . or any of the others who had lesser points.

This could be the bane of social media and influencers' "influence."

There were sponsorships and endorsements on the line, after all. They required customer stimulus. The right spokesperson with the right presentation.

This audience could be considered a consumer focus group to determine who might be more suitable for promoting products. It might not be Avery, after all.

Layla seemed to understand all the stakes and said, "Literally anything could happen here. The entire competition comes down to how the viewers related to and enjoyed Avery Reed."

*Jesus, like . . . hmm, no pressure there.*

He spared a glance at Jack, who gave a decisive *No worries* nod.

That wasn't how Avery felt.

He'd found himself on the ragged edge.

As Layla had said . . . *anything could happen.*

She didn't rush the results, relaying a few more tidbits about the top contenders.

Until Avery didn't think he could take much more.

As though she sensed this, she said, "All right. Moment of truth, y'all."

Yet she stalled out—conveying how crucial this was to *her.*

Then she seemed to force herself to move forward. "Seriously, best of luck to everyone."

She peeled apart the sealed flap.

Inhaled deeply.

Glanced down.

And said on the exhale, "Twenty-five points to Avery Reed."

His family exploded.

"For a perfect one hundred points," Layla continued, emotion tinging her voice. "Avery Reed, you are *Light Your Fire*'s Best Bunkhouse Cook!"

While his people further went wild, he stared at Layla.

She smiled sweetly. And added, "Congratulations, cowboy. You did it."

His heart wrenched. Excitement over winning warred with their bittersweet ending.

Todd reappeared on-screen and popped the cork on a bottle of champagne while Brodi tossed confetti in the air.

And that was what happened in all the perimeter frames.

Layla said, "Every supplemental camera crew brought along bottles of bubbly so that all the chefs can celebrate a fantastic season. Willet, kudos to you for such a close competition—and congrats for being our runner-up!"

More corks were popped, and the techs were the ones to sprinkle the confetti, so the entire production looked like one big New Year's Eve party.

Avery had difficulty tearing his gaze from Layla, but he had a huge group swooping in to hug him or pat him on the back.

Somewhere amid all the hoopla, he found Ritchie, pulled him to him, gave him a hug, then clasped his shoulder.

With gratitude and that fatherly emotion again, Avery said over the din, "I can't thank you enough for all you do, Ritchie. This victory is for you too. You earned more than aprons and gloves, son. You get another bonus. A *big* bonus."

Ritchie's eyes misted. "I keep tellin' you, it's not about the bonuses. It's about havin' a family again. Havin' a roof over my head. And havin' someone like you to trust and rely on me."

"That I do. Now . . ." Avery glanced around and said, "Someone get this man a glass of champagne!" And he wasn't talking about himself.

Regardless, his aunt delivered two flutes and kissed Avery on the cheek, then Ritchie. "You both make this ranch proud." A tear tumbled down her cheek. "Don't you ever forget that."

She hugged Avery, then Ritchie. Then went for her own glass.

Avery and Ritchie tapped rims and drank.

Layla's voice snagged Avery's attention as she said, "That's a wrap on this season. Keep an eye on socials for what's next to come! Thanks to all our contestants, the audiences, and our sponsors—which you'll find listed on our sites and also on-screen as soon as I'm done with this last cheers to y'all." She raised her glass. Sipped. Then said, "Go on now. Light your own fire!"

# Chapter Twenty

It was later in the evening, after supper and dessert had been served to the cowboys, when Avery retired to his bedroom, the space holding a palpable void.

Sure, he was high from his win. And goddamn, that was a lot of money. *So* much money.

He had a small salary from the ranch, most of which went to his personal essentials and some of the gadgets and cast irons he preferred to use in the chuck hall—that he didn't take out of his annual budget. But his house was paid for, as were the utilities. He did like having a housekeeper, so he paid for that himself. And whatever food and amenities she brought for him every week.

There wasn't a huge need for a "raise," given he got plenty in return for his job.

Thus, this prize money was substantial.

He'd run the tax implications through the ranch's accountant and hand over a chunk to Ritchie to put in a savings account, in the event he ever did decide to leave this place . . . or if he wanted to settle down here. With everyone pitching in, he'd be able to build a small home on the ridge for him and a wife—a family.

It was a scenario that warmed Avery's heart.

As much as the distinctive ringtone that jingled his phone.

He connected with Layla, who had a pretty smile for him and a twinkle in her eyes.

"I waited until you were done with your work," she said, "knowing you wouldn't slack off, even after your coup. Way to go, cowboy. You were perfect all the way around."

He grinned, despite the tightening in his chest.

She was just . . . so damn beautiful.

And so damn far away.

He asked, "Any particular reason you opted to shoot the finale in Kansas City?"

"BBQ Capital of the World. I had a large conglomeration for an in-person audience. Interviewed a lot of the greats after the show, and even before, while I've been in town. Collected plenty of bonus content that's being edited for a special segment tomorrow."

"Then you're off to where?"

He could have kicked himself for asking. But needed to know.

"Got some meetings lined up," she told him, her expression turning somber.

His gut clenched with something akin to hope. "You don't look too excited about them."

"Oh, I am," she quickly said.

The hope turned into dread.

"I have meet and greets with company representatives for those sponsorships and endorsements I mentioned," she told him. "All over the country. Plus, I'm working on a proposal for my next project."

"Always got irons in the fire," he commented. Feeling a twinge in his soul.

Jesus, being in love wasn't supposed to be this painful.

But maybe he'd get over her.

With Layla off doing what Layla did, perhaps this gaping hole in his heart would seal and he'd forget that he'd ever experienced it. That he'd been desperate to see her. Was so freaking close to begging her to come to the ranch.

She had her own life to get on with, though. Her *new* life.

And given that Avery understood she needed to be freed from those bonds of the past, he wouldn't attempt to tie her down further.

The bird adage came to mind.

He didn't even have to open the cage door. She did that just fine herself.

She softly said, "It was good to see you."

Maybe *she'd* already gotten over *him*.

"You too, darlin'. I'm gonna call it a night now."

"Early morning, I know."

They both lingered on the line.

He let out a puff of air. "No point to drawing this out," he told her.

She nodded. Then said, "Goodbye, then. Take care of yourself, cowboy."

"Same to you. Safe travels and good luck with . . . everything."

He dropped the call. Before either of them added something that would make it even harder to part.

This was tortuous enough.

He was already gutted. He didn't need to be filleted.

There'd be nothing left of him.

Layla knew a heavy agenda would help to keep her mind off Avery.

Or so she continued to tell herself. That hadn't happened while she was hosting the last segments of the show or while she'd prepped for the finale. Even being on the "road" now (though she was mostly flying here and there) didn't help to contain him in a shadowy part of her brain. Too many things had him jumping front and center.

It didn't help matters that all the opportunities she explored were related to the BBQ world. Which not only had her thinking about Avery but also her daddy.

And when there was a break in her schedule, she found herself on that long driveway that split the farm in half. Gravel crunched under the tires of her rental. To the right were rows and rows of cornstalks. To the left was a lush lawn with shady trees that gave way to a vast garden.

Ahead was the house, a detached garage, and a barn for equipment and supplies.

A tractor pulled out of the upper quadrant and circled behind her in the roundabout, which had perennials planted in the middle. These were new additions. She paid them little attention, however.

Her gaze flitted to the rearview mirror as her daddy, as strong and sturdy as an oak, cut the engine on the tractor and hopped to the ground, bringing tears of relief—and other emotions—to her eyes, covered by sunglasses.

She pulled in deep breaths to compose herself. But they were fragile at best. Her heart all but seized up. When people said an overwhelming amount of stress made it feel as though an elephant sat on their chest . . . she now understood the expression—and the sensation.

But since she was actually here, she wouldn't pretend she had the wrong address and drive off without talking to him.

She exited the vehicle, just as he was stuffing his hands into the pockets of his overalls.

He gave a friendly grin, his eyes squinting against the afternoon sun, showing some wrinkles against his tanned skin. Though in truth . . . the man had barely aged.

There were obvious signs, of course. But they were minimal. In fact, he looked damn good for someone who worked long days outdoors. He still had broad, set shoulders. A casual though confident stance, warmth exuding from him.

He said, "Welcome. Are you here for Addie's book club meeting? She moved it to next weekend, and I'm afraid you must not have gotten her call or voicemail message."

Ah, the perfect excuse for Layla to get back in her car and disappear from his life again.

With all the feelings choking her up so that she couldn't even speak, it might be the sensible thing to do. Give him a wave and be gone.

She'd seen in person that he was well. That the farm was in excellent condition. That the clapboard house and outbuildings all had a fresh coat of sage paint with crisp white trim. And, apparently, he had a woman in his life.

All of this filled her heart with joy. Eased some of the pressure and tension within her.

He gave her an expectant look, if not a curious one.

Perhaps the more accurate word was "concern."

She realized her hands were shaking, and the corners of her mouth quivered. She wanted to smile. She wanted to say something. Anything.

But damn. She could barely even breathe.

"Shall I get Addie?" he asked in a lower tone, one meant to assure her that being out in the middle of nowhere with a man of his physical stature was nothing to fear.

That thought almost had a laugh slipping from her parted lips—of the hysterical variety. Not in the funny way.

He took a step back.

"No, no, no!" she suddenly blurted out. "I'm not afraid of you. And I'm not lost . . . at least, not anymore. And I'm not here for Addie's book club. I'm here for . . . you."

Her tears started to spill behind the dark lenses.

His jaw clenched for a moment. Then he shook his head, his expression turning to confusion.

Did he recognize her voice?

Figuring she was all in at this point, she removed the sunglasses and stared up at him.

His gaze narrowed. His mouth opened, and his jaw worked, like he was a fish attempting to expel a hook.

And succeeded.

He regained the step between them. Held her gaze and said, "I know those eyes."

She gave a slow nod as more tears fell.

"And the voice," he said. "But the face and the hair . . . you're not who I think you are."

"Oh, but I am!" she cried. "Today, I am, Daddy. I can explain everything. I just . . . I just want to look at you a few minutes more."

"Tess . . ." Now it was *his* eyes that watered, tugging even harder on her heartstrings.

"Yes," she said on a fractured breath. "It's really me, Daddy."

"Oh, good Lord, girl." He swooped in to gather her in his arms.

She flung hers around his neck and sobbed.

For how long, she had no idea. And he was in no hurry to release her.

She had so much to say, so much to apologize for. She'd even committed to telling him the truth about New York and Christopher—because he deserved to know what had lured her away. What had kept her away.

And that she was safe now.

For these endless moments, however, she let her daddy hold her and console her. Giving as much love to him as she received.

Another three weeks passed, and not so much as a speck of inner peace filled that hole in Avery's heart that his separation from Layla—and their subsequent breakup—had torn wide open.

Didn't keep him from losing concentration at the chuck hall, though.

Nor was the agony assuaged when Wyatt came from town with a box and handed it to him at the dinner table.

"Picked this up at the post office," she said. And wagged her brows with intrigue and excitement.

Avery noted that the return address label was from Todd's production company.

More reminders of love lost.

He used his pocketknife to slice through the tape and pushed back the flaps. The inside had a protective bubble roll that he discarded for the twins to destroy later.

He pulled out a plaque with his name on a gold plate and "Best Bunkhouse Cook" underneath it. Above that was a belt buckle with gilded edges mounted to the wood.

"I'll be damned," he murmured. "Didn't know they were going to give me something official."

"Why wouldn't they?" Chance asked. "Those were notable judges with their own titles. And the entire production turned into a national— maybe even an international—phenomenon."

True fact. Ale had set up a Facebook page for Avery, and his timeline and DMs were flooded with fans' comments and messages. After about the twelfth marriage proposal, he'd given up on social media.

Didn't have the time for it anyway.

He handed the plaque to Chance, who admired it before passing it around the table.

"You did good, little bro," Chance told him with a grin. "Not that I expected anythin' less from you. You don't really know how to f-up."

Aunt Brett grimaced.

Ale whispered, "I think that one's on the list, too, Uncle Chance."

Avery chuckled. Needing these brief moments of levity because, Christ, even his soul felt like deadweight.

He returned his attention to the box and extracted an envelope. Inside was a check.

For an amount he still couldn't wrap his mind around.

He gave it to Jack, at the head of the table.

Jack held it, eyeing it, as his other elbow was propped next to his plate, his arm crooked, his finger sweeping across his bottom lip as the pad of his thumb pressed to his jaw.

Very contemplative-like.

Avery sighed. "There's nothing to deliberate over, Jack. I never go back on my word, and you know it. So let me take what I need after

287

I pay the taxman. I'll dole out a portion to Ritchie and get us some state-of-the-art equipment for the chuck hall. The remainder goes to the ranch."

"We could put those funds in the bunkhouse account," Mateo offered in his diplomatic fashion, "and keep it as a buffer. We get lean years sometimes, Jack. No need to make the cowboys suffer. They don't stop ranchin' just because we're inching toward the red."

"I don't really see that happening in the future."

A new voice joined the conversation.

*The* voice.

The one that haunted Avery's dreams and whispered to him when she wasn't even there.

His shattered heart leaped. Truly leaped.

As did the rest of him. He was out of his seat in a nanosecond, spinning around to face the entrance to the dining room.

While a collective gasp rippled behind him.

Layla wore another of her flared dresses, this one in a floral print. She had on ankle boots and carried with her a leather portfolio, cradled in her arm.

"What the hell?" he muttered.

Aunt Brett sighed. "That one was warranted," she told the boys.

Layla gave Avery her brightest smile, her eyes shimmering with unshed tears.

"I have news," she announced. "I asked Todd to hold off on sending you that box until I had all my ducks in a row. Most of them anyhow. The ones that'd make this ranch enough cash to line all the coffers, not just the chuck hall account."

"I'm interested in hearing this," Wyatt stated with enthusiasm.

"I think y'all will be. May I join you?"

Ale hastily vacated his chair and said, "You can sit here, Miss Layla." Then he pushed his brother out of the seat next to his and told Hunt, "Go sit by Mom."

Hunt didn't argue because it got him that much closer to Jillian, who he still crushed on, despite it being a hopeless venture.

*Feel my pain, boy.*

Avery shooed Ale away and held the chair out for Layla. Didn't scoot her in since she had that thick portfolio in her lap.

He settled into his own seat, fighting for a breath.

She didn't leave them questioning her unexpected arrival.

"Avery gave me the gate code that was recently changed. I'm guessing that came about after Luke delivered Caleb's letters and the cash."

"That man is still not welcome here," Avery said, his tone sharper than usual when it came to this subject—because she knew about the letters. "You went to see him, didn't you?"

"Yes, I did," she told him without hesitation.

"And you failed to mention that during the times we talked?" He tried to curb the angst. The shock. The . . . whatever it was that he was feeling.

"I did it on impulse," she explained. "I'd said that I didn't believe he was threatening me, when I put more thought into it."

"What's this?" Jack asked, concern tinging his tone.

Avery waved him off. "Different story for a different time." To Layla, he said, "You shouldn't have done that, honey. You had no idea what he might have been up to, and—"

"Too late for the lecture, Avery," she commented. "And I'm sorry I didn't divulge this before or after I went. I didn't know how it would all play out. But I sensed, primarily from his online profile, that there was something to investigate. I learned a lot. Whether you want to know about it is up to you."

"Avery didn't read his letter," Chance commented.

"Neither did you," Avery countered.

"Mine's in a drawer. Yours is gone forever."

Aunt Brett cleared her throat. All eyes flashed to her.

"Not exactly," she said. "I pulled it from the recycle bin. Just in case you changed your mind down the road, Avery. Regretted not opening it."

Avery got to his feet again. To pace.

"That's not the reason I'm here," Layla said. "What I've collected over the past weeks are official offers from organizations wanting Avery's—and Jack's—face on their marketing campaigns. As well as mine." She unzipped her leather case and retrieved a file folder. She stood and rounded the table to Wyatt, handing it over. "I know you have other offers on the table, but as Jack's marketing manager, you might want to also look these over, then consult with a lawyer if y'all make any decisions. That's the extent of my involvement."

"I thought they were BSing me when they were posting to my socials," Jack murmured.

"Not at all. These are vetted," Layla assured him. "As for Avery..." She had a folder for him too. "Sky's the limit on what you want to pursue. As I mentioned previously, they contacted me before you put up a website, and a lot of the offers are joint ones—for you and me to act as a spokes*team*. The reason I've been taking all these meetings."

His head snapped back. "Thought you were off to explore other pastures for the show."

"I have been. I will continue to do so. However . . . the thing is . . ." She gazed up at him, her lashes fluttering. "I'm game for this sort of collab—with you. In fact . . ." She selected another file and gave it to him. "This is my proposal for season six. Filmed on the ranch."

*"What?"* He stared at her.

She smiled. Softly. And said, "It's an excellent platform. Check it out. Ranch living, ranch cooking, ranch—"

"What are you saying?" he quietly demanded, emotion tearing through him.

"It's not like Jack and Jillian's show, Avery. Instructional to a degree, yes, but it's more about the lifestyle and the techniques. What you can do with the tools you've mastered, including the trenches. I am recommending a cookbook, absolutely. But, again, it'll be primal grilling, not similar to *Rub It In*. This'll be more earthy. There's more of a . . . oh, heck. Read the proposal."

His brow knitted.

She groaned and said, "Okay, let me give you a little something to nibble on."

That was precisely what he wanted. But they weren't there yet.

*Yet.*

She flipped open the cover and pointed to a list of figures on the first page.

"Your salary," she said as she indicated the top line. "My salary." The next line. "Ritchie's salary, and a miscellaneous budget for food and supplies, plus a temporary cook to assist you or Ritchie when you're away from the ranch."

"I'm not planning on being away from the ranch, darlin'." He was quite adamant about that. To hell with the endorsements. He'd contended all along that his place was here with his family—and running the chuck hall. He'd stay true to his word.

"I understand, cowboy. Though . . ." She closed the folder and took all the paperwork from him, setting it on top of her chair. Glancing back at him, she said, "I want you to go somewhere with me."

"A honeymoon might be nice," Chance muttered.

Avery shot him a look. Because his brother wasn't helping matters. Avery was a bit twisted around by all of this. But he wouldn't be manipulated into changing his mind, his course of direction. Or going against his own grain.

"Darlin', I'm not gonna go see Caleb Reed. That's a done deal. And while I respect your initiative, because it's your prerogative to know him or not, and"—he glimpsed at his aunt—"I appreciate you being considerate enough to preserve something you think I might want to read in the future. But the bottom line is that I carved that man out of my life the day he left here. I'm good with that decision."

"And that's all up to you," Layla said. "What I want, cowboy," she told him as she stepped closer to him, her voice lowering, tears filling her eyes, "is for you to meet *my* daddy. Maybe ask him for my hand."

"Aw, Jesus." Emotion crested over Avery, though he still managed to gesture to the boys to not say a word about his swearing.

Layla splayed her palms over his pecs and stared up at him again. "Didn't take but being out of your bed even one night to know it's where I belong. Where I want to be. I just had to work some things out so that I could come back to you, cowboy."

The gesturing swung toward Chance, telling him to shut it, when Avery knew he wanted to let out an *I told you so*.

Avery brought that hand to his face, dragging it downward and then rubbing his jawline.

"I'm a bit perplexed," he confessed.

"She's proposin' to you, jackass." This from Jack.

"What is this, a free-for-all with the cussin'?" Aunt Brett admonished.

"I think one night is acceptable," Mateo said, always the voice of reason. "Given the circumstances."

Layla smiled through her tears.

"What do you say, Avery? Still in love with me?"

"You know I am."

"Still want me?"

"You know I do."

"Still—"

"Layla." Everything inside him finally unraveled. And his heart swelled. He got to one knee, taking her hand in his. And said, "Marry me."

Not even a question.

It didn't need to be. He realized that now.

All this time, she'd been working her way back to him.

Back to *them*.

She said, "You giving me the time to figure out where I'm supposed to be also let me decide who I want to be going forward. It's a no-brainer," she said on a broken breath. "I want to be here, on the ranch. With you."

He stood. Swept his fingers over her cheek. And told her, "Honey, all I want is for you to be mine."

"I always will be, cowboy." She kissed him, then murmured against his lips, "I *always* will be."

# Acknowledgments

I'm thrilled to have been able to expand upon the world I created at the TRIPLE R and bring more characters to life, while revisiting the ones from *Spiced Right*. Both Avery and Layla had much to struggle with before they could find their happily ever after. Those struggles also made the family stronger. I hope to continue on with this series, working with the Montlake team. Thanks again to my editors, Lauren Plude and Krista Stroever, as well as to everyone who contributed to the shaping of this story and its marketing. Additional gratitude to my agent, Sarah E. Younger of the Nancy Yost Literary Agency.

Above all, I want to express my deepest appreciation for my readers. You are the reason I do my best and strive to do even better with each book! Hugs!

# About the Author

With works ranging from contemporaries to rock star romances to romantic suspense to paranormals, Gigi Templeton is an international bestselling author. Her novels and novellas have been published under three pseudonyms by traditional publishers, including St. Martin's Press and Hachette Book Group/Forever; digital publishers such as Harlequin's Carina Press; and serialized fiction apps like Radish and YONDER. Templeton's *Spiced Right* won the Mid-Michigan Romance Writers of America Best Banter Contest in November 2022. She was also a finalist for the *Romantic Times* Best Book of the Year and Seal of Excellence.

Templeton lives in Arizona with her real-life hero and her rescued Maltese, and she is currently studying culinary arts and food photography. Read her blog and sign up for her newsletter at www.ggtblog.com, and follow her on Facebook and X, formerly Twitter: @ggtbooks.